DON'T LOOK BACK

BACK

DCI ROHAN ROY SERIES

BOOK 3

ML ROSE

Copyright © 2023 by M.L. Rose

All rights reserved.

The right of ML Rose to be identified as the author of this work has been asserted by him in accordance with the Copyright, Designs and Patents Act 1988.

No part of this book may be reproduced in any form or by any electronic or mechanical means, including information storage and retrieval systems, without permission in writing from the author. Infringement of copyright by copying.

(1) The copying of the work is an act restricted by the copyright in every description of copyright work and references in this part to copying and copies shall be construed as follows.

(2) Copying in relation to a literary, dramatic, musical, or artistic work means reproducing the work in any material form.

This includes storing the work in any medium by electronic means.

(5) Copying in relation to the typographical arrangement of a published edition means making a facsimile copy of the arrangement.

(6) Copying in relation to any description of work includes the making of copies that are transient or are incidental to some other use of the work.

This book is a work of fiction. Names, characters, places, and incidents either are

products of the author's imagination or are used fictitiously. Any resemblance to actual

persons, living or dead, events, or locales is entirely coincidental.

Table of Contents

CHAPTER 1

Tracy Barrett clutched the strap of her handbag tightly. It wasn't cold, but she still shivered, feeling the breeze on her legs. Her skirt was short, on purpose, and the rest of her attire was similarly revealing. She looked up the road at the lights of The Cliffe Sauna and Massage Parlour where she normally worked. Too many ladies in there tonight, so Tracy was on the street. She knew it was risky, especially as she was alone, but she needed the money.

The derelict, dark street was full of boarded-up shop windows, and cafés that had shut some time ago. A car streaked past, its headlights blinding her briefly. She raised her eyes to the car, wondering if it could be driven by a punter. The car slowed but didn't stop.

Tracy resumed her beat, walking up and down near the traffic lights, but not straying too far from the sauna. She should've booked her slot in advance. A good night's work could mean several hundred in earnings. She was younger than most of the ladies in there, and she knew Karen, the owner. But the parlour was full up; Karen's place was getting popular.

Another pair of headlights pierced the gloom as a car turned the corner. It moved more slowly, and Tracy stiffened. The car stopped at the kerb. It was a black car, with dark tinted windows. The windows remained raised, and she couldn't tell if the driver was watching her. Slowly, the window went down. Loud music thrummed from inside, then faded, as the volume was lowered. Tracy shuffled forward, bending to get to the window. She could see the dark silhouette of a man inside.

"Thirty quid for half an hour, fifty for the hour. There's a car park behind that sauna." Tracy jerked her thumb to the lights behind her.

The man's neck moved a fraction as he glanced at the mirror. She couldn't make out any of his features.

"What do you want?" she asked, impatient. She didn't want to miss other punters if this one was on the fence. He stared at her in silence, then resumed his forward gaze.

"See ya then." Tracy straightened. The window remained down. The music remained low. Tracy peered into the dark car. "You movin' or what?"

She saw the man's neck move again, and a pair of invisible eyes stared at her in silence. Her skin crawled, and the hair stood up on the back of her neck.

"Get in," the man said.

Tracy felt conflicted. This man was weird, and she was getting a menacing, strange vibe from him. He looked muscular and young, different from her usual fat, middle-aged men.

"I'm alright. Sorry to waste your time."

She felt the dark eyes stare at her.

"Fifty for half an hour," he said.

Tracy swallowed. That was a good deal. She could put up with his weirdness for thirty minutes. "Make it seventy and I'll do everything."

The man nodded. "Get in."

Tracy got on the passenger side. She could see his face clearly now. Smooth-shaven, and young, with short, dark hair. He stared straight ahead, ignoring her. He started the car as the lights changed to green. With a startle, Tracey recognised him.

"You? Why didn't you just call me?"

The man said nothing.

Tracey raised her voice. "What're you doing? I can't be arsed with this anymore. Stop the car."

The car kept moving. Tracey clenched her teeth. She said, "Take the next left. That leads to the car park behind the sauna."

The man zoomed past the left turning and carried on down the road. Fear spiked in Tracy's spine as she stared at the man.

"Where are we going?"

The man said nothing. His hands tightened on the steering wheel.

CHAPTER 2

There are moments in life that break you. Snap you in pieces like you were made of cardboard. Some people who experience them never become whole again and those who do, live in fear of those moments coming back.

For DCI Rohan Roy, that moment had been watching his daughter Anna in the grips of a vicious killer. Luckily, Anna was okay. She was a tough cookie. He watched her now, as the sunlight shone on her jet black hair, her head bent as she read a book, lying on the couch. He breathed in the peace, the quiet joy, of seeing Anna relaxed and safe. He had learnt to take nothing for granted in life, not even this fleeting moment of bliss.

He walked around and sat opposite her on the sofa.

Anna glanced at him. "Oh, hello, Dad."

"You okay?" He smiled. "Want some breakfast?"

"Had some porridge, thanks."

He nodded, and she went back to her book. It was July, and the summer sun was glorious outside, washing away the dirt and grime of the last few days. Given the trouble Anna had been through, Roy was surprised she wanted to stay in Sheffield for a while longer. But she did, and he was over the moon, unlike his ex-wife, Marissa. He didn't blame Marissa at all. He would be mad as well if something bad had happened to Anna in London. That was strange in itself. What had transpired over the last week was the last thing Roy, or anyone else, would've expected in the relative calm of the picturesque Peak District.

Roy had asked for his quarters to be moved from Hathersage, in the Don Valley, just past Sheffield's eastern borders. They had moved into the village of Dore, which was right at the city limits, and which blended the best of village life with access to the nearby metropolis. Dore used to be a part of the Peak District, but since the A57 was built decades ago, the village was now more like a small town. It was still beautiful, with its old stone houses. The River Sheaf, from which Sheffield derived its name, gurgled through the centre of Dore.

Roy felt safer here. It wasn't as remote as Hathersage. The South Sheffield police station, his workplace, was closer too; twenty minutes if he drove fast. He also had more neighbours, and he was making a point of getting to know them, for Anna's sake.

"Would you like some tea?" he asked, rising.

"Uh-hmm," Anna said, eyes glued to the page of the crime thriller she was reading.

Roy's phone buzzed. He went into the kitchen and then looked at the text he had received.

You didn't reply. Guess you don't want to know where your brother is.

Roy grit his teeth together. He rang the number back, but it went to answerphone, as he knew it would. He had been getting these messages since last week. Another prankster, like the one who left the neck chain that had belonged to Roy's missing brother, Robin, at his door.

Steve Pickering, the sick bastard they just caught, denied it was him. Roy didn't know whether to believe him. Pickering would be in prison for life, what reason did he have to lie? Unless, of course, he wanted to increase Roy's discomfort. A pain he'd carried for twenty-seven-years. Not knowing what happened to his eight-year-old brother.

One thing Roy was certain of: it wasn't Pickering who was sending him these messages. He was in jail, and didn't have access to his phone, or a laptop. And if it wasn't Pickering who left that necklace, then who did? The same person who was sending the texts, or someone else? Whoever it was, they knew his deepest, personal secret. His mission to find Robin, alive or dead.

The dilemma remained, like a cloud settling on his head. The vapours drenched his thoughts, obscuring his mind. He knew Burns and Burgess had a network of depraved child-killers. Most of that network had now been dismantled, once Burns was behind bars.

Roy stared at the screen for a few seconds, then wrote back.

I want to know. Tell me where Robin is.

He waited, but there was no response. With a sigh of frustration, he put the kettle on, then went out into the garden. South Yorkshire Police had now given him bigger quarters, and while he had to pay rent, it was a fraction of what it would cost down south. Not to mention the garden and the peace, which no money could buy. He had lived up north for a few years as a child, before his parents moved down south. He'd never thought he'd leave London again, at least not as long as Anna was in school.

He lifted his face to the warm sunlight, savouring it. A bird tweeted in the trees, and there was no sound of traffic. He breathed in, the air smelled of the bracken and heather in the far hills. The green and blue smudge of the peaks were a dim outline in the horizon.

He went back in to make the tea and checked his phone once again. No response from the mystery caller. He went through the three missing persons services he subscribed to, and none of them had anything new to report. Roy sighed, and got busy making tea, by which he didn't mean dinner, like most here did.

CHAPTER 3

Detective Inspector Sarah Botham wasn't prepared for the man standing at the school gates. It was drop off time, a flurry of children running in through the gates, parents waving goodbye and offering last-minute kisses to embarrassed kids. Botham stood still, her mouth hanging open as she watched the man who leaned casually against the gates, his eyes searching. To her frustration, he spotted her. She held her son, Matt, tightly by the hand. She knelt and kissed him.

"Nan will pick you up, okay?" she said. "Don't go with anyone else," she added, for the first time.

Matt looked a little confused, but then nodded.

"Okay, Mum." He dashed off, a bundle of energy, and Sarah walked behind him, making sure he went inside. Her eyes were hooked on the man, who was now walking towards her. He kept looking back to watch Matt. He stopped in front of Sarah, who glared at him, then looked away.

"Hi Sarah," the man said.

"What do you want, John?"

John Garnett spread his hands. "No hello? Come on." He tried a smile, showing his white teeth. He had cleaned up nicely, Botham noted. His clothes were new, and the black shoes were gleaming. At least externally, he was a far cry from the man he'd been.

"Hello and goodbye," Botham said, thrusting her hands in her pockets, and turning around. John fell in step beside her, and she seethed with irritation.

"That's my son back there," John said quietly. "I want to see him. You owe me that much, Sarah."

She stopped and turned to face him. Her teeth ground together. "I owe you fuck all, John. Matt's the son you turned your back on. You left us when we needed you. You've got a fucking nerve, turning up at his school. How did you find out, anyway?"

John shrugged. "It's the closest school to where you live so it wasn't hard."

"You've been following us around?" Botham shook her head. "Get a life, John." He knew what she did for a living. He'd left, and good riddance, when she was a uniformed constable. He hadn't seen her come up the ranks, and change track to detective. She didn't want to use any threats of reporting him, that could come later, if necessary.

She started walking again, and he followed her.

"I want to see Matt. He should have a father figure in his life."

Botham stopped again and stared at him for a while. John looked alright, but she'd rather trust a pack of howling hyenas than him. And she didn't want it for Matt.

"How will Matt feel when you leave again? He was two years old then, so he doesn't remember. I'm not letting you mess his life up." She stepped forward, and put two fingers on his chest, and pushed hard. He stepped backward.

"For ten years, you do nothing, and now you suddenly want to be his dad? Doesn't work like that, John."

She wasn't expecting the contrite look on his face.

"I know. I'm sorry, I've been all over the place. I had to be abroad for six years with work. But that's no excuse, and I'm not offering it as one. I don't expect to rush back into his life. All I'm saying is that I want to be there for him, if he wants me. And I'm prepared to do anything for that. That's all."

Botham was slightly mollified, but her bullshit meter was still surging in the red zone. John used to be a builder, a foreman at a construction company. "Where have you been?" she asked cautiously.

"In Dubai. My company sent me there. I've got the papers, passport to prove it. Honest." He spread his arms, and she got a whiff of nice aftershave. She had to grudgingly agree that he looked like he'd done well for himself.

"I'm not massively rich, but I'm doing alright. Got a house in Sheffield now, in Ecclesall. My company's doing renovations for Sheffield University on the halls of residence. I'm going to be here for a while. I've been wanting to come for ages, see how you two were doing. I'm sorry it's taken so long."

He pulled out a passport from the breast pocket of his jacket. "Here, look at the immigration stamps." He thrust the right page in her face.

Botham frowned, examining it. Then she nodded, satisfied with the stamp from Dubai Airport Authority and the dates.

"That still doesn't mean anything," she said. "You need to give me some time to speak to Matt. I'll see how he feels." In her heart, she knew Matt would want to see his father, and that made her feel vulnerable, and strangely sad. She'd been close to her dad till he passed away a few years ago. How could she deny that for her son?

"Take all the time you want," John said. "Please take my

number. Call me anytime. It might be better if I speak to him on the phone first, and then see him with you?"

Botham raised a hand. John had always been like this, rushing into things. "Leave it with me. I'll call you. And don't call me, I won't answer."

She took his number down, then strode off, heading for her car. She was about to get in when her radio crackled.

"Request urgent assistance at scene of homicide in Attercliffe. IC1 female victim found in abandoned garage. Request duty SIO and SOC to attend."

"Duty SIO Botham reporting. Do you copy?"

"Copy that, guv."

The uniformed sergeant making the call went on to give the address. Botham got in her car and started the engine. She was duty Senior Investigating Officer for the week. She waited to get a couple of blocks down from the school, trundling patiently behind the cars of the school mums, then blasted the siren, and hurtled down the road.

CHAPTER 4

Stephen Burns, convicted child killer, stared at the woman opposite him. "I didn't do it. He framed me for it, and here I am, rotting in prison."

Burns had his elbows on the table, and he leaned over the table, emphasising his thin, wiry frame. The glasses on his nose had slipped, and he pushed them up. "All the crimes he's put me in here for are lies. Just lies. He came to my house and messed me up. Shouldn't the police be doing the opposite? Protecting people?"

The woman wore an expression of pain. Her thin shoulders quivered, and her lips parted. There was frank desire in her eyes, but also deep regret.

"Unbelievable."

"Someone put those boys in that house. It wasn't me! It never *was* me. They found my DNA where the boys were killed, but that was just coincidence. I owned that farmhouse. Of course, it would have my DNA lying around. How can I be held responsible for what happened after I sold it?"

Burns flexed his jaws. He looked over at the burly prison

guards, keeping a close eye on the prisoners chatting to their loved ones. One of them caught Burns looking and he averted his eyes immediately.

"I'm so sorry," the woman said. She was leaning forward too, and their faces were close. In prison, visitors were not allowed to touch each other. Burns ached to touch and feel her. From the hot fervour in her eyes, he knew she felt the same way.

The woman's name was Lydia, and she used to be in a relationship with Stephen. They broke up a long time ago but had remained friends. Recently, Lydia had got in touch through the Good Samaritans prison network, which provided support for convicts who suffered with depression and anxiety.

Many prisoners suffered with depression, and the informal network was very useful for mental health patients. Burns had claimed he was depressed and was started on an anti-depressant by his psychiatrist, Dr Parsons. Of course, being a psychologist himself, Burns knew the symptoms of depression very well. It was a condition he had treated many times over. He knew exactly how to mimic the physical signs of depression, and what to tell Dr Parsons.

"That bloody detective Rohan Roy," Burns seethed. "He thinks I took his brother. I never! All I wanted was to be left alone." He squeezed his eyes shut, then clutched his forehead. "They planted the evidence, because they needed to catch someone."

"Surely you can ask for a retrial?"

Burns spread his hands. "How? I need new evidence. Evidence that shows that DCI Roy stole my DNA from police records and planted it. I can only do that if I get out of here and confront him. Make him pay for what he did."

He gazed at Lydia intensely, and she stared back, hypnotized. "But I can't. I'm stuck here, for something I didn't do."

Lydia shook her head, her eyes melting with grief. "I know. That

Rohan Roy will pay for what he did. He has to suffer the torment you're going through."

"Yes," Burns whispered. "He has to suffer the torment."

"You helped me so much. I wish everyone could see what a wonderful person you are," Lydia sniffed, emotion brimming in her eyes. She had suffered with depression herself, and Burns had done a lot of counselling with her. His previous life as a clinical psychologist meant he was well-trained, and it had worked wonders for Lydia. She now looked at life in a new light. She felt positive. It was amazing what a change in perspective could do.

Burns smiled and watched her eyes lower to his lips. "You did all the hard work, Lydia. I took you to the river, but you drank the water. You made yourself better and you can do it again. You know I'll always help."

Lydia swallowed, and then sniffed. She wiped moisture from her eyes. Burns got so close now their foreheads were almost touching.

"Imagine how many more people I could help if I was free. Instead, this travesty of justice has landed me in jail for life. Do you know about the Cardiff Three? Three men who were held on a murder charge for twenty two years before they got free. Guess where the killer was? He lived a few roads down from where the murder happened."

Burns conveniently neglected to tell Lydia about the two boys found in his basement. He knew she wouldn't have access to his confidential records. She could only read his sentence, in the public court documents. He was lying about his past crimes as well, but lying through his back teeth is what he'd done all his life.

"I didn't know about the Cardiff Three? Did that really happen? Six men were jailed for that long on a false charge?"

"Yes. All because the media and everyone else made a huge fuss about the murdered women, the police thought they had to do something. They found evidence these men used to see that woman. Read about it online. Now, the same thing is happening to me, and no one seems to be in the least bit interested."

"I am," Lydia breathed. "And I'll tell everyone what's happening. Just tell me what to do."

"There is one thing you could do," Burns purred. He lowered his head to his hands, and when he looked up, he was close to tears.

"That man," he gasped, his eyes becoming red. "That DCI Rohan Roy. He thinks he's untouchable because he's a senior cop. I want him to know what he's done to me."

Lydia dabbed at her eyes, then her jaws hardened. "Tell me what you want me to do."

Burns rubbed his eyes hard, aware that made them redder still. He thought about the suffering he had endured, and self-pity surged inside him. Like all narcissists, Burns was good at that. His pain was much more important than anyone else's. His thoughts mattered the most, and others had to think like him. And do like him. If they didn't, he could make them do what he wanted. At least, he liked to think that he could.

His hands covered his face, and he sobbed. Tears trickled down his cheeks and he wiped them.

"Oh, Steve," Lydia said, her heart breaking. Burns liked the lost look on her face. It was working. By god, he was good. Even at this low point in his life, when all he had was a room and a loo to his name, he could make her do what he wanted.

That was power. Some people wanted money, but they didn't know shit. This was real power. The ability to make Lydia do what he wanted. He strengthened the emotion inside him and tried to cry harder. To his amazement, it worked. He sobbed like a child deprived of his favourite toy.

Lydia touched his arm, then squeezed it. Burns knew he had to stop. This could go too far and then Lydia might be denied visitor rights.

"I'm okay." He wiped his face on his sleeve.

Lydia dried her own eyes.

"I want to be out there, helping people. But one person has a vendetta against me. He wants to destroy me. Rohan Roy. Do you know he comes to see me every now and then?"

"What?" Lydia gasped.

"Yes. He just sits there and taunts me. He likes to think I know where his brother is. When I tell him, for the millionth time…" Burns looked skyward, and his head moved as if in prayer to an invisible god. "When I tell him I don't know, he still pesters me. As if putting me here on a false charge wasn't enough. I have to suffer his visits as well."

"But surely… Surely you can complain about that? He has to stop it."

"I have tried, Lydia." Burns gripped his hands together, and his eyes closed. "Believe me, I've tried. But he keeps taunting me."

"He needs to be taught a lesson."

Bingo. Burns opened his eyes slowly. He looked at the table, following the wooden grains with a finger. He wanted to act the victim for a while longer, get her totally on his side.

Ready to wage war for him.

He said nothing, just stared down, aware his sunken posture was doing the trick. He could feel her eyes on him.

"What should we do?" Lydia whispered.

Burns shook his head. "I don't know. I just… want him to stop coming here and bugging me. Even the sight of him is terrifying."

They were silent for a while. "If only he could leave me alone. Not come here…" Burns frowned, pretending to think.

"Yes?"

He looked up at her, holding her eyes. "Maybe, if someone told him they know where his brother is. Then he might leave me alone."

Lydia's stare deepened; her pupils constricted. Her lips parted, but she didn't speak for a few seconds. "You mean a random person calling Rohan Roy to say they know where his brother is, like that?"

Burns shrugged. "Don't know. Maybe. What do you think?"

Excitement coloured Lydia's voice. "Yes, that might work. I could get in touch and pretend to know about his brother. Do you know his brother's name?"

"Robin Roy," Burns said without hesitation. "He was seven years old when he disappeared and has never been found. I have no idea where he is, and that's the truth."

"Right," Lydia smiled. "Leave it with me."

Burns stroked his cheek. "Actually, there's one more thing." He gazed at Lydia thoughtfully. "He has a daughter."

CHAPTER 5

Truth be told, Roy was enjoying his compassionate leave. After personal trauma, which Anna's abduction was considered as, all police officers were offered it. *Too damn right*, he thought, as no one really cared about the women and men in the front line, exposed to all manner of sick, evil crap that the rest of the world was thankful never to see. But he had initially gone against the leave, because he wanted to get back to work; his work was far from done. Pickering was behind bars, but the person contacting him, taunting him, was still at large.

That said, he would never forget the peace of sitting opposite Anna in a sunlit room, cup of tea in hand. He couldn't remember the last time he'd spent quality time with her. And no, saving her from a sadistic killer didn't count as quality time. Quite the reverse, in fact. An awful, harrowing time neither would ever want to repeat.

He went to ask how long she wanted to stay for, then thought a better way to put the question.

"Do you like it here?"

Anna's eyes were still on the book, and she nodded. Roy sipped his tea. "Your mother asked me how long you wanted to stay."

Anna put her book down slowly. "I know. She sent me a text as well. I said maybe another week."

Roy considered that. Anna, like most teenagers, liked her independence. That was probably at play here. He was grateful she was still with him, considering that a week ago she almost died, thanks to the culmination of an investigation he was leading. But he wondered if there was something else going on at home. He decided to ask her.

Anna shrugged. "Yes. Why do you ask?"

Roy stared at her for a few seconds. He could tell when she wasn't telling him everything. "Does Mummy have a new boyfriend?"

Anna's eyes flickered to her hands, which she inspected like she'd never seen them before. "Yes, she does. He's alright, I guess."

"Look at me."

Anna dragged her eyes from her nails, but not before she held them up to the light, frowning. Evidently, she wasn't happy with the state of her nails. The frown faded as she looked at Roy.

"You don't like him, do you?"

Anna shrugged again.

A few more questions elicited more information. His name was Greg, they met on a dating app, and no, he hadn't moved in, but he did spend a lot of time there. Whole weekends, and also a couple of days in the week.

Roy frowned. "That's a lot of time. How long has this been going on for?" He knew it was none of his business, but Anna's welfare certainly was his lookout.

"Last few months. He's not always there, but he's there a fair bit, if you know what I mean."

"Has he ever looked at you funny? Or said anything?"

Anna rolled her eyes. "Oh please, Dad. No, he hasn't. I'd tell Mummy if he had, obviously."

"Why don't you like him, then?"

"I never said I didn't. It's just… weird having another man around there. He's alright, I guess."

Roy couldn't shake off the feeling there was more behind Anna's words. He also wondered if this the real reason she was staying here – she had more space here than she did at home. He made up his mind, he would have to speak to Marissa. That would be like pulling teeth – there was no love lost between him and his ex, given the legal battle she had kicked off. It was old hat now, but the bitterness still lingered. However, this was about Anna, and he hoped Marissa wouldn't slam the phone down after two monosyllables.

He pulled out his phone, just in time for it to ring. He saw Botham's number. He answered.

"DCI Roy."

"Ey up, guv. Got a murder case in Attercliffe. Young IC1 female. Someone's done a real job on her. Poor lass."

"I'm on leave," he said. He hesitated, then rose and went to the kitchen for some privacy. Anna returned to her book.

"How old is she?" Roy asked, when he was out of Anna's earshot.

"Early-to-mid-twenties. One of the ladies of the night in Attercliffe, I think. The place where she was found is Sheffield's unofficial red light district."

"Never knew Sheffield had one. All the brothels are now online, correct?"

"Been looking, have you?" Botham teased, and he could hear the joke in her voice.

"Everyone gets lonely," he said, then changed the topic. "How does it look?"

"Bad," Botham's voice lowered. "The killer bled her to death slowly. Cuts in all the major arteries. SOC are on their way, as is Dr Patel."

"Sounds like you have it under control. Don't need me, right?"

"No, but thought you'd like to know as you're still head of MIT."

The Major Investigation Team was in charge of all the murder cases and other serious crimes like child abduction. For South Yorkshire Police, or SYP, Roy had become the newly-anointed head after the capture of Steve Pickering. Funny that happened while he was on leave. Knowing Nugent, his boss, the D Sup, it was probably done on purpose, so Nugent didn't have to give him the news in person.

Roy felt something else too. The leave was all good, but he did feel rested, and ready to get back into work. Then again, he still had Anna here.

"Thanks, Sarah. Let me call you back in a bit."

He strolled back to the living room. Anna was still reading.

"I might have to go out for some work thing. Have you got any plans for the day?"

Anna closed the book, keeping a finger on the open page. "Can you drop me off at town? I could head into the library and do some homework there."

Roy nodded. "And I can pick you up from there when done. Let's go."

CHAPTER 6

Roy told Sarah he was on his way, and she immediately felt surprise and a little guilt.

"Sorry guv, I didn't mean to disturb your leave. I honestly don't expect you to turn up."

"You're not disturbing," he glanced at Anna, who was now looking at her phone. Probably on TikTok, Snapchat, or the latest incarnation of ten-second video apps. "We needed some fresh air."

"We?"

"Yes, Anna's coming with me." He had his headphones on, as his rusty old VW's Bluetooth was older than him and didn't work. Anna looked up at the mention of her name, and Roy mouthed 'Sarah' at her, to which Anna nodded. She had met Sarah, and the rest of the team.

"What? Oh Jeez, look I'm sorry—"

"Yes, all your fault. Anna's going to the library, and I'll drop by the nick to pick up my radio and warrant card. Then I'll see you at the scene. Keep the doctor there for me."

"Dr Patel? Oh, she'll love that. Waiting for you, I mean."

Roy had had a few skirmishes with Dr Patel, who had a sharp

brain, and a sharper tongue, and who took no prisoners. He liked her work ethic, and suspected there was mutual professional admiration. Not that either of them would ever admit to it.

"Has she arrived yet?"

"Nope, but I'll pass your message on."

Roy hung up. He dropped Anna off at the city centre, and the teenager made her own way to the library. Roy told her to stay in the public areas, and not to talk to strangers, at which she did her usual head-shake and eye-roll.

In some ways, Roy thought as he drove back to the nick, *it was better that Anna was here, where he could keep an eye on her*. He needed to ring his ex-wife to find out more about this boyfriend of hers. He still thought Anna wasn't telling him everything.

Detective Constables Rizwan Ahmed and Oliver Walmsley were at their desks when he walked in.

"Ey up guv," Oliver said. "Aren't you meant to be on leave?"

"I was until DI Botham decided to call me up for the good news. New victim in Attercliffe?"

"Aye. Looks bad too. Young lass, cut up badly, then left on the pavement. A motorist saw it this morning and called it in."

"Do we have the motorist's details?"

"Aye, DI Botham spoke to him. He was in shock like. Hospital porter, on his way to work."

"Whereabouts in Attercliffe?" Roy asked. Rizwan answered, because he was up by the big map on the wall, circling a section.

"Road next to the Don River. Liverpool Street." Riz turned, and there was a glint in his eyes as he glanced at Oliver. Roy didn't miss it.

"What's special about Liverpool Street? Apart from the fact that it's in the wrong city?"

"It's known to be a place frequented by ladies of the night. Or was."

"Yes, Sarah mentioned it might be. I'm going over. One of you can come with me, the other stay and liaise with traffic to get the CCTV up."

"DI Botham said there's no CCTV in that stretch, guv. Just bad luck."

Roy frowned. "Maybe it's the red light road for a reason. No one wants to get arrested for soliciting, after all." He looked around him. "Where's Melanie?"

Detective Sergeant Melanie Sparkes was the latest addition to the Major Investigation Team. She was an experienced detective, transferred from Lancashire when she moved with her husband's job.

"Gone to the canteen, I think," Rizwan said. He looked behind Roy at the same time they all heard the heavy breathing and footsteps that preceded the arrival of the Detective Superintendent, Michael Nugent.

"Thought I saw you. You're meant to be on leave," Nugent rasped.

Roy turned. "Nice to see you as well, Sir," he said, no trace of irony in his voice. He watched as Nugent's eyes narrowed, and his nostrils flared once. The two DCs were very quiet.

"In my office, now." Nugent didn't bother to see if Roy followed. He turned and marched off. Across the small hallway, they saw him leave his office door open. Roy sighed, and walked in, then shut the door. Nugent was by the window in his room, looking impatient. As soon as Roy shut the door, Nugent took out a packet of cigarettes, and lit one. He blew smoke out of the window, leaning out, and resting the hand bearing the cigarette on the windowsill.

"You're supposed to be taking it easy," Nugent said, without looking at Roy. "Have you seen the psychiatrist?"

"Not yet."

Nugent glared at him. "Then you better get a move on. Without a psych assessment I can't let you start."

Roy frowned. "I wasn't told that, Sir. I'm on compassionate leave, but I didn't have any restriction on working."

"PSC recommendations," Nugent wheezed, then coughed. He crushed the cigarette against the outside wall, then waved ineffectually at the smoke. He made a funny figure: short, squat and barrel-chested, his arms waving in the air like he was crying for help. He slammed the window shut and sat down behind his desk.

Roy groaned inwardly. Professional Standards Committee, or the PSC, was a new body that regulated police officers. Every officer needed an annual MOT of their behaviour and conduct.

"I saved my daughter from a serial killer. Why does the PSC have to be involved?" Roy asked plainly.

From the smug look in Nugent's beady blue eyes, he knew the fat bastard was enjoying this.

"Don't ask me." Nugent tapped a yellow fingernail on a slim folder on the desk. "They sent this report through. You're personally involved in cases, which is affecting your judgement, apparently. You left without any warning when Anna was abducted. It could've ended badly. Your radio distress signal was traced to Jacob's Ladder, count yourself lucky help got there in time."

A flare of irritation spread slowly through Roy's body, warming his stomach. He knew better than to say anything. It would only make things worse.

"You've not found your brother as yet. That's also affecting your head. They said, and I quote, *DCI Roy can be dangerous and unstable, his operational judgement affected by his personal situation.*"

Nugent raised two meaty hands. "Again, don't ask me, this is all them." He folded his hands against his ample belly, and looked at the report like he was telling Roy 'I told you so'.

Roy pulled up a chair and sat down opposite Nugent. The D Sup didn't invite him to sit, but there was a flicker of sympathy in the man's eyes. Or maybe Roy imagined it. More chance of the latter, he knew.

The two men stared at each other without blinking. Nugent was the first to speak. "Unless you want to lose your job, I suggest you follow their advice. The PSC is powerful, Rohan. You know they've looked at your previous record. You broke a child trafficker's jaw once."

"I should have blown him a kiss, Sir. I'll remember for next time."

A red glow appeared in Nugent's eyes, like life returning to a dead robot. "Leave it out."

"I didn't ask for this, Sir," Roy said. "But I have to deal with it. You would do the same, if you were in my shoes. My brother's long gone, and we both know Mr Burns knows what happened, but he won't tell us." Nugent went to speak but Roy raised a hand, and his voice, not caring about the consequences. He would gladly take his leave and get the hell out of here.

"But to come after my little girl, that's lower than low." His lips curled upward in a snarl. "And I'm not going to apologise for not doing things by the book. Anyone would've done the same in my shoes, for Christ's sake. I don't need no shrink to tell me that." His lips twitched in a mirthless smile. He tapped the side of his skull. "I made sense of myself a while ago."

Even as he said the words, he knew he couldn't hide from

26

himself. The guilt of losing Robin, engraved into his soul as a teenager, was a little sharp-toothed critter that chewed away inside him as an adult.

The shame, the nightmares. The bitter pill that came up like acid burps from the whisky. Every time he swallowed that pill back down, sent the guilt back into its dungeon.

The last thing he wanted some fancy psychologist bringing it back up.

"I don't make the rules, son," Nugent said, in the most reflective mood Roy had ever seen him in. He was surprised Nugent hadn't had an outburst when Roy talked over him. From experience he knew that from there, things would spiral downwards. This time, even the D Sup seemed to realise Roy had reached his limits.

"See the psychologist. Make it easy on yourself."

Roy nodded. "Not hard. That makes sense."

The perpetual low growl returned to Nugent's throat. "Just bloody do it."

CHAPTER 7

18 Years Ago

Fifteen-year-old Jayden took a deep drag on the cigarette, watching the red tip burn. The hit of nicotine made him a little lightheaded. His father told him it was because he didn't smoke regularly. Jayden wanted to; he was getting used to the taste of a fag, as they called it in school. He had graduated to smoking some weed as well, or cannabis. The older, sixth form boys did it outside school. A group of them went past him, shoving and pushing each other in a play fight. Jayden tried to make eye contact, but none of them were interested.

Jayden saw the grey Honda approach, then slow down. His father, Jerry Budden, never picked him up from outside school. It was always on this back street, where no other parents ever picked up their children. Jayden had never figured out why. His dad said he hated the traffic. Jayden thought there was another reason.

His father's eyes rested on him, and at this, Jayden came off the wall he was leaning against, and slung his schoolbag over a shoulder.

"You're late," his dad observed as Jayden climbed into the passenger seat. The familiar smell of old leather, sweat, and stale beer hit his nostrils. The back seat was a mess of cigarette burns and dark stains. Jayden had never asked his dad what the stains were from. He knew he wouldn't like the answer.

"Put your seat belt on," Jerry rasped. "How was school?"

"Not bad. Same old."

Jerry drove the car around to the main entrance of the school and stopped a short distance from the gates. He watched the boys coming out. Jayden watched him staring, and distaste and nausea started churning in his guts. He hated it when Jerry sat in the car and watched the younger boys. Jayden knew it was easier for Jerry when he was in the car. Having another, albeit older, boy in the car meant no one would look twice at them. It was just another father and son waiting for their younger brother to come out. Jayden glanced at Jerry, a sudden, futile rage spiking in his veins. Too many bad memories.

His right foot slammed down on the floor, and he flung his fist against the side of the door.

"Can we go now, please! I want to go home."

"Alright, fucking hell." Jerry cast him an evil look. "What's the rush? You ain't got nothing to do when we get home."

"I'm tired. I got homework for tomorrow."

"As if you do any bloody homework." Jerry shook his head and carried on watching. A smile crept on to his lips. Jayden followed Jerry's lecherous gaze to a little boy, no more than seven or eight, who was standing near the school gates. The boy was clearly waiting for a parent to pick him up. It made Jayden feel physically sick.

"Listen now, lad," Jerry whispered. "See that kid over there? Here, give him this." Jerry took out a chocolate bar, and some sweets. "Go on, take it. Give it to that boy and tell him we'll drop him home."

Jayden stared at his so-called father, disbelief battling with fury in the pit of his stomach.

"You must be fucking jokin'," he said, raising his voice, and squaring his shoulders. Him and his father had never come to blows, not since he got bigger. Before that... Jerry had done unmentionable things for many, long, slow, tortuous years. Those cruel memories filled Jayden with shame, ripped his heart with torment.

"No bloody way am I doin' that," Jayden seethed. "No way."

"Look at me, lad."

Jayden wouldn't. He folded arms across his chest, his thick black jacket making his arms puff out. He stared resolutely out the window. Jerry had tried to make him chat to younger boys before, and initially he had gone ahead with it, but he stopped when he realised what was happening. There was no way he would allow the torment he had suffered to be visited upon another poor soul.

"I looked after you all these years. Gave you shelter when you were out on the street. Your folks were dead, and there was no one to look after you. You would've ended up a junkie or a burglar. I gave you my house. Me." Jerry pointed a finger at his chest.

Jayden wanted to say the words, but shame and hurt spun tight fingers around his tongue, stopping him from speaking.

What you did to me no man would do to another child. Never mind their own son.

Those horrible images and memories were burnt deep down in his soul. He couldn't escape the scars. He didn't want to think about them.

"I know it's not always been easy. But we cared for each other. Comforted each other. Eh?"

The words made Jayden shiver with disgust. Jerry tried to touch him, but he moved away.

"I want to go home," Jayden repeated. "Or I can get out and walk."

"It's a long walk, and it's going to rain soon."

"I don't care."

"Look," Jerry coaxed. "Just go and talk to that boy. Tell him we can give him a lift home. Go on."

Jayden cast his so-called father a look of pure venom. "I said no!"

Jerry swore loudly and profusely. Then he started to drive. Slowly, he turned the car around and stopped next to the boy on the opposite pavement.

"What're you doing?" Jayden frowned.

"Shut up." Jerry wound his window down. The little boy gaped at them. If he had a phone, it wasn't visible.

"Ey up there little fella," Jerry said in a silly, sing-song voice that nauseated Jayden. He looked away so the boy couldn't see his face.

"It's going to rain soon. You waitin' for your mum to pick you up?"

"Er, umm, yes."

"This is my son, Jayden. I've seen you round the school. I used to work here, you know. I know the principal and a lot of the teachers. What's your name, like?"

The boy looked around, then down at his feet, unsure. Jerry

carried on. "I'm sure I know your dad. Seen him around too. Here, have a choc." He handed a chocolate bar to the kid, who didn't take it, but looked at it longingly. "Go on, take it. It's alright."

Jayden had seen enough. He leaned over and spoke to the boy. "Go home now. Or go back inside the school and ask reception to call your parents." He got out of the car and stood next to the boy. "Come with me." He pulled the boy away, dragging him to the school gates. They went in, and Jayden dropped the boy at reception.

When he walked out, his evil joke of a father had gone. The rain started, a whispering drizzle at first, then the heavens opened up. He was drenched, shivering cold by the time he got back home.

The door flung open before he could knock. Jerry stood there; his teeth bared in fury. He grabbed Jayden's collar and pulled him inside, then slammed the door shut.

"How dare you do that to me?" He raged. "What did you say to that boy?"

"Nothing. I just dropped him off at the reception. Then I left."

"Don't lie to me," Jerry advanced on him. Jayden's back hit the stair banisters. His face was mottled, eyes glittering, rage contorting his face. It was strange, Jayden thought, that he didn't mind this fury. If his father was angry, he might hit Jayden, and that was okay. But at least he wouldn't be touching him, doing the shameful, weird things that he used to when Jayden was younger. Thank god he lost interest in that as Jayden got older. Thank god.

"I'm not lying." He didn't speak to anyone about what happened to him. A lot of the past made no sense to him because he had coped by forgetting. Pulling a shroud over his noxious, terrifying memories had become a habit for him. He didn't know who he had been before he started living with Jerry. His father. Yet, he knew in his bones that Jerry wasn't his father. He never would be.

"Are you sure? I've told you before, lad, no one's gonna believe you if you say owt. You hear me?"

Jerry snarled, his yellow teeth showing. Jayden moved away, but Jerry grabbed his arm.

"You hear me?"

"Yes. Now let me go."

CHAPTER 8

Roy put the phone down slowly, like he was putting the pin back in a grenade. The clinical psychologist had been soft-spoken and warm. Roy had nothing against Meredith Wilson. She'd been doing her job. But he shuddered at the prospect of answering her questions. Then he would have a follow-up with two inspectors from the PSC. In a perverse way, he was looking forward to that meeting. He could tell them exactly what he thought about the bloody PSC. The prospect made him smile grimly as he opened his desk drawer to get his radio and warrant card. The damn radio was out of battery, as usual.

The two detective constables were at their desk, and Sergeant Melanie Sparkes walked in with a steaming mug of coffee. Roy nodded at her, then indicated the mug, his jaws hardening, eyes serious.

"Where's ours then? I could do with a brew."

Melanie was used to his moods. "I did ask, guv. The lads didn't want any, and you weren't here."

"Never make assumptions." Roy smiled. "You alright? The

girls okay?"

"Girls are fine. Alexa's got a boyfriend, I think. She walks to school and back with him. She's always getting weird emojis on her phone."

Alexa was Melanie's fifteen-year-old teenager. Her younger daughter was eleven.

Rizwan looked up from his screen. "Weird, how? Do you mean rude?"

Melanie rolled her eyes. "Kind of, yes. I won't bore you with details. Stuff you can send on phones these days honestly."

"And how do you have access to your daughter's phone?" Oliver piped up. "Surely she guards that with her life."

"When she leaves it on the kitchen counter, or the sofa. This lad's always sending suggestive GIFs and emojis."

Roy caught Melanie's eyes. He could see the faint tremor in her face, and, as a parent, he knew instantly what she was thinking. Their last case had involved an app, and it had shown how vulnerable some teenagers could be.

"All harmless fun though?" he asked gently. "You talked to Alexa about it?"

Melanie nodded. "And I know the lad, and his family. It's all okay."

Roy nodded, then turned back to the DCs. He pointed at Oliver. "You, come with me. Riz, get me some CCTV footage. I know there's no cameras on that street, but I don't care where you get it from – house cameras, car dashcams, anything. Liaise with traffic if you have to. Pull up the cold case records. Find out if similar murders happened in the past, around Yorkshire, and remain unsolved." He turned to Melanie. "What would you like to do?"

"I'd like to come with you, guv."

Roy nodded. Melanie was a safe pair of hands, she had more than shown that in the last case. Her opinion on the crime scene would be useful.

"In which case," he told Oliver, "You stay and give Riz a hand here. We'll be back soon."

"Give him a hand he'll want the whole arm," Oliver said in exasperation and glared at Riz. "You lazy bugger."

"Shut up," came the inevitable reply from Riz. "The only work you done this morning is gel your hair."

Roy stuffed the dead radio in his belt, aiming to pick up batteries from the front desk on his way out. "I want to see some new stuff when I'm back. So, as the man says, less talk and little more action, alright?"

*****

The blue and white tape fluttered in the breeze, blocking off the entire street. Two squad cars guarded the mouth of the junction, uniformed officers directing traffic away. Car windows lowered as they drove past, inquisitive eyes trying to look down the street. Melanie ducked under the tape with ease, and Roy lowered himself stiffly, feeling the ache in his back.

He had been this way since rescuing Anna. The falls and jumps had taken their toll on his late forties body. He was working on his fitness, but the spate of recent injuries hadn't helped. Melanie watched him straighten slowly, grimacing.

"Bad back?" she asked, sympathetically.

"And knees, ankles, shoulders, you name it," Roy frowned, stepping forward gingerly. They headed for the cluster of police officers up ahead, to their right. Roy walked slower, taking in the road, and properties around him.

Many of the shopfronts were boarded up, but some were open. There was a café, and a man stood outside, speaking to a

36

uniformed sergeant, waving his arms in the air. Probably complaining about his lack of business today, which Roy couldn't blame him for.

Above the shopfronts, the terraced and semi-detached houses were presumably divided up into flats, as several windows were open, curtains drawn, and shapes visible inside. People were staring at the crime scene. The presence of witnesses was good news.

He knew they turned a blind eye to what happened here after dark, but the chances of someone spotting the victim or killer were now a lot higher. *That would make up for the lack of CCTV*, he thought, his trained eyes skimming the lamp posts and corners of houses for discreetly placed cameras. He found none.

His eyes came to rest on the parade of shops to his left. There was a bike repair joint, a newsagent, and a hardware store, which looked out of place. But what got his attention was The Cliffe Sauna, a massage parlour, as the neon sign rather proudly proclaimed. The gaudy neon lights, now turned off, looked like they belonged to a strip joint in Vegas, and not inner- city Sheffield. He watched as a shadow moved across one of the windows facing the street. A man, watching him.

He had to walk a good few minutes to get to the crime scene, despite his long legs. He looked back as he got there – the sauna was a distance away now, and round a slight bend in the road, obscuring the line of sight. At night, no one would be able to see what happened here from the sauna.

Two figures in blue Tyvek coats went into the white tent, where the body lay. It was good to see Scene of Crime already here. He recognised one of the Tyvek-coated figures as Justin Dobson, the head of SOC. He lifted the flap of the white tent and disappeared inside. A lightbulb flashed inside as photos were taken, prior to the body being removed.

The tent flap shifted again, and the familiar, petite figure of Sarah Botham emerged. She took her mask off, and then ripped off the plastic apron. She stuffed them in the black bin liner by the tent and did the same with her gloves and shoe coverings. Then she walked over to Roy. Melanie was speaking to one of the uniformed sergeants by the tent.

"Now then. Dragged you out at last," Sarah said, rubbing her hands together.

"I'm not out of hibernation yet. The PSC think I'm a headcase, and they want a psych evaluation before I return full time. Nugent's putting his foot in it, as usual. Although he claims it's got nothing to do with him."

Sarah made a face, and her green eyes glowed. Her button nose was red, and the morning's brisk breeze put a shade of pink to her cheeks. He looked away, not wishing to stare.

"That sauna back there. Is it what I think it is?"

Sarah nodded. "Aye, I think so. The uniforms have knocked on all doors down the street. A woman opened the door and said they're shut, and that was that. I'm going to have a word."

"We need to. Were they shut last night?"

"Apparently. That's what they told Gary," Sarah pointed to the uniformed sergeant Melanie was speaking to. "He was in charge of the door to door. I guess we can revisit the places of interest."

"Why was the massage parlour shut last night? That makes no sense. Surely that's when they make their money."

Sarah shrugged. "Worth asking the question." She tucked a strand of blonde hair behind her ears.

"What do you think of the body?" Roy asked.

A shadow passed over Sarah's face. It was never easy, Roy knew. One never got used to it, seeing another human being lying there, messed-up and desecrated beyond belief. Sarah

38

blinked, twice.

"Bad, aye. Bruising around the neck, maybe that's how she died. Cuts all over so she bled out. Cigarette burns on the skin too."

"I'll take a look," Roy said, and walked past her. He nodded at Gary and Melanie. He'd seen Gary in the past, he was rising up he ranks. The red-haired, freckled-faced sergeant said 'hello' and Roy replied.

"Did you speak to the massage parlour owner?"

"She didn't identify as the owner. Her name's Debbie. She said she's the caretaker for the owner, who's called Emma Birtwistle. She's in Spain apparently."

"Convenient, that. Just in case they have a police raid, eh?"

Gary grinned, showing his dimples. "Yes, guv."

Roy put on his apron, mask, gloves, and shoe coverings. Then he braced himself and went inside the tent.

CHAPTER 9

The woman lay on her back, her arms and legs bent at an unnatural angle. Her dress was ripped in places, and almost transparent. She was younger than Roy had imagined. Early twenties at the most. Her eyes were dark, staring wide into nothingness. Her neck was turned to the right, not by accident. The body had been shaped, left in this position on purpose, to suit the killer's evil mind.

One more look at the young face and Roy squeezed his eyes shut. The mask and apron gave him some detachment, but not much. He wanted to close the eyes; the poor girl deserved that much. The sooner she was out of here, the better.

"Ey up," came the muffled greeting from his left. Justin was by the woman's feet, taking samples from the ground. He tapped an invisible watch on his left wrist.

"What time do you call this then?"

"Fashionably late, mate," Roy said.

"Too late for this poor lass, that's for sure." There was a tinge of gravity in his words, weighing them down.

Roy nodded at him and carried on with his inspection. The head was carefully turned to the right, there was no doubt. Sarah was correct about the neck bruising; he could see the ugly blue and black welts spreading. But he wasn't sure if it was the cause of death. For one, he couldn't see a deviated windpipe. That took air to the lungs, and in most strangulation cases, it was broken. A broken trachea, or windpipe, was always obvious, as it was such a superficial structure. He knelt to take a closer look. With a gloved finger, he gingerly lowered the lower eyelid. He couldn't see the jagged black marks in the whites of the eyes that would signify the blood haemorrhages which happened when the neck was squeezed to the point of no return. Another mark against strangulation being the cause of death.

Roy had picked up these little nuggets from his mentor, Arla Baker. To this day, he hadn't met a detective who knew their way around a dead body better than her.

Roy was assuming the killer was a man, as most violent deaths were carried out by men. But he could be wrong. He went to the other side of the body, stepping around the head. Her short, dark hair was tucked in under the shoulders. No blood around the head. The pathologist would confirm, but head trauma was unlikely.

The sleeves of her short dress were cut off. Roy could only imagine the only intention was to show the deep cuts on the elbow and wrists, where the arteries came up to the surface. He looked down the body, where Justin was still brushing the ground carefully.

On the legs, Roy saw cuts at the ankles, again where he knew the arteries crossed over the top of the ankle bones. There were deep gashes at the back of the knees, and in the groin. Blood congealed in clumps at the tops of these wounds, and had flowed down her hips, pooling on the floor. These brutal injuries were never easy to see, and Roy shook his head, wondering at the cold brutality with which the wounds were inflicted.

"A pensive mood doesn't suit you, Inspector," a firm female voice said. He looked up to see the prim and proper Dr Sheila Patel, her short hair combed neatly to the neck. She wore a dark trouser suit, and flat shoes which didn't do anything for her height, but he suspected she didn't care. Her dark eyes glittered at him, then lost the hardness as they swept down to the body.

She was in the apron already, and lifted the mask to her face, and knelt on the floor with her briefcase. She opened it and took out a long probe that looked like a torture instrument. Roy was tempted to comment on it but held his tongue. He knew it was a rectal thermometer.

Dr Patel assembled the gizmo, then approached the body. She tutted in her throat lightly as she felt the skin, then looked in the eyes, and inside the mouth. Roy gave her a few minutes to examine externally.

"Time of death?"

"Rigor mortis is present in the large muscles, and advanced, so I would say twelve hours." Dr Patel pressed two fingers on the chest, then withdrew it slowly. The purplish-blue colour on the skin didn't change much.

"Livor Mortis is also advanced. Definitely twelve hours-plus."

Roy had heard that term before. Another thing he'd learnt from Arla Baker. "Livor is the colour of the body after death?"

Dr Patel paused and looked up at him. Her face betrayed no emotion as she nodded.

"Correct. It's this dark purple colour that all dead bodies get, and the bluish tinge is from haemoglobin leaching out of the blood vessels. It's fixed, as you can see, which only happens twelve-plus hours after death." She pressed on the arm once, and the colour didn't change.

"When was the body found?" The pathologist asked.

"This morning around 8 am. It's eleven now. Safe to say she died before midnight last night?"

Dr Patel thought for a while, then nodded. "Between ten and twelve, but let's check the core temperature first. Here, help me, will you?"

"He'd be doing something useful then, eh right? Not just standing around and watching." Justin offered a comment from his position.

"Don't mind him," Roy said to Dr Patel, ignoring Justin. "We only let him out on certain days. He's stopped taking his pills."

Sheila shook her head as Justin grinned behind his mask and got back to work. Roy moved as the pathologist came over to his side. He grabbed the hips where Dr Patel asked him to and pulled gently. Dr Patel used the rectal probe, then pulled it out, and took a reading. She pulled off her gloves and entered the number on her phone.

"I'd say between 11 pm and midnight. Last night the temperature was about seventeen degrees. This woman's thin, her body would lose heat quickly. Core temp is about eighteen degrees. I'll know more when I use the spreadsheet at the morgue."

"We can work with that," Roy said. He made a mental note of the time of death. He watched as Dr Patel checked the body, donning new gloves.

"No external signs of sexual activity. But again, I'll only know more when I take a proper look. And this…" words failed her as she looked at the wounds in the hips. Roy knew she'd seen it all. Twenty years in this business and it gives you a hard skin. But often, there were simply no words. She did her examination still, going through the motions.

"He went crazy here. Total contrast to the clean cut in the elbows and ankles. He sliced and chopped at random. In the process he cut the deeper femoral vein and arteries."

Her words fell on silence. Justin had also stopped working, listening.

Dr Patel said, "He did it on both hips, and I think it was an attempt to reach the blood vessels, but it could also have been frustration." She looked around the body. "There is an element of ritual her, with the positioning of the arms and legs, and the way the head is turned. Like he wanted her to face that way. Assuming it's a he." She glanced up at Roy.

"Sarah thinks she's a sex worker. So, her killer might be a he," Roy said.

Dr Patel pointed at the arms. "See those track marks? They're needle tracks. She was an intravenous drug user. If you look at her face, the cheeks are full, she doesn't have the sunken cheeks or starved look of a typical heroin user. I'd say she kicked the habit. These needle marks are old." The pathologist shrugged. "Not sure if that helps."

"All of it does, thanks." Roy looked at the entrance as the tent flap lifted and Sarah entered, wrapped in her white apron. He nodded at her, then focused on Dr Patel again.

"What about the neck? Could strangulation be the cause of death?"

Dr Patel took a closer look. "No deviation of the trachea," she said, confirming Roy's observation. "That doesn't mean she wasn't strangled – it means asphyxiation might not be a cause of death. I mean, there's marks on the throat, she was assaulted here."

"He was eager to get his hands on her," Roy said. "Any prints?" He asked Justin.

Justin spoke up from the rear of the tent. "None, soz. Not done with the legs yet, but not seen any so far." Soz was short for sorry, another Northernism that Roy had got used to.

44

"I don't think you'll see any, either." Dr Patel agreed. "No tell-tale bruises, apart from the face and neck. I'd say this started as a crime of passion, then he came to his senses, and put gloves on."

Sarah's phone rang, and she went outside to answer it. She came back presently, her attractive face grim, the normal sparkle in her sea green eyes absent.

"The lads have found a cold case, with similar injuries. Young female found dead seven years ago, not far from here."

CHAPTER 10

Roy came out of the tent, followed by Sarah, leaving Dr Patel and Justin to do their thing. A fine drizzle had started, the kind of rain that's barely visible, or audible, but still gets you annoyingly wet if you stand outside for a couple of minutes. Sarah lifted the hood of her jacket. Roy had no such luxury; the whispering drops began to plaster hair to his scalp. He watched the uniforms manning the roadblock, and the constables on the other end of the road. He estimated about half a kilometre had been cordoned off. He pointed northwards, away from the direction he'd come from.

"That leads to Meadowhall and Rotherham, right?" he asked Sarah.

She nodded. Meadowhall was the largest shopping centre in Yorkshire that Roy knew of, and Rotherham was a nondescript, industrial town. Meadowhall formed the eastern border of Sheffield.

"Shut down the whole road," Roy said. "Divert traffic in a loop. I want a door to door in every house on the street, all the way up to the main junction. There will be CCTV up there, and chances are we get more witnesses."

"Lots of disruption, guv. What about people who live here, can they drive?"

Roy shook his head. "Not till we do a search. Uniforms on the case already?"

"Aye, I've set their tasks. Door-to-door in progress, as you can see. Justin's got one of his men searching with the uniforms, for anything on the street. Bloody rain's not going to help."

"That's why I want the entire road shut." Roy looked at Sarah approvingly. They both knew water was the biggest enemy of evidence. Scene of Crime officers hated it with a passion. Damn drops washed away all manner of prints too – finger, boots, tyre treads.

He spotted Melanie in front of a small door next to a closed store, with a uniformed constable. They were talking to a woman in a dressing gown, who held a cigarette in her hand, and shivered inside the doorway. Roy and Sarah walked towards the Cliffe Sauna.

"Tell me about the cold case," Roy muttered.

"Good job you asked the lads to look. I remember it now as well. I was a constable then, but it stuck in my mind. The woman was found in Attercliffe, just across the river."

Roy nodded. Attercliffe was another renowned run-down part of Sheffield. Sarah continued. "She was found on the canalside. It was summertime. That part of the canal towpath is shady, runs through Victoria Quay. You know what goes on around there."

"Drug dealing, pimping and sex work. Correct?"

"Yes." Sarah took her phone out and flicked to the email Riz had sent her. "Her dress was torn, injuries in the elbow, wrists, hips, and elbows. Knife wounds, she bled to death. Unconfirmed reports of her being a sex worker. Tracy Perkins, her name was. Lived in a council estate up in Loxley. Single mother, left her baby with her mother. Only one reason she'd be down by the canal at night."

They'd arrived at the Cliffe Sauna, and they both stopped, watching the building. It was a semi-detached three-floor, large, squat building. Plenty of rooms inside, they could see. The neon sign was attached to the side of the first floor bay window, and the rusty fittings needed replacing. The building had a lick of paint, and looked alright, in comparison to many of the other houses on the street.

"She was also strangled, but that wasn't the cause of death. She bled out. No witnesses. No prints. No DNA matches. A couple of arrests were made, young male drug dealers in the area, but there wasn't enough to charge them."

"We still have their records on file," Roy muttered. "Might as well check on them, see if they're still around. You never know, these bastards like to surface every few years, don't they?"

"That they do, guv."

Melanie approached them from behind. "Man who reported the crime. Shall we let him go?"

Roy looked at Sarah, as she'd spoken to him. Sarah nodded. "He's coming later to give us a statement. Name's Andy Pike. I've got his number and address. Lives with his wife and kids nearby. He's not going anywhere. Is that alright?" She glanced at Roy, who nodded. He trusted Sarah's judgement.

"What time does he get to work?" Roy asked, referring to Mr Pike. "He's a porter at the hospital, right?"

"Yes. He does shift work and he was starting at 8 am today. He saw the body at seven-thirty. Uniforms were here by seven-forty-five."

"Alright, I want to see him when he comes for the statement." He turned to Melanie. "Anything from the door to door?"

"This place is dodgy," Melanie pointed to Cliffe Sauna. "Been here a few years. Used to be a tanning salon before. Now it's this, a massage parlour" Melanie raised her hands, and made apostrophe signs with her fingers.

"Hmm," Roy said, stroking the stubble on his cheeks. "Any witnesses?"

"None yet. I'll carry on, shall I?"

Roy and Sarah nodded, and Melanie walked off to join the uniforms again. Sarah went up to the tall red door. The sign, in red letters, was stamped above the doorway: 'Cliffe Sauna and Massage Parlour'. Sarah knocked and waited. When nothing happened, she raised a fist and hammered it on the door. It was a thick, tough wooden door, with a round brass ring on the side. She raised the ring, and let it fall, twice. That made a louder sound than her knocking.

They waited, and Roy went to the side, trying to look through the bay windows. The glass panes had massage and sauna deals stuck on them. The white blinds were down, and he tried to peer through the edges, but only darkness met his eyes. He rejoined Sarah and shrugged. Then he stepped forward and hammered with his large fist. The big door shuddered.

"Police!" Roy shouted. "Open the door or we open it. Up to you."

He moved away, and they heard a sound from inside, the whisper of rushing steps.

A bolt slid on the other side, and a few more locks clicked open. The door opened smoothly, and a woman's face appeared. She had no make-up on, and her cheeks were puffy, her hair straggly. She was in her mid-to-late-fifties, Roy thought, but the lines and creases on the woman's face marked her out as a sun-worshipper, which probably made her look older.

"Sorry luv, I was in the loo," she said. Her accent was thick south Yorkshire. "What's goin' on 'ere, like?"

"A dead body." Roy didn't mince his words. "Young woman killed and left out on the street. That's what's going on. We're not here for fun, or to waste your time. Can we come in?"

Sarah had already put her foot on the porch, not waiting for an invite. The woman stood her ground for a second or two, then gulped, and thought better of it. She opened the door wider.

The interior was dark, but then their eyes got used to it. The lobby was surprisingly luxurious. Deep, soft purple felted sofas lined the space, with small tables in front. The reception table was covered in similar purple felt, with gold letters proclaiming the name of the place on the wall above. Dark blue wallpaper, with dark flowers, hung on the wall, giving the place a cosy, intimate air. Someone had spent good money on this place.

"Are you Debbie?" Sarah asked. Roy was looking at the exits from the room. There was a door behind the reception desk, covered in wallpaper, the door handle flush with the wood panel. He would've missed it unless he looked carefully. There was another door at the far end, which was shut.

"That's right. And you are…"

Sarah held up her warrant card. "DI Botham of South Yorkshire Police. This is DCI Roy."

Roy was still looking at the door at the far end of the room. A sliver of light came in through the bottom, and he saw a pair of feet there. There was a little creak as the feet shifted. Someone was listening to them.

CHAPTER 11

"Are you the manager here?" Sarah was asking. Roy moved past them, trying to tread softly, helped by the deep pile carpet on the floor. Next to the reception there was a bar, and the carpet gave way to a wooden floor. The door, with the feet still visible under it, was a few paces next to the bar. Roy's big feet creaked on the wood. He watched the light change under the door, as the feet moved, and he heard steps receding.

"Where're you going?" The woman asked.

Roy turned. "You'll find that it's us asking the questions. What's behind this door?" He pointed at the metallic grey coloured door, which merged with the wallpaper.

Debbie was gearing up for a retort but thought better when she saw Roy's expression. His jaws ground together as he stared her down.

"That leads to the stairs... Goin' up I mean."

"Someone was listening to us. Can you open the door?"

"I can like, but... you 'ave no right to come in 'ere, do yer? This establishment is closed now, but even when it's open—"

"Open the door or there will be a dozen officers searching the place top to bottom. How about that?"

Debbie looked to Sarah, as if for support, then gulped. She came forward and opened the door. Roy stepped past her, into a wider than expected hallway, with two rooms ahead of him, and another door at the back, leading outside. A staircase went up to his right. The rooms were shut. He put a foot on the lowest rung of the stairs and listened. The house was still. He knew someone was up there, probably the man's shadow he'd seen from the street.

He heard a door open and close softly, the sound dimmed, but still carrying through the walls.

"Do you want to get him, or shall I?" Roy put a hand on the banister.

"Wait," Debbie raised a hand, panic clear in her eyes. "I'm not the owner. I look after this place. The bloke upstairs is Karen's partner. He keeps an eye on the place when Karen's not around."

"Karen's the owner?" Sarah asked. Debbie nodded then moved past Roy and started climbing the stairs. Roy followed, as did Sarah. Debbie looked behind; her eyes wide.

"Keep moving, or we go upstairs," Roy said, not stopping. Debbie was clearly scared of something. She had stopped, wringing her hands, her eyes wide open. As Roy stepped past her, she held an arm out.

"Wait, I'm going." She moved past Roy, and he glanced at Sarah, who was trying to look at the top of the staircase. A frown flitted across her face, and Roy followed her gaze. Debbie was on the landing, walking rapidly to the door at the end. Rooms opened up on either side, and the doors were all shut. The deep pile dark carpet was still here, as was the wallpaper.

"Did you see something?" Roy said, as they followed Debbie.

"I thought that door was open, but someone shut it."

Debbie was fiddling with the handle, and she gave up with a tired expression on her face. "It's locked."

"Where's the keys?"

Debbie looked like a rabbit in the headlights, only her eyeballs swivelled sideways a couple of times.

"Ah, I, this door is normally locked, and Kevin has the keys."

Debbie had a habit, Roy could see, of saying the names first, and introducing them later. He asked, "Kevin is Karen's partner?"

"Uh, yes."

"So, you don't have the keys?" Debbie shook her head. Sarah was trying the handle already, and it was locked.

She looked at Roy, who took two steps back. Sarah pulled on Debbie's sleeve and the two women moved out of the way. Roy rushed at the door and kicked it with all his might. It was sturdy, but he was aiming for the lock at the handle. The blow was jarring to his foot, sending tingles of pain up to his right hip. He grimaced, regrouped, and smashed his boot into the door again, and this time was rewarded with a sharp crack. He struck with his shoulder, staying on the door, refusing to bounce back, leaning on it till the lock splintered, and he almost stumbled into the room.

The room was dark, blinds down and curtains drawn at the bay window. Roy had seen the man in this room, when he looked up from the street. Sarah flicked a light switch on the wall, and a lurid, reddish light came on. *The cliched red light*, he thought, shaking his head. Sarah flicked another switch, and this time, a table lamp came on by the bedside, a normal yellow glow lighting up the wall. The large bed looked comfortable, with a fluffy purple duvet. Roy swung around, looking. There was no sign of the man. Sarah had opened a door opposite the bed and stepped inside an ensuite bathroom. It was empty and she emerged from it quickly.

Roy had spotted the door on the other side. Like the door behind the reception table, it was barely visible, covered by the same wallpaper, no handle. Before he could move, the door flew open. A tall man stood on the other side, large enough to stop a tank in its tracks. He walked in, ducking underneath the door frame. His face was pockmarked with scars, and he had wild stubble on his cheeks. His clean shaven-head had a tattoo on the side, and he wore a ring on his left ear. The snarl on his face was from the gutter, and a gold tooth flashed when he bared his teeth like a hyena. His voice was low and raspy.

"Wot the fock do you want, eh?"

CHAPTER 12

Roy stepped up to the man, who bunched his fists, spittle flying from his lips as he advanced. He stopped within touching distance. If he was trying to intimidate Roy, it wasn't working. Ignoring the man's broad girth, and gnashing teeth, Roy reached inside his pocket and calmly retrieved his warrant card.

"DCI Roy from South Yorkshire Police. And you are?"

"Get the fuck outta here now. Go on!" the man indicated the broken door. "And I want compensation for damage to the property."

Roy thought of a suitable response but checked himself. No point in aggravating the situation. He needed answers, and the civil way was best to begin with. If force was needed later, so be it.

"We can discuss that. We're looking for a murderer, and I was under the impression there was a suspect here." He raised his eyebrows. "Is there?"

The snarl etched deeper into the man's face, til it looked like his teeth were actually protruding.

"What the fuck are you talkin' about? No suspects here. This is legitimate business. Ain't you seen the sign outside? You fuckin' blind or wot?"

"Are you here for a massage? Or is it the sauna?"

"Shut up," the man roared, spit flying from his lips. Roy moved slightly to avoid the onslaught. "Get off my premises, now."

"Not until we've searched the rest of the house and spoken to everyone here. Got it?" Roy angled his head to one side, and his eyes bore into the man's. "We can do that now, or I can get some officers in here, and arrest you for resisting a police operation. Which is going on, just outside. You know that 'cos you were looking out that window a while ago." Roy jerked a thumb at the bay windows.

The man looked like he was going to burst like a balloon full of hot water, then he breathed with his mouth open. Roy grimaced as the foetid breath, reeking of old cigarettes, hit his nostrils.

"Wot do yer wanta know?"

"Your name, for starters. Are you the owner?"

The man's blue eyes flicked to Debbie, who cowered behind Sarah. Then he looked back at Roy, scowling.

"Aye. Kevin Rawlinson. Now pay for that door and fuck off."

Roy chose to ignore Kevin's wishes. "Is there anyone else here?"

"No."

"Mind if we have a look?"

Kevin's eyebrows wiggled, and his brain appeared to register something. He gave Debbie another dirty look, which let her know she'd messed up. Then he stepped aside. Roy and Sarah walked out the side door, and into another small landing. Stairs went up and led to another three rooms, one of which was unlocked. It was a carbon copy of the bedroom downstairs.

Roy put gloves on and raised the blinds. He was on the highest floor and could see the street below. To his left, and way up the street, he could see the small knot of uniforms, two white vans, and the white tent at the crime scene. To his right, and closer, lay the junction with the main road, and the squad cars and sergeants manning the roadblock.

He dragged his eyes back to the crime scene. It was slightly around the bend, and although visible, that was only because of the white tent and numerous figures. At night, the lights of a car would be noticeable, but nothing else. Sarah was looking around in the rest of the room. She opened the bedside table drawer and pulled out a pair of handcuffs, covered in fluffy pink feathers.

"Can I arrest you?" she asked, shaking them; they made a jingling sound. Roy didn't answer. She chucked the handcuffs on the bed and pulled out other stuff. A whip, black satin sheets that clearly had many uses: to tie hands together, to tie someone to the bedposts, or as a blindfold. Sarah rummaged around the drawers with gloved hands and came up empty. She looked under the bed, then straightened.

"Nowt." she put her hands on her hips and blew away a strand of hair by her lips.

"We need to check the other rooms," Roy said, making for the door. "But first, let's have a chat with Mr Rawlinson."

The bedroom downstairs was empty. They walked down the corridor, trying out the handles of the other rooms, only to find them all locked. Downstairs, Debbie had turned the lights on in the reception, but the blinds were still down.

"Where's Kevin?" Roy asked, looking around.

"He… He left." Debbie looked hapless, and scared. And she wasn't the kind of woman who was scared easily, Roy thought.

She had to look after a brothel, after all. Sarah was on the radio, asking uniforms to scour the area. Roy stepped out to the front, while Sarah checked the back. He jogged over to the sergeants by the squad cars, but they hadn't seen anything.

When he returned, Debbie was at the reception, where she'd been told to stay, and Sarah was in the small garden, by the back wall. It was a couple of meters high, and Sarah was speaking on her radio. She turned when she saw Roy and pointed at the trampled flower bed by the wall.

"They can't see him. He clearly climbed up here and went over."

There was a shed to one side. The door had a lock. Roy peered in through the window but couldn't see a ladder. He put a foot on the window ledge, and grabbed hold of shed roof, and hauled himself up. The structure creaked, then tilted alarmingly. For a split second, he wondered if the whole thing would collapse on top of him. But then it stabilised. Gingerly, Roy heaved upwards, and was able to clutch the top of the back wall. One knee bent on the shed roof, other on the shed window, he was able to raise his chin over the wall and take a look. There was an alley, and another row of terraced houses opposite. Two uniformed constables and Melanie were running down the other end of the alley. Roy hopped back down.

"Nothing," he told an inquisitive Sarah. He wiped his forehead with his sleeve.

"There must be an entrance from here into the alley. Kevin's a big bloke. If you found it hard to get up to the fence…" She left her sentence unfinished and looked around the back of the shed. She knocked around there for a while, and then shouted out triumphantly. Moments later, Roy heard a door creak and then shut. Sarah's voice came from the other side of the wall.

"I'm out here, guv. He must've come out this way."

Clever, Roy thought, *to hide the gate behind the shed.*

He went back inside to speak to Debbie. Sarah remained outside, chattering on her radio.

"What's your last name, Debbie?" Roy asked, flicking open his notebook. Debbie wrung her hands together, her eyes wide.

"Mcpherson. What happened out there?"

Roy looked at her. Her cheeks were pale, and her eyes darted around til they settled on Roy's face.

"Like I said earlier, a woman's died. Her body was found out there. I want you to look carefully at this," Roy took out his phone and scrolled to a photo he'd taken of the victim. He showed it to Debbie and watched her expression closely. Debbie squinted and moved the phone around to get a better angle of view. Then she went abruptly still, and she couldn't look away from the screen.

"Someone you know?" Roy asked. Debbie was still glued to the phone, and when she slowly raised her face, it seemed she was seeing Roy for the first time. She blinked, and put the phone on the reception desk quickly, then wiped her hands like they were dirty. Roy put the phone back in his pocket.

Debbie touched her forehead, like she was trying to get her thoughts together. "She... uh, worked here sometimes. I've seen her around. Think it's her, anyway."

"What's her name?"

"Tracey. Can't remember her last name."

"Could it be written down somewhere?"

Debbie gaped at Roy like he'd asked her a trick question. Then she fumbled on the desk, pulling open a drawer. "Let me check, hold on."

Sarah came back in, and the look of disappointment and slight shake of her head meant one thing – Kevin Rawlinson had vanished.

"Positive ID," Roy whispered as Sarah got closer. They both looked over at Debbie who was skimming through a diary. She stopped at a page.

"Yes, here we go. Tracey Barrett. She last came here... two nights ago. She had some clients."

"For what?" Sarah asked. Debbie's face made the answer plain, but she fought valiantly to make her expression deadpan.

"Massage, as it says on the board outside. That's what we do." She pressed her lips together and shut up.

"How many women, like Tracey, work here?" Sarah pressed. "Are all their details in that diary?"

Debbie looked down at the green leatherbound diary, and stared at it like she realised her mistake. Slowly, she replaced the diary inside desk drawer.

"Uh... that's confidential information. About the masseurs, I mean."

"We would have to see that," Roy said. "This is a murder investigation, and you just told us the victim's name was Tracey, and she worked here." Roy smiled a little. "You did the right thing. Unlike your boss out there. Any idea where he's gone?"

Debbie shook her head.

Sarah asked, "What happens here, Debbie? It's more than massage, isn't it?"

Debbie looked around like a cornered rat. Her head moved sideways slowly. "You'll have to speak to Karen, the owner. The ladies come here, book a room, and treat their clients. That's all I know. Karen does the advertising and spreads the word. It's a massage parlour. The sauna's out the back before you go into the garden."

"What sort of a massage parlour"—Roy waved his hand

around—"Looks like this? Purple fluff everywhere, love and heart signs, and tart's boudoir wallpaper? Sorry if we're not making ourselves clear, but a woman's lying dead on the road outside. She worked here. And if this is a massage parlour, then I'm the Archbishop of Canterbury."

CHAPTER 13

"What the girls do in the rooms is their own business," Debbie said. They were now sitting at one of the tables, Sarah, and Roy opposite Debbie. "The men come in and look through the brochure to choose which masseur they want. Or sometimes they know from before. The girls contact their clients on social media. Don't ask me where, and how."

"Did Tracey see anyone specific that you remember?" Sarah asked. Debbie frowned as she thought. Then she shook her head.

"Quite a few girls come and go. The men all become a blur to be honest. They change so often. Sometimes the girls have a regular guy every week. But it changes."

"Was Tracey worried or angry last time you saw her? And when was that? I need a date and time."

Debbie lowered her head and sniffed once. When she looked up, her eyes were red-rimmed. Her lips moved a couple of times before she could speak.

"Tracey had a little girl. I've got one as well, and we used to talk about them. She left her girl with her mum when she came here to work the night. She lived up in Loxley. She worked in the packing factory in Burngreave, I think. Feel sorry for that child, but maybe best she's not old enough to understand."

Debbie took out a tissue and dabbed at her eyes, the tip of her nose red. Sarah asked gently, "When did you last chat to her?"

"Saturday evening, it was. I'd just had my dinner when she came in. After 6 pm. Can't remember the exact time. She seemed fine, normal, like. She had a bloke I'd never seen before."

"Can you describe the man she was with?"

"I'd say slim, about six feet. Dark hair. He wore a blue jacket, I think, black jeans and white trainers. In his thirties. Young bloke."

"And you've not seen him before?"

Debbie thought a while, then her eyes widened. "Oh shit, yeah. It was 'im. He wore a suit, like, and glasses, that's why I got confused. He were drunk the week before, and I heard him and Tracey shouting outside. I had to go and stop it. Not good for the business, the girls fighting with their clients outside the premises."

Roy and Sarah exchanged a glance. "Are you sure it was the same guy?" Sarah asked.

"Yes. When they came back in, she told him to stop pestering, and then Kevin came back from wherever he was, and that bloke buggered off. Never knew his name. I'm surprised Tracey came back with him on Saturday."

"And today's Monday," Roy said slowly. "You didn't see Tracey on Sunday?"

"No, the house was full. Weekends are busy for us. Girls respond to Karen's ads, and they come in, and show me a link on their phones that Karen sends them."

"Think carefully," Sarah said. "Before last week, did you see that man with Tracey? Did she mention you to him?"

Debbie's eyebrows knotted together as she thought. "She mentioned a guy from here who saw her on the street. She said she saw him more than once. She was out shopping, with her girl. He came up to her. She told me the name as well. I can't remember now."

"Is there any CCTV here?"

Debbie shook her head. "There's alarm buttons everywhere for the girls to press. In the bed panels, on the walls in the bedrooms. For obvious reasons, we're not allowed to have cameras here."

She looked from Sarah to Roy, and to both of them, that was an admission this was a brothel. She'd made it plain already, in fairness.

Roy said, "Tell us about the charming Mr Rawlinson. How often is he here?"

"Once a month, I'd say. Or every six weeks. Him and Karen come together sometimes. Mostly, though, Karen stays in Spain. The girls say Kevin has businesses here he comes to see."

"What sort of businesses?"

Debbie's eyes darted around, not looking at either of them. She gulped, and her hands moved on her lap.

"Don't be scared," Sarah said, her voice low. "He can't do anything to you."

Pain spread across Debbie's face. She thumped a fist on her thigh and looked heavenward once. She also glanced around, as if fearful someone was listening. She lowered her voice.

"That's what you think," she whispered. "Kevin's men know all about the girls. They come here and make good money compared to what they'd get in the supermarket or cleaning someone's house. But Kevin knows where they live. He's got photos of them, and he blackmails them later if they don't keep coming back. I don't know why I'm telling you this." Debbie covered her face with her hands.

"So, there are cameras here?" Roy asked. "How does Kevin take the photos."

"I think you need to go now," Debbie suddenly stood, indicating the talk was over. "I can't do this anymore. I've got mouths to feed."

"Did Kevin and Tracey ever have a fight?"

Colour left Debbie's cheeks, and her face crumpled. "You should go now." She backed away from the table. "I shouldn't have spoken to you. Please go."

"One last thing," Sarah said, both her and Roy also rising. "Do you know where Kevin might be?"

Debbie shook her head. Sarah said, "We need to search the premises. And I need that black diary you looked through, and the brochure you mentioned."

*****

Sarah and Roy stood outside in the rain, still that irritating light drizzle that was now making puddles on the road.

"Well, well. At least we have two leads to chase up. Kevin being the first one." Sarah looked at Roy.

Roy thrust his hands inside his pockets. "I wouldn't be surprised if Rawlinson was a part of an organised crime network. His partner, Karen, could even be the head of the gang. That's why she spends all her time abroad."

Sparkes, and Inspector Jonty Adams, one of the veteran uniform inspectors, walked up to them.

"Can't see that bugger anywhere," Jonty breathed. "He's a big fucker, right? He's bloody vanished. Didn't hear a car or nowt, did yer?" He looked at them. "And there's roadblocks on either end of the road. Where could he have gone, like?"

Roy looked up at the house next door to Cliffe Sauna. It had a pizza joint on the ground floor, now shut. It was also semi-detached, one half attached to the sauna. He noted the windows with curtains drawn. A top floor window was ajar.

"Have we looked in there?" He pointed at the small door that led to the property upstairs, most likely divided up into flats.

Melanie said, "Yes, I did, with Gary. Four families live up there. Three flats, each with a family of four, one's even got six living in a two-bedroom flat. It's a tip. They haven't seen nothin', which I don't believe. They must know what goes on next door."

"Aye, they do. Probably too scared to open their mouths," Sarah said. "The only reason Debbie did is because she's more scared of getting arrested than she is of Kevin."

Roy did a 360, looking at all the houses around. "Kevin's somewhere here, I think. Let's keep the roadblock in place. Keep the uniforms here over night." He looked at Jonty, who nodded. "Kevin definitely had a problem with Tracey. He wouldn't have scarpered like that otherwise. And this might just be his area, where he knows people. Someone could be hiding him."

They walked towards the white tent, where Roy wanted to do a last check of the site around the body. Dr Patel came out of the tent and saw them.

"Thought you'd gone already," Roy said.

"There's a paucity of bodies in the morgue today. Unexpected deaths, anyway."

"Wonders will never cease. Anything to add?"

"Not a great deal. I managed to have a look with a vaginal speculum. Definitely so signs of sexual activity. I should have more for you by tomorrow morning."

"Look forward to it," Roy said, his face blank. He watched as Dr Patel clicked her heels away on the tarmac and got into her car, next to the white SOC vans.

"Time to see what the lads dug up for us," Sarah said.

Roy was still looking at the houses. "Kevin's here. I can feel it."

A voice shouted from somewhere, catching his attention. "Hello detectives." Roy frowned and turned around. Behind the white tent, there was a black iron fence, separating the pavement from the grass verge that rose up to a small hillock. A man stood there. He was young and dressed in a dark jacket and trousers. His hair was black, and short, and he was an Asian man. Something about him shouted 'journalist' to Roy, and he couldn't believe the man had the gall to sneak all the way up here. He must've found a way somehow through the back.

"Who's he?" Sarah whispered.

"Looks like a media vulture," Roy scowled. He walked over, irritation surging inside him. The man gripped the waist high fence, observing Roy warily as he approached.

"What do you want?" Roy demanded, stopping a few feet away from the fence.

"I live around the corner, on Mansell Road. Just the other side. I was on my way to work and saw all this. Thought I'd stop by and ask."

That explained how he knew his way around here. But he still wasn't off the hook.

"Do you work for a newspaper? Or a radio channel?"

"Who me?" The man smiled. "No, mate. I'm a garage mechanic. Never seen nowt like this around here, like. What happened?"

Roy ignored the question. If the man lived around here, he could be useful as a witness. Also, a new suspicion was tingling in his mind. Malignant narcissist killers often returned to their crime scene. He noted the man's hands. Rough and calloused, a working man's hands. He didn't have any tattoos visible, or any other identifying marks.

"How long have you lived here?" Roy asked.

"Me? More than ten years. Moved down here when me old gaffer opened up a new garage here. He used to live in Riddlesthorpe before."

"What's your name?"

"Jayden Budden."

Roy was more relaxed. Something about the man still bothered him. Although he smiled, there was a tension in his body, a hard look in his eyes.

"How did you know I was a detective?"

Jayden shrugged. "You're in plain clothes, but you're obviously a police officer. Otherwise, you wouldn't be here, right?"

"Hmm. Is this the way you normally go to work?"

"Yes, I cycle across that path." Jayden pointed to the crest of the hillock. A woman was walking across, eyeing them. "It's not very well used. Gets muddy and that."

"So why do you use it?" Roy cast his eyes back on Jayden.

"It's up slope, so gives me a bit of exercise, you know." His attention flicked to the white tent. "So, what happened here?"

"I can't tell you, but I'm sure you knew that already. Do you live alone, Jayden? Or with someone."

68

"Alone. Why?"

"Where were you last night between ten and midnight?"

A frown creased the man's forehead. Roy now realised he wasn't as young as he looked. He had minor wrinkles in the corners of his eyes, and lines on his forehead. Mid-thirties, instead of late-twenties, he thought. He looked at the man's shoes. Trainers, and they were worn with use. Not a mechanic's choice of footwear, but maybe he got changed into boots when he was at work.

"I was actually cycling home this way. Went to the pub for a drink after work. Then cycled back home. Left the pub around 10 pm."

"What time did you get back home?"

"Takes me about half hour. Why you askin'?"

"When you were cycling back, did you see anyone on this road? Or a car? Anything, really?"

Jayden thought for a while. He indicated the row of houses up the road. "There's a massage parlour up there. It's active at night, if you know what I mean. I don't see any ladies out on the street. But I do see men going in and out of there. Last night..." his head lowered on his chest as he thought.

"Yes, I saw a car. It was a black car, two-seater. Might've been an Audi or a BMW, not sure."

"I know you were cycling then, but any idea of the time?"

"Around twenty past ten? My house is ten minutes cycle from here, and I was home by half ten."

"And again, I know it's difficult, but did you notice the car's registration number? Or how many people were inside?"

Jayden drummed fingers on the side of his leg. "I remember the car was stopped by the massage parlour. That place had its lights on. The car had its lights off, but then they switched on. A woman was speaking to the driver."

Roy leaned forward, sensing this was important. "What did the woman look like?"

"She had a dress on. I didn't stop to look, like, so don't take what I'm sayin' as gospel. Alright?"

"Yes, carry on." Roy checked out the flat top of the hillock. There was no tree cover. The path provided a good view of the road below. The path was deserted now, and this man was probably right about it not being well used. The hillock sloped down to the left and disappeared behind the row of houses.

"I think she got in the car, and they drove off. Driver and passenger only, don't think there was anyone in the back. But I can't be sure like."

"Which way did the car go?"

The man pointed to his right, where the road curled around, and went under a railway bridge. "That way. Joins the A612, I think, from a roundabout."

Roy watched Jayden as he spoke. His lips were dark, and fingernails stained yellow from nicotine. He was clean-shaven, and there was nothing unusual in his appearance. But the most unassuming men could be the most vicious of killers.

"Did you see anything else?"

Jayden shook his head. Roy nodded. "Okay. Will you please come to the station and give a statement? It will be useful."

"Sure, no problem. I can't do now, like, but can drop by after work, around five?"

Roy took out his notebook and took down Jayden's details. "See you at 5 pm."

"Aye." Jayden nodded, then smiled. "Never met a real life

detective before. Nice to meet you." He stuck out his hand. After a moment's hesitation, Roy shook his hand. A warm, firm grip. Then Jayden went back up the slope, to where his cycle was resting on a dry spot on the ground. Roy watched him cycle off. Something about that man didn't rest well with him.

He walked over to Sarah, who was chatting to Mel. He told them about Jayden. The ladies saw him as he cycled down the path, and then went down the slope, disappearing from sight.

"Look into him," Roy said. "I want to see if there's anything of interest."

CHAPTER 14

The man watched the policemen milling around. He had been here for a couple of hours now. When he first arrived, he had been thrilled to see the white tent, and the blue and white police tape. It meant his work was being recognised – again. It had been a long time, six years now, and his work had been forgotten. Not anymore. He was back, striking a blow at the heart of the matter, telling the world he wouldn't stand for it.

His fists clenched and his pulse boomed against his ear drums. He had joined the group of neighbours who had gathered close to one of the police cars that had set up a roadblock. He stood close so he wouldn't stick out, but he paid little attention to their chatter. Like most people, they weren't worth listening to. He knew far more than any of them ever would.

He watched as the big plainclothes officer, who had just come out of the tent, strolled up to the brothel. A woman followed him, petite, her blonde hair tied into a ponytail. Quite tasty, she was. He smiled to himself. He knew they were both detectives. He liked to know these things.

The big guy looked like he was in charge. He stopped to speak to a couple of officers, and he was clearly giving them orders. The man tried to think if he'd seen him before. An Asian man, Indian or Pakistani. Perhaps a Latino. He searched his mind, frowning. No, he couldn't place him, and that was good. He needed to find out more about him though. He could be trouble.

The door opened, and the detectives went inside Cliffe Massage Parlour. The man watched the two police officers standing at the roadblock. They were chatting to themselves, one of them showing the other something on his phone. That was good. He separated from the neighbours, and walked down a little, stopping before the blue and white tape, fluttering in the wind. From this angle, he could see the space between the brothel and the other houses, and the street beyond. He saw movement at the back fence. A man emerged through the fence, then peeked back over it, perhaps standing on his tiptoes. His scalp was clean-shaven, and he looked familiar; maybe he was the man who sometimes worked there as the pimp and guard. Then he was gone, perhaps escaping before the cops could question him.

As he looked at the brothel, shards of memory punctured his heart, making it bleed. The sunlight rusted into darkness. Visions from a life he desperately wanted to forget reared their ugly heads. His mother had worked in one of these places. All through his miserable childhood, he hadn't known the truth. As a teenage boy, he remembered taking her dinner there as she couldn't leave for the night. He hated everyone who worked there. All of them pandering to a sick fantasy. So many of them, addicted to drugs, and off the streets.

He shivered when he thought of his mother, skeletal and shivering, injecting herself in the bedroom. He watched through the keyhole, fascinated. When she died from an overdose, he felt nothing. He managed to break open the door, and then stared at her still body. He touched her arm once, but it was cold.

That was the only time he felt she was at peace. Her colourless face, her lips blue. A part of his broken heart was glad she was gone.

He had stood by the grave on a cold, rainy day soaked to the bones, as the priest read the prayers. He was alone. No one came to see his mother but him. When he walked home, soaked to the bone, he realised death was the answer for some people. Only death could heal their problems.

His ideas became an obsession, then an urge. He started following sex workers around the city. He realised quickly, that the police didn't care about them. He could hurt a sex worker, but it was bad for their business to get the police involved.

In every one of them, he saw the bone-white, deadened face of his mother. When he saw them, he wept tears. But when he killed them, he felt no emotion. As he cut them to death, letting their poison bleed out, it was like he was watching his mother's grave being lowered to the ground, soaked in an acid rain. He was the solitary son watching his mother's death. The rain washed away his memories, leaving him shivering and alone.

"Excuse me."

He jumped at the voice and whirled around. A uniformed police constable was standing there, hands tucked inside his chest rig. The man blinked. There was no rain, it was warm, but the sky remained cloudy.

"You can't stand here. Can you please move back," the constable said, watching him.

"Oh yes of course, sorry. I was driving along but couldn't get through. So stopped to check. What happened here?"

"Can't comment, sorry. You will see it in the news soon enough."

"That white tent is a forensic tent, isn't it?"

The constable looked at him for a few seconds without

speaking. The man didn't want to push his luck, but he also loved playing with the police.

"A forensic tent means a serious crime. I live nearby. I need to know. Has there been," he dropped his voice to a conspiratorial whisper, "like a murder or something?"

"Can't comment, I'm afraid. All will be revealed soon."

A man came out from the brothel. He was the tall detective. Another officer called out to him.

"DCI Roy, can I have a word please?"

DCI Roy. Now he had a name. He smothered his smile. "Thanks for all your hard work," he said to the constable. As he walked away, he glanced furtively at DCI Roy, who was deep in conversation with the uniformed inspector. He thought a lot of himself, that DCI bloody Roy. Well, the bastard was in for a shock. It was about time Roy was taught a lesson or two.

CHAPTER 15

18 Years Ago

Jayden watched Jerry get ready for work. He spruced up nicely in the mornings; that was noticeable. He wore a clean shirt and a light jacket. He never told Jayden what he did for a living, despite Jayden asking. The answer was always an evasive one. *At the warehouse. In an office.*

Jerry was well liked by the neighbours. An elderly couple lived to their right and a young family on their left. Jerry was helpful towards them. The young housewife looked after her two babies. They were both girls. Jayden knew Jerry wouldn't be interested in them, even when they grew up. He liked young boys.

Ever since that incident with the boy at the school gates, Jayden had noted his father had been quieter. He was more wary of Jayden. He got home from school one day and found his stuff all over the place. Clothes in the cupboard were moved, books and papers taken out of drawers. No one lived in the house apart from Jayden and Jerry. His father had been through his stuff.

The bottle of rum he had hidden in his cupboard remained there. Jerry didn't mind Jayden drinking, and this was his secret stash. He bought a bottle every now and then by saving his lunch money. Alcohol had become an escape from the nightmare of his memories.

Jayden got ready for school. He still had some time, about half an hour, before he started to walk. He could wait for the bus as well, but often he walked. He stopped outside Jerry's door. He tried the handle, but the door was locked. This was also new. It was as if Jerry, his so-called father and guardian, wanted to keep his life separate.

Jayden went downsta,irs and searched for keys. He found a bunch in the kitchen counter drawers, but none that fit Jerry's bedroom door. His small study was also locked. Jayden went in the garden and rummaged around in the shed.

He was looking for old photo albums. Maybe a phone book, or a diary. Anything that pointed to the past. He did this search occasionally, because he remembered nothing of what had happened. His childhood seemed like a dream to him, obscured by a dark veil. Nothing was clear, he only saw shadows, and hints of shapes.

There was a time when he had a mother. He knew that. He also had a brother. Jerry told him they had died, and he had found Jayden in a care home, then adopted him. He had showed Jayden the papers a few years ago, when Jayden asked questions. He wished he had taken photos. Jerry didn't allow him to have a phone, and they never took photos. Not even when they went on holidays. They went to a secluded villa in the south of Spain. It seemed strange to Jayden, how they saw virtually no one on holiday. Certainly no families. They went to the beaches that were almost deserted.

Jayden stopped searching and flopped down by the garden shed. He lowered his head into his hands. Who had his family been?

Jerry had showed him photos once, but that was a long time ago. Apparently, they had the same last name as Jerry – Burns. Jayden didn't know their names, but from the dim recesses of his memory, he vaguely recalled the memories of his mother. He also had a brother, and another father. He couldn't remember any of the names, or where he used to live. Jerry had told him his family came from Dumfries, in Scotland. As he got older, Jayden found that dubious. Why would his family live up there, and die from a car crash, but he ended up in Leeds?

When he asked Jerry, he got vague replies – children in social care often moved around. Some got lost in the system or ran away and ended up on the streets. Jayden was lucky to have Jerry.

Casting his thoughts aside, Jayden had some cereal for breakfast, then left for school. He was halfway there when he heard a voice behind, calling his name. He stopped and turned. It was Karen, a pretty, brown-haired girl he shared a few classes with. She was always very friendly, and Jayden thought she liked him. He liked her too, but he was awkward and clumsy with girls.

"Hiya. I was calling you for ages, but you didn't hear me." Karen grinned and almost bumped into him. He looked into her wide, open eyes.

"Come on," he said, licking his dry lips. "We'll be late."

"You playing football this Saturday?" Karen asked.

"How did you know I play football?"

Karen had a mischievous smile on her face. "I've got my ways. You play centre-forward, don't you?"

He was confounded, and Karen put him out of his misery. "I know you practice at school during lunchtime, and my brother plays on Saturday morning. He's in year five though, still a little kid. Mum takes him to school."

"Oh, right."

"You like football?"

"Yes, I do. Scored a goal last week. That were good. I'm not a forward so I don't get much of a chance."

Karen was walking very close to him, and their arms brushed against each other. Jayden moved away, self-conscious.

"Have you chosen your subjects for GCSE?" Karen asked.

"Yeah, I have."

"What did you choose?"

He told her, and Karen shared hers. "Which one's your favourite?"

He shrugged. "I like maths."

"Oh, right. I'm no good at maths. Get confused." She laughed, and it was a light, tinkling sound. Jayden looked at the top of her head. Her brown hair was combed down straight past her shoulders, and even in this cloudy, cold day, it looked nice. He felt like he should appreciate her more, but he felt strangely dead inside. It had always been like this when he met girls. Karen wasn't the first one to pay him attention. In the last year, two more girls had wanted to be friends with him. Each time, he felt cold and weird inside, not aware of what to do.

Jayden nodded in silence.

"What do you want to do for A-levels?"

"Don't know."

Karen kept up a steady chatter about history, her favourite subject, teachers, and her sport of choice, netball. Jayden remained mostly silent.

"Don't talk much, do yer?" Karen asked. Jayden shrugged. She looked at him and held his eyes. Then she smiled. Again, Jayden felt that sensation, like he should feel something deep in the pit of his belly, but nothing happened. He felt cold, empty inside.

They were getting close to school. Karen slipped her hand into his. "Come here." She pulled him into a deserted alley. Gently, she pushed him against the wall, then pressed herself against him. Desire blossomed in her eyes as she stared up at him. Her lips parted.

"Kiss me," she whispered.

Jayden's stomach did a somersault. A cold fist descended in his belly, and his spine shook. It was that weird turmoil he always felt when he got close to a girl. He didn't feel any desire. He knew he should feel it. His mind told him so, but his body didn't respond.

Karen was pretty, gorgeous. He should be all over her, like the other boys did with their girlfriends. But he couldn't even bring himself to touch her. What the hell was wrong with him?

"Come on," Karen said. Her leg rubbed against his. "Don't be shy."

Frustration hit Jayden's chest like a sledgehammer, fracturing his fragile peace. He felt numb with pent-up anger, and he didn't know what to do. He moved away, and Karen stumbled. She frowned at him; her eyes full of hurt.

"I'm sorry," he mumbled. "I can't do this."

Anguish sent barbs inside his heart as he looked at her confused face. He slung the schoolbag on his back and ran away.

CHAPTER 16

Kevin Rawlinson had an angled view of the road from the attic where he was hiding. He could see the white tent, then not much else as a house blocked his view. He stiffened as he saw the two detectives, the woman and man, walk down the road. The man stopped, put his hands on his waist, and raised his head, looking around like he expected to see something.

Kevin sneered. Bloody pigs. Let them look all they want. He was on the road behind, and he had jumped over a fence, then used a back alley to get where he was. This placed used to be a crack den, till Kevin bought it, and made it respectable. Now he housed immigrant families who paid in cash and lived in cramped rooms. It was a double bonus for Kevin. He used the women in his so-called massage parlours and got the men to ferry his drugs around. On top, they had to pay him rent.

But Tracey… Kevin flexed his jaws together. His fists bunched up tight. That girl was asking for trouble. His eyes followed the detectives as they appeared a distance away, now near Cliffe Sauna and the roadblock. They stood there, chatting to the uniformed sergeants, then got in their car and drove away.

But the danger was still here. A police van arrived, off-loading several uniformed officers. Kevin swore under his breath. The officers took instructions from their boss, and fanned out, knocking on doors. Kevin glanced at the top of the road; the traffic block was still in place. This was bad news. He slumped against the wall, thinking. He had already turned his phone off and removed it from the battery. He took out the burner phone and called Karen.

"Kev, is that you?"

"Yes. I got bad news. Tracey Barrett is dead. That silly cow who made hassle for us. I told you not to give her a slot. Now the heat's on us. The cops came to Cliffe Sauna today. Asking questions. One of them even broke down a door when they couldn't find the keys from Debbie. That stupid bitch. Another one of your hires."

"Whoa, whoa. Calm down. Tracey's dead? You sure? I told you not to—"

"Too late for that now. Now I'm stuck here, cops crawling everywhere. I can't use my phone. Call Debbie and tell her to shut the place. In fact, shut down everywhere."

He heard Karen swear and then she was silent for a while. "Damn this. We can close down Cliffe, that makes sense. But the other places? Why?"

"Because I bet you any money Debbie's told the bloody pigs about us. She's got a big mouth that one. You need to fire her. Or I will."

"Oh god, Kev. Haven't you done enough?"

"Hey, this wasn't my fucking fault," Kevin ground out. "You know that. That bitch knew too much."

"She didn't. You overreacted. Anyway, nothing we can do now. Jesus, what a mess. Did the cops speak to you?"

"Yes. I could've done a runner immediately and I think I should've. I spoke to them just to see what they know."

"Yes, you shouldn't have waited. Who were the cops anyway?"

"Some bizzy called DCI Rohan Roy. Also, a DI Sarah Botham. She looked familiar actually. Might have seen her around when she was younger."

"You need to get out of there, Kev. It's too dangerous. Where are you now?"

"Statin' the bleedin' obvious, are yer?" Kevin growled. "I'd get out of 'ere if I could. Too many coppers out there now. I need to wait till nightfall."

"Where are you though?" Concern tinged Karen's voice, and Kevin's heart warmed a touch.

"Best not to tell you, in case someone's listening. But I'm okay. Safe for the time being. You need to be careful. The Spanish Police might come asking questions. Send some feelers out."

The Costa Del Sol, where Karen and Kevin lived, was commonly known as Costa Del Crime. One of the reasons so many dodgy Brits lived there was that the local police could be easily bribed to look the other way.

"I will. Take care my love."

Kevin hung up and looked out the window again. He was sitting on a mattress on the floor, and there was a sleeping bag here. Another van load of cops had arrived, and they were swarming down the street. Kevin swore loudly and smacked a fist into his palm. His wait here would be a long one... But it could get a lot worse if the filthy pigs actually came inside. Kevin frowned, thinking for a while. Then he got up and went downstairs.

CHAPTER 17

Major Incident Room 1, or MIR 1 as it was abbreviated, was less than half-full, but those present paid attention to Roy as he spoke. Behind him, the whiteboard had a photo of the crime scene, and the woman's face in close-up.

"Name is Tracey Barrett, and while we don't have definite evidence, chances are she was a sex worker. Council tax records, electoral rolls, and passport records show that a woman matching her name and appearance lived in Grimesthorpe, where Debbie, the manager of Cliffe Sauna, said she lived. Her mother lives in the same tower block, and she's been notified."

Roy paused, and then waited as Sarah switched the projector on, and an image appeared on the screen. It was a video of the street, with Cliffe Sauna and Massage Parlour at the top, and the white tent of the crime scene much further down, round the bend. It was a drone view, rising above the terraced houses.

"A bird's eye view of the scene, if you like. Note the River Don to the left. Cross that and you're into Burngreave. We've got the Boat Squad looking in the river, right?" Roy turned to Sarah.

"They're going in later today," Sarah confirmed. "There's also a dual carriageway, the A6109, that runs parallel to the river. There's CCTV there, traffic has confirmed, and they're looking at the footage as we speak."

"With any luck," Roy said, "we should be able to find a car that exits Liverpool Street, or at least comes from that direction, between ten and midnight last night. We don't know what car we're looking for, but there won't be that many. Now to return to Cliffe Sauna." Roy pressed a button on his remote, and the view changed to a close-up of the brothel.

"No CCTV here, although Debbie alleges the owners kept secret cameras in place to blackmail the workers, and, presumably, their clients. We haven't found any yet?" He looked at Sarah. Riz was sat next to her, and they both looked up, and shook their heads.

"But we do know Tracey, the victim, was seen with the same man twice, including the night before her murder. She was also approached by this man in public, at the supermarket. If we can get the date and time of that encounter, we should have CCTV footage. We're looking for an IC1 male in his late-twenties or thirties, last seen wearing a dark jacket, jeans, and white trainers, but he might also wear a suit. Which makes me wonder if he's a professional of some sort. A professional who frequents a brothel. Anyone know one of them?"

His question was received with muttered replies and snorts of laughter. Oliver, who had been quiet for so long, clearly couldn't resist any more.

"He was in his birthday suit not long after. Let's get an eyewitness description of that." He laughed, Riz and Sarah rolled their eyes, as did Roy. Only Oliver found his own jokes funny. Oliver realised the room had gone quiet, and his spine folded lower down in the chair. Roy continued, after a shake of his head.

"So, we have our work cut out. Kevin Rawlinson, who's a local hoodlum, and also the partner of Karen Powers, the owner, managed to escape, which I'll admit is my fault. I should've cuffed the bastard as soon as I saw him."

"He was cooperating, guv," Sarah reminded him. "Or at least looked like it, for starters."

"We should have seen that looks were not deceiving – he looked dodgy, and we need to get him quick," Roy grated. He was still upset at not having Kevin in custody. "When's Debbie arriving for her statement?"

"In a couple of hours. She's not asked for a solicitor."

"Good, now the cold case." Roy pressed the arrow on the remote, and the picture of a waterfall appeared, followed by the SYP logo.

"What the hell," he muttered under his breath, and went back, and the screen now showed a photo of Sheffield from a hill on the Peak District.

Sarah rose and plucked the remote from his hand. She went to the laptop and changed it to the right PowerPoint presentation.

"You'd moved to the welcome presentation for new recruits," she said under her breath.

"Thanks," Roy whispered. Aloud he said, "That wasn't the cold case, but you knew that." The room tittered.

"Maybe it was a cold waterfall," Oliver piped up, and Riz frowned at him. Thankfully, Oliver didn't respond, which was a mercy in itself. Instead, he patted down his expensive suit collar and flicked an imaginary speck of dust from the breast pocket.

Roy pressed the remote arrow again, and now the screen showed a disturbing image of a woman lying on a grass bank, her dress in tatters, patches of blood all over her body. Her head was turned to the right, and the knees and elbows were bent in an exact replica of Tracey Barrett's final position.

Roy looked at the sheet of paper on his hand. "This is Bianca Wilkins. Aged twenty-two, found near Victoria Quays three years ago. MO is the same as our current victim. She was also a single mother. No DNA, no prints on her body. She was wiped clean, apart from the knife wounds. Her killer was never caught."

"Geographically, it makes sense," Roy said. He pulled up a map of Sheffield on the screen. "The first woman, Bianca, was found near Victoria Quays, close to Attercliffe and Meadowhall, by the riverbank. Our current victim, Tracey, was in Attercliffe. For now, we continue to search the area around Liverpool Street, the river, and Burngreave. Kevin Rawlinson is the key man to find, and so is the guy who was last seen with Tracey."

Sarah rose and passed a sheet of paper with Tracey's photos and details. The meeting dispersed. Roy and the team headed out to their desks. Melanie had set up a whiteboard next to her desk, and stuck photos and a timeline to it.

"Bianca Wilkins was found in Victoria Quay, right on the towpath. No CCTV there, one of the reasons for its informal status as Sheffield's red-light strip," Sarah said.

Melanie looked at Oliver and Riz, and Oliver spoke. "Bianca worked at a couple of these so-called massage parlours as well. It was called Sunrise Massage, and it shut down a long time ago. I looked through the statements and found one interesting name. Debbie McPherson. She was the manager of one of the parlours. This was seven years ago, and the parlour's shut down now. No photos of Debbie, but what are the chances it's the same Debbie you two spoke to today?"

Roy and Sarah looked at each other. "She didn't mention anything," Sarah said. "And she must've known. I'll speak to her again."

"What does her statement say?" Roy asked.

Oliver squinted at his screen. "Literally two lines. An admission of the fact that she worked there, and the times she checked in and out. Nothing else."

Rizwan said, "I've got Debbie's address and phone number here. Shall I give her a call and ask if she worked at Sunrise?"

"Do that, but she's coming here later anyway, so we can ask her."

"I need someone to come with me," Roy said. "To go and see Tracey's mother. The rest of you, keep digging up more on Bianca."

CHAPTER 18

Roy was leaning back in his chair, two folders, bearing the records of the two dead women, on his desk. He thought about the invisible thread that tied them together. Bianca Wilkins and Tracey Barrett.

Rizwan had called Debbie McPherson, and she had reluctantly admitted she used to be the manager at Sunrise Massage.

Debbie McPherson was the biggest link. Despite what Debbie had told them, she had suppressed what she knew about Bianca. Roy knew she wouldn't have forgotten. If anything, that's the first thing that would've sprung to her mind. And yet, she didn't say a word.

Oliver whistled from his table, and clicked his fingers at Rizwan, sitting opposite. Riz went over and looked at Oliver's laptop screen. Oliver glanced at Roy.

"Come and see this, guv."

Roy went over, and a mug shot of Kevin Rawlinson met his eyes on the screen. Oliver scrolled down the page. Kevin had been arrested a few times, but not in the last five years, since he'd been living in Spain, presumably. He also had two prior convictions for GBH.

"His real crimes are hidden. Well, to the extent that we've never got enough evidence to take him to court. He's well known, as you can see. He's the son of Shaun Rawlinson, head of the Loxley Boys gang." Oliver clicked, and the mug shot of an older man appeared. He was bald like his son but had a goatee beard. He looked to be in his sixties, with sallow, sunken cheeks and a dead-eyed stare.

"Guess where Shaun now lives?"

Riz said, "Costa del Crime?"

"Yup."

"And Karen Powers, Kevin's girlfriend lives there as well. In Fuengirola, not far from Marbella. That's Karen, not Kevin's dad, Shaun. Not sure where Shaun lives. No one knows, in fact."

"Ask the NCA," Roy said. "I'll do it. I wouldn't be surprised if Shaun lived close by to Karen and Kevin, a happy family of sorts."

"Can't they be extradited, guv?" Oliver asked. "It's well-known that they're criminals."

"You need evidence, son," Roy muttered. "Either for a current case, or something historic. Without that, we can't do anything. Besides, we tell the Spanish police, and these guys have a remarkable talent for disappearing as soon as that happens."

Roy sighed and shook his head.

"Anyway. What are the Loxley Boys up to?"

"A number of things. Just read through these reports. Extortion rackets, gambling dens, drug smuggling, and prostitution. Their companies run a number of these so called massage parlours, like Cliffe."

"Guv," Riz said.

Roy looked up and caught Riz staring over his head. He turned, and saw a woman standing there, looking around expectantly. She held a small leather bag in her right hand and was dressed in blue slacks and a brown jacket. Her gaze alighted on Roy, and her eyes narrowed. Roy groaned inwardly. Then he stood, aware he needed to bite the bullet and get this over and done with. Time was an issue. He had to pick up Anna as well. He checked his phone. The teenager had sent a text. She was doing homework in the library and was fine till 3 pm. That gave him a couple of hours.

He stood and approached the woman. "DCI Roy," he offered a hand. The woman smiled and shook it.

"Meredith Wilson. I'm the Clinical Psychologist for SYP Occupational Health."

Her hair was whitening at the temples, and she had prominent crow's feet around her eyes. Her dark hair was combed to her shoulders. Her brown eyes were sharp and attentive, with a hint of warmth in them that deepened as Roy introduced himself. She was an attractive older woman.

Meredith looked around, and Roy was aware that everyone was watching them. He said, "Should I be attending your office? I wasn't provided any details." Which was typical of police department organisation, he thought. Part of him couldn't escape the feeling Nugent had set it up like this.

"I was told to come here," Meredith said, deepening his suspicion. "You're welcome to come to my office, it's across the road."

Sarah was next to him. He turned to her and saw the question in her eyes. "Something I got to do," he said, the awkwardness coming off him in waves. "You take one of the lads or Mel and talk to Tracey's mum. See if you can find out who her bloke was."

Sarah's eyes flicked to Meredith, gave her the quick once-over, then went back to Roy.

"Take your time," she said. "Call me if you need anything."

"Where I'm going," he whispered. "I'm going to need all the help I can get." He smiled stiffly, and Sarah didn't respond, her eyes watchful on his retreating back.

"Shall we go?" Roy asked Meredith, who nodded.

*****

Sarah wheeled the black Ford Titanium CID car into the parking space. Melanie got out, and together, they walked down the large courtyard of the council estate in Grimesthorpe. Tall, needle-like grey concrete buildings rose high around them, almost blocking out the sky. The Wincanton Estate was one of the largest housing projects in eastern Sheffield, built in the 1970s.

The two detectives followed the signs for apartment 23, block 4. Melanie pressed on the buzzer at the door, and a woman's voice answered. Melanie introduced herself, they had rung in advance. Soon, they were knocking on the green door of a flat at the end of a bland, grey cement corridor. Sarah heard the shuffling of feet, then a lady opened the door.

She was in her fifties, at the most, Sarah guessed. Her hair was white in places, mousy brown in others, and needed a dye and wash. She had other things on her mind clearly, obvious from the bags under her eyes, and the look of exhaustion deep in the lines of her face. Her lips were dark with nicotine stains. There was a faint odour of old fags, and a whiff of alcohol on her breath.

Sarah and Mel held up their warrant cards and introduced themselves. The woman stared at them, unmoving.

"Where is she?" she asked, simply.

"Can we please come in?" Sarah said, gently.

The woman's face spasmed in a sudden contortion of pain, like she'd been knifed in the gut. She knew.

"No," she said. She seemed to recede in size, slowly bending at the waist, seeming to fall in slow motion, but her legs managing to hold her up. "No, please, no."

Sarah held her under the arms, and Mel helped. They stepped inside a postage stamp-sized landing, that led to a living room on the left. The TV was on, and a children's cartoon was playing. On the carpet, a toddler was playing with Lego, and he looked up with astonished eyes as the three adults came in. He was about two years old, Sarah thought. She smiled in what she hoped was a reassuring manner, then focused on putting the woman on the chair at the dining table. The toddler stared at them for a while, then went back to his Lego.

"You must be Mrs Barrett?" Mel asked.

The woman pulled out a tissue and wiped her nose. "Yes. Call me Cathy." Her face remained downcast, and her body shook like she was being battered in a storm. Slowly, she raised her eyes to meet Sarah's.

"Just tell me," she whispered. Sarah asked if Tracey Barrett was her daughter's name, and the woman closed her eyes, and kept them shut. She continued to tremble. Sarah took that as a yes.

"A woman matching your daughter's description was found on Liverpool Street in Sheffield. It's just south of Attercliffe. I'm afraid she passed away. I will show you some photos now, please be prepared. We also need you to come and identify the body."

Cathy lowered her head into her hands, then to the table. She remained liked that, her shoulders shaking. The boy seemed to realise something was afoot. He left his Lego and tottered over to Cathy.

Sarah whispered to Mel, "Call the FLO." Mel nodded and left. Sarah cursed herself. She should've thought of that earlier. Cathy was beside herself in grief, and hadn't noticed her grandson, till the boy pulled at her clothes. She lifted him in her arms and held him as she wept.

Sarah knew anything she said or did would be wrong. There was no easy way to do this. She simply gave Cathy some time. The older woman dried her eyes, and kissed her grandson, who was fascinated by the tears in her eyes. He wiped them, trying to grab the tissue from Cathy's hand.

Sarah had to ask the obvious question. "Is that Tracey's son?"

"Yes. His name's Billy. Robert, but we call him Billy."

"Hello Billy," Sarah said. Billy completely ignored her, still trying to catch the tear drops on Cathy's cheeks.

Mel came back, and nodded in silence as she took her seat next to Sarah.

"I know this is a difficult time for you. But if I can ask you a few questions that would be very helpful."

Cathy stared at her, sniffing. "How did she die?"

There was no point in mincing words. If anything, brutal frankness was what Cathy needed. She needed the truth.

"She died from knife wounds. Her body was found on Liverpool Street early this morning, and we were notified. She worked at the Cliffe Sauna and massage parlour, and the manager there, Debbie McPherson, identified her."

"I told her not to go there. That damned…" Cathy spat out, then checked herself as she was still clutching Billy. He didn't want to let go, happily playing with her hair now. Cathy rose, and with Billy, went into the kitchen. She came out, having got some sweets for him. She placed him on the carpet again, and he got busy with his snack.

"She shouldn't have gone back there," Cathy said. "Not after what happened."

"What happened?" Sarah asked. Both she and Mel had their notebooks out and ready.

"A man followed her around. I saw him once, when we were in the supermarket. He came up to us and started chatting to her. She didn't want to speak to him. But he followed us around, till he got the message and left."

"And where did she meet this guy?"

"I asked her about it, and eventually she opened up. She met him at that Cliffe Massage Parlour." Cathy looked down at her hands. "I was ashamed she were doing that. Goin' there and stuff. We might be poor, but we don't have to do mardy shite like that." She was silent for a while.

Sarah said, "When did this happen? And which supermarket?"

"A couple of weeks ago. At the big Tesco in Grimesthorpe. Even Billy was with us. I got proper scared, like. He'd been watching us for a while. I saw him again once, around here. Sure it was him, anyway. I was out with Billy in the pram."

"What does this man look like?" Sarah asked.

"Medium height for a bloke. Dark hair, and pretty sure he wore a dark jacket and black jeans. White trainers."

So far, that description fit the man Debbie had described. "Any distinguishing features you noticed about him? Was he clean-shaven?

Did he wear a ring? Any tattoos? Think closely, Cathy. This is important."

Cathy lowered her head, and her lips pressed together. "He was clean-shaven. Although his clothes were casual, they looked alright, I mean good quality, if you know what I mean. He didn't wear a cap, and at the back of his head, above his neck, to the side, there was a tattoo. It was a picture of something, in blue ink. Sorry I can't be more precise. It wasn't that big, and my eyes aren't what they used to be."

"Which side of the head, do you think, right or left?"

Cathy's eyebrows met in the middle. "He was speaking to her, and I was behind him. To his left, yes, left."

"And you saw him again around here? In the estate?"

"Tracey did shifts in the hardware store in town. When she started late, Billy and I walked her down to the bus stop. That's where I saw him. He was dressed smart this time around, in a suit. But I recognised him."

Sarah asked a few more questions about the colour of the suit, and the man's general appearance. Then she tapped her pen against the notebook page.

"When did Tracey start working at the massage parlour?"

"A few months, she said, but I don't know if she were speaking the truth. She knew I was angry with her about it."

Mel spoke up. "Is Billy's father involved in his care? Does he come around, or does Tracey take Billy to his?"

"Aye, he does come around. Once every fortnight, Billy spends the weekend with him. He brings Billy back, or Trace used to collect him." Cathy clutched her forehead. "God, I'll have to tell him as well."

"Can we have his name and address?"

Cathy looked up slowly. "You can. But you might have him on your books already. He only came out of prison last year."

CHAPTER 19

Lydia Moran watched from her parked car as Rohan Roy dropped his daughter off. He had parked in the side alley, but Lydia didn't follow him there, as it would give her away. She had pulled into the car park by the one way system, and it offered her a good view of the entire are. The teenager got out of the car, as did Roy. He hugged her, then they spoke briefly. Roy got into his car and drove off. Sheffield City Library was next door, and the teenager came out on the main street, then went inside the library. Lydia got out and locked her car. She made sure that Roy wasn't coming back, then she hurried across the street.

Her heart was pumping, knocking against her ribs. Anyone could walk into the library, but she needed a card to take books out. She asked at the counter, looking around for the teenager. Anna, her name was. She was distinctive, tall, slender, with jet-black hair. Lydia finished her enquiries at the counter, filled up a form for the library card, then walked around. She found Anna at the rear, behind the book collections. There was a large study area, with desks arranged in rows. A number of people sat with their laptops, working, or reading.

Anna was taking things out of her backpack. Then she rose and walked over to one of the bookshelves. She vanished behind a book rack and Lydia hurried over. It was the history section, and Anna was searching through the titles. Lydia walked past, noting Anna was looking at the Tudor period. She stood next to the teenager, pretending to be interested in the books.

She picked out a book, then dropped it on purpose, by Anna's feet. Anna picked it up.

"Oh, thank you," Lydia smiled. She was five-five, short compared to Anna, who was at least three to four inches taller. Anna wore glasses, and her brown hair was shoulder height. She had a bookish, serious expression, and the glasses accentuated that.

"I've been looking for this book for ages, and then I drop it as soon as I find it. Typical."

Anna smiled politely and kept on browsing. Lydia said, "Really interesting period of English history. My students love it."

That caught Anna's attention. Lydia wasn't lying, she was a teacher. She taught in a secondary school, and her subject was English. She had a good idea about history as well, and she used to teach humanities.

"Are you a teacher?" Anna asked.

"Yes."

"Whereabouts?"

"At a secondary school in Totley, called Totley High School How about you? Do you go to school, or college?"

"Oh yeah," Anna grinned. "I'm doing my GCSEs next year. Got to write essays on the Tudors, so revising for it now."

"Oh right. I teach GCSE and A-levels, history and English. Do you like the Tudors? Or history in general."

"I do, actually. Some people find it boring. But I find the way people used to live quite interesting. As in, what would I feel like if I was alive then?"

"Wow, that's a really good way to think about it. I'm going to tell my students. You must be good at your studies, right?"

Anna smiled, a little self-conscious. "I get along okay."

Lydia disagreed. "No, to have the kind of insight into history that you do, it's more than just getting along. You're a good student, I think." She smiled. "What other subjects do you like?"

Anna shrugged. "I like a bit of everything, apart from physics. I didn't used to be good at maths, but now I'm better."

"Oh great. What do you want to study at university? I'm assuming you want to go to uni, right?"

"Yes. I want to do law."

"If you're good at history and English, that's a great foundation for law. As a lawyer, you have to read long documents, and do it quickly. A couple of my students did law. One of them stays in touch. She's a solicitor now in London."

"Oh really? Whereabouts?"

"Linklaters or something like that." Lydia was making all this up, but it seemed to be working. "One of the big firms in the city. She's doing really well. She studied history at Manchester. Loved it."

"Nice."

"Have you thought about what you want to do for A-levels?"

"Maybe English, psychology and maths."

"That's a good combination. It gives you a broad base. University admission officers will like that."

"Thank you."

Lydia smiled. "You're welcome." She introduced herself, then shook hands with Anna.

"Nice to meet you," Anna said. "See you later."

Lydia thought for a second. She knew she couldn't push too hard on their first meeting. "Sure."

She browsed for a while longer, noting Anna's black jeans, her trainers, the green nail polish she had on, and her well-combed long hair that came down to her mid-back. Then she waved goodbye and moved away. She watched from behind a bookshelf as Anna went to her desk and sat down with the books. The table next to her was empty. Lydia decided to seize the chance. Acting disinterested, she sat down, and pulled out a notepad from her handbag and started to make notes from the pile of books she'd collected. She pretended not to see or acknowledge Anna next to her. She angled her chair, so she had her back to Anna.

The teenager got up and walked from her desk. Lydia watched as she went to the counter, and then to the loo. When she was sure Anna was coming back immediately, Lydia acted quickly. She took out the voice-activated transmitter and made sure it was switched-on. It was a tiny grey object, no bigger than a coat button. She put it inside Anna's backpack, making sure it was in one of the empty side-pockets. That device could pick up any conversations within a ten-metre radius, and all Lydia had to do was log into it remotely and download the voice files. She could even do it in real time and follow live conversations.

Lydia zipped-up the bag, then sat down on her chair. She looked around. The surrounding desks were empty, and no one had seen her. Heart thumping loudly, Lydia went back to her books, pretending to read.

When Anna came back, Lydia was facing her. She said 'hello', and Anna waved at her.

"How's the work going?" Lydia asked, indicating Anna's open laptop.

"Not too bad. It's going to take me a few reads before I can do it."

"What's the essay about?"

"Political life in the Tudor Courts, and how that influenced Henry the Fifth's thinking."

"Ah, interesting. I set my A-level students an assignment like that before the break."

"Hmm."

Anna was interested. Lydia went in for the kill.

"Which school do you go to?"

"Oh, in London. Clapham High School."

"I thought so. Your accent isn't from here." She smiled. "Well, I live here, and come to the library often. Let me know if you need any help."

"Sure," Anna grinned.

Lydia watched the teenager as she sat down.

Soon, I'll know a lot more about you, she thought. And then, I'll tell you the truth about your father.

CHAPTER 20

L uke Hammond," Mel said on the radio. They were driving back to the nick from Cathy's flat. "He spent a-year-and-a-half for armed robbery. Pleaded guilty and got out with a lighter sentence. Yes, I'll hold."

Mel spoke to Oliver for a while longer, then hung up. Luke was Billy's father. "He's been in and out of prison for the last ten years. He's now 28 years old. Started with burglaries and now armed robbery. Put a security guard in the jeweller's shop in hospital last time. Surprised he got out so early."

"Judges can be lenient if convicts have children," Sarah said. "The security guard didn't die, did he? Luke would've spent longer in prison otherwise."

"No, the guard had a concussion, that's all." Mel's phone rang again, and she spoke to Oliver, then hung up.

"Luke's never done time for sexual offences or killed anyone. I've got his address and number. Shall we pay him a visit? Tracey went around to his house Sunday the week before to pick up Billy. The week after her stalker harassed her in the supermarket."

Sarah nodded. "Let's go see him."

Mel entered the address on the sat nav, and it appeared on their dashboard. She called the number Oliver had sent her, but it went to voicemail. She left a message to say they were coming around.

Luke lived in Loxley, which was in northern Sheffield. Sarah was in Grimesthorpe still, and she pulled up in the Tesco car park. It was a sprawling supermarket, and it took them a while to speak to the manager, who took them into the security office. Sarah was surprised by how well organised it was. The wall of TV monitors looked into every aisle and checkout, and also in the massive car park out and back. Staff sat watching the screens and making notes.

"It's not just this store," the manager explained. "We keep an eye on our chain across the city. But we are the biggest branch. So, what did you need?"

"July fourteenth," Melanie said, looking at her notes. "There was an altercation between a man and a woman at the main shop floor. That woman has now been murdered. We need to find the man urgently. You must have CCTV footage from that day."

"Sorry to hear that," the man looked shocked. Then he scratched his neck. "We do, but it will take several hours of trawling through CCTV from that day. Do you know if the security guards were called?"

Mel and Sarah exchanged a glance. Mel said, "I think the man left before that happened, but he was threatened with it."

"Like I said, we can have a look, but it will take a good few hours. Our CCTV is 24-hours and rolling. You're lucky, because after four weeks we delete all the data."

"If you send us the files, we can look through them ourselves," Sarah said. "There's a chance this man has been here before, either to follow our victim, or he lives nearby and shops here."

The manager gaped at her. Sarah said, "We want to put up posters, once we've identified him on CCTV. Is that okay?"

She could see the doubt on the manager's face. He scratched the back of his neck. "It's not great for business, to be honest."

"It might be worse to have a known killer hanging around your shop. Imagine if something more serious than an argument happened one day." Sarah raised her eyebrows, and the man seemed to get the message.

"Okay," he acknowledged.

*****

The part of Loxley where Luke Hammond lived reminded Melanie of the worst parts of Belfast, where she'd grown up, during the Troubles. No armoured car patrolled the streets here, and there weren't gangs of teenagers throwing stones at them. But she saw the burnt-out cars, raised on bricks because the tyres had been sold for the rubber. The graffiti on the walls, sprayed on house fronts even, was loud and proud, denoting the presence of rival gangs. Windows were smashed in, and shopfronts were vandalised, presumably those that didn't pay the gangs protection money.

Luke's house, a narrow terraced two up and two down, was sandwiched between one with boarded-up windows, and another with two girls playing hopscotch in the front pavement. The whole street was formed of brown brick terraced houses. Judging by the curtains that twitched, Melanie knew their alien presence was noted. People who lived here knew an unmarked police car when they saw one.

The door was scruffy and had once been green. Now it looked like someone had vomited on it repeatedly, and let rain wash it away. The bricks were chipped in places, and large patches of fresh damp appeared under the windows. Melanie shuddered when she thought of a toddler being here. Sarah pressed the calling bell, which didn't make a sound. After two tries, she knocked on the door. She had to thump on it loudly before they heard a sound. Steps came down the stairway and stopped at the door. There was no eyepiece, but the letter box flap lifted. Sarah bent, and she could make out a pair of dark eyes observing her.

"Luke Hammond?"

"Who wants tae know?" The Scottish voice was raspy and low, like its owner had spent a lifetime on twenty a day, and cheap booze.

"Detective Inspector Sarah Botham, and Sergeant Melanie Sparkes. Can you open the door, please?"

"Get tae fock! I ain't don' nothing wrong. I cannae believe you're here."

"I think you'll want to hear what we have to say."

"Awa wi' ye! I ain't talkin' nae more. Ye wannae talk? Talk tae ma probation officer. Now piss aff!"

The flap dropped as Luke walked away from the door. Sarah put her mouth to the letterbox and shouted, "It's about your son, and his mother."

Movement stopped inside the house. Then the floorboards creaked again. The letterbox flap rose again, and the eyes regarded them quietly.

"Whit aboot them?"

"Let us in and we'll tell you."

There was silence for a while, then slowly, the inside bolt slid, and the chain rattled, then the door opened a crack. Mel saw a pale-faced, stubbled, sunken-cheeked, sinewy young man, who looked older than his years. His blue eyes were flat, teeth yellow when he grimaced at the sight of them. He wore a yellow string vest, Caribbean style, which was several sizes too big and hung low on his waist, looking ridiculous. His jogging bottoms were loose and marked with black spots from cigarette burns. He scratched his stubble, and his eyes were watchful.

"Whit aboot me son and his ma?"

"Like I said, let us in," Sarah put a foot on the porch and heaved herself up, making Luke step back.

"Ye dinnae show me your warrant card?" He screeched, his back hitting the balustrade of the staircase.

Mel came in behind Sarah, and both women showed their warrant cards. Mel shut the door. The floor was bare boards, but in its defence, the boards were polished and firm. The walls were whitewashed, and the interior looked marginally better than the dilapidated exterior.

"Can we sit down, Mr Hammond?" Sarah asked. Luke grumbled under his breath, then opened the door on their right, which led to a living room. It had a flatscreen TV, and two cheap, brown faux-leather sofas on either side. The shelves behind the TV, on either side, had framed photos of a baby in Luke's arms, flanked by an elderly couple. Slim, upright speakers stood on either side of the TV.

Mel took a look at the photos. The baby was Billy, and she assumed the elderly couple were Luke's parents. When she asked him, he confirmed they were.

They remained standing, til Sarah said, "Let's sit down." Mel followed her example, and after a while, so did Luke. He frowned at them and spread his hands. His body odour came off him in waves, and Mel tried her best not to hold her breath or crinkle her nose. The stench of cannabis mixed with sweat was almost overpowering.

"Weel, go oan then," Luke rasped. "Whit's happened na?"

Sarah said quietly, "Tracey Barrett's died. Her body was found on a street in Attercliffe this morning. She died from knife wounds."

Luke stopped breathing. His pallid cheeks went paler still, and his eyes flared wide. His lips parted, and he said words which never made it out of his mouth. Then his eyebrows creased, and he shook his head like he was trying to swat away a fly.

"Whit urr ye talking aboot?"

Sarah repeated herself, and Luke interrupted her. "Boot… boot, she wis 'ere lest week. She took Billy. She wis braw…" He stopped suddenly, and his spine lashed straight. "Where's ma son? Is Billy a'richt? Is Billy a'richt?!" He shouted the last words, his eyes wild, neck veins engorged.

"Billy's absolutely fine," Sarah said, raising her hands. "Please don't worry. We've just seen him, with his grandmother, Cathy."

Luke sagged, the tension in his spine dissipating. The wildness in his eyes remained. The blue-grey pupils swivelled left and right, his drug addled brain trying to make sense of what he was hearing.

"Howfur… Whit happened?"

Sarah looked at Mel, who took over. "Mr Hammond, Tracey was knifed to death. I'm sorry to say."

Luke stared at Mel, dumb. Mel said, "Do you know anyone who might've done this? Did Tracey have any enemies?"

Something shifted in Luke's face. A shadow, slipping across his mind, coming to the fore briefly before he controlled himself. He blinked, and then shook his head vigorously. Too vigorously, Mel thought.

"Na, na. She wis a good lassie, me Trace wis, a good lassie. Ah cannae imagine wha did this tae her." His head lowered. "Ah cannae jalouse…"

Sarah frowned and leaned forward. "Did you say jealous?"

Mel touched her sleeve, and Sarah looked back. "No guv,

jalouse is 'think' in Scottish. Isn't that right, Luke?"

Slowly, the young man raised his head, the dullness back in his eyes. He looked a million miles away, his brain spinning on a different track. "Eh?"

"Don't worry," Mel said, giving Sarah a wink. "You don't think Tracey had any enemies?" she asked Luke. Slowly, this time more composed, Luke shook his head.

Mel knew Sarah also sensed Luke was holding back. She could tell by the way Sarah sat forward, hands clasped, and tense.

Mel asked, "Think carefully, Luke. This is important. Whoever did this to Tracey is a very dangerous person and could be out to hurt others. Think about Cathy and Billy's safety as well."

Luke stared at her, and that shadow slithered across his face again. Spots of colour appeared on his cheeks, like the beginnings of doubt in his mind.

Mel spoke softly. "If you know something about Tracey, then tell us now."

"Ah donnae know." Luke licked his dry, cracked lips. "Donnae know."

"Did you know that she worked at a massage parlour? It was called Cliffe Sauna and Massage."

Luke shook his head. "Nah."

"And did you know she was a sex worker there?"

Something flitted across Luke's face, and his spine seemed to tremble, moving his body. His drooping eyes narrowed. "Nah, I dinnae know that."

"Are you sure?"

"I jes' told yeh, I dinnae know!"

"So, she had no fights or disagreements with anyone recently, nothing that she was worried about?"

"Nah. Like I said, she wis' a good lassie." Sadness cast a veil over his face then, and his cheeks sagged. His lips trembled, and his voice shook when he spoke. "I cannae believe it."

He sniffed and wiped a hand over his eyes. Sarah glanced at Mel, and both knew what they were thinking. If this was an act, then Luke was worthy of an Oscar. After a few seconds, Mel took up the questioning again.

"Where were you last night between the hours of ten and midnight?"

"Why?"

"Just answer the question please."

"Ah wis workin' down the pub – mah mucker owns it."

"What's your friend's name? And people saw you there, so they can provide an alibi?"

Luke licked his lips slowly again, and Mel could see the cogs in his mind turning slowly.

"Aye, sure they can. But you dinnae tell mah whit fer you wannae know?"

"That was approximately the time when Tracey died last night. You are not a suspect at this stage, but we will need to speak to you again. Can I please have your friend's details, and the address of the pub?"

"Aye." Luke observed them closely. "I wan tae see mah son. Can I do that today?"

Sarah glanced at Mel and spoke before she could. "I think it's best if you leave them alone for a couple of days. We might need to speak to you again. By the way, did you last see Tracey when she came to pick up Billy?"

"Aye. Last Sunday that wis."

"What time?"

"After lunch. I'd say aroond two or three."

"And she seemed fine to you? Not worried, or anxious about anything?"

"Na. She were a'richt. Her normal self."

Sarah stared at him for a while, and eventually, Luke looked away. "Stay local, Mr Hammond. We will need to speak to you again."

CHAPTER 21

18 Years Ago

Jayden had started spending more and more time outside home. One of his friend's brother's owned a printing press, and he could forge IDs. That meant they could now buy drinks illegally. He got home late one evening. He had picked up a few cans from the off-licence and was feeling the effects of the booze by the time he knocked on the door. Jerry took his time to answer. When the door opened, it was a stranger who was standing there. Jayden had never seen the guy before. He gaped at him, and the man stared back. Then he heard Jerry's voice, behind him. The man let Jayden in. In the living room, Jerry was sat watching TV. The man stood, his eyes roving all over Jayden.

"Who're you?" Jayden asked.

The man smiled. It was a strange, knowing kind of smile, and it made Jayden shudder. "Hello Jayden," he said. The man had a shaven head, and a stubble on his cheeks. His shoulders were wide, and he was a big, tall man. He was bigger than Jerry, who had a slim, but wiry and strong, build.

"I'm Keith Burgess," the man said. "Your dad's friend." He came closer. Jayden didn't flinch, but it took all his strength to stand his ground. "Would you like a drink?" Keith asked.

"What sort of drink?" Jayden eyed his father, who appeared to be watching TV with his girlfriend and ignoring them. His girlfriend's name was Lydia. Jayden didn't know her last name. Lydia came around and stayed the night sometimes. He didn't like her. She stared at him often, and was too quiet. She was a small, brown-haired, waspish woman with glasses, who looked like a schoolteacher, and he found out later that she actually was one.

When she spoke, it was the perfunctory hi and hello. He couldn't figure her out, but when he asked Jerry, he was told Lydia was Jerry's girlfriend.

Neither of them paid any attention to what was happening between him and Keith.

Keith smiled and moved to the kitchen counter. Jayden didn't follow. He didn't like this man. He was like a big bear, but a dangerous one. He moved slowly, like he owned the place. He opened the fridge and took out a can of beer.

"In a glass?"

Jayden shrugged. "I don't mind. I'll come down in a bit." He went upstairs and shut his door. He was getting changed, when he heard steps coming up, and there was a knock.

"Who is it?"

"I bought your drink upstairs. Thought you might want it here." It was Keith. The door moved like Keith was trying to open it. "Sorry. Do you want me to leave it down here."

Jayden had finished getting changed. "Yes, leave it there please." He listened by the door as steps faded downstairs. He

112

opened the door and was shocked to see Keith standing close by. He tried to shut his door, but Keith was fast, for a big man. He pushed the door, and Jayden stumbled backwards.

Keith shut the door behind him. A sickening, lascivious grin appeared on his face as his eyes roamed all over Jayden.

"Oh, you look nice in those. Here." he held out the can of beer.

"Get out of my room," Jayden said. He tried to brush past Keith, but the man stopped him, and tried to put an arm around his waist. Jayden flung his arm away.

"I said get out!"

"Now come on, don't play hard to get." Keith wiggled his eyebrows. He was still holding the can, and he tried to grab Jayden again. Jayden pushed him, and Keith fell back against the wall. The smile vanished from his face, replaced by an angry leer.

"Don't be like that. I was just being nice." He came up to Jayden again, and he tried to push him on the bed. His hands roamed all over Jayden's body.

"Stop it," Jayden shouted. When Keith didn't listen, he bent his elbow, and hit Keith in the face. Keith stopped, and a trickle of blood appeared by his lips.

"Why, you bastard…" He gripped Jayden hard now, and they fell on the bed, wrestling. He was bigger, but Jayden wasn't weak, and he was more agile. He kicked Keith in the chest, pushing him to the floor. He was slower getting up, and Jayden picked up the table lamp, and smashed it hard on Keith's head. Then he took a well-aimed kick at Keith's face, and the man grunted, then fell backwards.

Jayden ran down the stairs. His father was standing in the living room, and so was Lydia. Her glasses were off, and her mouth was open.

"What's going on?" Jerry shouted.

"Your fuckin' friend just tried to rape me. That's what happened." Jayden screamed back.

Rage spiked in his heart, and he cursed at the sorry excuse of a father in front of him. "You bastard!"

Then he grabbed his coat, opened the door, and ran out into the cold, gloomy night.

CHAPTER 22

Meredith Wilson's voice was quiet and measured.

"The child trafficker was handcuffed but refused to answer your questions. You hit him in the face, and then kept hitting till his nose and jaw broke. You continued even when he was unconscious, and unless one of your colleagues stopped you, you might have killed the man. Is that correct, DCI Roy?"

Sunlight streamed in through the tall, Georgian windows. Meredith had an office in the nicely maintained old building, opposite the modern cement and glass block that was the SYP Headquarters. Across the road, but it might as well have been a million miles away. He was in the comfortable armchair opposite Meredith, and the psychiatrists' couch always made him uneasy. Felt like he was being lulled into a false sense of security. Correction, he thought to himself. Meredith was a clinical psychologist, not a psychiatrist, but there was hardly any bloody difference. It only meant she couldn't prescribe the tablets he had once taken and had come off as soon as he could. They messed with his head right from the start.

Roy knew he had to answer. "I don't think he would've died. I mean, I was interrogating the man. He wasn't complying. He was alright after a spell in the hospital."

Meredith shifted, and her relaxed posture belied that carefully cultivated look that all shrinks had, in Roy's opinion: a blankness close to boredom. The 'whatever you say will not phase me' look. Her large eyes drew him in, and he could tell she knew that he saw her as an attractive older woman.

"That wasn't the first time though. There was the teenage grooming gang in Croydon, and the paedophile in Clapham. Two of the gang members ended up in a coma, and both sued the police when they recovered. The paedophile suffered cracked ribs, and a punctured lung, and was in intensive care for two months. He could also have died."

What a shame that would've been.

Aloud, he said, "They came after me. I had to defend myself."

Meredith pursed her lip and looked down at the report in her hand. "That's not what it says here."

"My word against theirs. You're probably reading their lawyer's report. In any case, they didn't win the case, did they?"

Meredith folded hands over the report and looked at him. Her blue green veins stood up on her hands. Her nail polish was green with black polka dots.

"That's not the point, is it? The point is the regularity with which this happened. Still happens, if Keith Burgess and Jerry Burns are to be believed. Yes, I know how you feel about them." She nodded, and her kind eyes bore into his. She smiled a little. "I'm not trying to be difficult. I want to understand how you feel when this happens."

Roy shrugged. "Well, they're just getting what they deserve. Sorry, but that's how I see it."

"And what do you think they deserve?"

"They're scumbags who abduct children from their families and sell them on. Also abuse them. Scar them for life. They deserve to be locked up, and..."

"And?"

"Kept away from society. They shouldn't be a part of humanity in general, because their brains are wired the wrong away. They're diseased. Evil. Plenty of scientific evidence that shows their brains pathway are structured wrong. I'm sure you know all about them."

Meredith smiled slightly again, saying nothing. "Tell me about your brother."

Roy closed his eyes. "Please. I've been through this many times. With at least three professionals like yourself. What I do has nothing to do what happened to Robin."

"I didn't ask you that," Meredith said. "I just wanted to know about your brother."

"Know what?"

"Anything." She moved her hands in the air. "Anything about Robin that comes to your mind."

The glitter of the gold necklace as Robin ran away from him that day. The last time he saw him. Vanishing into the darkness between the trees. Shouting, catch me if you can.

Those impossibly big, angelic eyes. The mildly questioning look on his face as he squinted up at him. Robin hung on every word his older brother said.

Roy felt the weight spreading across his chest like a wave of sheet metal. His throat constricted as he tried to swallow. He stood.

"Excuse me. I just need the loo."

"Sure. Out the door, on your right."

Roy nodded and walked out of the spacious study. He got into the bathroom, and heaved a sigh of relief when he realised that he was alone. He gripped the edges of the counter, leaning over the sink. He looked at himself in the mirror. He felt, and looked, tired. These stupid talks made him that way. No way could he spend another second in that room.

Then suddenly, without warning, he burst into tears.

CHAPTER 23

"He's lying through his back teeth about Tracey," Melanie observed about Luke as Sarah drove. "She was in some kind of trouble, and he knows about it."

Sarah agreed. "We need to bring him in. He's shook up enough to spill the beans. The only problem is he's going to get the duty solicitor, and if it's Keenan, or one of his boys, they'll mess things up."

James Keenan was the veteran, and expensive, criminal law solicitor and barrister-at-large in Sheffield. He loved poking holes in cases and getting murderers out of custody.

"With any luck, Luke will think of his son and come to his senses. If he knows anything that's worth knowing, that is."

"The house was empty," Sarah observed. "He said he was alone and I didn't hear any sounds. Did you?"

"I got the same feeling. Only one pair of shoes and slippers. One towel hanging from the stairs railing. I looked in the kitchen, only one plate in the sink."

The pub Luke had mentioned was still shut. They drove past it.

It was in a brown brick building that looked like a Scouts outpost that had seen better days. It was called the Bullock Arms, and a picture bearing the words, and the faded brown image of a bull, hung over the entrance. No one went in or out from the doors. The windows upstairs were shut, and there was no sign of life.

"Let's come back later," Sarah said, driving away. "One of the lads can come in the evening and speak to the punters."

Mel was looking at her phone. "I've got the number here." She called, but it went to answerphone. They both knew it was important to know where Luke had been last night.

*****

When they got back to the nick, Sarah parked the car, and her phone buzzed. It was John Garnett, Matt's father. They had exchanged texts a couple of times the previous day. John wanted to come over and see Matt, and he wanted to know if tonight was good. Sarah didn't think so. She had to speak to Matt after school today, and perhaps over a few days, just getting him ready for the big meeting with his biological father. Matt had last seen him when he was two years old. Nine years was a long time. Yes, Sarah had the conversation, when Matt asked him in the past. Sarah had always said his father had gone away, and she didn't know where he was. It had been heart-breaking, seeing the disappointment on his face. She would never forgive John for what he did to her son.

And now he couldn't just waltz back in their life. To be fair to John, he was giving them time, and being cautious himself. She had looked him up online. He was a quantity surveyor, and in charge of the renovations at Sheffield University. His CV also said he had worked in Dubai. All of that tied in with what he'd told Sarah. She had phoned his employer and spoken to his boss. He'd done alright for himself and that was good, because she wanted a good role model for Matt, IF, and it was still a big

120

if, John was going to come back into Matt's life.

Not tonight, she texted back. *Maybe this weekend. I'll let you know.*

Mel had gone inside already. Sarah stuffed the phone back in her pocket and thought as she walked back slowly inside. A couple of passing uniforms said 'hello', and she greeted them absentmindedly. She really had to manage this carefully. Her mother didn't want John to come back into Matt's life. She said when John left again, Matt would be worse off. Sarah wondered that even if John lived elsewhere, that was no barrier to the two having a father and son relationship. A long distance one, but at least the gaping hole in Matt's life would be closed. He would know his father was there, and in his own way, cared for him.

She had asked John if he was in a relationship or had got married with children. He had denied both of those and was currently single. But Sarah had her own ways of finding out. She had done a search on HOLMES (Home Office Large Major Enquiry Systems), and on the PCN (Police Crime Network) database, and not seen anything untoward. She had then checked John's details for a change of name, or an alias.

So far, she'd found nothing. No marriage certificate in his name. Of course, that didn't mean he hadn't fathered children without marriage. She had looked up his previous addresses and searched for anyone else named on his utility bills, or council tax. So far, she'd only seen his name. However, John had lived abroad recently, so she didn't have all the records. She knew there was no hope of getting information from Dubai. She would keep looking, til she had satisfied herself that John was speaking the truth.

As Sarah walked into the office, she saw Rizwan, leaning over Melanie's desk, speaking to her. He looked up as she entered.

"Ey up, guv. The boat search party came back. Nowt in the Don River. Door-to-door is still going on. No sign of Kevin

Rawlinson."

Sarah thought about what Rohan had said. Uniforms were already on the street, and they didn't hear a car leave. Even if Kevin got into a car, the roadblocks were in place.

"Tell them to carry on. Have they asked in every house? Have they gone inside and looked, if they have suspicions?"

Rizwan scratched his head. "Don't think so. They're asking questions, but that's it."

Sarah shook her head. "Not good enough. I want searches inside the houses, withing a three block radius. He could be hiding there, like the guv said."

"On it," Rizwan said, picking up his phone to call the uniforms inspector in charge.

Sarah heard a sound and looked behind to find Roy lumbering into the office, a washed-out, exhausted look on his face.

"You alright?" she asked.

"Hmm," he said, typically tight-lipped. She knew something had happened, probably at the psychiatrist he was forced to see, or with Nugent. She also knew he would never talk about it.

"How was your interview with Tracey's mother?" Roy asked, hooking his thumbs on his belt, and spreading his feet.

"Difficult, but productive. We met Tracey's son as well, a little toddler. Cathy, her mother, knew what Tracey was up to. She also mentioned a man who accosted Tracey in the supermarket. Seems like the same man as Debbie mentioned. We went to the supermarket and should be getting CCTV footage soon. And"— she raised a hand as Roy went to speak— "We got hold of Tracey's ex-partner. An ex-convict in Loxley, called Luke Hammond. He knows stuff he's not declaring. We might need to bring him in."

"You have been productive." Roy smiled, and his eyes slid to

Melanie, who was listening with one ear, her attention split between the laptop and them. "Both of you."

Melanie's eyes remained on her screen, and she said, "I've just got the CCTV through, from the supermarket. Sending it to the researchers now. We have the date, and approximate time, so hopefully they can get us something.

Sarah looked hard at Roy, at the chiselled jaw line, and the strange but palpable emptiness in his eyes. He was thinking about the case, but she could tell he was forcing himself. The lights were on, but no one was home.

She got closer to him, and lowered her voice, out of earshot. "What happened?"

Roy frowned at her. "A woman's dead, and the killer's on the loose. What more do you want?"

She went to speak, but he stepped away, avoiding the question in her eyes. Sarah watched his back as he went into his office and shut the door. She shook her head internally. What was Rohan so afraid of?

CHAPTER 24

Detective Superintendent Michael Nugent appeared in the office. He pointed at Roy. "Can I have a word please?"

"Carry on as you are," Roy said to the others, standing. He looked at Ollie and Riz. "Can you two chase up Luke Hammond? I know he was in the pub the night of Tracey's murder, but something about him doesn't sit right. Dig into his record sheets. See if you can speak to him again."

He glanced at Melanie and Sarah; aware Nugent was fidgeting behind him. Well, he could easily have called Roy and asked. Roy had work to do, and he wouldn't let Nugent disrupt his rhythm. He knew the Super liked to throw his weight around, and walking across the corridor to order Roy, and expect him to obey immediately, was exactly the kind of thing Nugent would do. Well, Roy was secretly enjoying feeling his boss's eyes boring into his back.

"Debbie McPherson," Roy spoke to Sarah and Mel. "She's here, and let's make the most of it. She'll be out today but squeeze her as much as you can about Kevin and Tracey, and of course Bianca."

"Kevin and Tracey," Oliver said. "Isn't that like a sitcom on TV?"

"No, that's *Gavin and Tracey*, you muppet," Sarah scolded him.

"There's something about Kevin on TV," Oliver frowned, drumming his fingers on the desk.

"Kevin Spacey?" Melanie asked, intrigued. "God, I fancy him."

"*Something about Mary*," Riz piped up. "Great film."

Roy sighed. "Can we please get back on track. If Debbie has more dirt on Kevin, I want to know before I speak to him. Got it?" He raised his eyebrows at Sarah, who gave him a thumbs up."

"I'll be back in a minute," he said. Then he turned to Nugent, who had a face like a poisonous fart trapped inside a balloon. That pleased Roy no end. He smiled as nicely as he could. Nugent glared at him for a second, then turned and stalked towards his office. Roy followed. He went inside Nugent's office and shut the door as the Super opened the window and sparked up. He took a deep drag from his Marlboro Red, then blew smoke out the window. His hand dangled outside, holding the cigarette.

Nugent's barrel chest heaved, and his baleful eyes glittered at Roy. "Kevin Rawlinson. He's a big fish. What you got on him?"

"We got hi-tech surveillance cameras at his brothel. Massage parlour, I mean. He did a runner when we tried to question him. He wouldn't run if he wasn't guilty. I think we can make a charge stick."

"Have you spoken to Mark?" Mark Spencer was their CPS man. He was a paralegal who offered advice on what sort of evidence would work and might lead to a successful court prosecution.

"Not yet. But even if we don't get Kevin for the murder, there's a whole lot else. He knows that hence the Spiderman show over the roof top. He could've killed himself, the stupid prat."

Nugent finished smoking and threw the cigarette away. "The Loxley Boys have big lawyers. A case against them will take up a lot of manpower. Are you sure you've got this right?"

"I need to speak to Kevin first. Can I just get on?"

Nugent sat down on his desk and fixed him with a stare. "Just run things past me. Okay?"

"As always, Sir." Roy smiled. Nugent narrowed his eyes. Roy shut the door softly behind him.

Oliver and Riz were at their desks, engrossed in Ollie's laptop. Sarah and Mel had left, presumably to question Debbie. The two DCs didn't look up till Roy was almost next to them.

"We got him," Riz said, a triumphant smile on his face. "The bloke who harassed Tracey at the supermarket. The skipper's taken his mugshot to show Debbie downstairs. If it's the same guy who was arguing with her at the massage parlour, we have our man."

Ollie turned the laptop so Roy could see and pressed play. The black and white CCTV screen was divided into four squares. The top right square showed a slim man in a dark suit stop next to two women, identified as Tracey and her mother, Catherine. Catherine was pushing a pram with a baby in it, and Tracey held the shopping trolley. The man stopped, and started talking to Tracey, which rapidly escalated into an argument. Tracey moved away, wheeling the trolley, but the man followed.

Oliver switched to the box below, and now they saw the man facing the camera. He was young, in his late-twenties-to-early-thirties, with a light beard on his cheeks. He had short, dark hair, and was of average height, just under six feet. His hands moved in the air as he gesticulated. Tracey did the same, and then tried to walk away again, but the man followed.

A security guard got involved, presumably attracted by the

shouting. Soon, two security guards were removing the man forcibly, because he wouldn't listen. In the end, three guards kicked the man out. A camera outside the supermarket showed the man argue with the guards, who formed a barrier, stopping him from entering again. They walked him to his car, a black Audi A5. The man got in the car, and the guards waited til he drove away.

"Traffic got the car reg, and checked with DVLA," Riz said. "His name's Damien Russell. If he's the man on the screen, that is. He could be a friend driving Damien's car. Anyways, Damien lives in a place called Heeley, down south near Meersbrook. Council tax and electoral roll documents show he lives alone. No PCN seen so far, but we're still looking."

"Where is he now?" Roy asked. "Have we sent uniforms around?"

"Not yet. Waiting for the skipper to confirm with Debbie it's the same guy. Ah, there she is."

Roy turned to see Sarah walking up to them fast, her cheeks tinged with colour. "It's him, alright," she panted, clearly having run up from the custody cells downstairs. She glanced at the laptop. "Same bloke that Debbie saw with Tracey, and she had to break up a fight. Almost got physical, she said. He was holding on to Tracey's arm, and she had to kick him."

Riz said, "Guv, I just did a search for Damien's name in the Heeley area. There's twenty-odd with that name, but only one that fits the age. As long as he was driving his own car, we have our man."

"Send uniforms in, and you two can go with them," Roy said to the DCs. "I want him in custody now."

CHAPTER 25

"**M**r Russell," Oliver shouted through the letterbox. "Could you please open the door?"

It was their third attempt, with the same result. No response. Rizwan was standing behind Oliver. He moved, and peered in through the bay window that faced a small front garden. With his cupped hands, he could make out a sofa facing a wall-mounted TV, and two armchairs. If no one was home, he wondered why the curtains weren't drawn. Unless the occupant had left in a rush.

One of the uniformed sergeant's voices crackled on the radio. "Nowt back here, guv. We walked in through one of the houses opposite. His back garden's overgrown and quite a state. Back door seems locked. Curtains open in the upstairs window. Can't see anyone. Do you want us to go in?"

"I'll call you back," Riz said. He joined Oliver, who was hammering at the door again. "Leave it lad. He's not in. Car's not here."

Oliver stepped back, and they both craned their necks to look at the upper floor. The curtains blocked any view, and the windows were closed. The street was a row of terraced properties. Riz watched as a shape moved across the ground floor window of the house to his right. He pulled on Oliver's sleeve, and they went out of the small, rickety, wrought-iron gate that leaned to one side. Riz knocked on the door, and a few seconds later, they heard the sound of shuffling feet. The heavy door yawned open to show a small, wizened old woman in a bathrobe, peering at them through thick-rimmed glasses.

"Sorry to bother you," Riz said. "We're the police, and we would like to speak to the man who lives next door." He showed his warrant card, and so did Oliver.

"What's your name?" Riz asked.

"Dotty. Well, Dorothy, but everyone calls me Dotty, you see." She smiled and a couple of teeth were missing. "I forget things, so the name fits. Would you like to come in?"

"No that's fine, thank you. Now, this man, Damien Russell, have you seen him around recently?"

"Not really. I see him in the morning sometimes. When he's at home, that is. At the weekends, you know.

"When was the last time?"

"Oh, maybe last week. Or was it the week before, I can't be sure. Won't you come in? I can't stand for too long."

Reluctantly, the two DCs went inside. The place had seen better days. The carpets were threadbare and paisley, relics of a bygone era. Wallpaper had faded on the walls, and cobwebs hung in the corner.

"Do you live alone, Dorothy?" Oliver asked.

"Shows, doesn't it," The old biddy said, leaning on her walking stick. Oliver and Riz exchanged a glance. She was sharper than she looked, clearly. Dorothy opened the door of the living room and settled on a sofa. The men stood by the door.

"Oh, sit down, please. Make yourselves at home."

"You have family around, Dorothy?" Oliver said.

"Not really. I've got a son, and he's got two boys, but they live down south in Surrey. Not seen them for a while. My son wants me to move, but I can't be bothered at my age. My husband passed away last year."

"Sorry to hear that."

They were silent for a while, out of respect. Rizwan said, "So, you were saying you saw Damien, the man next door, last weekend? What was he doing?"

"Either last weekend or before. He was washing his car, he was. He looked after that thing. He waves at me and so on. But he's not very chatty. Don't know much about him."

"Did he live alone?"

"Think so, yes. Never saw anyone else live there. Oh, he had some women come around. I sit out here in the front room with the lights off at night, you see. I can't sleep very well these days. I can see the outside, but no one sees me."

Riz tensed his shoulders, and Oliver smiled. Riz asked, "Tell us about these women you saw."

"To be honest, it might have been the same one. She wasn't very tall. Came at night, in his car. Late, it was. Can't tell you the exact time, but it would be after 10 pm. I saw her in the porch light. Pretty young lass. I've seen her at his place a couple of times. They used to argue."

"Can you describe her to us?"

"Like I said, not very tall—"

Oliver raised a hand. "Dorothy, we want to know if she was black or white, the colour of her dress, her handbag, anything that caught your eyes."

Dorothy frowned at Oliver, then her forehead cleared. "Oh, I see. She was white. Petite, you know. Wore a blue dress, and a cardigan over it. Can't remember the colour."

Oliver looked at Riz, and he nodded. He took out his phone and showed Dorothy a photo of Tracey Bennett.

"Is that her?"

Dorothy took her time, and Oliver enlarged the image, showing it from various angles.

"Ooh er, that's her like, you know. That lass I saw. Hang on." She peered at Oliver; her eyes hazy behind the glasses.

"Why do you have her photo, like?"

"How many times did you see her, Dorothy?"

"She was the lass from last weekend. Saw her a few days ago as well."

"Did she only come at night, or did you see her in the daytime as well?"

Dorothy frowned, the wrinkles on her wise forehead etching deeper. "Think I saw her leaving one morning while I was having breakfast out here." She turned to Oliver. "What's happened to her, like?"

Oliver looked at Riz. Dorothy smiled at them. "If nowt were the matter, you wouldn't be askin' me all them questions, would yer? Don't worry like, I'm too old to get scared. He's done summat to her, has he? Is she missin' or owt?"

Riz said, "Dorothy, we can't go into details about that now, but we are looking for this woman. Her name's Tracey Bennett. If you see her, or you see Damien, please let us know." Both of them gave Dorothy their cards, which she examined with great interest.

"You know, a detective man's never given me his card, and now

131

I get two in one go!" Dorothy laughed, and Oliver got the impression they had made her day. He touched her shoulder. She really was a heart-warming character.

"Stay in touch, okay? And let us know as soon as you see Damien."

"Aye. I'll do that."

"We'll see ourselves out."

The men went out and met up with the team of uniforms outside. "Set up a perimeter," Oliver said to the sergeant on duty, a man called Darren. "Our victim was here. This is now a crime scene. Any news of Damien?"

"Neighbour opposite saw him the day before. He left early in the morning. Way early, like around 6 am. She saw him from her bathroom window. He had a big rucksack on his shoulder and left in his car. It's a black Audi A5."

"Did the neighbour know where he works? Or what he does for a living?"

"Nope. We asked in a couple of the other houses." Darren indicated the houses on either side. "They saw him around but didn't know much about him. He was seen wearing a suit, looking like a professional. The neighbour opposite said he's lived here for a few years. Single man, lived alone."

"Okay, good. Set up the perimeter please."

Riz was speaking on his radio to Sarah. "Victim was seen here, guv. Setting up a crime scene here, now. Shall we go in to have a look? No sign of Damien. He's not answering his phone. Traffic are looking for his car on CCTV around Sheffield."

"Yes, go in," Sarah said. "But be careful not to disturb evidence. I'll let Justin know."

Justin Dobson was the head of SOC, or Scene of Crime. Riz thanked her and hung up. He relayed the information to the others. Oliver put both hands on his waist.

"Let's try with the keys first." He went to his car and came back with a selection of Chubb lock keys that the police carried with them to see if any of them fit. He tried them on the door, watched by Riz. After the tenth attempt, Riz lost patience.

"Get the portable battering ram. Unless we can get in the back door."

"Just wait," Oliver said, still fitting another key into the lock. He twisted it with a grimace, and nothing happened.

"Right, that's it. I'm going around the back," Riz said.

CHAPTER 26

Roy shut the door and locked it. He sat down at the table, and stared at the cheap, fake wood grain. It was alright. It was fine. He had a wobble with Meredith Wilson, but he got through it, like he always did. Meredith didn't know any better, and that's the way he wanted it.

No one had to know. He had his game face on. He would snarl, jibe, grimace his way through the day. Another day. Not long to go. Just another day, then he could sleep. At least Anna was here. He checked his watch, then his phone. He had half an hour left to pick her up. Then, depending on how the case went, he had the evening with her. Not alone with his frustrations, walking in the lonely mountains, getting lost, soaked in the rain.

Roy sighed and opened up his laptop. He replied to a few emails, and spoke to Nugent, reassuring the D Sup that he had done his psych assessment, and that Meredith would submit a report to Professional Standards.

Then he clicked open a map of Sheffield. He zoomed in on the section of Attercliffe and Burngreave, where the Cliffe Massage Parlour was located. He noted the close cluster of houses. He jotted a few things in his notebook, then went outside. The first person he saw was Sarah, who was looking at his office like she'd never taken her eyes off it. He stopped, hand still on the door handle. They maintained eye contact for a few seconds, then she let him go. He didn't see anger or reproach in her eyes, only concern, tinged with confusion. He felt bad. Sarah was worried about him, and he owed her more than putting up a front.

He put it to one side and approached her desk.

"The black book from Debbie McPherson. Anything in it of interest?"

She craned her neck to the side and looked at him in silence, then pointed at Oliver and Riz. "I gave it to the lads."

Riz glanced up and nodded. "No names of any customers, if that's what you're after. Only the women who worked there, and that too only first names. Tracey's name appears quite a few times. She was a regular there."

"The place has cameras, according to Debbie. Did the uniforms find anything?"

"Search still ongoing, guv. Debbie's here now, by the way, in the interview room. Shall we interview her?"

"I don't mind," Roy looked at Sarah, who shrugged. He said, "I need to get Anna from town. Will be back in fifteen minutes, no more." He sat down on a chair and faced the team.

"There's something bothering me. Our killer is methodical. He has a style of cutting, and he leaves the body in a certain position." He moved his hands in the air. "Knees and elbows bent – head turned to the right. He wipes the bodies clean, leaves no marks anywhere. Victims are fully dressed. I want to know if there's any cold cases with the same MO. The reason being, sick bastards like him might well have done it before, but the case wasn't solved. And he might do it again, if he's come back."

Oliver said, "You want me to look in the cold cases database?"

"Yes. Start with Sheffield and Yorkshire, then expand to the whole country. Let's see what we find. If we get nothing, then we can carry on as we are. But at least we know."

"We'll get something ready by the time you're back," Rizwan said.

Roy said, "After I drop Anna off, I'm going back to the crime scene. We need to find Kevin; he's got to be around there. And I also want to search the Cliffe Parlour again."

Oliver and Rizwan looked at him expectantly. Roy nodded. "One of you can come with me, and the other can follow if that's alright with Sarah." He glanced at her, and she nodded.

Sarah said, "I'll interview Debbie with Riz. See you at the crime scene."

Roy said goodbye and headed out to the car. His old VW was still in one piece, but every time he pulled the driver's door open it creaked and wobbled like it was going to fall off. He sat down, and the seat groaned, and descended a few inches more than usual. His arse was now used to the lack of springs, but it was getting more uncomfortable. He felt like he was sitting on one of those jelly cushions, with pokey springs sticking up and into potentially alarming regions of his backside.

The ignition whined like a horse being strangled, and then died. He tried again, hoping the engine wouldn't flood from shoving the clutch down. Finally, the engine sputtered to life, in bits and drabs, then coughed and belched smoke as he pulled out of the car park. The only reason he kept this car was its spaciousness, and the fact even with his long frame he could stretch and sleep with the back seat pulled down. He had done that a few nights when he was homeless or travelling. That seemed like a long time ago because it was. Perhaps he did need a new car after all.

He picked up Anna, who was waiting for him outside the city

library. He couldn't stop there as it was a one-way street, and wisely, Anna had chosen one of the side streets. He took her back to Dore. Anna had made friends with the neighbour's daughter, Pearl, who was the same age as her. Pearl wanted to come over, and Roy was happy that Anna wouldn't be alone.

Dore wasn't as isolated as Hathersage, where the horrendous nightmare had happened to Anna. Pearl and Anna were becoming mates, and Roy had spoken to her parents, who lived three doors down. They were good people and had invited Roy and Anna over one evening.

"No boys," Roy told Anna before she shut the door. Pearl, who was shorter than Anna, and standing behind her, giggled. Anna rolled her eyes and frowned.

"Seriously, Dad. As if I know boys here."

"And no house parties."

"Too late. I've sent out invites on Snapchat already. You're not back till tomorrow, right?"

"Very funny," Roy grumbled. "Call me, okay? And if you can't get me—"

"Call the switchboard. Yes, I know, and I've got the number."

Anna and Pearl waved as he went back to his car. He got back in, and after the usual rigmarole, the car started, farting acrid smoke. Roy hoped he wasn't pissing off the neighbours too much. He droned away; glad Anna wasn't on her own. He got to Liverpool Street and parked by the squad cars. He was about to get out when his phone buzzed.

Guess you don't want to see your brother again, do you?

Roy clenched his teeth together. As usual, there was no number to call back. He sent a message.

Stop this crap. If you knew where he was you would've told me by now.

137

He got a message back instantly.

Oh, I know where he is. But you never will, that's the whole point.

Tell me then.

You'll have to try a lot harder than that.

With that mysterious reply, the messages stopped. Roy threw the phone down, and it hit the footwell, then bounced off the door. He slammed a fist into the side of the door and put a dent in the flimsy metalwork. The car shook as he gripped the steering wheel and roared, almost ripping the wheel off. Then his head sank into his hands. He stayed like that for a while. Then he picked up his phone and got out.

He creaked his neck sideways. His fists clenched and unclenched. He wanted to spit bullets and knock some heads together. He walked past the two uniform sergeants, responding to their greeting with a curt nod. He ducked under the blue and white tape and stalked down the road. Ahead, he could see the white tent, and the white forensic van was still there. He couldn't see around the bend, but hoped the other roadblock was still in place.

He stopped short as he walked past the Cliffe Sauna. The door was shut, and all the curtains were closed. A young, uniformed constable was walking nearby, his eyes on the ground, head lowered in thought. His hands were folded behind his back, and he looked like he was bored out of his skill. He looked up quickly when Roy approached.

Roy didn't waste any time. "You're not paid to look at the road, constable. There's a dangerous man on the loose, or didn't you know?"

The constable gaped, then frowned at Roy. He clearly wasn't aware who this man in civilian clothes was, taking that rude tone of voice with him.

"What dangerous… Who are you?"

"DCI Roy, of the Major Investigations Team, and SIO in this murder case."

The constable's eyes widened, and his spine snapped straight as he practically saluted. His name badge said Hillyard. "Sorry guv, didn't recognise you."

"Don't worry about that," Roy snapped. "Look sharp. We chased a man who's the chief pimp in that brothel," Roy jerked a thumb in the direction of the Cliffe Sauna. "He's not gone far. Didn't have a car. He must be in one of these houses. Here, come with me."

Roy headed for Cliffe Sauna not bothering to look back. Hillyard ran close to his heels. Roy got to the door and slammed his fist on it.

CHAPTER 27

oy waited for a while, but no one came to the door. He pounded the tall door with his fist, making it shake. He remembered Debbie was at the nick, so someone else better be here, or he would have to find access some other way. After a few minutes, and lurking through the windows, there was still no response. He even tried the calling bell.

"No one here, guv," Hillyard said.

"We'll make a police officer out of you, yet. Come on, let's go round the back."

Roy jogged towards the white tent till he saw an alley between the row of houses. He took a sharp left, and ended up in the alley that ran around the back. Up ahead, he could make out the Cliffe Sauna, and the fence over which he had climbed. Kevin Rawlinson's escape route. He jogged up to it, then glanced at the houses to his left. Uniforms had been here already, he was sure.

"Your lot done a door-to-door here?" He asked Hillyard, indicating the houses, whose entrances were on a different street, accessible from this alley.

"Yes, guv. No one seen or heard anything."

"Have you been inside the houses?"

Hillyard opened his mouth, then shut it. "I... No, I don't think we did, guv."

"There's a dead body on the road out there, and no one here saw anything?"

"That's what they said, guv. I was on the other side actually, and we did take two statements from witnesses. Those houses we went inside."

Roy nodded and looked around carefully. If Kevin came out the hidden back gate, his only option was to turn left, and head down the road that led away from the crime scene. Hillyard was right, these houses didn't face the road where the body was left. There might not be any witnesses.

But Kevin had to be somewhere around here. Within minutes of him vanishing, uniforms were crawling in this alley, and in the road ahead. Roy walked down, and the alley curved, then opened into the road. It was pretty much the same as Liverpool Street, mostly terraced houses, with some larger semidetached.

"Was your team here?" Roy asked. Hillyard nodded. "Did you check all the houses on the street?"

"Yes, Sir."

Roy walked down the road. If Kevin had to hide, this place would be ideal. He noticed some of the houses had rear loft developments that looked out to the houses on Liverpool Street, and the crime scene. A good vantage point to hide and observe. He whipped his head around. This road ended in a cul-de-sac. There was no way out. Something tingled at the back of his neck.

"Have you, or any of your team, been inside any of them?"

"No, guv."

A sixth sense was buzzing in Roy's mind, the sound getting louder by the second. He looked at Hillyard.

"We'll start our own door to door, now. You and me. But before that, call two more of your team here."

Hillyard, nodded, and pulled out his radio. He spoke briefly on it, and his Inspector's voice came on it. Roy recognised it as Jonty's and stretched out his hand. Hillyard gave him the radio.

"DCI Roy speaking. I want a search in the houses here, including the loft and rear gardens. Broadmoor Street," he said, glancing at the road name sign.

"Search, guv? You think the man's there?"

"Yes, I do."

Roy hung up. He asked Hillyard, "Is it mainly families on this street?"

"Some of them have young people as well. I thought they might be students. That house there, had two young women who answered the door. They both had accents, like Polish or something."

Eastern European. Roy frowned. The brothel was next door, and it was a sad fact that some women from Eastern Europe were trafficked to work in the sex industry.

He could be wrong, of course. Might be just a house of flat sharers. But still worth a look.

"Which one?"

Hillyard pointed to a mid-terraced house. Roy had noted it was one with a loft conversion that looked out to Liverpool Street.

Roy followed Hillyard as the young constable went up to the house and rang the bell. It was a big, tall, terraced house, the type built at the turn of the century. They had three floors, each designed to house a family. Now they were all smaller flats, and the loft conversion had added a fourth floor. The house had seen better days. The bricks needed re pointing, and the wooden window frames had rot in them.

Hillyard was about to ring the doorbell again, when the door opened on the chain, and a pale face appeared. They could only see a fraction of the woman's face, her eyes darting over them, not opening the door any further.

"We're police officers. We came to speak to you a while ago. Can we come in, please?" Hillyard said.

The woman said nothing for a while. There was a sound behind her, followed by another voice, speaking in a foreign language. It sounded urgent, like it was scolding the woman who answered the door.

Roy had seen enough. He pushed past Hillyard. "Open the door now, please. We need to speak to everyone in the house."

There was another rushed conversation inside, then the door shut once, and the chain slid across. Hillyard and Roy stepped inside. The floorboards creaked under the threadbare carpet. The kitchen was at the end of the hallway, and a staircase went up to the right. A woman stood on the last step, hand on the banister like she was about to run up the stairs. The woman who opened the door stood next to the coats hanging from the hooks.

They looked pale, haggard, and anxious. Roy noticed the bruise on the arm of the girl standing on the step.

He showed them his warrant card. "DCI Roy. Have you seen anyone running down this street? Or has anyone tried to come into the house?"

Both women shook their heads. They still hadn't said a word. The one who opened the door looked at her feet.

"What's your name?" Roy asked.

The woman raised her head, her eyes watchful. "Katie." She

pronounced it like saying the initials 'KT'.

"Is that your real name?"

The woman glanced at her friend, who was staring at Roy. Then she looked at the floor again and nodded.

"And yours?" Roy turned to the woman on the stairs.

"Monica."

"I think that's your real name. Correct?"

Monica, who seemed the bolder of the two, nodded.

Roy said, "Are you from Poland?"

Both women shook their heads in agreement. "Moldova," Monica said.

Roy pointed upstairs. "Who else lives here?"

The women exchanged a glance again, and it was Monica who spoke. "Another girl. She is out now. Will be back later."

"Just three of you in the big old house?" Roy asked. "You sure."

"Yes," Monica said, not sounding sure of herself at all.

"We're going to have a look around, if that's okay." Roy said. "We'll stay out of your way." He smiled, trying to put the women at ease, but from their frightened stares, he wasn't having much luck. He pulled Hillyard to one side.

"Call for a female staff member. You stay down here. I'll have a look upstairs."

Roy excused himself and went up the stairs. Monica had gone up ahead of him, and he caught sight of her, closing a door. He came on the landing and knocked softly on Monica's door. At the same time, the doorbell went. Roy heard the voice of a female officer, and he leaned over the banister.

"Up here."

He was surprised to see Sarah. "Mel is interviewing Debbie," Sarah explained.

Roy nodded. "I think he might be here," he whispered. "Call it a hunch. Monica's in there, you have a look around here. I'll head up into the loft."

He left Sarah to it. She knocked on Monica's door and went inside. There was a bathroom next to it and Roy had a quick look inside. Three toothbrushes in a cup on the sink. He opened the cabinet door that had mould on it. He had gloves on now, and picked up an orange medicine bottle, with writing in a foreign language. He twisted the lid open and saw small brown pills inside. He put the bottle back in the cabinet. He went out and tried the other two bedroom doors. He could hear Sarah speaking to Monica inside. The other bedroom doors were locked. Before he went up, there was another smaller room next to the staircase. The door opened to reveal a study of sorts, with a beanbag on the floor, and a table with a laptop on it. The window curtains were open, and he could see the street, and the two uniformed constables who had just turned up.

He heard a creak from upstairs. It was subtle, but he heard it alright. He glanced at the ceiling once. He pulled out the baton from his belt line and went up the stairs.

CHAPTER 28

There was a good-sized landing, which opened out into three doors. Two were closed, but the smaller bathroom door was open. Roy had a quick peek inside. Tiles on the floor had cracked, and the rickety shower enclosure was rusting in the corner. It was empty, and Roy knocked on the white tiled walls, making sure there wasn't a cavity big enough to hide someone.

He went into the room at the other end, the one that faced the rear, and which would have the window that allowed views of the crime scene. The door opened smoothly, to reveal a good-sized bedroom. No bed was present, and the floorboards were bare. There was a table and chair in one corner, and an old scenery print on the wall. On the floor, there was a mattress, with a bed cover and duvet, and it looked slept in. Roy went out and had look at the room next door. This one was similar, and the window faced the side of the house. There was also a mattress on the bare floor, but without any bedding. The room was devoid of any other furniture. He shut the door and went back to the rear bedroom.

He could hear all the sounds now, the faint voices from the

floors below, the water pipes as they gurgled briefly under the floorboards. His heavy boots crunched on the wood as he bent lower and moved the mattress on the floor. There was nothing behind it, and it was up against a wall. Roy raised the mattress and had a look on the underside. He found nothing. His eyes fell on the window, whose blinds were pulled down. He raised it, and saw a good view of Liverpool Street, visible between the houses. He saw the white tent of the crime scene and both the roadblocks, sealing off the road. He left the curtain raised and looked around him carefully. There was nowhere to hide in here, and yet, someone had slept in this bed recently. It was warm.

He opened the Velux window all the way and leaned out. The fall down below was vertical, broken only by the eaves. He saw the L-shaped courtyard, and then the garden started. The lawn was overgrown with weeds, it was practically a jungle. There was a strip at the rear of the houses, which joined the alley that ran behind Cliffe Sauna. The back garden of this house would be easily accessible from the brothel.

Roy turned and heard steps coming up. Sarah appeared at the doorway. Roy raised a finger to his lips and beckoned her over. Sarah looked at the scenery and nodded.

"Where is he though?" she whispered. "I didn't hear owt, and there's nowhere to hide. We looked everywhere."

Roy pointed at the wall. Sarah frowned at him, confused. He walked over to the table, and she helped him move it. Behind the table, there was a panel on the wall, the kind that opens up into the eaves for storage. Sarah grinned at him.

Roy reached for the handle, and Sarah handed him her flashlight. He opened the small panel door and switched the flashlight on. The beam lit up a large, cavernous space. A mouse scurried away. There was a water tank in the middle, a remnant from years gone by, when combi boilers didn't exist. It was built to store hot water, and now the brass surface was rusting. Boxes were scattered around and piled in one corner. Roy put his head inside, and the musty, damp smell hit him immediately, a powerful blast of old wood, and animal waste. He held his breath and crawled inside. Dust rose around him in a cloud. He heard Sarah on the radio, calling for reinforcements.

He crawled to the piled up boxes and pulled his legs up into a crouching position. The boxes were a mix of light and heavy, and he wondered what they contained. He grunted as he moved the top layer, then shone his light into the rest of the space.

He spotted the sleeping bag immediately, and behind it, the shaft of light that slanted in through the hole in the roof. He scrambled over the last box and grabbed the sleeping bag. It was empty. The hole in the roof was just about big enough for his shoulders to squeeze through. He pushed his head through it. The tiles of the slanted roofs of the houses on either side met his eyes.

As he whipped his head to the right, he caught sight of fingers holding next door's chimneystack, and a man who moved his head behind it.

"Kevin," Roy shouted. "There's no way out. Give yourself up, now."

In response, the man stood, and tottered his way across the pitched roof, arms held out on either side for balance.

CHAPTER 29

"Bloody hell," Roy seethed. He tried to crawl out of the hole in the roof, and his feet immediately slipped on the tile, scattering a few loose shingles.

"Guv, you alright?" Sarah's voice came from behind.

He grunted in reply. He watched Kevin totter his precarious way across the pitched roof. The man sat down, and bum-shuffled his way across to the next chimney. If Kevin got to the last house on the terrace, he could potentially get down to the garden, and escape from the cul-de-sac. There were a lot of ways this could go wrong for him, but he seemed to have decided it was his only option.

"Kevin," Roy called out once again. "Stop where you are. There's no escape."

Roy craned his neck to the right and was just about able to see one of the uniforms standing in front of the house.

"Oi you! Yes, you there, look up here. DCI Roy. Can you see that bastard up on the roof?"

The uniformed constable leaned to the left, searching up for the voice. Then he appeared fully into view. He gaped at Roy, with his head sticking out of the roof. Roy waved a hand, pointing to his right.

"He's there, up there. Can you see?"

Confusion reigned supreme on the constable's face. "Who, guv?"

"The bloke on the roof god damn it. There's only one! It's not a bloody bird. Can you see him?"

Finally, the constable twigged. He ran out of vision, and then ran back in, excited.

"Yes, yes! Seen him!"

"Alright then. Keep an eye on him. And put a man in the garden of the last house, and behind this street. He's headed into the woods at the back."

The constable ran off to do his duties. Roy went back into the loft, banging his head on some roof tiles in the process. It hurt like mad, and he cursed and grumped his way back over the duty boxes, the mice poo, and cobwebs that clung to his face. He came out of the panel, his head dusty and cobwebs in his hair. Sarah grinned when she saw him.

"Good police work, guv. You found him. It's like that movie, *Fiddler on the Roof*."

"Pimp on the roof, more like," Roy grumbled, brushing dust off his limbs. "Come on then, let's get him."

They went down the stairs. "Did you find anything in the rest of the house?"

"Got a laptop on the second floor. Another on the first floor. Three girls live here, but as many as ten were here last month. All trafficked from Moldova. Sad, really. Katya told me."

"Who?"

"Oh, she said her name was Katie, at first. The other woman,

Monika isn't talking. She speaks better English, but she might be higher up the gang chain."

They went past a couple of uniforms moving beds and wardrobes in the first floor bedrooms.

"Toothbrushes in the bathrooms. They'll be good for DNA samples."

"All bagged, guv, don't worry. We're knocking on walls, lifting floorboards. SOC will be here soon."

Roy grunted his approval, and they went outside. Like a group of tourists watching a flock of birds in murmuration, five constables were standing there, watching the roof of the house next door. In the houses opposite a couple of windows were open, and fascinated neighbours had joined in.

Kevin Rawlinson was evidently trying to be Spiderman, Roy thought. He now had his arms around the chimney post, and his right foot was feeling for a landing spot. He found it, and moved to the other side, sitting down on the gabled hip of the pitched roof.

"Kevin!" Roy shouted, cupping his hands over his mouth. "You're surrounded. There's no escape. You could fall and kill yourself. Is it worth it?"

As expected, the man didn't reply. He shuffled along, holding on to the pitch of the roof for support. His feet slipped, and he screamed as he slid down the roof. His progress was halted by a Velux windowsill, where he jammed his feet in. He tried to climb back up but slipped down again.

"This is the gift that don't stop giving," Roy shook his head. "Right, get him down, enough time wasted." He walked over to the constables, who were grinning, watching the show.

"Who's at the back?" He asked Hillyard, who stood to attention promptly.

"The guv is."

Roy asked for Jonty Adams on the radio. "DCI Roy. Can you keep a couple of men there, please? His aiming to climb down the other side, but I think he's going to fall and kill himself. Call an ambulance. I need him alive."

"Ambulance on its way," Jonty said.

A gasp went up from the constable, and the neighbours across the road. Roy looked at the roof, where Kevin had slipped again. Kevin screamed once and tried to hold on to another window ledge. It didn't work this time. His momentum carried him all the way down to the rood edge, and he tried to grab the gutters. He managed, and they bent, ripping off their ties to the wall as they held him for a few seconds. He dangled precariously, then fell like a sack of potatoes to the hedge down below.

The constable rushed to get him, and Roy heard the whine of an ambulance siren getting louder.

CHAPTER 30

Kevin had a concussion, and he was put in the back of the ambulance. Roy and Sarah left, and as they walked past the rear of the Cliffe Sauna, he said, "I wish we could get in there. I'm tempted to break in the back door."

"That would be unnecessary as I've got the keys from Debbie." Sarah smiled and patted her coat pocket. "Always rely on a woman."

Roy muttered something inaudible as they went around to the front, and Sarah tried the keys. The third attempt worked, and they went inside. The entire place was deserted, and their shoes thumped on the stairs as they went up and down, searching everywhere. Roy knew the uniforms and SOC had already been here. He could see the white marks on the floor, where the forensic officers had collected samples.

He joined Sarah inside a bedroom on the second floor. They had shoe coverings on, and markers were present on the floor, spots for them to avoid. Both of them knew the cameras that Debbie spoke of hadn't been located as of yet, despite adequate searches. It was possible Kevin had removed them already.

Roy knocked on the walls but didn't find any hollow spots. He bent under the bed, and found only dust, and bare floorboards. The deep pile purple carpets had been lifted and rolled up on the hallway. He stood and put his hands on his waist. Sarah had left to check the next bedroom, and she returned soon.

"Looked around this floor. Nowt," she said, shrugging. "I was with the lads when they looked upstairs. Same story. Debbie might've been bluffing to get herself off the hook."

"We'll get the truth out of Kevin soon enough. Let's go."

Sarah left, and he grabbed the door handle to shut it. That's when he noticed it. One of the four screw holdings that held the handle and lock in place. The tiny black bump on it, so small it was barely visible. He stopped and knelt by the door. The other three screws were also coloured black, but only the bottom left one had the tiny protuberance. It was so easy to miss that even if the handle was dusted for fingerprints, this would've been overlooked, which it clearly had.

Roy didn't have a screwdriver, and neither did Sarah. They went downstairs and rummaged around in the utility room behind the reception. They found a box of tools, and Roy carried it upstairs. When he took the handle off, they gazed at the tiny camera within the steel casing. It was state of the art. The lens was barely visible, and the whole camera was round, and the size of a green pea, but black. He prised it out of the lock and held it up to the light between two fingers.

Sarah put her hands on her thighs and bent closer to have a look. "What sort of a brothel is this, guv? Spying on their punters?"

"To blackmail them later," Roy said. "But you're right. There's more going on here than meets the eye."

"Do you mind if I swing by my house, guv?" Sarah said. "Got to pick up a change of clothes. My locker's empty. Matt should be home from school as well. He wanted to get on the bus back with his mates and I said yes."

Roy nodded. "Sure, no problem."

It was a detour to the outskirts of Totley, where Sarah lived. As they drove, Roy checked the missing persons schemes he subscribed to. Every day, they posted possible sightings, or links, across Europe, but they had contacts all over the world. Today, they had nothing.

Many missing persons changed their names and settled in Spain or Portugal. Most of them remained missing, but every now and then, these schemes managed to find a lost loved one. Those stories were advertised prominently on their websites. What was not so well advertised was the failure rate, which, in Roy's case, was still one-hundred-percent.

After twenty-seven-years, he had found a better chance of finding his brother than these missing persons services. He had Burns, Robin's abductor, in prison, but the man wouldn't talk. As Burns's psychiatrist Dr Parsons was fond of saying: you can't get water out of a stone.

Steven Burns had tortured Roy and his parents for a lifetime, and Roy now knew his parents would carry that hurt to their graves. And yet, there was no legal way of making Burns spill the truth. If Robin was dead, why wouldn't he admit it? It didn't make a difference if Burns killed Robin, Burns would be in jail for the rest of his life.

Burns' silence left the sneaky suspicion in Roy's mind that Robin was alive. Since Burns was caught, that suspicion had ignited new life in his mind. Or perhaps it was nothing but cruel torture, a way to make him suffer more. Burns knew very well he could continue to hurt Roy and his family from his lock-up; all he had to do was maintain his silence.

The utterly vile, evil bastard. Denying him, and his poor, elderly parents any closure. If his parents died without knowing... Roy didn't want to think anymore. The guilt corroded his soul like acid, and that would never stop. His teeth clamped together;

nostrils flared as he looked out the window. The hills were blue green in the distance, greyish clouds floating between them. He wished he could feel some peace. Some way of easing out the thorn stuck in his heart.

"Penny for your thoughts, Rohan," Sarah remarked.

He stirred and blinked. "Getting to be a long day." He passed a hand over his face.

"How's Anna?"

"She's good. Neighbour's daughter's with her. I shudder to think what they're up to. Probably trashing the house as we speak."

"Yes, got all the boys round, smoking drugs and playing loud music. Saw an invite on Snapchat last night actually."

"You should go," Roy grimaced. "Hang out with the kids."

Sarah grinned as she slowed down to take a bend in the road. "Be reyt. Don't worry."

Be reyt was the universal Yorkshire phrase for it's going to be alright. "If you say so," he rolled his eyes, then smiled. The smile faded as his earlier thoughts came back. He had to make an appointment to see Burns, and maybe Burgess, his accomplice, as well. He hadn't seen either of the evil twins for a while, and maybe Dr Parsons wouldn't mind, but previous skirmishes had taught him it was wise to speak to the psychiatrist first. Dr Parsons, to be fair, understood the situation. He was all for putting pressure on Burns to find out about Robin, but in a compassionate, and legal, way. Those two words rubbed Roy up the wrong way.

Compassion for a child killer. God give him strength. What was wrong with the laws of this country? How could an evil, twisted bastard like Burns have rights? Any bloody rights at all.

His fists clenched on his thighs, and the rage gathered at the

156

corners of his mind. A silent snarl split his lips.

"Let it go, Rohan," Sarah said quietly. They had stopped at a red light. She turned to look at him, and their eyes met. Her large sea green eyes were always frank, direct. She didn't have to say that she knew what he was thinking about. She knew.

"Be reyt, okay? Give it a little more time."

The lights changed, and the moment passed. She drove, and Roy stared at her face. A few whites had appeared in her blond locks, tucked in behind her right ear. She didn't wear earrings to work. Only mascara for makeup. That was enough.

"Yes," he sighed. She glanced at him and offered a tight-lipped smile. They arrived at Sarah's house, which was on a street of bungalows and semi-detached houses. Totley, and the area around it, was nicer than the eastern parts of the city.

Roy heard Sarah mutter something under her breath as she parked. Then he noticed the man standing outside.

"Won't be long, Rohan. Stay here," she got out of the car, looking tense. Roy put his window down so he could hear her speaking to the man. He caught snippets of the conversation. Sarah's hands were moving in the air, and she was agitated.

"… Not this evening… Sent you a text. Didn't you get owt?"

"He's my son. I tried to reach you…"

The man wore a light blue summer suit, and he was clean-shaven. He seemed relaxed, leaning against the stone front wall. His eyes flicked over to the car once, and Roy knew he'd been spotted. Behind them, the net curtains of the front bay window twitched. Probably Sarah's mum.

The man was arguing, and Sarah was having none of it. She tried to move past him, but he blocked her way. His tone was entreating now.

"I'm sorry. I really am. But…"

Sarah didn't look happy at all. Roy knew she could handle her own fights. He didn't want to get involved. But something told him Sarah could do with the support. He got out of the car and crossed the road. The man had clocked him already and stood up straight. Sarah turned, her face a mask of exasperation.

"You alright?" he asked Sarah. He nodded at the man. "DCI Roy. Sarah's colleague."

"John Garnett, Matt's dad." The man stuck out a hand, and Roy shook it.

Sarah was seething. She had blotches of colour on her cheeks, and her neck was red. "John was just leaving. Weren't you John?"

"I'm going out of the country tomorrow with work. I just wanted to see my son once before I left."

"I told you no already. I haven't spoken to Matt about this. You can't just turn up here."

John's eyes went to Roy, who towered above Sarah, and him. His eyes lost the hardness, and his Adam's Apple bobbed up and down. He raised both hands.

"Okay, I'm sorry. I don't want to make a fuss. I just wanted to see him that's all."

"And you will, John, okay? But at the right time. You can't just turn up after ten years and start making demands."

"I'm not. Guess I'm a little confused about it all as well. I just want to make amends. Look, I'm sorry."

He came off the wall and took a step back. "I'll speak to you later? Is that okay?"

"Yes," Sarah sighed.

"Nice to meet you," John said to Roy.

He inclined his head. "Likewise."

They watched as John turned and walked down the road. He turned the corner and vanished from sight.

CHAPTER 31

18 Years Ago

Jayden slept rough that night. He went into a park in central Leeds and found a bench. It was under a tree and kept the rain away. He couldn't sleep for ages, and then passed out. He woke up when a hand shook him by the shoulder. He blinked to find bright sun rays burning his eyes. He smelt the man before he saw him. An overpowering, awful, humid, deep stench. The man had a beard up to his navel and wore a tattered long black coat. He hadn't washed in years it seemed, and his face was streaked with grime. A homeless man.

"That's my spot." The man shook him again, and Jayden flung his arm off, and sat up on the bench. "You're lucky I wasn't here last night," the man said.

Jayden stood, wrapping the coat around him. "You can have it mate. I'm not coming back."

The man sat down, a cloud of sweat, stale beer, and general unwashed smell assaulting Jayden's nostrils. He waved his hands in front of his face and stepped back.

"Yeah," the man grumbled. "That's what they all say. This is my spot. Just remember that, like."

Jayden left the park and walked towards the town centre. He had barely any money, only a couple of pounds in change. He didn't feel hungry. He felt sick, and above all, he felt hurt and angry. He was torn between crying, and screaming and hitting someone, or something. He got to the bus station, and sank down on a bench, and held his head, trying to think.

He had nowhere to go. No family apart from Jerry. His school friends couldn't put him up. His clothes were back at the house. In the end, he decided to go back. With any luck, that evil bastard Keith would be gone by now. He could go to the police, but what could he say? It's not like he had any proof. He didn't even know if the police would believe him. He was under eighteen, and he smoked cannabis and drank alcohol. What if the police put *him* in jail?

And regarding his abusive past… The shame layered inside him like ice would forever freeze his tongue. He could never talk about it. Jerry used to tell him how no one would understand. It was their own, secluded world. If Jayden told anyone, they would make him homeless, and no one would look after him. Jayden was young then, and he went along with it.

Now he knew the truth. He felt that dumb, ballooning pain inside, overcoming him. He gripped his head again, unable to think. It felt like his skin was getting stripped off. He was burning inside, in a hell of shame and guilt. Eventually, he rose, and made his slow way back to the house. He had to collect his things. He had to face Jerry. Tell him for once and for all, that he was leaving. He didn't want anything more from him. He knew it would be difficult. Jerry might threaten him. Or beg him to stay. If he begged, that might be harder.

Jayden approached the house, his heart thumping loudly. Jerry's car wasn't in the drive. He had gone to work. The door was locked. He looked in through the windows and saw the living room was empty. He didn't see the TV, which was strange. He went around the back, but that door was also locked.

"Ey up, you back already?" A woman's voice said over the fence. It was the neighbour from next door. He turned quickly. There was a gap in the fence, and he could see her, holding a baby.

"I saw your dad leave this morning. He packed up all the stuff in the house. There was another guy with him, helping him."

Jayden's mouth hung open, and he shut it with an effort. "This guy who helped him. What did he look like?"

The woman was looking at Jayden strangely. "Big bloke, with a shaven head."

Keith Burgess, Jayden thought to himself. The woman said, "Why are you back?"

"Uh, umm, I thought I left something here, but I was wrong. Sorry, got to go."

He ran off, before the woman could ask him anything else. So, Jerry was gone. Jayden tried to make sense of it all as he walked. Keith and Jerry had clearly paired up, and that didn't sound good at all. Jayden was glad he didn't have to see either of them anymore.

As he walked, he realised this was the start of a new life for him. When he thought of Jerry, he didn't feel sad. He felt conflicted, and horrible, but not sad. He was glad to be rid of him. Now, he had to find somewhere to live. He knew where the big church was and headed in that direction.

CHAPTER 32

Melanie and Oliver were interviewing Debbie McPherson. The veteran arsehole, James Keenan was sat next to Debbie. He looked smug as a fat Cheshire cat, which bothered Oliver. He wore an expensive cut of suit, which gleamed like blue satin. Oliver was also fond of his nice suits. He had to grudgingly admit James looked sharp in his.

James smirked at him, and Oliver gave him a thin, cold smile back. He suspected James and Debbie had a good chat, and James had told her she'd be out in no time. Well, they'd see about that. He glanced at Melanie, who indicated the machine. Oliver flicked the switch and introduced everyone.

"Miss McPherson," Melanie said, "Please have a look at these photos." She took out photos taken by forensic officers earlier, which were printed. They showed the victim in close up and longer range photos. Debbie had identified Tracey Barrett from the image Roy had taken on his phone. But this was the first time she was seeing the larger photos. Breath hitched in Debbie's throat, and her eyes froze. Melanie sifted the photos, laying them out side by side.

Debbie averted her face, snapping her eyes shut. She sat further back in her chair.

"You knew Tracey, and you had spoken to her that night, is that correct?"

Debbie didn't answer. She touched her forehead, then rubbed it. Melanie prodded gently. "According to the statement you gave us at the Cliffe Massage Parlour, you were working the night before."

Debbie nodded in silence. Mel continued. "You've already told us Tracey seemed like her usual self. But she was also pestered by a man. He came wearing a suit once, looking smart. Then you found them having an argument outside. Is that right?"

Again, Debbie nodded in silence. Oliver said, "Debbie McPherson confirms her agreement. Can you please say yes or no next time, Miss McPherson."

Debbie sighed and sat up straighter in the chair. "Yes."

"Why was Tracey out on the streets that night? She normally had a room in Cliffe, didn't she?" Mel asked.

Debbie cleared her throat before answering. "The house was full up. That happens sometimes. Sometimes the girls take their business outside."

"And you don't mind because if they get arrested, it's nothing to do with Cliffe."

"It's never anything to do with us," Debbie said carefully, looking at Melanie. "We operate a massage and sauna business. What the ladies do in their rooms is entirely up to them."

Melanie had already spoken to Sarah, who had informed her about the micro-camera.

"But the ladies are filmed doing what they do. Is that correct?"

Debbie looked at James, who nodded once. She said, "I don't

164

know about that. I've never seen it."

Oliver liked that. Debbie was refuting her previous statement. She was digging herself a hole, and James had probably advised her without being aware.

Mel pressed her lips together. "That's not what you said the first time, Miss McPherson. You said, the owner's partner, Kevin, had installed cameras."

"That was a rumour." Debbie defended herself. "I didn't see nowt. Someone chatted about it, that's all."

James nodded, his eyes flicking from Oliver to Mel. Both of them ignored him. Mel said, "Who did you chat to?"

"A couple of the girls. Not sure which ones, and it was a long time ago. Like I said, I never seen owt."

"And yet, you were happy to tell us that Kevin planted cameras in the bedrooms."

A flicker of irritation passed across Debbie's face. She raised both hands. "But I didn't see owt. Yer not listenin' to me."

James intervened. "My client has made it very clear what her position is. She heard a rumour that's all. She was in shock when she was first questioned. She also didn't have any legal representation at the time."

Both Melanie and Oliver looked at James deliberately, and he held their reproachful eyes. He said, "She does now, and while she is not refuting her previous statement, she is making it very clear that she has never seen such cameras." James was relaxed in his chair, and the smug look on his face remained.

Melanie nodded and moved on. Oliver noted that Mel was keeping knowledge of the cameras for later, to see if Debbie could be drawn into it again. It was a useful move. Debbie was the manager after all. She was trusted by Kevin, and his partner Karen. The cameras could be used later.

"The victim, Tracey Barrett, was found with lacerations where the major surface blood vessels area, and her limbs were twisted in a certain position. We looked for any previous cases that were similar and found another victim. Her name was Bianca Wilkins. Her body was discovered near Victoria Quays, six years ago. Does that strike a bell?"

Debbie's face was slowly turning the colour of the whitewashed wall. Her eyes flared wider, and she looked around the room as if the answer to her question lay hidden somewhere.

James Keenan was losing his smug appearance. He glanced at his client, then leaned over to whisper something in her ear. Debbie blinked a couple of times, then nodded.

"No comment," she whispered.

Oliver and Mel sighed. Mel went for it. "Bianca also worked in a massage parlour called Sunrise. It was near Victoria Quays and was similar to Cliffe. Most of the masseurs there were sex workers. And you were the manager. Are you denying that now?"

James whispered again in Debbie's ears. This time, Debbie didn't respond. Her eyes were fixed at her feet, and she sat still like a stone, staring. Mel gave her some time. Oliver glanced at the brown envelope in his hand. He had printed out the case details for Bianca, which contained her photos as well.

"Debbie?" Mel asked. "Did you work at the Sunrise Massage Parlour six years ago?"

James slid his eyes towards his client. He looked nervous now, and Oliver was enjoying every minute of it.

"Yes, I did," Debbie said quietly. Her eyes remained on the floor. "And I was there when Bianca died. I mean, I worked there. I didn't know Bianca well, only in passing. But I remember her death. The police came in and shut the place down. I was asked questions, and I didn't hear anything after that."

Mel glanced at Oliver, and he took the photos out from the envelope. He spread them across the table for Debbie to see. The photos were of the crime scene, from the riverside towpath near Victoria Quays where Bianca's body was discovered. They were grisly, and Debbie looked away after a brief examination.

"I must say," James cleared his throat, "This is not something my client should be questioned on."

Debbie raised a hand. "It's ok. I've got nothing to hide." She looked at Mel in the eye. "I didn't know much about Bianca. Her death was a shock to us all."

"What about Sunrise Massage Parlour? Who was the owner there?"

Debbie sighed and resumed her downward stare. "I don't know, and that's the honest answer. I was interviewed by a woman called Lydia. Can't remember her last name. I didn't ask if she was the owner."

"Do you have her number? Did they send you a contract?"

"Might have her number on my phone, but not sure. There wasn't any signed contract."

Mel nodded. "We'll get your phone back, and we want that number, or any contacts you had at Sunrise.

A shadow passed across Debbie's face, and a light flickered in her eyes.

"Til tomorrow, you will remain in custody."

Debbie gaped at Mel, and James protested. "What? You can't do that. Either you charge her or let her go now."

"There's a twenty-four-hour detention rule in murder cases," Mel said, "And you know that."

Oliver smirked at James, who scowled at him and Mel. Oliver

knew James didn't have any time to lodge a bail petition, and get a hearing done before tomorrow.

"That's settled then," Mel said. "We will see you again tomorrow. Your phone will he handed to you for the purposes of information retrieval, then taken back till you're released."

And hopefully, Oliver thought, a night in custody will refresh your memory.

CHAPTER 33

R oy wanted to wait in the car while Sarah got her stuff, but she wouldn't hear of it.

"Don't be daft. Come on in, I won't be long."

Roy shook his head. "We have to get back. Lots to do, still."

Sarah put on a bemused expression, like she'd just been told the sky was blue. Which it was Roy thought, this being July. And not raining. They had to be glad for the small mercies.

"Me mum's in there, and she'll make you a cuppa while I get changed. She's heard about you, anyway."

He couldn't say 'no' anymore, it would be rude. But the last sentence made him stop. "Why has she heard of me?"

"I told you what a horrible man you were to work for. Know-it-all from down south."

"That's true. I do know it all."

Sarah grinned, and he followed her through the front gate, and the small front lawn, which was well kept. A little square lawn bordered with flower beds that someone looked after. Red, yellow, and purple flowers that looked pretty in the sunshine.

Sarah went up the steps and took out keys, then unlocked the door. It was a nice, comfortable space, with homely smells of food from the kitchen, and a faint odour of clean, washed clothes. The walls were bright, with light-yellow wallpaper. A staircase went up to their right, and straight ahead, an open plan kitchen was visible, the bi-folding doors opening out to a garden.

A door opened on the left, and an elderly woman came out of the living room. She had a troubled expression on her face. She looked at Roy and went still, putting a hand on the wall.

"Mum, this is DCI Rohan Roy, who works with me."

Sarah's mum put a hand on her chest. "Oh, I see. Sorry, I was worried about John outside. He was hanging around when Matty came back."

Sarah frowned. "What?"

"I went to the bus stop to fetch Matty. When we walked back, he was there. The bloke you talked to. He didn't approach us, he just watched. Seemed alright enough, but not sure why he was there. Then I realised it were John, and I couldn't believe it."

"He didn't try to speak to you?"

"I think he wanted to. But I was quick, 'cos you told me, didn't yer? I didn't want to hear owt from him, anyway."

"Glad I told you an' all," Sarah said. "Can't believe he turned up, when I told him not to. Right mardy pillock, he is."

"Say that again. I'm sorry, love," Sarah's mother said to Roy. "Do come in, won't yer? Can't keep you standing out here all day. Would you like a cuppa?"

"I'm Rohan," Roy extended a hand. "Hello." He felt a little self-conscious, and a bit awkward.

"I'm Clare."

They went inside the kitchen and dining area. Roy was impressed. With his salary, he could never afford a nice semi-detached like this in London. Clare went to the granite top kitchen counter and put the kettle on.

Sarah put her keys on the counter and got closer to Clare. "Mum, have you seen John around before today?"

"Can't say I have love, no. You said he came to the school, didn't yer?"

"Yes, he did." Sarah gave her mother the cups. "Day before yesterday. I didn't recognise him, he looked so different. Right posh, like. Think he's done alright for himself."

"That don't give him the right to come up here, though, does it. How did he even know where you live?"

Sarah frowned, then crossed her arms across her chest. She was leaning against the counter, and her eyes found Roy's, who was sitting at the table, facing them.

"He must've followed you," Roy said. "Do you know what car he drives? He walked off today – I wonder if he was driving. He doesn't seem the sort to take the bus."

"I don't know his car, and that's a good point. Time to do a DVLA search."

Roy shrugged. "He doesn't look dodgy though. Today, I wondered if he was going to kick off, but he seemed alright. But you told him not to come here, and he still did, because he's going off abroad tomorrow."

"I don't believe owt he says," Sarah grumbled. She looked away, and from the grim expression on her face, he realised there was a lot of hurt behind those words. Sarah sighed, and then put a hand behind her neck, massaging it.

"He says he's different now, and that might be right," she sighed. "And I do want Matt to have like a father figure. I just don't know."

"Take it easy, love," Clare advised, bringing Roy his cup of tea, which he accepted with thanks. It was a nice brew, strong and milky, just the way he liked it.

"It's only been a couple of days, right?"

"Yup. Alright, ta. I'm going to get changed." Sarah took her cup, winked at Roy, and left. Shortly after, a young boy walked into the kitchen, and with a mutter of greeting to Clare, he opened the fridge.

"Say hello to DC, I mean Detective…"

"Just Rohan is fine," Roy said, putting Clare out of her misery. He turned to the boy. "You must be Matthew. Hello."

"Aye. Hello." Matt looked at Roy, then drank noisily from his bottle of Diet Coke.

"That's enough now," Clare said. "I'll get into trouble for buying you that. He used to be addicted to Coke," She explained. "Even the Diet Coke's stopped now, but he gets it sometime.

"I was never addicted," Matt protested. "What does that mean, anyhow?"

Clare went silent, and Roy could tell she regretted using the words. He said, "It means you get very used to something that's not good for you. Like burgers. Too much and you get fat."

He wouldn't have used that last word if Matt had been a girl. Matt shrugged, then nodded as if Roy just said something very wise.

"You from down south? Whereabouts?"

"London."

"My football coach is from London. He used to be in the Chelsea Academy. Now he's moved here."

"All good people do, eventually."

Matt looked confused.

Roy smiled. "Only messing. Do you like football?"

Matt's face became animated, and his eyes sparkled. "Oh, I love it. Got practice tomorrow. I play central midfield, and it's great. Do you play?"

"I used to, yeah. Played as a forward."

"Cool." Matt came closer. "Did you score a lot of goals? Where was your club?"

"Banstead, in Sutton. We played in the Fuller League, third division. It was club level, not county."

"Still good though," Matt's eyes were shinning. "How long did you play for?"

"Into my twenties, actually. I played at university, then for the Forces Team after I started working. We won the United Forces Cup three years in a row. We had a good team of some ex-league players. Then we got too old." Roy grinned.

"You look alright, still," Matt said generously. "Would you like to play sometime?" He indicated the garden. Roy had already seen the goal posts and net.

"Maybe one day, sure," Roy said. "Your mum and I have to get back to work."

"She's not here yet. She takes time to get dressed. One time, like, she took so long I fell asleep in front of the TV."

"That might've been for going out, but now she has to work. Don't think she'll take that long."

"She will," Matt said solemnly. "I heard the shower running. That's why she asked you to come in."

Clare smothered a laugh, which didn't escape Roy's notice.

Matt nudged him, then indicated the door. "Come on. Five minutes, that's all."

"Alright," Roy sighed. He stood up and stretched. "Let me get my shoes."

Matt had run off already. "I'll get them," he shouted back. "You go outside."

"He's nuts about his footy," Clare said. "Goes to practice four times a week, even Sunday morning."

Roy went outside, into the sunshine. He checked his phone, then sent a text to Anna. She replied back swiftly, which was a relief.

We're busy with the party. Lots of boys here xx.

Very funny x

Roy put the phone back in his pocket with a smirk. Until recently he didn't know that an x meant a kiss. Anna couldn't believe his ignorance.

He saw the football and put it on his bare feet, then played it on one foot. Matt came back with his shoes, and they went into the grass. They passed the ball to each other, then Matt took the ball, and dribbled past him. He was eleven, but still little, compared to Roy. For a small kid, he was good. He went past Roy twice and scored once.

"Don't go easy on me," Matt said, getting the ball back from the net. "Tackle properly, alright?"

There was no getting past children. Roy opened his mouth then shut it. He nodded.

"I see you two are getting on well," Sarah called from the door. She had put on a fresh blouse and dark trousers which hugged her petite figure. Her hair wasn't tied in a ponytail for once and fell over her shoulders.

"He played league football, Mum. He's good," Matt said.

"Got to go, son. Enjoyed that." He gave Matt a high five, and the boy jumped up to slap his palm against his.

As he walked back into the kitchen, his phone pinged. *Anna*, he thought. But it wasn't Anna. When he saw the message, his blood ran cold. The sunlight faltered and went dark as night.

Playing football with a child when you should be looking for your brother. Shame on you.

Roy halted, then spun around, his eyes going to the back and side fences. His head jerked around, noting the gaps between the trees on either side, and at the rear. He saw nothing. No movements in the trees, no sounds apart from the tweeting of birds.

Sarah was by his side. She put a hand on his arm. "What is it?"

Roy remained rock still, eyes still scanning the fences. Then he turned and looked at the rest of the house. There was a side entrance, with a garden door. It was locked, and about two metres high. He walked over and looked over it. The side passage was empty.

"Rohan?" Sarah called.

"It's nothing," he said, his voice stiff, discomfort tickling his spine. A slow rage was warming his chest again. "Thought I heard something. Come on, let's go."

CHAPTER 34

Y ou alright, guv?" Sarah asked as she started the car's engine. Roy's face was like thunder. He chewed his bottom lip as his nostrils flared.

"Someone's watching me," he spat out. "The same bastard who keeps sending me texts about my brother. He knows I'm here."

Sarah stopped the car. "What?"

Roy took out his phone, scrolled to the messages and handed it to her. She checked them and tried to look at the number. There wasn't any.

"You need to triangulate this. Have you filed a PCN?"

"No," Roy growled. "Don't want to bring this mess into work, but now I don't have a choice. This dickhead knows I was in your garden. He's got to be around here somewhere."

Sarah sat there, thinking. "How could they get hold of your number?"

"Your guess is as good as mine. I know it goes back to Jerry Burns somehow. Or Burgess. But neither of them is talking."

"When did you last see them?"

"Couple of weeks ago. The messages never really stopped, but they've got more frequent now." He turned to her. "I'm sorry about this. Nothing's going to happen to your family, I promise."

Sarah nodded. She pointed at her neighbour's houses. "I know we need to get on, but worthwhile asking them if they saw anything?"

"Good idea. You handle your side, and I'll ask on the other. Then we can go around the back, if there's any access?"

"I'm afraid there isn't," Sarah said, then pressed her lips together in thought. "But there's a couple of houses on the other side that are empty, I think. We should check there first." She started the engine up again and drove around the block, circling her street, and then taking a left turn. This street was similar, with both terraced and semi-detached houses, even a couple of detached ones. Sarah pulled outside a detached property that had seen better days. The front garden was overgrown with weeds, in stark contrast to the houses on either side. The waist high double gates on either side of the small, circular drive were leaning on rusty hinges. Roy opened one of them, and they walked through. He rang the bell, then knocked on the door. Sarah looked in through the windows. The downstairs curtains were open, and she cupped her hands over the glass trying to get a view inside.

"Nowt in there," she observed, moving from one bay window to the other. Roy thumped the door hard enough to make it shake. He came out of the porch and craned his neck up. The windows were shut as expected, and his hammering hadn't aroused any interest.

"You take the left, and I'll go right," he said. The side gate was tall, and locked. He could break the rotting wood frame with a heave of his shoulder, but he wondered if there was any point. Sarah joined him.

"Locked on the side too. Here, gimme a crogger." She put both hands on his shoulders and placed her right foot in his cupped palms. Roy lifted her up, and Sarah grabbed the top of the door frame which didn't have any spikes. She swung her leg over, then dropped deftly to the other side. She was virtually silent as she ran up the path, and Roy watched through a crack in the door frame. He would've made an almighty thump as he landed on the other side, but Sarah would give no warning to anyone hiding in the house, or garden.

His radio crackled, and it was her. She was panting as she ran around. "Nowt in the garden. Right skaggy here, all weeds and that. But…" her words trailed off as she panted harder, and Roy heard a scratching sound.

"This house does look right behind ours. I can see Matty playing in the garden. So close. Bloody hell."

Sarah tried to get in the house, but all the rear doors were locked. She came back and found a window ledge on the side she could scramble on, and she jumped over the side fence into the neighbour's garden. Roy met her out at the front.

"Miss Nimble, aren't you?"

"Used to do gymnastics when I was little." She wiped her sleeve across her forehead. "Muscle memory, guv."

Roy nodded and looked over the street. "Good work. Those houses might've seen something. Worth asking?"

Sarah nodded, still catching her breath. "You go left, and I'll go right."

They jogged off, aware of the time, and the fact they had a few houses to cover between the two of them. They could call the uniforms to do a door to door, but it seemed like a waste of time and resources.

Sarah struck gold with the third house she knocked on. The occupant took a while to answer, then an elderly woman opened the door. She wore a blue house gown, with food stains in the front, and slippers. She adjusted her glasses, then squinted at Sarah.

"Hello, I work for the police. My name's Detective Sarah Botham," she showed her warrant card, which the woman checked with great interest.

"Have you seen anyone on the street today acting suspiciously?" Sarah stepped to one side and pointed at the detached house opposite. "Or going in and out of that house?"

The woman padded out and went past Sarah. She moved well, Sarah noted. Her legs were stronger than her own mother's. Sarah stood next to the woman as she walked out on the pavement.

"Shilpa used to live in that house. My friend. She died last year. Poor Shilpa."

"Sorry to hear that," Sarah said gently. "But did you see anything this morning?"

The woman squinted back at Sarah. She was almost a foot taller than her, back now bent with age, reducing her height.

"Aye. I keep an eye on that place, you know. Her boys want to sell it, but they might also do it up. Not decided as yet. I did see someone jump over the side gate an hour ago. A small man it was, or maybe a kid. There's some teenagers always up to no good, you know."

"What time did you see this?"

"I was sat by the window like, havin' me tea and biscuits. I've got diabetes, but I don't take no tablets, I diet control." She peered at Sarah like she was testing her.

Sarah nodded. "Oh yes. That's good. So, what time was that?" She wondered if biscuits were the right form of diet control in diabetes, but she kept that to herself.

"About half-four, I think. That's when I like a cuppa."

Sarah's radio crackled, and she turned the black knob to the right, and told Roy where she was.

"So, half-four," Sarah entered the time on her phone. "And what did this person look like? Please think of what colour clothes they wore, what type of shoes, any hats, or glasses?"

The woman frowned and leaned against the stone fence. "Aye, it was well strange like, you know. He was wearing black clothes, and he jumped on the side door just like you did now. That was you, weren't it?"

Sarah blinked a couple of times. "Yes, it was. Sorry, I forgot to ask your name."

"Fiona Alderson. You can call me Fi. All my friends around here do."

"Thank you, Fi. What else can you tell me?"

"He had a baseball cap on, pulled down low. He also had a hoodie top on, and despite the sun, he had the hood pulled over his head. I could barely see his face."

"How tall was he?"

"Not very. Taller than you, mind. Less than six feet, definitely."

Roy approached them quickly. Sarah introduced them and said, "Fiona saw a man climb over the side gate. Has to be our man."

"I saw him get out as well. Came out the same side and ran down that way."

Sarah asked, "What colour shoes was he wearing?"

"Black. Can't tell you much more than that. I saw his hands – they were normal colour."

"Do you mean white?"

"Aye. It were a white lad, dressed in dark clothes. Thin and wiry, not big like your bloke here. Sorry, I mean your colleague."

"That's alright," Sarah said. "Have you seen that bloke before?"

"Come to think of it, I have. He walked up and down the street around the same time yesterday, when I was havin me cuppa. I remember 'cos I never seen him before, and I know everyone who lives here."

Roy said, "Was he wearing the same clothes?"

"He were, aye. That's another thing that struck me. Who wears a hoodie in the summer, like? Not even my teenage grandson."

Roy pointed at Fiona's house. "Do you live alone?"

"Aye. You get to my age, that's all you're left with. My son visits with his children. They live in Scunthorpe."

Sarah took down Fiona's phone number, then they bid her goodbye. Fiona had their cards now and promised to call if she saw that man again.

"Any luck at your end?" Sarah asked Roy, after Fiona went back inside.

"Nowt, as you would say. Tried three houses, no one saw anything unusual. We could send uniforms around, but the farther out you go, the less close you are to this house. Fiona's place was perfect. Just opposite."

"Aye, and she's a sharp one. Clocked me as I went over the side door. Kept that to herself til the end."

"We might need her services, after all," Roy remarked. Sarah's phone pinged, and she answered. Her face twisted as she stared at the message.

"Oh no," she whispered.

"What?" Roy demanded, stepping closer.

"It's Kevin Rawlinson."

CHAPTER 35

Flashing blue lights blazed in the sky, and there was pandemonium outside the entrance of Northern General Hospital, where Kevin Rawlinson was admitted after his fall from the roof.

Two police riot vans were parked next to the two squad cars, and visitors were being directed to another entrance via the main A&E.

A bunch of thuggish skinheads stood smoking outside the entrance to the wards, watched by a group of burly uniforms who had been drafted in for the possible showdown. The skinheads wore leather jackets, and spat on the floor, and hurled curses at the uniforms.

Inspector Jonty Adams came up to Roy and Sarah as they approached the groups.

"It's worse inside. They've blocked us from getting inside the ward. It all kicked off when we tried to move Kevin to the nick. He was stable, and the doctor said he could be moved as long as he had regular checks with the FMP tonight." The Forensic Medical Physician was a local GP called Shauna Edwards, and

Roy had met her before.

"How did they know he was here?" Roy growled. "We confiscated Kevin's phone as soon as he was arrested, correct?"

"Beats me," Jonty flapped his arms. "He had nothing else on him. There's no leak from my team I can assure you."

That had been the other only other option Roy was suspicious about. After what happened last time, they couldn't be too careful. Jonty read the look on Roy's face.

"I only told my skipper, and I sat in the front. Only two of us knew where we were going."

"Clearly someone else did. Maybe someone at the hospital leaked it. Kevin might know people who work here." He shook his head. "Anyway, let's go upstairs."

"Before we knew it, there was like a dozen of them," Jonty said. "They blocked the ward doors. Security was called, but hospital security's pretty useless."

"Was there a fight?" Sarah asked. In response, Jonty took off his hat, and they saw the ugly welt on the side of his head.

"Windows got smashed, and instruments were broken. I radioed for help. Then this lot appeared," Jonty indicated the skinheads at the gate. "They're like reinforcement for the thugs upstairs. Kevin's a big bastard in the Sheffield underworld. His dad's Shaun Rawlinson."

Sarah made a clucking sound in her mouth. "I should have twigged that. No wonder his name's familiar. They're the Loxley Boys, aren't they?"

"That's the name of their gang, aye," Jonty said. "This lot aren't saying who they are, but we got them on camera, anyway. Anyway. We can't get Kevin out without a riot, guv. What do you want to do?"

Jonty and Sarah looked at Roy. He sighed, then kicked his foot on the tarmac. "Let me speak to him."

As they stepped out onto the third floor, Roy saw Jonty wasn't wrong about the possibility of a riot. Barrel-chested, thick-armed thugs lined the lobby outside the lifts and stood outside the ward door. The uniformed officers standing guard looked pensive, watching them closely. A group of hospital security officers stood next to a uniform sergeant, speaking in a low voice. A woman in a suit rushed up to Jonty as they tried to get inside the ward.

"Jenny Sinclair, Hospital Trust Operations Director. What's going on here?" Her cheeks were sunken, and eyes glittering. Her blue dress suit was ironed crisply, and everything about her, down to the gleaming blue-heeled shoes, said privileged, but harassed hospital manager.

Jonty looked at Roy, who showed Miss Sinclair his warrant card. "We've got a criminal in there who needs to be taken into custody. Unfortunately, his men are trying to stop us. This doesn't happen normally. Apologies for the commotion."

Jenny crinkled her nose like there was a bad smell coming from Roy. "Commotion? Are you joking? Our equipment was damaged in the brawl inside the Hewitt ward. There's sick people in there, who need urgent medical attention."

"To be fair," Jonty said, "this lot aren't stopping the medical or nursing care. But they won't let us take Kevin Rawlinson out from there. They say he's still unwell, but your doctors have said he's good to go."

Jenny turned on Jonty. "With all due respect, I doubt you have any experience of running a busy acute admission ward. When I say sick people, I mean people who need to be moved in and out of there, from theatre, and for investigations like scans. That's what these goons"—she waved a hand at the thugs standing and watching—"are stopping from happening. The porters are so scared now they won't come up here."

"You can ask them to attend," Roy intervened. "I am the Senior Investigating Officer here. I can guarantee no one will hurt the porters, or any of the medical staff."

The corners of Jenny's eyes relaxed a touch, and she appraised Roy up and down. "What was your name again?"

"DCI Roy."

Jenny sniffed and her nose turned up a touch. "Well, DCI Roy, you better make sure nothing happens to my staff. We have a zero tolerance policy for this kind of behaviour."

"Understood," Roy nodded. "Open the doors and ask your staff to resume their normal functions."

Jenny narrowed her eyes again, then turned on her heels. She spoke to a group of nurses near the ward gates, then pointed at Roy.

"Right then. Let's sort this out," Roy said. Jonty and Sarah followed him. Instead of heading for the ward, Roy went up to the thugs hanging out in the corner. They noticed him, and one of them patted the shoulder of a wide, squat man, built like a tank. He wore a black puffer jacket, had a gold earring in his left ear, and tattoos up his neck. He had a scar on both cheeks, as if a butcher had sliced him up with a knife, then used the same skills to stitch him as crudely as possible.

"Who the fock are you?" The man snarled. His battle scars, and aggressive posture marked him out as a leader of the group. He clearly fancied his chances against the three cops facing him.

"I'm here to help you make sure Kevin Rawlinson doesn't spend the next ten years in jail for arranging a riot."

The man's mangled face became even more hideous as he frowned. He bared yellow teeth like a hyena.

"You what?"

"Public Order Act 1986, Section 266. Anyone proven to arrange a riot will be indicted and if convicted, spend the next ten years in jail. I think Kevin's got a good chance of getting convicted, as you lot are hanging around. Isn't that right, Sergeant?" Roy asked Sarah, without taking his eyes off the thug.

"That's right, Detective Chief Inspector. A riot in a place of medical care is especially harmful for the indicted, and incarceration in a high security prison is almost guaranteed."

"And what a shame that would be, as Kevin might well have gone home tomorrow after we questioned him. He's not a suspect, we just want to interrogate him. Now"—Roy pointed a finger at the thug, and raised his voice so his followers could hear him—"He's almost certainly going to do some jail time, because you lot are kicking up a fuss here. In which case, it will be my pleasure to bash your fucking face in." Roy towered over the man but bent lower to get his face within inches of his. "Do you understand?"

The man blinked, and his mouth opened, then shut. Roy pressed his point home. "I hope Kevin has a lawyer ready. The Public Order Act is enforced much quicker than any other court order." He stood straight, as the man glared at him.

"Of course," Roy said, "You could make it easier on Kevin by going home and let us conclude our investigation. But you won't so I'll let Kevin know. What's your name by the way, in case he asks?"

Now the bloke was clearly ruffled, the danger of pissing off his boss starting to filter through his thick skull. His followers had shuffled closer, intrigued by the exchange.

"What's your name?" Roy raised his voice.

One of his followers, a massive, round tomato-shaped giant in a black overcoat, answered. "His name's Gary."

Gary spun around like he'd been electrified. "Shut the fock up you blitherin' stupid scallywag," he screamed. The giant gasped and stumbled backwards. Roy tried not to laugh, and Sarah covered her mouth with her hand to hide her mirth.

"Get back there," Gary shouted, and his followers scrambled to the wall. Gary turned back slowly, scratching his head.

"Alright then, Gary," Roy said. "Are you lot going to clear out of here, or do you want me to arrest Kevin?"

Gary made a sound like a Pitbull growling. "We're off." He motioned to his followers, then had a quiet word with them. One by one, the filed out of the double doors, into the staircase. Soon, the lobby was empty, save the hospital staff and the police. There was a lightness in the air, a palpable sense of relief.

Roy walked past Jenny and gave her a wink. She turned down the corners of her mouth.

"I see your methods are effective, DCI Roy."

"At your service. Hope that lot didn't disturb the patients too much," Roy pointed at the ward.

Jenny smiled for the first time. "Don't think so. Thank you."

"Right charmer, aren't yer?" Sarah hissed at him as they walked into the ward. There was a hard glint in her sea green eyes he couldn't quite fathom.

"A lot more where that came from." He intended it as a joke, but Sarah, for some reason, didn't see the funny side. She huffed and turned away to speak to the matron. The matron led them to the cubicle which housed Kevin.

"The constable outside is downstairs for the trouble," Jonty explained. "I'll call him back up now."

Roy nodded, and Sarah knocked on the door, then entered. A female doctor in a white coat turned from the foot of the bed. Kevin was awake, and he glared at Sarah and Roy as they walked in. Sarah showed her warrant card to the doctor, whose

ID badge said ST2 Nicola Hayward

"He's alright now," Dr Hayward said. "He was lucky, he landed on a hedge that broke his fall. No fractures on x-rays. Blood tests and vitals are all normal."

"Lovely," Roy rubbed his hands together. "The man who thought he could fly. Shall we have a little chat then, Kevin?"

CHAPTER 36

D r Hayward opened the door to leave, and Kevin called out to her. "You can stay, doctor. These two have no right to be here."

"I think you will find we have every right, as the arresting officers," Sarah said. "Thank you, Dr Hayward."

The doctor shrugged, then left. Kevin turned his hateful gaze at Roy as he pulled up a chair for Sarah, then sat down on another himself.

"I'm not saying a bloody word without a lawyer," Kevin ground out. "So, you two can fuck right off."

"What about the cameras, Kevin?" Roy asked. "The ones hidden on the door handle. Real tiny, almost microscopic. State of the art. Must've cost a fair whack. Those ones."

A veil seemed to pass over Kevin's face. His eyes flickered once, and Roy felt something in his glance. Then Kevin looked away and clamped his jaws together.

"I know nowt about that."

"We saw them, Kevin. They're in the lab, right now, getting

analysed."

Kevin didn't turn to look at him. He closed his eyes. Roy said, "Cooperate, and you get off with a lighter sentence. Plead guilty. You know how it works. I'm being generous here, Kevin."

The criminal turned to stare at him once, and again that look flashed over his features. It bothered Roy. Kevin knew something he didn't. He got the suspicion Kevin was searching, probing.

"No comment," Kevin said.

"When we get the films from it, you'll be in much more trouble than you are now, Kevin. We'll have evidence, and you're going in for a long time. Your organisation will be in trouble, too."

Kevin kept his neck turned away from them and shook his head. "You lot and your empty threats. Never changes."

"Your dad, Shaun. And your girlfriend Karen, in Spain. We will drag them into this too. They'll be in custody soon."

Kevin turned back slowly to look at Roy. A superior, sickening grin spread across his lips.

"Call them in all you want. You got nothing on them, and you know it. You lot are unbelievable."

Roy felt Sarah stir, and she slid her eyes to him. He knew what shew as trying to say. The threats weren't working. Kevin was a seasoned gangster; he knew the law well.

Sarah spoke up. "Your men have gone, by the way. Didn't stick around long to protect you. Time to head for a cell, Kevin. And you'll be there for more than twenty-four-hours, given the murder case on your doorstep. Isn't that right, guv?"

"Absolutely. You're the number one suspect in the murder, and in case your barrister makes a petition to let you out after twenty-four-hours, any judge will uphold your detention. We're talking a few days, by which time we'll have enough evidence to build a case against you."

For the first time, Kevin looked bothered. His eyebrows lowered, and the frown returned to his face.

"I ain't got nowt to do with the murder, and you know it."

"Then why did you run, Kevin?" Roy asked. "Not only run, you tried to fly across the roof, like a bird."

"Maybe fear gave you wings," Sarah said.

"Exactly. And what were you afraid of?"

Kevin glared at them, his eyes skipping from Roy to Sarah. He lingered on Sarah, and he frowned, then looked away. Roy didn't miss it. He glanced at her, and she was staring straight at Kevin.

"That's right, Kevin. We've met before. I arrested you once, many years ago. A drug bust in Loxley. Remember now?"

"Had nowt to do with it, and you got nothing," Kevin smiled. "That's what I remember." He looked fatigued, and tried to shift his body, then winced in pain.

"You need to go now. I want my solicitor here."

"What do you know about the dead woman, Tracey Barrett?"

A shadow flittered across Kevin's face, and he looked askance. Neither Roy nor Sarah missed it.

"Nothing?"

"She worked at your place. We know she was moonlighting as a sex worker. Was she threatening to get you into trouble? Expose your blackmailing racket?"

Kevin closed his eyes and breathed heavily. "You need to go now." He reached out with his right hand and grabbed the red button hanging from a thread. He pressed it twice.

"Talk to us," Sarah urged. "We've got Debbie McPherson in custody. She's talking about you. It's only a matter of time, Kevin. Once we get the video evidence, it's all over. Help us and we can help you."

"Just go!" Kevin shouted, dragging an arm over his face, and sinking further down in the bed.

The door opened and the matron came in. "What's going on here?"

"They're harassing me, that's what," Kevin shouted, elbow slung across his face. "Tell them to get out."

The matron shook her head firmly. "You need to leave now, Inspector. Visiting times are over, anyway."

Roy stood, followed by Sarah. "Have it your way," Roy said to Kevin, who ignored him. "I'll see you at the nick."

CHAPTER 37

DC Rizwan Ahmed leaned over the chair of the traffic officer's desk. A bank of screens faced him, four in total. But that was nothing in comparison to the scores of screens that took up an entire wall to this right – the individual feeds from the entire network of CCTV cameras of Sheffield. The room was big, almost like a theatre, with the wall of screens acting as the stage. Instead of seats, rows of desks occupied the space. Some of the TV screens on the main wall were blank, due to faulty cameras, or new locations that weren't yet operational. But they were few. Almost every corner of Sheffield and the surrounding region was visible here.

"I can't see it." The traffic officer, whose name was Darren, puffed out his cheeks. He clicked on some more buttons, but all four screens on his desk remained stubbornly blank.

"What does that mean?"

"It means we're not getting a triangulation signal from the phone. Are you sure you got the right signal?"

"Yes, it's what I gave you." Rizwan had received the text messages from Roy's phone, and they were trying to get a location on the phone. Every time a mobile phone was used, it sent a signal to the nearest cell, or mast, which were dotted around everywhere.

Roy had opened up a Police Crime Notice, or PCN, for the texts he was getting about Robin. It was the only way he could get the phone signal triangulated, and with any luck, discover the phone's location.

Luck that now seemed to be in short supply. "Nope," Darren said, after trying to match the phone's signal to every known mast. "No dice."

"What does that mean?"

"It means they're using a signal blocker."

Riz knew about those. A signal jammer was often used to hide a phone's connection, and to stop eavesdroppers. It meant a certain degree of technical ability, which was concerning. This wasn't some random nutcase after all.

"So, they use the phone to send the text or call, then turn the jammer on to disguise the signal. And it's on right now?"

"Exactly. The good news is he can't keep the jammer on all the time or he'll end up blocking his own signal. I can keep trying, and if I have any luck, I'll let you know."

"Thanks Darren."

Riz went downstairs to find his corner of the office empty. The Major Investigation Team was nowhere in sight. He Sarah Botham's radio on her desk, getting charged. So, they must be back. He knocked on DCI Roy's office door, but it was locked and there was no answer. He tried the Major Incident Room, and everyone was there. The MIR had a partition down the middle, which made it longer when opened up. It was closed now, resulting in a much smaller room, but still big enough for a dozen people. Or five of them, all of whom looked up as he entered.

"That geezer sending you the texts is using a signal jammer," Riz told Roy. "But Darren from traffic says he can get through to him eventually." He handed the phone back to Roy, who took it from him with a murmur of thanks.

"Right," Melanie said, "Now that we're all here, let's get going." She went up to the whiteboard, which still stood with the names and photos from the morning meeting. Three photos of Tracey Barrett, stuck next to her name, DOB and address. Melanie wrote on the whiteboard.

"Tracey's mum, Catherine. Tough lady, obviously grieving. The FLO, Emily Hodgkinson, is there, and will stay the night. Any update on the CCTV from the supermarket?" She looked at Ollie and Riz, and Oliver shook his head.

"The researchers are going through some of it, and Riz and I are doing the rest. The bloke we're trying to spot is IC1, dressed in a suit, medium height, light beard, no other distinguishing features."

"The same guy she had a fight with outside Cliffe Massage Parlour, presumably. He fits the description, anyway. Cathy also led us to Luke Hammond, Tracey's ex-partner, and father of her son."

Rizwan looked at Oliver, and said, "We went over to the pub in Loxley where Luke said he spent last night. He was there, according to a couple of the punters, and the owner, Jim Flagg. Dodgy pub though. It was late afternoon, but already almost full. Some colourful characters."

"Yes," Ollie grinned. "The music kind of stopped when we walked in and showed our warrant cards."

"The music stopped when they saw you dressed up like a peacock," Riz snorted. "You stuck out like mud on a white wall."

"Get off, you," Ollie grimaced. "Anyway. The pub's got CCTV, but the manager said it's not been working recently. Which sounds convenient, but we've managed to pick Luke up on the street CCTV, which shows him entering the pub at 9 pm and leaving after eleven. He goes home after that. His house is ten minutes' walk away."

"Good work," Mel said. "Does he come out after that?"

Oliver shook his head. "Not till the next morning, when he gets into his car and drives to the supermarket."

"That eliminates him then."

Roy said, "What if he went out the back door, and jumped the fence. Have we looked in the streets around? He might have not used his car."

The blank stared told him what he wanted to know. Oliver said, "We'll get on that, guv."

Rizwan was looking down at the table on his hands. He had scrolled to the right page now and revised what he had read a couple of hours ago.

"Two witnesses on Liverpool Street saw a black car pick up a woman. The woman fits Tracey's description. The car is a standard four-seater. The witnesses couldn't identify the car's make or brand. It drove down the road, towards Meadowhall. Traffic have got back to us with a list of cars coming out onto the A156, just left of the crime scene, and across the river. Quite a few black cars between ten and midnight. Unfortunately, everyone they've seen so far has one driver and no passenger. We're checking with DVLA to see if any of the drivers have a police record."

Sarah mused, "So he picked her up. Drove away, then did he come back to drop the body? Or did he walk back? I think that's too risky for him. He'd be spotted."

"Yes," Melanie said. "Either he drove back, or he went around the corner, where there's no houses, hence no potential witnesses. He kills her there and drives back."

"But," Rizwan said, "No witnesses to say the car came back. They're still doing a door-to-door, but most of the street's been covered by now."

"It's a short walk around the corner," Roy said. "He could've killed her, then taken her back. Took his chances as it was late, and dark. Tracey was five-three and light. Wouldn't be hard to carry her back on his shoulder."

There was silence for a while. Their thoughts ping-ponged against the walls, and each other.

"How did he get away?" Roy asked softly. "It had to be in a car, because he picked her up in one. We need the DVLA information from traffic of all the cars seen on CCTV." He looked at Oliver and Riz, both of whom nodded.

"Definitely done by tomorrow morning, guv," Riz said.

Sarah asked, "Shall we put e-fit posters up in the supermarket? They're already around Liverpool Street."

"Good idea," Roy said. "Unless Kevin Rawlinson killed Tracey, this unknown man is our other main suspect. Not to mention number three, Luke Hammond."

"Kevin's in custody now," Melanie said. "We've also sent out feelers into NCA and Interpol to see what files they have on Shaun Rawlinson and Karen Powers, Kevin's dad, and girlfriend. So far, they haven't sent anything."

Sarah stifled a yawn, and said, "It's too late to start questioning him tonight?" She looked at Roy, who nodded.

"He's refusing to talk anyway, so let's deal with it tomorrow." He switched attention to Mel. "Thoughts on Debbie McPherson?"

"I haven't told her we know about the cameras. Speaking of which, they really are state of the art. One-hundred-percent remote, long battery life, and all footage is stored in an encrypted cloud location. The cyber lab are having a field day trying to crack the code."

"Hopefully they have something soon," Mel continued. "I think Debbie's hiding something. She admitted working for Sunrise Massage Parlour, but she didn't know Bianca Wilkins well. Not like she knew Tracey. But she clammed up, and I think there's something more there."

"Me too, guv," Oliver said solemnly. "We'll ask her again tomorrow."

Mel nodded. Roy asked, "Phone call lists all back? I know voice data will take a while."

Oliver said, "Tracey's phone sent a signal last night at 11:30 pm. Nothing after that. Mast signal triangulates to within 200 metres of Liverpool Street. Her phone's still there somewhere, but we didn't find it."

"I'm sure uniforms will be looking for it tomorrow," Roy said. "We have one suspect in custody already, that's a good day's work. Have a rest, everyone. See you tomorrow."

"One more thing," Melanie said, and sighed. All eyes turned to her, but she was looking at Rizwan. Riz felt a little flutter of discomfort in his belly.

"Shaun and Kevin Rawlinson's gang, the Loxley Boys, are connected to the Wrexham Hill gang, another OCN up in Liverpool."

Riz felt like he'd been punched in the guts. He could feel everyone looking at him. In the last case, the Wrexham Hill Gang had killed Paul, his wife, Sharon's brother. Sharon was lucky to be alive, and so was Riz. The threat from the Wrexham Hill Gang had never gone. Riz and the others suspected the gang kept an eye on Sharon, still. Paul might have told her things that made her vulnerable. Sharon denied it, and Riz of course believed her. But the gang were a different story. The entire event cast a shadow all over them. Not only did Sharon lose her brother, but her own life remained in danger.

Mel's voice was low. "The Loxley Boys have been the local enforcers of the Wrexham Hill gang for a long time. Their drug supply network branches out from Liverpool, and Sheffield is a big market for them."

Riz sighed. "What does this mean? Does Sharon have to be careful?"

Mel shook her head. "I doubt it. This is about the murder of a young woman, and nothing to do with Sharon's brother, Paul." She looked at Roy and Sarah, both of whom nodded.

Roy said, "I know Kevin is a suspect, but would he really kill Tracey and leave the body on his doorstep? This is like career suicide for him. And this happens on his trip back home. Seems a bit coincidental to me."

"Good point," Sarah frowned. "Kevin might well be the fall guy here. But that means, we need to think of who might want to frame him. Correct?"

Roy nodded. "Someone who wants Kevin out of the way. Someone in his gang? Or another OCN?"

"Like Wrexham Hill," Oliver said slowly, his eyes on his friend and partner, Riz.

"Oh god," Riz said, and leaned forward, gripping his forehead.

"Either way," Roy said, "I can't see this being of any danger to Sharon, or you, Riz. Home now, people. I want you bright and early tomorrow morning. Lots to do."

One of the uniformed constables came into the office and asked for Roy. "There's a man out there to see you. Name of Jayden Budden."

"Ah yes. The bloke I met this morning at the crime scene. He

lives around there. Remember? I wanted you to dig into him."
Roy looked at Sarah, who nodded.

"Yes, I did. He's squeaky clean. No PCN, no skirmish with the law." She pulled up her laptop and looked at the screen. "Got his details from the council and electoral roll. His driving licence and passport is also in order. Nothing from the Home Office. He went on holiday to Mallorca, Spain, last year. Nothing out of the ordinary. He's self-employed, and files his taxes every year on time."

"Thank you." Roy looked at his watch. "He's late, should've been here by 5 pm." He nodded at the constable. "Tell him I'll be out in a minute."

The constable left and Roy turned to his team. "This guy's clean, but he bothers me, for some reason. He knew we were detectives." He glanced at Sarah who nodded. "He lives in the neighbourhood and knows the area well. He definitely knew what went on in Cliffe Massage Parlour. He also saw a man pick up a woman who matches Tracey's description – and probably was her."

"You think he's the killer? The man who's here now?" Melanie asked. "Surely he wouldn't be that stupid."

Sarah and the two DCs showed their agreement by nodding. Roy raised a hand. "I'm not saying that. I just found it a bit weird for a member of the public to approach us like that. Anyone else would just ask at the roadblock, or one of the uniforms."

"Maybe he was passing by the crime scene, and thought he'd stop and ask," Riz said. "The stretch where SOC put their tent up is not easily accessible for pedestrians. You said he knows the area, and that's why he was cycling on that path."

Roy spread his hands. "It could all be very innocent. But just remember what I said. Don't stop digging into him."

He left and walked down the corridor. Through the glass doors, he could see Jayden. The man was looking down at his phone. Presently, he put the phone back in his pocket and folded arms across his chest. He sat still, and there was a small backpack next to him. It looked like the same backpack he had on his shoulders that morning.

Roy placed his card on the reader, and the door buzzed, then slid apart. Jayden looked up as he approached. He stood, looking pensive. Roy nodded at him, then at the duty constable, who was the same man that came to call him. Roy showed Jayden into one of the interrogation rooms.

"I need to record this. Is that okay?" Roy pointed to the machine. He watched Jayden, apprehensive the man would now ask for a solicitor. To his relief, Jayden didn't mind. Roy spoke on the machine, and they sat down facing each other.

"Recording statement of Jayden Budden for case number A5820. DCI Rohan Roy present."

"Please tell me what you saw on Thursday night as you cycled home around 10 pm."

"I saw a woman on the street, wearing a dark blue dress. It was short and came up to her thighs. She wore a cardigan over it and had high heels. The man drove up in a black two seater, maybe an Audi but it could be a BMW. They seemed to chat for a while, then the woman got in the car. The car drove in the direction of the main road, past the railway bridge."

"And what did you do?"

"I carried on home. I didn't think about it til this morning, when I was cycling to work again, and I met you."

"This is your normal route to work, is that correct?"

"Yes."

"Have you ever seen that car before? Or the woman?"

A shadow passed over Jayden's face. He shifted in his chair and pressed his lips together before replying.

"No, can't say I have. It was late last night, and there was nothing else on the road, hence I noticed. During the daytime, I'm going to work down that way. But no, I've never seen that car, or that woman before."

"Have you been to Cliffe Massage Parlour before?"

The shadow remained on Jayden's face, and the corners of his eyes crinkled. "No, I have not. Do I need a solicitor?"

"No, you don't. You're not a suspect, you're a witness giving his statement. However, you do have the choice of having a solicitor if you wish to."

Jayden appeared to relax more. "Alright then. Is there anything else you want to ask?"

"You've lived in Attercliffe for more than ten years, is that correct?" Jayden nodded. Roy asked, "And how long have you lived on Mansell Road?"

Jayden thought for a while. "Around four years, I'd say. I bought the house about five years ago, but it were a dump like, and I had to do renovations."

"In the last four years, what have you noticed about Cliffe Massage Parlour? When did it start?"

"That place has been there for the last couple of years, I'd say. Everyone knows what goes on in there. What sort of a massage parlour stays open past midnight? There's a few of those knockin' around."

Roy went to speak, and so did Jayden. Roy allowed him first. "There's one thing I should tell you. A lot of Eastern European women have moved into that part lately. I know a couple of houses on my street that has these young Bulgarian women. The lady who cleans my house also cleans theirs."

"How do you know they're Bulgarian?"

Jayden smiled for the first time. "My cleaner's from there. She said they arrived a year ago." His face became serious. "She also said some of those girls had no one here. They don't have any money. She doesn't know how they got here."

A suspicion tingled at the back of Roy's mind. He remembered the Eastern European women at the house where Kevin was hiding. Kevin knew them clearly and was using them. Were they sex workers? And had they been trafficked into the country?

"Thank you, Jayden," Roy said. "You've been very helpful. If there's anything else, please get in touch."

CHAPTER 38

The man was sitting on a park bench opposite the police station's rear entrance. He knew the officers left from the rear car park, and he knew what car DCI Roy drove. He watched them leave, one by one. Finally, he saw DCI Roy's car approach the barrier at the gates. He jumped up and ran across the short distance to the park fence and jumped over it. He got into his car and fired the engine. He gave Roy a few seconds head start, then followed him. With the evening traffic, it was easy to hide a few cars behind. Roy's car wasn't hard to see, it was easily the oldest on the road, and the rear bumper almost scraped along the asphalt.

He had seen Debbie McPherson go from Cliffe Massage Parlour into the police car. Liverpool Street and the road behind was full of police still, and he suspected something had happened. If they'd got hold of the man who ran away in the morning, that made things interesting. Would they try to accuse him of the murder? The man smiled, his fingers happily tapping on the steering wheel. He could see Roy three cars ahead. These stupid coppers were going to frame the wrong man. That would be bloody fantastic, but also a tad disappointing. He wanted to be known as the killer. He wanted a name for himself. Like…

The Death Artist. He wanted to remain invisible but be a constant threat. That way, no one would forget him.

Kevin Rawlinson was the pimp's name. He wasn't sure if he saw the same guy run away from Cliffe this morning, but he looked familiar. The man had only seen Kevin once. In any case, the police thought they had something, so it was time to give them something new to worry about.

Traffic got lighter as Roy left the city. He headed for Dore, and the man hung back further now. Eventually, he drove past Roy's car. Roy had stopped on a residential street, and the man parked up ahead, then watched as Roy went inside a house. He gave him some time, then got out of the car. Leisurely, he walked past the row of terraced houses. As he got closer, the door opened, and two teenage girls stepped out. They went down the steps and out of the front garden. The door behind them opened and Roy appeared. The man averted his face quickly.

"Anna," Roy called out. "What time will you be back?"

The taller of the two girls turned and spoke to Roy. The man walked slowly, but he couldn't stop. He didn't hear exactly what the teenager said. From the corner of his eyes, he could tell Anna was related to Roy, probably his daughter.

Well, well, he smiled to himself. That certainly made things more interesting.

*****

Roy shut the door, then sat down in the living room. He didn't buy alcohol anymore, but he was desperate for a beer. He made himself a cup of tea instead. Odd, how he'd got used to that now. A few sips of the scalding tea, some mindless crap on TV, and his veg and protein for dinner, was enough to keep his mind off the booze.

Today, dinner was a stir fry and sliced chicken in soya sauce. Cooked by Anna, earlier, before she went out. Although he was too late to eat with her, he was grateful she'd made it. He left the noodles alone, as he was trying to stay off carbohydrates. Then he gave in and put some on his plate. What was a chicken stir fry without noodles? He'd only have a few strings, that would assuage his guilt.

Giving up carbs, which meant not buying bread, pasta, rice, potatoes for home, had definitely helped. Okay, so he hadn't given up carbs completely. He still ate an odd chip here and there, and a slice of pizza when Anna ordered a delivery. But only a slice or two, no more. And he had to admit he felt better. Bread and rice made him feel bloated and tired. He felt nicer without it.

He finished eating, then with the mug of tea, he went back to the living room. His mind didn't stay on Netflix for long. The thought of someone watching him again, and even worse, being at Sarah's house, was bothering the hell out of him. He picked up his phone and called Sarah. She didn't answer but called him back.

Roy said, "Hi, it's me."

"Ey up guv. I was going to ask business or pleasure, but then realised it might sound bit dodgy." She laughed. She didn't sound stressed, and that was good, he thought.

"Business, I'm afraid. Did you manage to do a door-to-door on your street?"

Sarah sighed, and it sounded as though she sat down. "As a matter of fact, I did. None of the neighbours saw anything. It's possible this person looked through the back fence and saw you playing with Matt." She paused. "Creepy, though."

"I'm sorry," Roy said, and meant it. "For the next few days, maybe you should do the drop- offs and pick-ups. Although your mother seems more than capable."

"Yes, I'd be lost without her. Don't worry, we'll be safe. I'll keep an eye on Matt. I asked a squad car to do some rounds around the neighbourhood tonight."

"Well done."

"Mum likes you, by the way. You made a good impression."

"I fell for the family trick. You had a nice shower and got ready while I played football." He grinned. "Tell Clare I said 'hello'."

"I will do."

There was a pause. "Who do you think this could be?" Sarah asked, referring to the phantom texter.

"It's odd. From the description the old lady gave us, it sounds like a young lad. Slim, about your height?"

"Could Burns have a son we don't know about?"

Roy thought for a while. He'd been asking himself the same question. But they'd been through Burns's history time and time again. Still, there was a chance they might've missed something.

"Don't think so, but worth checking again." He didn't want to mention the awful thought gnawing at his mind. Burns was a celebrity in the sick, depraved world of violent child abusers. On the dark web, he had a website with a fan zone, for crying out loud. But his so-called fans had no way of contacting him. His emails and phone calls were screened. His previous followers – Burgess and Pickering, were also in jail, and would never be let out.

But... Roy knew, as well as any policeman, that the prisons were a universe unto themselves. Money exchanged hands regularly, under the table. Guards could be bribed, but it wasn't easy in high security prisons, like where Burns was. It was possible that one of the trio had someone on the outside. Someone who matched the description of the person the old lady saw today.

"I think we need to get a list of visitors not just for Burns, but also Burgess and Pickering," Roy said. "We might get this guy's identity that way."

"I'll call tomorrow." Sarah paused for a while. "Are you okay, Rohan?"

"Why wouldn't I be?"

She paused again, and Roy sighed. He was no good at this. Meaningful silences and subtle hints were not his thing. A bellyful of food was also making him sleepy.

"Well spit it out then," he growled. "What is it?"

"You saw that psychologist today. How did it go?"

"Fine and dandy. I put up with her psychobabble for a while, then left. She tried to wink at me a couple of times."

"Please Rohan, be serious. I'm…" She seemed to struggle with her next words. "I'm worried about you. I mean, a lot's happened over the last couple of months. And I know… I mean seeing the psychologist is probably a good thing."

"You sound like Nugent."

"You know what I mean," she said quietly. She didn't have to utter the words that got filled in by the static and silence. His day and nights were blighted by not knowing what happened to Robin. In some ways, capturing Burns, dismantling their horrible network, had made the lack of closure worse. If getting The Lily Man, as the press had dubbed Burns, didn't reveal the truth of what happened to Robin, then what would?

He suddenly wished Sarah was here. Some thoughts couldn't be conveyed over the phone, or even on a video call. He abolished that feeling as soon as it came. Sarah was a colleague, and it was best to keep it that way. But she had also become a friend, and the only person, apart from his parents, he could talk to about this stuff. Well, she did most of the talking, and he tried to avoid it.

The sound of a key rattling in the door distracted him. The door opened and shut.

"Anna, is that you?" he called out. "Hold on," he said to Sarah.

"No, It's Father Christmas," Anna replied. She stuck her head in through the living room door. "Oh sorry. You on the phone?"

"Yes. You alright?"

Anna gave him a thumbs up. "I'll be up in my room."

Roy waited till Anna had shut the door behind her. "Sorry," he said to Sarah.

"Was that Anna? Say hello."

"I will." He felt bad as Anna had only met the team in the station and got on well with Sarah and Melanie. He needed to organise a more social occasion.

"How long is she staying for?" Sarah asked. "You must be glad she's there."

"Can't wait till I get the place back to myself," he grumbled, then smiled. "She's here for a couple of weeks more but might go down to London for a couple of days to see her mother." He didn't want to think what would happen when Anna left for good and wouldn't be back for the rest of the summer. Then school from September. He'd miss her like mad. Well, that was life.

"Anyway," he said, listening to her yawn. "I'd better let you go. See you tomorrow."

"Yes, boss. Remember what I said. Look after yourself."

He thanked her, then hung up. His mind went back to the case, and what happened through the day. It was eventful, to say the least. Getting Kevin had been the highlight, but something told him Debbie McPherson was still being frugal with the truth.

Kevin wouldn't spill any beans, he was a career criminal, and he'd let his solicitor do the talking. It was Debbie they needed to focus on, and Luke Hammond. Roy hadn't seen Luke yet, but the fact that he had done time for armed robbery wasn't just a coincidence.

Roy got off the sofa and went to the table. He pulled up his writing pad and wrote down the names of everyone connected to the case, including Tracey's mother, Cathy. She'd provided the biggest clue about the unknown man who was pestering Tracey. Hopefully, by tomorrow, there would be more CCTV photos of the man. In any case, Roy was determined to have uniforms swarm all over the supermarket, asking questions. If it had been a loud argument, then other shoppers would've noticed.

Then there was Bianca Wilkins. Her case was now a cold one. But Roy didn't think it was again sheer coincidence that Debbie McPherson had been the manager of the massage parlour when Bianca died. He frowned, and drew a line from Debbie to Bianca, then back to Tracey.

What was he missing here? What connected these three women?

Perhaps Sunrise Massage Parlour was also owned by the Rawlinson lot. The Loxley Boys gang. Were they silencing the sex workers if there was a dispute? Then why on earth would they display the bodies?

No, there was something else here. Roy stared at the white space between the black letters. The pieces were coming together in his mind, but parts of the jigsaw were still missing. Not missing, he could see them, they just didn't fit. He would have to scramble around the corners of his brain for more inspiration.

He thought of what the witness, Jayden Budden had told him. Young women from Eastern Europe had moved in, like the two women he spoke to in that house.

His eyes narrowed as a sudden thought hit him.

He opened up his laptop and logged into the South Yorkshire Police database. He searched for a while, then his fingers stilled. Breath caught in his lungs. He stared at the screen like his eyes were probing inside the machine. A sense of disquiet was spreading across his bones.

"Bloody hell," he whispered to himself.

CHAPTER 39

The man waited until the lights were getting switched off, one by one. Attercliffe was one of the seediest parts of Sheffield. It was packed with council houses, and the high street was littered with pawn shops, betting joints, and pubs where a Friday night without a fight, or really any day of the week without one, was almost sacrilege. But Friday and Saturday nights were special. That's when the punters blew their betting wins, and their lager lout, jealous neighbours laid into them. The inevitable brawl was almost a ritual in the Attercliffe pubs.

The massage parlours had sprouted in recent years, and while everyone knew what happened behind closed doors, they turned a blind eye. In fact, there was now about a dozen massage parlours, or brothels here, and their success had spawned new establishments across the river. Like Cliffe Sauna and Massage Parlour on Liverpool Street.

The shabby buildings over the shops were now cloaked by the diesel-clad, grimy night, and their inhabitants were turning in for the night. It was half-past-eleven, and the three pubs on the high street were finally kicking out the last of their vocal, and utterly sloshed, punters. Some of these men would end up in the massage parlours tonight, those who had the money. Some would end up in a custody cell overnight. Right on cue, a police car trundled slowly down the street. The man retreated further into the shadows behind an alcove. For tonight, he couldn't be seen by the cops.

He relaxed as the police car went to the end of the road, and then took a right, disappearing from view. He emerged, and walked in the same direction, going past a pub. A drunken slob almost bumped into him, muttering curses. He went to the end of the road, where across the junction, there was the large bank building. He had no idea why Attercliffe needed such a large bank. It wasn't as if this area's inhabitants could afford substantial deposits. Maybe because the land was cheap, like most of Attercliffe.

He walked past the bank, and then slunk into another dark corner of a building. From here, he could see the row of terraced houses on the street opposite. He had been coming here for a couple of weeks, trying to establish his target's pattern. He looked at his watch. Twenty to midnight. If the last few nights had been any indication, it should be any time now.

He stiffened as the door of a house opposite him opened, and a woman stepped out. She wore a short dress, with a summer coat over it. Her heels clicked on the pavement as she walked down, one hand clutching the strap of her handbag. The man's breathing quickened. He took off his hoody, revealing his face. He patted down his hair. He had put on a lot of aftershave and groomed himself well. He detached from the shadows and walked in the woman's direction.

"Hello Charly," he said, coming up behind her. The woman gasped, then spun around. She was on guard immediately.

"Who are you?" She backed away a step.

"Hey, you met me the other night. At the massage parlour." He told her his name. "Don't you remember? We had a good time. I gave you a good tip." He came closer. She was still wary but held her ground.

"Yes." Her eyes scanned the street around them anxiously. "What do you want? You coming to the place?"

He knew what she was afraid of. Street prostitution was illegal, and she could get arrested. He raised both hands.

"I just wanted to say hello, that's all. Yes, I am coming to the parlour. To see you, obviously." He smiled, showing his white teeth. He knew women liked his smile. Charly was still silent, and her face remained blank. She remained on her guard.

"Do you mind if I walk with you?" He spread his arms and smiled again. "I'm going there to see you anyway."

She thought for a while, then nodded. They walked past the bank, and then into the side street that led towards the canal, and the bridge over it. Lights were bright on the bridge, and even at this time of the night, people were crossing it. That wasn't good for him. He had hoped the bridge would be empty now. He thought quickly. His eyes were drawn to the oily, black waters of the canal, and the lights shimmering on it.

They got closer to the bridge. He kept up the conversation, hoping to keep her interested.

"You're such a nice person. I know you do this for money, but what if you could do something else for the same money?"

She looked at him. "Like what?"

"I run three barber shops. Women can cut men's hair too, and one of the shops is for women only. I'd pay you well."

She shook her head. "Won't pay the same as this."

"Oh, you'll be surprised. Here, let me show you the salons. We're the real deal and charge good money."

214

From the corner of his eyes, he saw the path was sloping up towards the bridge, but there was another smaller track leading down to the canal.

"Here, look." He got closer and held out his phone. Curiosity won Charly over, and she looked. He hooked his other hand around her mouth, stifling her scream. He shoved the phone in his pocket. He grabbed a kicking and squirming Charly against him and dragged her down the path. Charly wasn't tall, and he had chosen her carefully. They always fought back, and he wanted to be sure he could overpower them.

He pulled her into the canalside. No lights here, only faint beams from the bridge above. She kicked his legs, and he grunted in pain as he lost his footing. He slipped down to one knee, but his arms were strong, and they didn't let go of her. He held her down, and then on her back. He was on top of her quickly, and he grabbed her hair, and slammed her head down a couple of times. Charly's eyes rolled back, and her struggles diminished. He smacked her head once again, and she went limp.

He got to work quickly, putting his gloves on, then his mask. He put tape over her mouth, winding it round her neck a couple of times to make sure it was tight. He also tied her feet together.

Then, with gloved hands, he squeezed her neck. As the pressure grew, Charly's eyes opened. He increased the tightness on her neck and watched the panic build in her eyes.

When it was over, and she was unconscious again, he couldn't stop looking at her face. It reminded him of his mother. They all did. All his victims. When they rested in final repose, and in total peace. It was his mother's face looking back at him. He was that solitary boy, standing in the rain, watching her body lowering into the grave. He relived that moment every time this happened, that slip in his life when he passed into another world. He patted Charly's cheek affectionately. Then he pulled

215

out the packet of instruments from his coat and got to work.

CHAPTER 40

Roy was at his desk early, sipping on a coffee. It was half-seven, and he'd had a restless night's sleep, waking up several times thinking he could hear sounds around the house. He'd checked Anna's door a couple of times to make sure it was locked. In the end, he gave up, and went for a run at 6 am. It was easier in the summer, and nothing beat watching the dawn unfurl over the Don Valley.

He looked at the paper in his hand, over the steam from his cup. It was good coffee too, from the canteen. The paper bore the call list from Tracey's phone, which was still not found. Phones emitted signals for five days after they were switched off. Triangulation of the last signal still showed the phone to be within a hundred-metre radius of where she was found.

Roy put the call list down and walked over to the large map on the wall. It showed the whole of Sheffield, up to the margins of the Peak District. He focused on the opposite, the east, where the crime scene was located. Two streets away lay the river, and over the bridge, the exit to the dual carriageway of the A61. Above that, lay the industrial areas of Grimesthorpe, then Burngreave and Attercliffe. To the right, the huge sprawl of

Meadowhall, one of Yorkshire's largest shopping malls.

Roy tapped a fingernail against the crime scene, brows furrowed. The place was close to the river, which was a small tributary of the once-mighty Sheaf, from which Sheffield got its name. Still, it merged with bigger bodies of water, and there would be large drains emptying into it.

"Morning guv," a voice said behind him. "Early bird gets the worm, eh?"

He turned to see Rizwan. The DC took off his light coat and hung it on the coat peg on the wall. Then he joined Roy, who had gone back to inspecting the map.

"Ordinance survey maps," he said. "They show the storm drains, don't they?"

"And power installations, transport hubs. Why?"

"I want to search the drains for the murder weapon, and also the victim's phone. First, let's make sure the drains exist at the murder scene, or nearby. Then we call the drain camera folk."

"No problem." He scratched the back of his head and looked around the room. A pair of detectives in another team sat at the other end, out of earshot. "Can I ask you something?"

"Shoot."

"I haven't told Sharon about the connection between Kevin Rawlinson, and the Wrexham Hill Gang. But I can't help being worried about it. Last thing I want is for Sharon to be dragged into this again."

"If the Wrexham Hill lot suspected Sharon of knowing anything, they would've acted on it already," Roy said softly, noting the concern in Rizwan's face. "But they haven't. They just wanted to get rid of Paul, because he'd spoken to us." Roy pulled up a chair and so did Riz.

"Besides, an OCN won't go around killing people. Especially

218

women who aren't connected to them. It's bad for their business. They don't want the NCA, or us, to pry into their affairs."

Rizwan nodded. "That makes sense. Sharon's heart-broken of course, that Paul's dead. But she knows what he was mixed up in. It had to happen sooner or later." Riz looked sadly at the floor.

"Sharon only knew where he was living, that's all. She didn't know owt else."

"Then she's got nothing to worry about. You've been keeping an eye around your house lately, though, right? Not seen anything weird?"

Riz shook his head. "Nowt. I've been observing for a while now. No dodgy cars or blokes."

Roy smiled. "I think Sharon will be fine, mate. Don't worry."

"Thanks guv," Riz looked relieved.

Oliver and Melanie walked in, both with cups of coffee in their hands. Riz rang the research team, asking for the ordinance maps. Roy addressed all three of them as he opened up his laptop.

"I've been doing some thinking. I know, have to do it sometimes. I wondered if a killer like ours has been operating for a while, but just been under the radar. The cold case got me thinking. What if he's done more like that, but no one knows." Roy shrugged. "Assuming the cold case and our current victim's killer is the same, but it seems likely."

The others nodded. Roy said, "I know the researchers and you lot have been through the cold cases over the last twenty years and found nothing else. But then I thought of missing persons."

All three of them sat up straighter. "If they're not home for more than a week, then chances of a death are high," Oliver said.

"Good thinking, guv."

"So, I looked into the missing persons database for Yorkshire, Derbyshire, and Lancashire. Basically, east to west of the country, up here. And I found this."

He turned his laptop screen so the others could see.

"A woman called Gemma Jackson, aged twenty one who was last seen in Meadowhall six years ago. She didn't have much of a family, but the investigation showed she was a sex worker, and also a single mother. Gemma's body was never recovered, but she fits the type our killer would go for."

The others looked at the woman on the screen. The image showed a young brunette, about five-feet-five, smiling for the camera, clearly a photo taken by friends and family. It was a close-up of her face.

Roy continued. "She was reported missing by her aunt, who lived with her, and looked after her baby. Gemma was last seen coming out of Meadowhall, taking the train back to her council flat in Grimesthorpe. She got out of the station, and then we lost her. Her aunt raised the alarm the next evening when she wasn't answering her phone."

The team was hanging on to every word Roy said. "Today, I'd like to speak to the aunt. Go and see her, if possible. The case is still open, which means Gemma wasn't found. There might be CCTV records from six years ago, we need to ask traffic."

Oliver rose. "I'll go and do that now guv." He wrote down the PCN number on a jotting pad, and the missing persons details. He tore off the sheet and left.

Melanie looked thoughtful. "I understand why you would look at this," she said to Roy. "But Gemma is a missing person's case. There's nothing to link it to our current case. After all, we could scour the whole country for missing sex workers."

"You're right, but I've got a feeling about this. She's the right age and vanished around the same area."

"Who did?" A female voice behind them said, and Roy turned to see Sarah. She shrugged off her coat and draped it over her chair.

"I had a brainwave last night," Roy said. "Happens rarely." He explained about Gemma Jackson and showed her the screen. Sarah stroked her chin, looking dubious.

"She's just a missing person, right?"

Melanie nodded. "That's what I said. Might be a wild goose chase."

Roy shook his head. "It's too much of a coincidence. Say this was in London, or Edinburgh. I'd let it go. But see where this woman was last spotted. Coming home from Meadowhall. Stopping off at Attercliffe, walking towards Grimesthorpe. And then she disappears?" Roy raised his hands. "And she just happens to be a sex worker who's also a single mother? You can literally see her as our victim. No one knows what happened to her, and that could be because our killer wanted to hide the body. Now he's grown in confidence and has started to display them."

Everyone looked at him in silence. Sarah said, "A few reaches there, guv. Some assumptions. You always warn us against making those."

"I know," Roy agreed. "But I just find this jarring. Gemma's profile is a carbon copy of our victim. It won't hurt to look into the case."

Sarah shrugged. Melanie went up to the whiteboard in the corner and wrote Gemma Jackson's name.

"Going back to Bianca Wilkins, the cold case with the same MO," Roy said, "Did we make any enquiries?"

"Yes," said Melanie. "The previous DI in charge was the SIO.

Inspector Pitt. I never met him." She looked at the others, and everyone, apart from Roy, averted their eyes.

Roy said, "Anyway. Carry on."

Melanie clearly understood there was an undercurrent of something, but she let it go. DI Pitt had been Roy's predecessor, and he had taken early retirement with PTSD. It happened more often than not to police officers but wasn't exactly publicised.

Melanie cleared her throat. "Well, Bianca was found on the canal towpath near Victoria Quays. No witnesses came forward. CCTV footage, bear in mind this was three years ago, shows a solitary man going down to the towpath an hour before she died. He doesn't come back up. He was the main suspect, and CCTV followed him as he walked from Burngreave Cemetery to the tow path. Before the cemetery, he wasn't visible. This was also at night, so views were limited."

"No other suspects?" Sarah asked. "Bianca didn't have any enemies? Jealous lovers? Family problems?"

"She was a single mother, who lived in a council flat. Her mother lived in the same block but in a different flat. Remarkably similar to Tracey Barrett, our first victim."

Sarah looked at Roy, and by now, he could sort of guess what she was thinking. He nodded. "Go on," he said. "Say it."

"It's almost like he checks the family background before he strikes," Sarah said, her eyes on Roy.

"Exactly. This is the reason why I looked at the missing person's database. Gemma Jackson was also a single mother." He looked back to Melanie. "Anything else?"

"Usual hardships. They lived on benefits. Bianca worked in the supermarket and had recently started night work at the Sunrise Massage Parlour. No enemies from what I can gather. It was also run by Karen Rawlinson, but Kevin was the figurehead. The same set up as Cliffe."

"Could the killer be targeting their massage parlours? The brothels I mean," Rizwan said. "The ones run by Kevin and his gang."

Roy frowned. "I can't see this being a vendetta. Against what? If the killer has something against the Loxley Gang, then killing sex workers doesn't help. It only brings more attention towards them. If they burnt down the building, or tried to attack Kevin, that would make more sense."

"I agree," Sarah said, folding arms across her chest. "We're not dealing with gang violence here. The killer chooses single mother sex workers, and the Loxley Boys just happen to run the largest number of brothels in Sheffield."

Roy nodded. "In this case, the coincidence is justified. Sarah's right. If this was gang warfare, then there would be a lot more blatant violence. No one would do a ritual kill."

Melanie said, "I spoke to Bianca's mother, Emily. She suspected what Bianca was up to, when she left her son with her at night. She confronted Bianca, and she confessed. Then she carried on," Mel shrugged, "I assumed as the money was good. By the way, Bianca was also an ex-IV drug user, like Tracey."

"And she also had a son," Roy said, head lowered. His mind was connecting the dots. He looked up at the team. From the corner of his eyes, he saw Oliver coming in.

"I don't want to be alarmist, but I think we have a killer who's choosing his victims with precision, because he's following a pattern. You know his type now. We need to send out feelers to all the brothels in the city. Any single mothers who are ex-IV drug users need to forget about working and stay at home. Til this blows over anyway."

"They have to stop blowing." Oliver chortled at his own joke. Then his face straightened when he caught the daggers from everyone else. "I was just saying. As a joke I mean…" His words died away. He scratched the back of his neck and looked down at his feet. "Right, er…"

"This better be good," Roy said softly.

Oliver looked around him, aware he was on thin ice. "CCTV. Traffic," he blurted. "I spoke to them about Gemma Jackson. They'll see what CCTV they have on the night of her disappearance from six years ago."

"You have some uses after all," Roy said.

Riz said, "Perhaps Ollie and I can start spreading the word in all the massage parlours. Eh, guv?"

"Yes, do that." Roy glanced at Sarah. "Shall we see what Kevin Rawlinson has to say?"

CHAPTER 41

Anna was back in the library when she heard a familiar voice behind her.

"Fancy seeing you here again," Lydia Moran said.

Anna turned and grinned. "Oh, hi. I was wondering if you were going to be around today."

Lydia indicated the books on Anna's arm. "How's the revision going?"

"Not great. The books on Henry the Fifth are mostly too critical. The ones I've read so far. I'm trying to get a feel for what he was like as a person, you know? And that's hard to get."

"That's an excellent attitude. I might just have the right book for you, as it happens. Have you read the book by Jane Carmichael? Hang on, I need to look for the title." She searched on her phone, but the connection wasn't great inside the library.

"I might have to use my laptop. Where are you sitting?"

"Same place as yesterday," Anna said.

"Okay, I'm on the other side."

"I'll come with you."

They walked to where Lydia was sitting, to the right of the entrance. Lydia had sat here so she could see everyone entering and leaving. She had seen Anna come in around 10 am, but deliberately left her alone. It was now close to midday.

Lydia checked her screen, and then showed Anna. The teenager wrote down the details.

"Let's ask the librarian. They can do a search for us," Lydia suggested. There was queue to see the librarian, and Lydia seized the chance to chat.

"So, how are you finding it up here?"

"It's great," Anna said. Then her face fell. "I mean, it can also be scary, the great outdoors. I'm kind of careful about where I go."

Lydia understood. Burns paid a couple of prison guards to supply him with information about the outside world, and his contacts. He had told Lydia about Pickering.

"Oh, I see," she feigned polite disinterest. "But it's nice out there, as well. I mean, I do like my long walks. We're very lucky, having such gorgeous countryside right on the city's doorstep."

"Hmm, yes," Anna smiled, and turned away, indicating the conversation was over. Lydia changed tack quickly.

"I last went to London in November to see a friend. She lives in Battersea. She's a teacher at Dulwich College. Do you know of it?"

"Yes, it's meant to be a good school. For boys though. Alleyne's, next to it, is for girls."

"That's right, but from the sixth form, it becomes co-ed. Janet's been there a while now. Almost ten years, I think. She teaches English." Lydia smiled. "Anyway, I best leave you to it. If you

226

need me, I'll be here."

Anna thanked her, and remained in the queue, while Lydia went back to her desk. She watched as Anna got the book from the counter, and then she pretended to be reading when the teenager looked at her as she walked back to her spot. Lydia craned her neck, observing Anna as she sat down at the back. Lydia knew she couldn't be too pushy. Anna was already on guard, given her recent experience. Roy must've told her to stay away from strangers. Slow and steady was the best way forward.

It wasn't easy to distract herself. Anna was the best way for her to get closer to Rohan Roy. But she had to bide her time. She started reading a crime thriller book and was soon lost in the story. She was surprised when Anna came and stood in front of her desk. She put her book down and smiled, adjusting her glasses.

"That book is so helpful," Anna grinned. "Honestly, it shows Henry the Fifth as a person, and that's just what I needed."

"Glad it's working. Not sure how far you've got, but it gets better near the end. I recommend it to all my students."

"Thanks." Anna started to leave, then hesitated. "I'm going for lunch. Do you want to get something?"

Lydia feigned disinterest, then looked at her watch. "Well, why not?" She grabbed her purse and stood. "Come on, let's go. I know a sandwich place that's really good."

"I'm on low carbs," Anna said, as they swiped their cards and walked out of the library.

"Get away. You're far too young."

"Maybe. That's what my dad says as well."

They'd walked out on the road, and the sunlight was warm on their faces. Lydia directed them down a busy alley bustling with cafés.

"So, your dad doesn't eat many carbs?" Lydia asked innocently.

"Oh gosh," Anna waved a hand. "He's like the anti-carb mafia. Doesn't buy bread, potatoes, or pasta. Although I suspect he has chips occasionally, as he gets them on his way back from work."

"Well, that's good of your dad. What work does he do?"

There was a slight pause, and Lydia closed her eyes. Maybe she'd gone too far.

"He's a police officer."

"Oh, very good. In Sheffield?"

"Yes." Anna shut up then and looked away. Lydia refrained from asking any more questions. They got to the café, which was heaving. They found a seat outside, which was nice.

"What would you like? My treat," Lydia smiled. Anna refused but Lydia waved it away. She went and ordered, then came back.

"You know, it's good to have met you," she said, after sitting down. "I live alone, and it gets a bit, you know, lonely sometimes."

"Oh," Anna said, sipping her tea. "You don't have a partner, or family?"

"No. Never happened really. Had a long term boyfriend for almost a decade. My third long-term relationship. We broke up recently." Lydia smiled but allowed a tinge of sadness to show on her face. The smile faded quickly. "Just the way my life panned out. Got two cats, though."

"What breed?"

"Ragdolls."

Anna clenched her fists in delight. "Oh god I love ragdolls. My friend Julie has one. They're so fluffy and cuddly."

"That they are."

"What are they called?"

"Beadle and Muddles. Muddles is getting older, she's twelve, and she forgets her way around the garden. She's always been forgetful though, hence the name."

"Is Beadle a girl as well?"

"Yes. Otherwise, I'd have a litter on my hand." She laughed and Anna joined in. "But Beadle is sharper. She bosses Muddles around a lot. But they're also good friends."

Their food arrived, and they started eating. Lydia pondered her next question, then decided to ask it anyway. "So, where do you live in Sheffield?"

"In Dore. That village a bit south from here."

"Oh, not far from me at all, in Totley. You should come around some time. Play with my cats."

"Maybe." Anna smiled, but Lydia saw the strong hesitation in her eyes. At least, Lydia thought, there wouldn't be another Rohan Roy living in Dore. She had something to tell Burns, after all.

CHAPTER 42

Roy watched through the viewing box as Mel and Sarah finished. Debbie was downcast. She rose and followed her solicitor out the of the room. The door opened and the two female detectives entered.

Mel said, "Debbie came clean. Tracey Barrett had found out about the cameras. She asked Kevin for more money. Kevin kept most of the cash the customers paid, and Tracey wanted a bigger cut."

"How did Tracey know about the cameras?"

"Debbie has no idea, but she did say Tracey's ex-partner, her son's dad, knew Kevin. Luke Hammond. Apparently, Luke introduced Tracey to Kevin. Debbie thinks Luke is the reason Tracey knew so much about Kevin's business."

Roy frowned. "So, Tracey was trying to blackmail Kevin? Is that right?" He looked from Mel to Sarah, both of whom nodded.

Mel said, "And Debbie also talked about Bianca Wilkins. She didn't know her as well as Tracey, but she was aware that Bianca also had arguments with Kevin, who was running the

Sunrise Massage Parlour. She'd lied to us earlier about not knowing Bianca at all. She's scared of Kevin, and what he might do to her when she's out."

They were silent for a while. Roy said, "All of a sudden, it seems Kevin had a motive for these murders. He certainly had the opportunity; he was in the massage parlour when Tracey was murdered. Correct?"

"Yes," Sarah said. "That's what he told us."

"As for means, Kevin's a hardened criminal. He could well be a malignant narcissist personality disorder psychopath as well. He kills in his own way, to get rid of the women who stand against him. Jeez." Roy rubbed his chin, leaning against the wall.

Sarah said, "It will be hard to build a case against him for Bianca's murder. It was six years ago, and the witnesses might not come forward."

Roy asked, "Anything else on Kevin?"

"Apart from his stints in jail? We know the rest," Sarah said, and glanced at Mel.

Mel was more circumspect. "Like the guv says, it's possible his criminal record's hidden the fact he's also a sick bastard. Maybe he has killed these girls, and everyone's been looking for someone else."

"Right then," Roy said. "We got everything?"

Sarah nodded, and they said goodbye to Mel, and went into Interview Room 3. Kevin sat up straighter when Roy entered. He dwarfed his solicitor, a bespectacled man in an expensive suit.

Roy had never seen the lawyer, but he took an instant dislike to him. The lawyer looked posh and respectable, which meant he was expensive, which in turn meant he would play low down and dirty to get his client off the hook. A lawyer's basic humanity was at an inverse relationship to his fees, Roy had discovered with time. A rich lawyer would get the worst criminals off the hook without blinking an eyelid. No one would ever be more corrupt than a lawyer who knowingly defended the indefensible. He bristled with contempt as the solicitor smiled at him condescendingly.

"John Rattner," he said, in a suave, well-modulated voice. "And you are?" His eyes moved from Roy to Sarah. They introduced themselves, then sat down.

"Nice to meet you," Mr Rattner said, his eyes cold. His accent was home counties and hinted at a private school education. *All the more alarming*, Roy thought to himself.

Sarah spoke for the machine, noting the names, date, location, and time.

They had decided Sarah would handle the questions. Roy could see the hostility in Kevin's eyes every time they met his. He remained statue still but didn't look away when Kevin glared at him.

Sarah spread out photos of Kevin's father so Kevin could see.

"Mr Rawlinson, can you please confirm this is a picture of Shaun Rawlinson, your father."

The question was meant to take Kevin unawares, and it worked. The bald criminal frowned, and the scar on his left cheek seemed to go deeper. He stared at the photos, then to his solicitor.

Mr Rattner, Roy was happy to see, looked a little flustered. "What is this about, Miss Botham?"

"It's pertinent to the case. Shaun is the founder of Sheffield's largest organised crime network, The Loxley Boys. Isn't that correct, Kevin? I hope you don't mind me calling you Kevin."

"No comment," Kevin said.

"So, you're denying this man is your father?"

"No comment."

"Are you now the leader of the network, and you run it in absentia, from Fuengirola, in southern Spain?"

The slight widening of Kevin's eyes was satisfying, as was the light jerk in his neck. He wasn't expecting that.

"No comment."

"Your father Shaun and girlfriend Karen both live there, don't they? Must be nice. Is it by the sea?"

Kevin's cheeks were mottling red. "No comment," he said through gritted teeth.

"So, you came over to check the businesses, didn't you?" Sarah maintained her seemingly casual chatter. "But you didn't expect one of the sex workers at the Cliffe Massage Parlour to die, did you?"

Kevin frowned. "No comment."

"You've told Karen, I think. We found the burner phone on you. You called a Spanish number. No one picks up. Is it Karen, or your dad you called?"

Kevin kept a stony silence.

"Suspect refuses to answer," Sarah said to the machine.

She continued. "I wonder what Karen would say when she learns how the girl died. Quite brutal, really. Karen won't like it."

Kevin glanced at his lawyer, who shrugged. Good, Roy thought to himself. Keep them guessing.

Sarah said, "The night of Tracey Barrett's death, you were at the Cliffe Massage Parlour. Witnesses have verified this.

However, no one remembers seeing you between the hours of 10 pm and midnight. Can you confirm where you were during that time?"

Kevin said, "In my room. I'd fallen asleep."

It was a good answer. He knew they couldn't press him any more on it. Sarah said, "How well did you know the victim, Tracey Barrett?"

"I didn't. She worked in the massage parlour, that's all."

"We know you had arguments with her, and she knew about the cameras you had installed in the doors."

Kevin went still, and his eyebrows lowered. "No comment."

"You blackmailed the men who came to the brothel, right? Or you liked to give yourself the option to do so, in case it came in handy later. But Tracey started to blackmail you, didn't she?"

The frown on Kevin's face was spreading like the ground cracking in an earthquake. "No comment."

"Tracey threatened to tell the punters, which would mean the end of your business. Worse, she could tell us, which meant we would look into your so-called massage parlour empire. Got a few of them, haven't you?"

"No comment."

Sarah made a show of pulling out other papers from the brown envelope that Roy handed her. She spread out crime scene photos of Bianca Wilkins from six years ago. Kevin fixated on them, and he breathed faster.

"Bianca worked at the Sunrise Massage Parlour, which you ran as well. Bianca was killed in the same manner as Tracey. According to witnesses, you also had altercations with Bianca, shortly before she died."

Rattner leaned forward. "Miss Botham, what does this have to do with the current case? My client has nothing to say about a cold case that remains unsolved."

"Given the MO is the same, and your client ran the establishments in question, I would say it's very relevant. The same person was likely the killer in both cases." Sarah stared hard at Kevin. "Was that person you, Kevin?"

Kevin was turning a shade of purple. "No comment."

"You had bad relations with both women, and they worked at your brothels. When we tried to question you, you did a runner. Can you see how bad this looks for you, Kevin?"

"No comment." Kevin snarled and sat back in his chair. He looked at his solicitor, who nodded at him, then focused on Sarah.

It was time, Roy thought. He touched Sarah's arm. "Soon," he said, "We will find Tracey Barrett's phone, and the murder weapon. I'm hoping the phone at least, as it's close by. The phone will have more information about Tracey's links with you, and your links with Luke Hammond."

Kevin's jaws flexed, and a vein throbbed on his forehead. Roy knew he was getting under his skin.

He said, "Once we have more evidence that you had motive to murder Tracey, we have enough to build a case."

Kevin's jaw dropped open. "What case?" he blurted.

Rattner didn't look happy at all. "DCI Roy, what're you trying to say? Either you charge my client or stop these empty threats."

Roy gazed at Rattner. "I would say entering a plea of manslaughter means your client would get away with a lighter sentence. If we charge, and prosecute, then he will be incarcerated for decades, if not for life, given the death of Bianca Wilkins six years ago."

Kevin's jaw looked like it might separate from his face and end up on the table. He blinked a few times.

Rattner said, "I don't understand. Can you explain?"

"In preparation for a murder charge, we are gathering evidence. The process should be complete within 48 hours. This interview was a means of giving your client some clarity about our intentions."

"What?"

"We explained on what basis we think a charge is valid. But we will only formally do so when we have more evidence."

Sarah said, "To make the case watertight."

"Exactly," Roy agreed. "We are confident of building a good case. Unless of course, Mr Rawlinson has something he wishes to share with us now." It was a statement, not a question, and Roy directed it to Kevin. He held up two fingers.

"Not one, but two murder charges Kevin. There's a good chance of at least one sticking."

Kevin looked like he'd been slapped, then stamped across the face with a spade. He opened his mouth, and his lips moved in silence.

CHAPTER 43

What's that?" Roy leaned forward.

Kevin wheezed. "I... I didn't... Yer off yer fuckin' rocker. I didn't kill those lasses. Load of bollocks this."

Roy stared at him calmly. For a man who ran a criminal network, Kevin wasn't very clever. He suspected Shaun called all the shots still, and Kevin was the muscle, because he was good at intimidating people. If Kevin had any brains, he wouldn't have run like he did. He would've cooperated and be out by now. He'd dug his own grave.

"You were there, Kevin. You wanted Tracey dead because she was blackmailing you. You had the means to kill her."

Sarah added, "She would've sunk your business. Did you catch someone important on camera? Did Tracey threaten to talk to them?"

Kevin turned his saucer eyes to Sarah. "You're bonkers."

"Really? Then why don't you tell us why you have those cameras, and why Tracey was arguing with you?"

"Bitch wanted more money!" Kevin roared, slamming a fist on the table. The legs were nailed down, but the steel top shuddered like a drum. "They all do. I told her to piss off. Nowt else happened. I didn't even see her that night."

"And what about the cameras?"

Kevin went back into his shell. "No comment."

Sarah continued. "So, you're denying killing Tracey?"

"Of course I bloody am, you fecking pillock!" Kevin howled this time. "Yer deaf or what?"

Rattner spoke into Kevin's ear, and his words seemed to have a calming effect. Rattner patted him on the shoulder, and fixed Roy with a stare.

"My client would like to terminate the interview now," Rattner said stiffly. "If you don't intend to charge him, I suggest you let us know your intentions soon, or he will be going home later today."

*****

Sarah and Roy sat in the office, two steaming mugs of tea on the table in front of them.

"Think he's lying?" Sarah asked.

"He's not talking about Luke, and he knows more about Tracey than he's letting on," Roy sighed. "But killer?" He shook his head. "Not sure, but it's a possibility. He was there, and he could've done it. We still need to find a murder weapon."

There was a knock on the door, and Mark Spencer, the CPS contact, poked his head in when Roy asked him to enter. He came and sat down. Sarah explained Kevin's arrest and possible charge.

"Difficult," Mark shook his balding head. He adjusted the glasses on his nose. Mark was in his fifties and was a veteran of the CPS and criminal court law. Before the police spent a small fortune on preparing a legal case, they asked his advice.

"On the victim, you don't have any DNA or prints that match with Kevin. She was in the same place as him that night, but that doesn't mean anything. She didn't die there. Her body was found outside. Regardless, to get Kevin in the frame, you need evidence. Have you searched his car? His house or flat? Anything there that might point to the victim had taken a ride with him, or stayed overnight?"

Sarah said, "Uniforms have impounded his car, and SOC are in his flat in Ecclesall. We will know more later tonight, or tomorrow."

"Anything on CCTV that shows he was in contact with the victim? Went to her house, or met her in the centre?"

Sarah said, "Kevin's phone data's been analysed. He sent some texts to his friends the day before yesterday. That puts him in a café near the university. Also, at another bed-and-breakfast in town, run by Polish immigrants. That looks similar to the house behind Cliffe, where he keeps the young women who come to work in the massage parlours. But Tracey's not been seen at any of these locations. CCTV shows him, but nowt else."

"You got a problem then," Mark blew out his cheeks. "Do you think he did it?"

Roy said, "That's what we were just discussing. He had the motive and opportunity. Not just for Tracey, but also the cold case victim, Bianca. I want to see what Tracey's phone data shows."

"Even if the phone data shows contact, or threats, that doesn't mean a murder charge will stick," Mark said.

"Yes," Roy sighed. "It boils down to evidence, I know. The problem is we have to let him go by tonight, unless we charge him. He's not done anything illegal, nothing that we got him

239

for, anyway. His lawyers will say his criminal past is behind him."

Sarah said, "What about the skinhead goons who turned up at the hospital? We can bring them in."

"And they'll say they were his mates, that's all." Roy felt dejected. "I can't see an option other than letting him go."

Another knock on the door, and Melanie entered. "Debbie McPherson's solicitor's signed her release forms. We've moved her to a safe house temporarily. I've told her to stay put, and not go out much."

"Good. We might need to bring her back for questioning."

Roy looked at Mark. "It seems we might not be able to build a case against Kevin, after all. I'll speak to Dobson to see if he got anything from Kevin's house and car that connects to Tracey. If not, we might have to let him go later tonight."

Sarah's radio crackled, and she answered. It was Rizwan. "Reporting from Damien Russell's gaff. Do you copy?"

"Go ahead Riz."

Sarah listened, and her eyebrows hiked north. "Bloody hell," she said softly.

CHAPTER 44

D ebbie McPherson jerked her head behind as she walked. She had heard the footsteps. A man was walking up to her rapidly. Debbie gasped and shrank against the wall. The man have her a quizzical look, then walked just as quickly past her. He didn't look back, but Debbie didn't relax til he turned the corner and vanished from view. This neighbourhood was quiet, and new to her. Debbie looked around fearfully. The mute, suburban houses stood still in the sunlight, the windows reflecting shard of light in her ears. A woman came out of the front door and arranged some flowerpots in her garden. She didn't glance in Debbie's direction. Debbie didn't relax til the woman went back in.

Then she pulled the baseball cap down lower and straightened. This area was called Ashstead, and it was on the outskirts of southwest Sheffield. Nothing like her area in Hillsborough. Proper posh this, with nice big semi-detached houses, lovely gardens, and clean streets. No burnt-out cars or tipped over bins here. No graffiti on the walls. For a second, she wondered what the posh people here would feel like if they knew she was living here, on the run from the Loxley Boys Gang. She could bring violence to their doorstep, and they were blissfully unaware. In another time, she might've been able to see the funny side.

But not now. Her spine shook, and she trembled as she took a few steps forward. She couldn't stay in that house anymore, with the FLO and a security guard. They might be the police, but Debbie didn't like the way the guard looked at her. She knew Kevin knew police officers. No one ran a criminal network like his without knowing senior cops. Yes, Kevin had told her that once. Sometimes Debbie had to wonder what sort of a mess she had got herself into.

She had ratted on Kevin. She didn't have a choice. She couldn't end up in jail, not with her children still at home. But was it the right decision? With shaky hands, she pulled out a packet of cigarettes and lit one.

Don't bite the hand that feeds you... The old proverb seemed to slap her across the face. Debbie cringed, then screwed her eyes shut. Why did that bitch Tracey have to kick up such a fuss? She thought she was tougher than Kevin? Really?

Remorse flooded in after the spike of anger. Tracey was dead, and... That just messed up everything. She couldn't help thinking Kevin had done it, given what he had at stake. Had Kevin also killed Bianca, all those years ago? Debbie had been new to the business then, and Karen had taken her under her wing. Introduced her to Kevin, and Debbie's so-called career as the modern age madam of the massage parlours had flourished. All she had to do was collect money from the punters and keep the girls in line. That wasn't a problem.

Debbie got to the crossing and looked over. It was a bigger road, but not busy, with hardly any cars. She crossed it easily, then went through a wooden gate in a fence that was the boundary of a park area. She sat down on a bench and lit another cigarette. She recalled what the female detective had told her. Sarah something, her name was.

Sarah said, there was a chance a killer was loose on the streets, searching for single mother sex workers. That made her shudder. It also made her sick to think it might've been Kevin, right from the start. Was that even possible? What about Karen, how could she not have known? Kevin was her partner for crying out loud.

Debbie took out the burner phone the FLO had given her. She'd spoken to her husband, Dan, already. Dan would take the boys and live with his mother in Armthorpe for a while.

She took out the handwritten list of numbers she had copied from her phone. Her old phone was still with the police. They wanted to keep it for now. Debbie traced a finger down till she got to Heather's number. Heather was her cousin. She worked in one of the parlours that Debbie had looked after.

"Who's this?" Heather's voice was hesitant.

"It's me, Debbie. Are you okay?"

"Debbie! Bloody hell am I glad to hear from you. What's going on? I heard a girl from the Cliffe died, and then you were taken by the cops. Is that right?"

"Yes," Debbie took a deep drag on her cigarette. Her voice shook despite trying to control it. "Listen love, you got to stop working for a while. There's a nutter out there, who's pickin' out women like you. Single mothers who do this shite."

Heather was silent for a while. "Eh? What you on about?"

"Just listen to me will yer? Don't go to them massage parlours anymore. The police think the sick bastard who killed Tracey might be out for others like her."

Silence followed, and Heather was thinking about it. "I ain't got no job right now," Heather said quietly.

"Then ask your mum for some money. She must have summat."

"No, I can't. She's skint as well. I need the dosh."

Debbie's feet stopped moving. "You're not back on the skag, are yer? Not using again?"

Heather had a history of taking heroin, and she used to inject in the past. After her son arrived, she had kicked the habit, but Debbie knew these terrible habits had a way of coming back.

There was a slight pause, and that told Debbie everything. "No, course I'm not." Heather sounded defensive. "I'm clean, aren't I?"

"Heather, just listen to me. Whatever you're doin', just stop for a while. The streets aren't safe. The massage parlours aren't either."

"I've got to go, Debs. You look after yourself, alright?"

Heather hung up.

Debbie held the phone against her forehead, breathing heavily. She rang another number, but there was no response. The third number worked.

"Hello?"

"Luke?"

"Aye. Who be this, like?"

"It's me, Debbie. Listen, we need to talk."

CHAPTER 45

Sarah was driving with the siren on, weaving in and out of traffic. As she approached Loxley, she cut the siren. There was no point in warning Luke Hammond of their arrival. A patrolling squad car had seen Luke come out of the betting shop. He had gone into the pub and was still inside.

"You sure of this, guv?" Sarah asked Roy without looking in his direction. She was gripping the steering wheel, sitting forward, eyes on the road. She took a sharp right to swerve past a lorry, then floored the gas as she overtook another car.

Roy wobbled in the seat, and put his phone down, unable to focus. Anna had just sent a message to say she was fine and was doing some window shopping post lunch. He swore as his head banged against the side.

"What's the rush?" He grumbled.

"Luke works for Kevin, you said. We need to grab him before it's too late."

"Yes, we do. I doubt that a layabout like him will go anywhere from the pub. He's made some money betting, now he wants to spend it." He turned on his radio and spoke into it.

"DCI Roy to base. Request backup for the Swan pub in Loxley."
Static crackled on the microphone, then a voice came on.

"All units on duty, sir. Will keep trying."

Roy hung up and put the radio back in his breast pocket. Their black Ford titanium was an unmarked car, fitted with all the mod cons, and invisible paint on the top that showed up on infra-red imaging from a helicopter above. But on the road, they were just a couple driving a normal vehicle. Sarah slowed down as she went through the grime and graffiti ridden streets of Loxley. She went past the pub and parked not too far away, as they might have to drag Luke in.

"You take the back," Roy said. "Let me know if he does a runner."

The rear exit was in the car park. Sarah found a spot for herself under a tree. A council apartment block reared its ugly head on either side. The walls had the ubiquitous graffiti. She couldn't see behind the wall. Roy found a rubbish bin and held it firm while she clambered on top. Over the wall, she could see a wooded area, falling down a slope into a canal. There was a towpath by the water, deserted now. Roy helped her back down.

"Taser him if he charges at you," Roy said. "But hopefully I'll get him first." He eyed the pub, which fitted in perfectly with the surroundings. The window frames were rotting, and damp spread on the walls. The back door was shut currently, a 'Do Not Enter' sign painted in red on it.

"This is a drinking hole for the Loxley Hill gang, guv," Sarah warned as she walked with him. "Be careful."

"We've gone past that now," Roy said.

With Sarah, he ducked in under the awning of the front entrance and stepped inside the pub. It was dim inside, despite the several windows letting in light. It took him a few seconds to realise why. The windows were shaded up to halfway height, not allowing easy visuals from outside. Despite the early afternoon hour, the place was reasonably full. Several heads turned to look at him.

Roy stood with thumbs hooked into his belt. As he scanned the punters, Sarah went up ahead, searching the tables. Roy returned the looks from several eyes. A big, bearded and tattooed man with a shaven head locked eyes with him. Roy recognised him from the hospital. One of Kevin's skinhead friends. He walked over, which the man didn't like. He put the pint glass down from his lips and looked hesitantly at his friends.

A wide-shouldered bloke who looked like he could carry a truck on his back glared at Roy as he approached.

"You lot are Kevin's friends, aren't you? I'm DCI Roy, the man who arrested him."

He got a sullen silence in reply, and it was deathly quiet in the whole pub now.

"I'm looking for a man called Luke Hammond. He lives around here, and drinks in this pub. Anyone know him?"

The four men sat at the table either glared at him or looked down at their drinks. Roy turned around, noting the bartender was staring at him behind the counter, and so were the men at the other tables. Roy spread his hands. He couldn't see Sarah, who had gone around the corner.

He spread his hands. "Anyone? We know he's here, so if you've seen him, do the right thing and tell me."

A woman with gold hoop earring so large they almost came down to her shoulders, stood. She was black, with red, green, and yellow beads in her hair. Her eyes flashed at Roy.

"Man dem good for nuthin', you get me? Why the fuck should we know where man dem be?"

"He might be useless, I agree," Roy said. "But we do need to speak to him." He raised his voice. "You see, it's about a woman who died night before last in Attercliffe. She was Luke's son's mother. Now you know why you need to speak to him."

A chair was dragged across the stone floor, making a grating sound behind him. Roy glanced to see the big skinhead standing up. He was wide, but it had all gone to rolls of jelly in his chest. Soft flesh hung down from his once thick forearms.

"Yer the scallywag copper in the hospital. Keepin' our Kevin for no reason. Yer got some nerve, turnin' up here, asking for Luke."

"Popular around here, isn't he?" Roy reflected. He looked at the black woman, who had placed her hands on her waist. She wore tight blue jeans that ended at her ankles, and pink pumps on her feet. A loud pink top was stretched tight across her ample bosom. It had the picture of a tongue hanging out between two red lips.

"But I sense a conflict of opinions," Roy said. "You don't like him much," he addressed the woman, "And I'd like to know why."

"Man dem not here, bruv!" the woman screeched. She kissed the inside of her cheek in a long drawn out sound like a wrapper tearing. "You not heard what I said?"

Roy was about to speak, when he heard a crash from the rear, followed by a shout.

"Stop. Guv!" It was Sarah.

Instantly, he charged down the floor, and a man stood up from his seat, blocking him. He spread his arms wide.

"Time you left mate, nowt goin' on—"

Roy didn't hesitate as he got within touching distance. He grabbed the man's collar, and headbutted him with savage force.

He heard the crunch of the nose bone, and the man howled in pain. Roy shoved him away, and he fell, covering his face in his hands. He fell against one of his friends, who also lost balance, and his pint glass, which smashed on the floor.

Roy jumped over the mess. To his right, he could see the back door, and it was now open. He caught a flash of movement, and a lanky man in a yellow string vest ran down the rear car park. Sarah was in hot pursuit. A shadow loomed to Roy's left, and another pair of arms reached out for him. A force crashed into his side, reeling him towards the bar counter. Roy fell against a set of bar stools that were empty, but he managed to twist and slide on the floor as he fell. He was up before his attacker, flicking out his baton as he did so. The man snarled and spat, and came for him again, but Roy was now behind him. He hit the man hard with the rubber baton, the resulting whip crack echoing around the pub. The man held his head and howled.

Roy turned on his heels and ran. The man in the ludicrous string vest was trying to scale the wall, and Sarah was holding on to one of his legs. Roy grabbed his waist and pulled him down. The man resisted, but it wasn't much use. They put him face down on the floor, and Sarah handcuffed him.

"Luke Hammond, you are under arrest," Sarah painted. She read him his rights.

"Nice to meet you, Luke," Roy said, wiping sweat from his forehead. "Let's go back to the nick and have a chat, shall we?"

He looked up and saw a group of the hooligan punters had appeared at the back door. They were in a fighting mood. One of them had a baseball bat in his hand.

Making sure that Luke wasn't going anywhere Roy got to his feet. With purpose, he walked towards the group. He could hear Sarah calling for back up on the radio. More men appeared behind them, and they walked out, snarling and spitting. Roy stopped when he was close.

"Luke Hammond is under arrest for suspicion of murdering Tracey Bennett. An innocent girl who was stabbed on the streets and left to die. You wouldn't like it if that was your girl, would you?"

Roy pointed a finger at the man he had seen inside. "What do you think?"

The question appeared to have taken the group by surprise. The angry, red-faced mob remained, but Roy had their attention.

"I didn't think so," he said. "And if Luke knows who did it, or he did it himself, then he should face the consequences. Now, we got riot police on the way. This place will get shut down in minutes, and you'll all be under arrest. Or you can let us leave quietly." Roy spread his feet apart and stood his ground. "What will it be?"

The bullish men looked at each other. A couple scratched their foreheads, and their beer bellies. Their earlier bravado was evaporating. They grumbled, and cursed, and started going back inside.

Roy called out to one of them. "The two chaps inside, who tried to stop me. Can you please ask them to come out? I'm calling them an ambulance."

He heard some mutterings of confirmation, and then Sarah and him were alone with Luke. He heard the sound of sirens in the distance, and they got louder. He jogged over to where Sarah had put Luke sitting upright against the wall. He stared at Luke's blonde dreadlocks, snot-nosed, snivelling pale face, and the dirty string vest. The smell of stale sweat, and cannabis was coming off Luke in waves. His hooded eyelids lifted, and he glared at Roy.

"Jesus Christ. Bob Marley's turning over in his grave, mate. I can see your nipples through that thing."

Sarah averted her face to hide her laughter. Luke didn't see the funny side of it. "Piss aff!"

As a young, uniformed policeman, Roy had sharpened his teeth on the streets of Brixton in south London, where there was a large Caribbean population. He had a lot of respect for those Islanders who made their home here.

Roy sat down on his haunches. "You a Rasta man?"

Luke made a sound in his throat like he was hacking up phlegm, then he spat on the floor. "Feckin' pig."

"Charming. Alright, then. Why did you run, Luke?"

"I was jes' goin' home. No' that's any of your bother, like."

"You had to run off in order to get home. Besides, home is in the opposite direction, right?" Roy looked at Sarah for guidance, and she nodded, then pointed towards the road, down where she had seen Luke yesterday.

"Gae feck yerself," Luke growled. "I was mindin' me own business till you turned up."

Sirens shrieked nearby, splitting the air, then stopped abruptly. Sarah raising her hand and waving at the SYP riot van that trundled up, was the reason. An ambulance had also arrived. Roy watched as the paramedics went inside the pub, directed by Sarah.

"The cavalry's arrived, Rasta man Luke," Roy said. "You've got a couple of minutes before we take you in. I'm offering you a chance."

"Ye call this offerin' me chance? Yer doolally!"

Roy was sat close to Luke, and together, they watched the uniforms and paramedics go in and out of the pub.

"You introduced Tracey to Kevin, we know that. Tracey starts working in the brothels. She finds out about the cameras that Kevin uses to spy on the customers. Or maybe you told Tracey about them. She starts to blackmail Kevin. How am I doing so far?"

Luke's jaw was set in a hard line, and he started to his feet. Sweat trickled down his forehead. Sarah approached with a uniformed sergeant, but Roy raised his hand, and exchanged a silent look with Sarah. She understood and moved away.

"We have witnesses and evidence, Luke. Kevin drank at this pub, right? You used to meet him here. Is this where he met Tracey, too?"

Roy wanted to ask what sort of man pimped out his son's mother, but for now, he kept that to himself.

"I know you worked for Kevin and the Loxley Hill Gang. Were you trying to move up the chain? Was Tracey helping you?"

Luke grimaced, then stiffened, his eyes still averted. Roy sensed a change in his posture. His hands were clenched into fists, and his breaths came shorter.

"Maybe you got rid of Tracey and told Kevin he doesn't have to worry. You become Kevin's right hand man."

"Yer feckin' off yer tits," Luke muttered, but his voice lacked the earlier venom.

"Or your ambitions were higher. You wanted to get rid of Kevin. Tracey agreed to help you."

Roy looked at Luke closely, but he turned away. His spine was taut, and a tension rippled across his cheeks.

"Go on, Luke. Tell us what really happened."

"Piss aff, will yer?"

"Who killed Tracey?"

Luke's head snapped in Roy's direction. A fire flashed from beneath his hooded eyelids.

"I donnae know! I told yer that already."

Roy tried a new track. "Damien Russell. The man who was obsessed with Tracey and followed her around. Did you know him?"

Luke was quiet again, ignoring him. Roy knew he had something here. Luke knew Damien, or at least, knew about him. He repeated the question.

"Feck off," came the reply.

Sarah approached with hurried steps. Her cheeks were mottling crimson, and there was a worried look on her face. She spoke on the radio, then focused on Roy. He stood and moved out of Luke's earshot.

"New victim," Sarah said, her eyes tinged with tension. "Same MO. IC1 young female, found on the canal bank near Victoria Quays just now."

CHAPTER 46

R oy pondered his informal chat with Luke as Sarah drove. She had the siren on for the second time this morning and whizzed in and out of traffic. It was close to 3 pm, primary school home time, and the roads to Sheffield central were clogged.

"He knew Damien," Roy muttered, almost to himself.

"Who?" Sarah glanced at him. "No woman no cry?"

Roy smiled despite the latest bad news. "Yes, our Rasta man." He pressed his lips together, thoughts tumbling over one another. "Damien Russell has a connection with Kevin and the Loxley Hill boys. He might be a part of their organisation, or a link to other OCNs."

"You think so?"

"Only guessing. But Damien was deep in with Tracey, that much is obvious from what the lads said. If she was staying over at Damien's place, and he went to see her Cliffe Massage Parlour, they were seeing each other, and also had issues to sort out."

"Luke might give up Damien," Roy continued. "We need to get

that out of him."

"We should ask Debbie and Kevin as well. I doubt Kevin will respond through his lawyer, but Debbie might know."

"Good thinking. Debbie's okay in the safe house?"

Sarah nodded. "Last I heard she was fine. Went out for a walk, but now back."

Sarah arrived at the crime scene, finally. It was at the end of a busy main road in Attercliffe, with a path that sloped down to the canals. The path lay between rows of terraced houses.

Roy got out and stretched. His phone beeped and he took it out to check if Anna wanted to be picked up. He couldn't go, but he could send her a cab. His teeth ground together when he saw the text. It contained a single photo of a gold chain that he knew only too well. He had an exact replica on his neck, and he never took it off. This one though, belonged to Robin.

The inevitable message followed.

He was wearing it when he disappeared.

Roy snarled at the phone, then shoved it back in his pocket. It would have to wait. He grabbed hold of Sarah, who had walked up ahead.

"Listen. That man who watched Matt and me at your house. Any feedback from the door to door?"

"The only thing we have is from the neighbour opposite. No other sightings. I followed it up before we left actually, forgot to tell you." She arched an eyebrow at him, a pensive look on her face. "Why?"

"Just curious. All okay at home?"

"Yes, fine. Mum's with Matt after school, obviously. And John's coming tonight." The sudden anxiety on her face told Roy everything.

"Is Matt okay with it? You must've talked about it."

"Yes, we did last night, for a while. He had lots of questions, the poor lad. We'll see how it goes."

"Yes, take it easy. In some ways, it's good that he wants to come back into his life. As long as he's a good influence on him, that's fine."

"Better bloody be," Sarah said darkly. "Or I'll do his guts for garters."

Roy nodded. His mind was on why he was getting the text now. He looked around, trying to spot anything of interest. Some bystanders had arrived by the blue and white tape, fluttering in the breeze. They were speaking to one of the uniformed constables. Roy watched them closely. No one looked at him or looked away suddenly. A few faces had appeared on the house windows, and a couple of women stood outside a door, talking.

Down the path, he could see two men changing into blue Tyvek coats. Justin and his men had arrived. But nowhere could he see anyone observing him. Hair stood up on the back of his neck. He had missed the bastard at Sarah's house. He wouldn't miss him again. If this guy knew where Robin was... He better watch himself.

Roy walked towards the crime scene, stopping to sign his name on the clipboard held out by a uniform constable. With Sarah, he put on shoe coverings and snapped on gloves. As they walked down the slope, the black waters of the canal rustled gently against the banks. There was a footbridge overhead, and two uniforms stood on guard, facing away from the crime scene, and redirecting pedestrian traffic.

Roy looked up at the bridge, and the gaggle of people trying to take a look after they'd walked past the uniforms. He clicked his fingers towards a constable who was standing around, looking despondent.

"Hey you. Yes, you. Come here."

The man seemed to recognise Roy. He stopped slouching and came over hurriedly. "In most ritual murders, the killers come back to watch the scene. Do you understand?"

"Yes… Yes, guv." The man licked dry lips.

"See up there," Roy pointed at the inquisitive onlookers on the bridge. "I want that bridge to be closed down to all pedestrians. Put up a sign if you have to. Who's your boss today?"

"Inspector Adams, sir."

"Tell Jonty that DCI Roy requests this to be done. And do it now."

"Yes, guv."

The man turned and practically ran up the slope. Roy joined Sarah, who was chatting to a uniform by the water's edge. Further to her right, the actual crime scene was within the tall grass that covered the land next to the tow path. Trees grew as well, shielding the houses from the canal. A brick fence ran along the edge of the houses.

The killer had hidden the body. Sarah came up to him. "A jogger reported the crime. He's still here. Do you want to have a word?"

Roy nodded, and they went up to the man. He was sat by the towpath, in red and blue tight Lycra cycling gear. Despite the nice weather, he was shivering. He had a light blonde beard, and his eyes were staring at the dark waters of the canal, like he could see something awful there.

Sarah sat down next to him, and Roy stood discreetly to one side, but withing earshot.

"My name is Detective Inspector Botham," Sarah said. "Thank you for waiting. What's your name?"

"Paul Rivett."

"Tell me what you saw, Paul."

"I was cycling down the path like I sometimes do. I have to go slow as there can be people on it as well. I saw two foxes, pulling at something. And then I saw a hand, an arm sticking out of the bushes…" Paul stopped speaking and his eyes widened with shock, and his hands became claws.

"I'm sorry you had to see that, Paul. It's okay, take your time."

"I stopped, because then I saw the body. It was a woman… She was clearly dead. I chased the foxes away. It was horrible."

"Was there anyone else on the path at the time?" Sarah looked at her phone. "You saw the body at 2 pm, according to your statement."

Paul nodded. "Yes. Just after 2 pm. I had a day off, and the sun was out so I came out for a cycle. No, I didn't see anyone else. There's not that many people on this path, it's a long way to the main road."

Roy heard heels coming down the path. It was the pathologist, Dr Sheila Patel. She nodded curtly at Roy, then walked over to where the white tent was now erected.

"I called 999, then spoke to your people," Paul said. He lapsed into silence. Sarah looked at Roy and he nodded. Paul was harmless, and he wasn't acting.

Sarah made sure she had Paul's details, then she let him go. They walked past the now fully erected white tent. A houseboat sailed down the canal. A man stood on the deck, watching inquisitively.

"I wonder if there was a boat last night, at the time of the murder," Sarah said. "Or anyone on the bridge."

"I can't see any lights anywhere," Roy said. "No streetlamps. No cameras either. This place must be deserted at night. Not safe."

"Nope. It's known for drug dealing. Most sex workers don't come here anymore though. It's safer for them to go to a massage parlour, or hotel. Couple of muggings here, in the last four months. People avoid it.

"And yet, this girl came down here. I wonder why. Was it to meet someone? Or was she with another person?"

Sarah said, "Let's see what Sheila found."

They got changed into aprons and masks before they went inside the tent. Roy snapped on shoe covers, then followed Sarah inside. Dobson was arranging a camera on the tripod, and Sheila Patel was looking at a rectal probe thermometer that she had just pulled out.

The body lay twisted in the same manner as Tracey's. The head was turned to the right, and the blonde hair formed a halo around. Her eyes were wide and staring. She was young, no more than mid-twenties. She wore a black dress that was ripped at the shoulders, and there was a gash in the abdomen, with dark blood staining it. She had several precise, small cuts at the sides of the neck, where the main arteries lay, and on the elbows, and ankles.

Roy noticed the needle track marks on the forearms. They looked fresher than on Tracey, but not recent. Her feet were bare, legs bent at the knee. She lay on her back with the head turned to the right.

"Cometh the hour, cometh the detectives," Dobson said. "Fashionably late, is it?"

"Keep taking pretty pictures Justin. Better than what comes out of your mouth," Roy said.

"You mean the valuable forensic evidence that helps you solve the cases?"

"Speaking of which," Roy said. "Have you got anything else on the first victim?"

"Aye," Dobson said, grinning. "I sent you an email before I came here."

"Better late than never. You have your uses."

Dr Patel shuffled around, putting the long rectal thermometer probe back into its sterile cap. "Will you two stop messing around?" Her nose and mouth were pinched together, and she looked like an angry schoolteacher. Her charcoal grey suit dress, neatly coiffured short black hair, and grey shoes went well with that image.

Roy pointed at Dobson. "It wasn't me. He started it."

Dobson spread his hands and looked suitably aggrieved. "I just asked a question."

"Like a pair of schoolkids." Sarah shook her head. "Ignore them, Sheila. Any idea of time of death?"

Dr Patel shot a glare at Roy, to which he smiled affably. "Around midnight, I'd say. It's almost 4 pm now, I'd say about sixteen hours ago. Rigor mortis is advanced in the bigger muscles. Skin colour is changing to waxy yellow of livor mortis. Close to midnight, or before one in the morning."

"So, between half-eleven and one in the morning?"

"Yes, I'd say so. I might be able to be more precise once I upload all the figures on the laptop."

"MO is the same as the victim from the night before?"

All of them looked at the body.

"Yes," Dr Patel said gravely. She went over to the head and crouched by it. She pointed at the neck.

"Bruise marks as you can see. He squeezed the neck, but not hard enough to break the trachea, which causes death from strangulation."

"Any prints?" Roy turned to Dobson. The head of SOC shook his head.

"No prints anywhere. Got a couple of boot prints. Should get the forensic gait analyst interested. I will see if the boot prints match the first crime scene."

Roy moved around, careful to keep his feet on the sterile duckboards. "Any blood drops? Torn pieces of jewellery?"

"If there was, he cleaned it," Justin said. "The place does look like it was scrubbed, and just the body left, like last time."

"I second that," Dr Patel said. "He wore gloves, and if there was any evidence on the ground, he cleared it. Plus, there's grass and shrubs around here, like the previous crime scene. We might get lucky though."

"That's me, Mr Lucky," Dobson piped up. "Once you guys have gone, my friend and I will scour the area. We might find something."

"You have a friend?" Roy raised his eyebrows. "Wonders will never cease. We're looking outside already, aren't we?" He glanced at Sarah, who nodded.

"Uniforms are doing a line search over the whole canal bank." She looked at Dr Patel. "Anything else?"

"No sign of sexual activity. Some bruising in the legs, but no lacerations. He did slice her in the abdomen – that looks like a jagged cut, done in a hurry. She probably fought back." The pathologist lifted one of the hands. "Look at the blood on the knuckles. She scraped them while trying to stop him. I'll find skin samples under her nails and should get some DNA from them."

"We need them soon," Roy said. "This is now a double-homicide, and we don't want it to become triple."

CHAPTER 47

Jayden had taken a break from work as he needed to buy a new padlock for his cycle. He had come into town, and walked quickly down the shortcut that was more like a food village, packed with cafés on both sides. It was a familiar haunt for most people who worked in Sheffield Central. It was a nice day, and Jayden was glad to be out. As he walked, he glanced at a café he knew well. His ex-girlfriend, Amy, used to work there. His heart saddened as he thought of Amy. She was a lovely, lively girl. A brunette who always wore a smile on her face. She came to get her tyres changed, and they hit it off almost immediately. But like every other woman he'd met, she soon found out his problems in the bedroom. His past abuse had left deep scars that might never heal. He was shy and awkward when it came to love-making. Amy had been more patient than any other. She had given him time, made him relax. It did work, and they had some good times together. But he would be kissing her, getting aroused, when suddenly the horrible memories of what Jerry did to him would come crashing back. The visions caught him unguarded, and his pleasure turned to ashes and pain. It was like a chainsaw ripped him in two, and he would fall back on the bed in a heap. Amy, like his other girlfriends, would ask him what it was – but it was impossible to say.

Gradually, Amy and him had drifted apart. It was a crying shame; she had been such a lovely person. He regretted not opening up to her, telling her everything. His shame lay on him like a tombstone, stopping him from uttering the truth.

As he walked past the café now, he tried to look inside, to see if Amy was still working there as a waitress. He couldn't see her. The café was packed, and people were sitting outside in tables. On an impulse, he wanted to go inside. If she was there, all good. If not, then well, he hadn't lost anything. He turned towards the café, then halted in his tracks.

His eyes zeroed in on a woman in her fifties, sipping tea and chatting to a teenage girl with long black hair. The woman was smaller than the girl, who seemed quite tall, even sitting down. Breath died down in Jayden's chest. His pulse roared in his ears, a booming pressure that blocked out all other sounds. He knew that woman.

It was Lydia, Jerry's girlfriend.

It had been years since he'd seen her, but he still remembered her face. Before Lydia looked up and caught him staring, Jayden turned and moved to one side. He retreated to a shop awning opposite, and stood under it, observing Lydia and the girl. Was that her daughter? No, the teenager was brown-skinned and looked like an Indian girl. They were deep in conversation. Lydia said something and the girl laughed. Jayden felt sick. A bad taste of bile was rising in the back of his throat. What the hell was Lydia doing here? And if she was here, where the hell was Jerry?

Breath rasping in his chest, Jayden looked around. His fists were clenched. The sunshine had suddenly turned to rust and rain. He took in the surrounding tables slowly. There was no sign of Jerry. He looked carefully at Lydia's left hand but couldn't see a ring. That didn't mean much. She could still be with Jerry; he had never been the marrying type.

Once, many years after he left that house in Leeds, Jayden had returned to see if Jerry still lived there. He did not, but the old neighbours were still there. A new family had moved into Jayden's old house. He didn't speak to anyone but left in silence. He had just wanted to see if Jerry would come back. He had looked up Jerry's name in the address books as well, and not found anything. Not in Leeds, or Sheffield. Not even in Manchester. In fact, Jayden had looked far and wide for Jerry Burns, but it seemed like he didn't exist.

Seeing Lydia here now was a jolt. But maybe he was getting ahead of himself. He had last seen Lydia almost a lifetime ago, and she was probably separate from Jerry. But an odd suspicion curdled in his guts. He recalled the strange way Lydia used to observe him. Then smile at him. It used to make him shudder. And here she was, with a teenage girl. Could this girl be in any danger? Did she know Lydia used to be Jerry's girlfriend? Probably not.

Jayden knew he was jumping to conclusions, but he had never trusted Lydia. Something told him he should watch out for this girl. He focused on her. She was beautiful, with that innocence of teenage years. Jayden watched them, then sat down at a café table opposite. He chose a seat inside, where he could see them, but they couldn't see him easily. He had a good half hour before he had to return to work.

After about ten minutes, Lydia and the girl finished their sandwiches, and left. Jayden paid hurriedly and followed. At the mouth of the alley, the girl said goodbye to Lydia. The girl stood there, like she was waiting for someone. Lydia crossed the road and went towards a car park. Jayden saw her get into a dark green Ford Focus and sit there. He could tell she was watching the girl, but the girl probably couldn't see her, engrossed as she was in her phone. Pretty soon, a car pulled up, and Jayden frowned as he saw the driver. He moved closer quickly for a better look. He was surprised when he recognised the man. It was that Inspector Roy he had met yesterday morning, by the white tent the police had erected, and where that woman had died.

The teenager, and Inspector Roy drove off. Jayden watched as Lydia drove her green car out of the car park and followed them.

CHAPTER 48

The nick was a whirlwind of activity. The two DCs and Melanie were busy working with the researchers, and Roy stayed with Sarah to prepare the multi-team briefing for later. Roy had filled Nugent in, and he would inform the Chief Constable.

Roy then went into town to pick up Anna. He didn't have time to drop her back home, but her friend Pearl was also in town, and would meet her at the police station, from where they would get a cab back to Dore. Leaving Anna in the reception area, Roy made his way back to the office.

"Sarah downstairs?" he asked Riz and Ollie, who were on the phone.

Ollie put his phone down. "Yes. Luke Hammond's got James Keenan as the solicitor." He rolled his eyes. "I know."

"Did Justin send an email with a forensic report?"

"Yes, and we also got the post-mortem report from Dr Patel. Riz and I went to see her at the morgue. Nothing new in the report, apart from recent sexual activity. DNA from the sperm didn't show any matches with Kevin. We haven't tried Luke's as yet.

There's another sample of DNA from under her nails. No match with that either."

"You guys got DNA samples from Damien Russell's house, correct?"

"Yes. There was a couple of pairs of boxers in the laundry basket he didn't take. As soon as DNA from those are available, I'll send it to Dr Patel."

"Bloody hell, Ollie. I think a compliment is in order."

"Sometimes I try, guv." Ollie grinned.

Rizwan came off the phone and got their attention.

"Debbie said she'd seen Damien Russell speak to Kevin at the massage parlour. On more than one occasion. I sent her Damien's photos. She's seen him around at the other parlour's as well. He hangs around Kevin. I called Kevin, but he's not answering.

"And he won't without a lawyer." Roy stroked the stubble on his cheek. "Did Debbie say anything more about Damien? Why didn't she say this earlier? We showed his photos to her?"

"She said they were CCTV images from the supermarket so she couldn't be sure. Now that we have DL and passport photos, she's more confident."

Ollie shook his head. "This Debbie. There's more to her involvement in this than meets the eye."

"I think so too," Roy agreed. "Is she using the burner phone we gave her? In which case, are we tracking her calls?"

The two DCs looked at each other. Roy said, "Get on it, lads. Find out who she's been calling. Track them. I want a call list, positive identity, and triangulation data. You never know, she's probably in touch with Kevin, as well as Damien."

Riz had a knowing grin on his face. Roy frowned at him.

"What?"

"You said lads."

"Did I? I meant chaps. Or guys. Whatever. Not lads."

"I think you're becoming northern, boss."

"Me? Never."

"I'll start tracking Debbie's calls," Riz said. "Anything else?"

Roy put both hands on the chair, making it creak alarmingly, but it still took his weight. "There's clearly a ring here. Kevin, Tracey, Luke, Damien, and Debbie. You're right, Debbie knows more about Damien then she's letting on. She must've known who he was from the beginning. She's afraid of Kevin, and what he could do to her family, hence she kept schtum."

Roy was thinking aloud. "Tracey must've found out something critical. But the new victim… That doesn't make any sense. Kevin was in custody then. So was Debbie. Only Damien and Luke were free."

He looked up at the DCs, who were hanging on every word he said. "Do we have a positive ID of the new victim?"

"Not yet, guv. HOLMES has nothing. Trying the Yorkshire Police image recognition software, but no hits so far. I don't think she has any contact with the police, home office, or border patrols."

"Have we asked in the brothels around the city? Sorry, *massage parlours*."

Again, the two DCs looked at each other, and more than a little embarrassed. Ollie coughed into a fist. "We were, uh, getting to that."

"First place I'd look at, to be honest. Given the nutter we have on our hands seems to be choosing sex workers who are single mothers, and ex-drug users."

Riz picked up the phone to do the honours. "Telling uniforms to start a door-to-door at the parlours, guv."

Roy left them to it and walked down the corridor. He was stopped by Nugent, who looked at him like he's just smelt something awful. Roy remained impassive.

"In my office," Nugent barked.

"Haven't got long, Sir. Suspect waiting downstairs."

"I know that."

They went into Nugent's office, and Roy shut the door. It stank of cigarette smoke as usual. Nugent didn't open the window and collapsed on his dog-eared brown leather armchair. His tabletop was a mess of files and papers.

"The Chief Constable's on my case. Is it the same guy?"

"Looks like it. Same MO. We have two suspects, one of them is downstairs. Kevin is still a suspect, though. He was there for the cold case as well. Bianca Wilkins. Bianca was found near Victoria Quays, close to our second victim." Roy sighed. "The pattern is clear, sir."

"But Kevin was in custody for the second victim so it can't be him."

"Hence, he's out for now. But Luke Hammond is a different story. So is Damien Russell."

"I need answers. And don't tread on any toes."

Roy levelled a gaze at Nugent. Eventually the Super relented. "I mean the NCA. If Kevin and the Loxley Boys have connections to the Wrexham Hill gang, and they're watched by the NCA—"

"Has the NCA been in touch?" Roy interrupted. Nugent shook his head.

"Not as yet. But I'm just letting you know."

"Thanks." Roy rose, nodded at Nugent, and left. As he walked out, he saw Sarah and Melanie on the corridor.

"I came up to see what's holding you up," Sarah said. "But Mel's got some news."

They walked over to the office. Ollie was absent, and Riz was speaking on the phone in a low voice.

Melanie said, "It's about the missing girl, Gemma Jackson. I went to see the family. The aunt still looks after the child. She didn't have a mother. Gemma didn't tell her aunt what she did for her night work, after she finished at Tesco. One of her friends knew. Gemma was out in a derelict building in Attercliffe, just after the Meadowhall roundabout."

"Good work," Roy said. "Six years ago, Gemma was last seen going home?"

"She came out of the station, and was walking towards Grimesthorpe, yes. There's no confirmation she reached home. Her aunt didn't see her that night. Maybe she shopped, but she wasn't carrying any bags. Then she went somewhere."

Riz had come off the phone and was listening to them quietly. They were all quiet for a while. Sarah asked, "Regarding where Gemma worked at night..."

Melanie pre-empted her. "Her friend didn't know. She was working the streets, which is dangerous of course, and she could get arrested. The friend's statement..." Mel clicked on the keyboard of her open laptop to retrieve the document. "It says she was thinking about joining a massage parlour. No names recorded."

Riz was looking intently at his screen. He raised his hand like a schoolboy. Sarah smiled at him.

"Go on then, our kid. You got summat?"

"It's about the cold case, Bianca Wilkins. Ollie got this from traffic, and he sent it to me. CCTV footage from the night Bianca died."

They gathered around Riz's desk. He played the video on his screen. It showed a young woman, identified as Bianca Wilkins, going down the steps of a path that led down to the canal path. The view changed, and it showed the street above. This time, a solitary man was walking on it. It was night, so his features were obscured. Riz zoomed in. It was a slim man, walking straight, head bent. He was walking quickly. He went down the stairs, the time stamp showed it was a minute after Bianca had walked down the same steps.

There was no CCTV on the canal path seven years ago, which was frustrating. Riz tried to zoom into the man's face, but the views were obscure.

"Is he wearing glasses?" Mel asked.

"Yes," Riz said. "That much we can make out, but nowt else."

Roy folded arms across his chest. "Do you have the CCTV from the supermarket that showed Damien Russell and Tracey arguing?"

"Yes guv."

"Bring that up and play it side-by-side. I want to see if Damien and this guy look similar."

"You had your Weetabix this morning." Sarah raised her eyebrows, her green eyes sparkling.

Roy tapped his forehead. "Nope, running on empty. Just on the ball, that's all."

Riz clicked several times on his keyboard, then pulled up the supermarket video, and played it side by side with the current CCTV.

Damien's similarity with the man from seven years ago was obvious. Riz played the footage, and they watched the man move. Riz slowed it down on the older CCTV, as there wasn't much of the man. But they had tracked him from the bus stop.

Sarah said, "Bus 47. That comes from the west, if I'm not mistaken."

"I think so, too," Riz said. He clicked on a bus route map and checked. "Bus comes from a place called Crookes. Goes all over the place like a bus does, but goes through the centre, then Kelham, and ends up in Meadowhall."

"Did traffic follow that bus?" Roy asked. "They must show where the man got on. Buses have CCTV."

Riz played the other files he had and got the images up again. The suspect had a yellow circle around his head on CCTV. He kept his head down, and the hood of his jacket was raised all through the bus journey. No visualisation of his head was possible.

Riz played the footage to the beginning of the bus journey. "He gets on the bus from Crookesthorpe. He walks to the stop, as you can see." They watched as the black and white image of the man appeared, strolling down the street. He joined others at the bus stop, but kept his hoodie on, and the glasses.

"He walked up here, and the streets before are in a CCTV black spot. Around Crookes, police put up posters and did a door-to-door, but no witnesses came forward."

"Where did Damien live then?"

"According to council tax records he was in Heeley, nears Meersbrook, that's down southwest. He didn't live around here."

Roy shook his head. "Bloody hell. Looks like the same guy. Can traffic superimpose his image and do their clever image recognition stuff. He's hiding his face, but his build and gait looks the same."

"Could still be a coincidence, guv," Mel warned. "There might be more people who match."

"Did I miss much?" Ollie sat as he came up to Riz's desk. He looked at the screen. "Ah yes. I got more CCTV from traffic, and it's good news. We got a visual on our victim from last night."

He lifted his chin, acting important. "So, who wants to see it? More importantly, what do I get?"

Riz folded arms across his chest and shook his head. Roy growled, "You'll get a clip across your ears if you don't hurry up."

Ollie rolled his eyes and opened up his laptop. The ensemble of detectives moved gracefully from Riz's desk to Ollie's. That involved Roy hitting his knee on the side of a desk and cursing loudly, then limping the last few steps. He stood at the back, muttering and rubbing his left knee.

With a flourish that was totally unnecessary, Ollie got the images from his email, then pressed play.

The black-and-white grainy image showed one of Attercliffe's streets. A man and a woman were walking, and the street was pretty much deserted, save a couple walking in the opposite direction to the high street. They were headed towards the canal. Ollie zoomed in. This time, traffic had enhanced the close-up images and attached them separately.

"The woman's definitely our victim." Sarah said.

"And the man also looks familiar," Melanie whispered. It was clear from the image who it was – Damien Russell.

CHAPTER 49

MIR 1 was full again. Roy opened the door to find all the chairs taken, and his team standing in front of the whiteboard, with photos of the two victims stuck onto it. The projector was humming softly in the ceiling, and a ray of light fell from it on the white screen opposite. The blinds were still open, they would have to be closed before he could do a presentation.

Roy took his position next to the whiteboard and took in the crowd. He recognised officers from North Yorkshire, and Derbyshire Police. The latter looked after the western half of the Peak District, while South Yorkshire did the honours for what was now a de facto part of Sheffield, the eastern Peak District. It was good to see so many of them here. Roy needed all hands on deck.

"Double homicide," Roy tapped the whiteboard. "You've not seen that for a while, I bet. Same MO. He's around here, folks, make no mistake. He's hiding in plain sight. You're all experienced officers, you know the profile by now. Malignant narcissistic personality disorder. What does that mean again?" The question was aimed at the junior staff.

A young DC from North Yorkshire Police, whose name Roy didn't know, raised a hand. "DC Andrew Sidebottom, guv. That means they think they are above ordinary human beings. They take pride in their crimes and like to show off."

"Indeed, Andrew. Our killer could well be someone the victims knew well. He's probably very charming, until he loses his temper. When he does, he can be vicious. In a way, that's good for us. That's when he makes mistakes. Blinds, please."

He looked at Oliver, who stood and frantically searched for the remote that operated the windows. He scrambled around the desktops, then the drawers. Finding none, he went over to the many windows, along with Riz. Together, the two DCs turned the blinds down, only to find several of the shutters wouldn't budge, and the room remained well-lit.

Oliver turned and scratched his head. Roy glared at both of them, tapping his feet.

"Sort it out, will you?"

"I was going to, but I had to take a call…" Oliver's voiced died out as he clocked the ferocious look on Roy's face.

"Well, do something," Roy whispered between clenched teeth. "We need to get a bloody move on."

In the end, Melanie came to the rescue. She came up to the whiteboard and moved past Roy to look at the shelf at the bottom of the board. She raised the remote, and her eyebrows. Roy sighed and laughter sprinkled across the room.

With a gentle whirr, all the electronic blinds turned down, casting the room into near darkness. Sarah clicked on the laptop and opened up the correct PowerPoint presentation. Roy peered at the laptop, wishing he had his reading glasses. With some difficulty, he could make out the slides. He started with the photo of Damien Russell.

"This man is our chief suspect now. He's been seen on CCTV

last night, with the second victim. The canal towpath has CCTV now, but unfortunately, where our victim died still remains a dark spot. It appears our killer knew that." Roy showed the CCTV footage on the screen.

The couple walked down the path, and then down the steps to the canal.

"We lose them after that. The man doesn't come back up, which means he escaped by another route." He showed the teams the magnified face, and then photos of Damien Russell from his passport and DL. The match was unmistakable, and whispers spread across the room.

"Mr Russell doesn't have any PCNs or a police record. However, he was close to the first victim, Tracey Bennett, who stayed at his house."

He showed a video of Damien Russell's house in Heeley. "He was last seen here in the early hours of this morning. He drives a two-seater black Audi, the same car seen by a witness from the night before. Traffic have traced his car, which was last seen going down a country lane down the A57, heading into the Peak District."

Roy changed the slide and played the CCTV image. A black Audi was streaking down a dual carriageway, overtaking other cars. It took an exit, then vanished from view.

"That was a country lane that not many people use, and it doesn't have any CCTV. Uniforms are already in the area?" Roy looked at Sarah, who stood up and addressed the crowd.

"Three squad cars are setting up roadblocks and scouring the countryside. It's all farmland there, after a golf course. That exit he took actually backs up on the golf course. Might be worth asking in the golf club if anyone playing saw the car."

Several heads nodded, and many of the officers were scribbling notes. "We need to find this man," Roy said quietly. "He's going to strike again, and we have to stop him before he does."

CHAPTER 50

Luke Hammond had changed his string vest, Roy noted with huge relief. No more pink nipple poking through a yellow hole. He was wearing police issue blue scrubs. His beard and hair was still scruffy, like he'd just been running his hands through them on purpose. He stared at the desk with a bored look on his face. His feet were tapping, but they stopped when Sarah and Roy walked in. He looked at them with barely-disguised fury.

James Keenan, his solicitor, and barrister, *dual-qualified*, as he liked to proclaim, was the picture of pin-striped serenity in his blue suit. Like a dark swan who could transform into a snake with the click of a finger.

Sarah spoke into the machine. They had already decided Roy would handle the questions this time around. He took his time to arrange the laptop, and the paper folders, aware Luke was staring at him. Then he looked up and smiled. Luke bared his yellow teeth like a hyena in response.

"Good afternoon, Luke. Hope you don't mind if I call you that?"

"Nah."

"Could you please confirm the last time you saw Tracey Barrett?"

"We've been through this already. Come on, like."

"Can you answer the question please."

"She came last Sunday, in the late afternoon, to pick up me wee bairn. That's the last I saw of her."

"What did you talk about?"

Luke looked at Roy like he was speaking a foreign language. "Talk aboot? Talk aboot? What the feck do yer think we talked aboot, yer feckin' swine. The weather? The fitball match?"

Roy turned his lips. "The Celtics beat Rangers, didn't they? 2-1, it was. Must've broken some hearts in Glasgow."

"Or heads," Sarah said.

"That too," Roy agreed. "Maybe you were upset at the time. The fact is, you introduced Tracey to Kevin, and from there, she met Damien Russell as well. Is that correct?"

Luke went still, his eyes on Roy for seconds longer than needed, like he was trying to judge his words. Roy hoped he would get a better response than he did at the pub.

"Nae comment."

Roy showed no emotion, but his hopes were dashed. He wanted to be out there, with the uniforms, searching for Damien. He had no doubt now Damien had killed all three women. Killers like him slipped under the radar. It was typical that he didn't have a police record, but still hung around men like Kevin, and Luke.

He said, "So you didn't talk about how things were going at the Cliffe Massage Parlour? We've seen the diary – she was there quite frequently. She got into arguments with Kevin, and even more so with Damien. You must have felt bad, because you introduced her to Kevin. Isn't that what you chatted to her about?"

"Piss aff."

"Sorry, can't. Got to do the job you see. Did you know that Tracey was spending nights at Damien's house?"

Luke stilled for a second or two. Even his chest stopped moving. Then his Adam's Apple bobbed up and down a couple of times. Everyone picked up on it.

Sarah said, "More than once. She was there two to three nights every week. They had a row two days ago, in front of his house. We got it all on tape." By the last comment, Sarah meant that they had the old lady's statement on tape, but Luke didn't know that. He was trying to act unconcerned, but something had clearly changed in him. There was a tightness in his shoulders, and his hands moved under the table.

"We have a new victim. She was killed last night. Damien was seen with her on CCTV, walking her down to the canal. We found her body this morning."

Roy pressed his lips together, thinking. "Where were you last night between the hours of ten and midnight?"

"Ah went tae the pub. Ask aroond. And then ah came back tae the hoos."

"Did you go to Attercliffe last night?"

"Nah."

"So, you wouldn't know what Damien was doing with this woman last night?"

"Nah."

Luke was trying to hold it in, act cool, but the strain was showing. His lips moved, and his jaws ground together.

"Where's Damien now, Luke?"

"Ah dinnae ken," he whispered.

"No, you do know," Roy said, holding Luke's eyes. "You met Kevin in the pub, and also Damien. The pub that we arrested you from. Half the Loxley Hill Boys were there. Don't lie to us anymore. Do you want another baby to lose their mother?"

"Wis yer talkin' aboot? Bairns lose their mother?"

"The women who have died recently were single mothers. The killer is choosing them. And that killer could well be your mate, Damien."

"Yer talkin' rubbish!"

"Am I? Damien was fixated on Tracey, and she turned up dead. Last night, Damien was seen with the latest victim, just before she died." Luke's eyes were roving, and Roy leaned forward to get his attention. "Where is Damien, Luke?"

"Ah dinnae ken! I told yer!"

"Tell us how long you've known Damien for. As long as Kevin?"

"Nae comment."

James Keenan extended a pin-striped arm. "DCI Roy, I think my client has answered enough questions about Damien. It's quite clear he doesn't know this person."

"Tracey was sleeping with Damien, and you had no idea." Roy shook his head. He ignored Keenan. He remained focused on Luke, and his words had an effect. Luke folded arms across his chest and looked to the floor.

"Damien probably killed the mother of your child, Luke. But maybe that doesn't bother you, given that you pimped her out anyway."

His barb had the intended effect. Luke breathed heavily, his upper lip contorting into a grimace. Roy settled back on his chair.

"We'll find him. Sooner rather than later." Roy reached out and tapped a finger on the desk. "He won't hide for long. We'll get him without your help. But you could've helped yourself a lot by helping us. Right now, we have good grounds to charge you for accomplice to murder."

Luke looked like he'd been shot. Roy said, "You knew Damien and Kevin, and that's how Tracey met them. You could easily have told Damien where Tracey would be night before last. A charge like that won't look good to your parole officer. Shame, that."

Sarah said, "You won't get out early this time, Luke. The judge will take a harsh view. No one likes a man who does that to his own son's mother."

"Especially not in prison," Roy said. "Let's hope you're in a secure wing."

Luke's swallowed hard, and his normally hooded eyes were wide and staring. He looked at Keenan, who was focused on Roy.

"Enough of this, Inspector," Keenan said quietly. "Either you charge my client or let him go."

Sarah's radio beeped, and she checked it, then excused herself. Roy spoke on the machine and took a break as well. He joined Sarah in the corridor. She was on the phone, nodding her head as she listened. Then she hung up.

"The basement in Luke's house is stashed full of bags of fertiliser. Inside, there's packets of white powder. There's like ten kilos of cocaine in there."

Roy said, "That's why he ran."

"He didn't kill Tracey. We know that much. And last night if he was in the pub, we can get CCTV or ask witnesses."

"He practically lives there," Roy snorted.

Sarah shrugged. "He's not getting out now, anyway."

"Yes, about that."

Roy narrowed his eyes at her, and she looked at him quizzically.

CHAPTER 51

Luke was fidgeting in his chair, and even Keenan was looking less than his usual polished and suave self. Sarah spoke into the machine, announcing their arrival.

"My client has the right to discharge himself from custody, DCI Roy," Keenan said, as soon as Sarah finished. "You have nothing to charge him with."

"Apart from possession of narcotics with the intention to distribute," Roy said. He glanced at Luke, who was turning a shade greener than the lime green lino floor.

"More than ten keys in your basement, Luke," Roy said. Where did you get that from?" Keys was the usual slang for a kilo of cocaine.

Keenan was looking at Luke intently. Roy said, "It's in your basement, pal. You better come clean. Is this Kevin's stash that you're holding for him? Is that why you did a runner when we came to question you?"

"Nae comment."

"I'm afraid that's not going to wash, Luke. We now have evidence to put you in for a long time. Your silence only makes you look more guilty."

Luke's gaze faltered, but Roy knew he had him now. He went for the kill. "Think about your son. Do you really want to do another five years for possession? Cooperate with us and you'll be out in two, even less."

Luke had a hunted look on his face – eyes sunken, staring into nothingness.

Sarah said, "Is this worth it, Luke? We know you're storing Kevin's stash. Why are you protecting him?"

Luke bowed his head and wouldn't look at them. Sarah said, "We can offer you protection. Your son will also be safe. Talk to us, Luke."

Luke raised his hollow, gaunt face, and stared at them like they were a million miles away.

"Nae comment."

Luke's head bent down to inspect an invisible point on the floor again and Roy examined him closely. The Rasta man's shoulders were slumped. He knew he was going in, and doing time, but he wouldn't give up his friends. That would earn him street respect – criminals were always more trusted after they'd done some time. But prison was nothing new to Luke. There was something more here. Luke was scared stiff. This was more than the drugs they found.

Roy said, "Did they kill Tracey for this as well, Luke? Is that why you're worried."

Luke wheezed slowly and shrank back in his chair. "Look at me," Roy commanded. Luke would not. He swung his head around like a trapped animal, nostrils flaring.

"I got nothin' more to say. I'm done here."

Roy went to speak but Keenan raised a hand. "That's enough, Inspector. My client has told you what he knows. He needs some time to rest."

*****

Sarah and Roy came upstairs to find the office empty apart from Melanie. She rose from her desk.

"You two look like you could do with a cup of tea."

"Thanks, Mel. Make mine a double," Roy said. "By that I mean two tea bags."

"Got it, guv. But be careful you don't get kidney stones."

Roy's forehead creased. "Drinking tea give you kidney stones? That's a first."

"If drunk in excess, apparently. That's my doctor says."

Roy grimaced. "Maybe that's what my back pains are."

Sarah shook her head. "Nope. You're just getting old."

"I'm maturing slowly like a fine wine. Good vintage, that's what I am." Roy sat down on a chair and stretched his knees, which clicked loudly. "See? All in good working order."

"In good sitting order, you mean," Sarah grinned. "Would be nice to see you in the Forces Half-Marathon this year, guv. It's in the Peak District. You'll love it."

Roy frowned at the two women who clearly thought this was rather funny. "Think I can't do a half-marathon? I've run ten miles in the past, without stopping, I'll have you know."

"Ten miles? Were you chasing burglars on foot down in London?"

"Yes, too much traffic. Keeps me fit," Roy muttered. Sarah sat down at her desk while Mel went to get the tea.

"Do we have a positive ID for the latest victim?" Roy asked.

"I believe that's what the lads are doing now. They joined the

286

door-to-door with the uniforms."

"And any news from uniforms of Damien, or his car?"

Sarah shook her head, then concentrated on reading something on her laptop. Roy pulled out his phone and called Anna. She was at home, and Pearl had just left. Roy said he would be back soon. He stood, and gathered his radio and stuck it on the belt. He also grabbed the baton from his desk drawer. Then he shrugged into his coat. Sarah looked at him inquisitively.

"Going somewhere?"

"To find Damien Russell," he said. "Tell Mel the tea will have to wait. Uniforms will need a hand before dark."

Sarah stood. "I'm coming with you."

"Isn't your boy's father coming tonight?"

"Yes." Sarah looked unsure of herself, which was unusual. Her normally direct sea green eyes were cloudy, and her shoulders a touch limp.

"It's a big evening for Matty. You need to go home."

Sarah shook her head. "No, guv, I—"

"You need to make sure you son is alright," Roy said firmly. "You'll regret not being there if something happens and you get stuck. Is Clare with Matt now?"

Sarah nodded. Then she sighed. "I guess you're right, guv."

"Good luck," Roy softened his voice. "It's going to be fine, don't worry."

CHAPTER 52

Y ou alright?" Sarah asked Matt, who was fidgeting nervously on the couch. He'd had his dinner but had left his plate half-full. She knew he was anxious.

"Yes," Matt nodded. Sarah sat down next to him and gave him a hug. "It's going to be alright, okay? I'll be here all the time. If you don't want to speak to him, or you want him to go, just tell me."

Matt looked down and nodded again. Sarah wondered if she was doing the right thing. She had met with John once again, and they had talked. He wanted to know what Matt liked – his sports, hobbies, favourite food. He had written everything down. Matt was a Liverpool fan, and he liked his toy cars. John seemed genuinely interested in Matt, and he wanted to be close to his son, as he said. He was now settled in Sheffield, had a good job in the construction company, and wanted to atone for his former absence. Sarah was cautiously allowing him. He still had to earn her trust fully.

"Mummy," Matt said, getting Sarah's attention. "How old was when he, I mean Dad, left?" The poor lad sounded so unsure when he said the word 'Dad' it broke Sarah's heart. She rubbed his back.

"You were two." She smiled.

"And he never came back?"

They had been through this before, and Sarah wondered why Matt was asking again.

"He did, but he didn't stay. And he stayed in touch, but then I didn't hear from him." She chose her words carefully, aware the eleven-year-old was listening with close attention. She was repeating what she had told him before, and she understood he probably wanted to get the facts right again, seeking some reassurance.

"He was working abroad. In Dubai. He came back sometimes, but he wasn't in Sheffield. That's why we didn't meet. Okay?"

Matt nodded. He looked down at his lap, and Sarah hugged him again. Her eyes moistened at the turbulence he must be feeling. She wished there was some way he could make it better for him.

"Do you think he loves me?" Matt turned his big, innocent eyes to his mother. Sarah was lost for words. Children often asked their parents questions that had no answers. But Sarah had never felt completely gobsmacked. She wished this didn't have to be so hard. Perhaps the hardest thing she'd ever done. Would she live to regret her decision?

"Yes," she sighed, not knowing what else to say. "In his own way, I'm sure he does."

The doorbell went, and she felt Matt stiffen. Her mother had gone home for the evening, and it was just her and Matt. She went to the door and looked through the peephole. John was standing there, holding two packages, one under each arm. She opened the door. He was dressed in a shirt and light blazer, with jeans. He looked smart casual, like she'd asked him to. *He had scrubbed-up for the occasion*, she thought, *clean-shaven, and well dressed*. They said hello, and she let John in. He followed her as they walked into the living room. As they had already agreed, Sarah sat next to Matt, and John sat opposite. John put the two packages, wrapped in gift paper, on the coffee table in front of them.

"I bought you some gifts. Would you like to take a look?" John asked, smiling. He looked at Sarah, who nodded. Matt looked at his mother as well. Then he reached for the packages and took the wrappers off. The first packet was a Liverpool Football Club official merchandise, and inside there was a familiar red uniform, in Matt's size, with 'Mo Salah', the name of Liverpool's premier striker, written on the back. Matt's eyes brightened, and his mouth opened wide. He took the jersey out and held it up.

"Wow!" He couldn't stop staring at the jersey. He looked at John. "Can I wear it?"

"Yes of course you can. It's yours."

"What do you say?" Sarah prompted.

"Thank you," Matt said. He started to unwrap the second package. It contained two radio-operated sports cars, with a controlling console. The operator could race the cars in the garden or a field, using the remote control. Matt was fascinated, and he picked one of the cars up, his eyes popping. He went to the floor and moved one of the cars around. He turned to John.

"How does the motor work?"

John showed him where the batteries went in, and how he could use the remote. Matt went into the side room to get changed into his red jersey, and then with John, he went into the garden to race the cars. Sarah watched them, leaning against the garden door. John and Matt were getting on like a house on fire. As the cars began racing, Matt jumped up and down with excitement. Sarah couldn't help but smile. She couldn't remember the last time Matt had been so happy.

The hours passed by, and it got darker outside. Matt had to be persuaded to give up on racing or playing football with his new jersey on. He was too excited in fact, Sarah thought, and needed to calm down a little. They had eaten dinner already, so they sat down for some cheese, bread, and snacks. Matt was too excited to eat.

John gestured to Sarah, and took her to one side, while Matt played with his new toys.

"I can get tickets for the next Liverpool match. A friend of mine has a season ticket, but he can't always go, and under-twelve go free for some matches."

Sarah thought about it. She wasn't sure about letting John take Matt on his own. John read the doubt in her mind.

"Why don't you come as well? I can see if I can get an extra ticket. Shouldn't be a problem. They're playing Sheffield United at home. Should be a good match."

Sarah knew she couldn't deny Matt going to the match, he would be over the moon. They had never been to watch Liverpool play. At the same time, she wondered if this was over-the-top, and if Matt's exposure to John was too overwhelming and sudden.

Then she considered that her son had never had a father figure. In truth, John had a lot of catching up to do. Perhaps this occasion was a fitting start. If she could go with them, that was acceptable to her.

"I would like to come," Sarah said.

"Of course. I'll get you a ticket straight away. There's still some spare."

They went back into the living room, where John said goodbye to Matt.

"Would you like to see Liverpool play?" John asked with a

smile.

"Oh yes," Matt gasped.

"Well, we might be going tomorrow. Your mum will come as well."

"Yay!" Matt leapt up. "They're coming to Sheffield, aren't they? United have just been promoted to the Premier League. But Salah won't be playing. He's having a scan on his left ankle. He should be alright for the next match against Newcastle."

Sarah and John smiled at the boy's enthusiasm. John said to Matt, "I've really enjoyed spending time with you. Are you happy to meet tomorrow?"

Matt nodded, suddenly shy. He looked at his mother, who patted his back reassuringly. Matt turned back to John. "Yes. I'd like that."

"Me too." John said. He went to say something again, but the stopped. Sarah could see the emotions flicker across his face. Too many regrets there, and too much wasted time. John lowered his head briefly, then smiled sadly.

"Thank you. I'll see you tomorrow, hopefully."

"Yes," Matt said eagerly.

Sarah was impressed with the way John had handled this meeting, and how well father and son had gelled. Well, John had a long way to go before he could be a father. But the first signs were promising. Sarah hoped fervently this would continue.

They walked John to the door. He stood outside and turned to wave goodbye. He looked his son in the eye. "Bye... Matt."

Matt waved back. "Bye." Then he suddenly blurted out the word. "Dad."

John froze, his eyes widening. Sarah also stiffened. Matt looked unsure of himself again, and shy. He leaned against Sarah's legs, and she held him.

John couldn't hold his emotions back this time. The tip of his nose reddened, and moisture creeped in his eyes. He sniffed, then nodded quickly.

"Thank you," he said in a hoarse voice. "See you tomorrow."

He turned quickly and left, not looking back. Sarah shut the door, wiping her tears quickly, so Matt wouldn't see.

CHAPTER 53

Roy was striding down the country road, Inspector Jonty Adams next to him. Quite a few slip roads came off the long and narrow A57 that connected Sheffield to the Peak District. This dirt track was one of them, and it sneaked into the heart of ancient hills and green fields that undulated down to the valley below. The emerald wave of land was divided into squares and rectangles by old stone walls. The track narrowed as it came up to a farm. It was a derelict yard, with two huge barns and a farmhouse with its roof caved in. The place was crawling with uniformed officers. The barn doors were open, and men went in and out. A squad car stood in the middle of the yard, its blue lights flashing unnecessarily.

"Turn that off," Roy said. "If he's around, he can see it from miles off." Jonty barked orders to a nearby constable, who scampered off to do it. The lights stopped flashing soon. Roy entered the yard. A sergeant came out of the derelict house and shook his head.

"Nowt in there but rats and mice," he hooked a thumb backwards. "Searched it top to bottom. Too dangerous in places, the roof's practically falling on our heads."

"Is there a basement?" Roy asked.

"Aye. It's empty apart from old farm gear, I'm afraid."

One of the constables came out, wearing a hard hat. The sergeant spoke to him briefly, then turned to them. "Sorry guv, nowt."

"Give me that," Roy indicated the hard hat. The constable hesitantly handed it over. Roy pressed it over his head, then strode towards the derelict house.

"Where you goin'?" Jonty called. "You heard what he said."

"Just want to have a look," Roy called back. "Carry on around the yard. If there's any animal pens in these fields, I want them looked at."

At the back of his mind, a memory was triggering uncomfortable feelings. Stephen Burns had a farm like this, not that far from here. It was true there was nothing to connect Damien Russell to Burns. But he still wanted to be sure.

The sergeant was right, the place was a death trap. Roy moved a piece of timber hanging down from the ceiling joist as he walked through the porch into the lobby. An awful stench of rotten animal carcasses violated his nostrils. The smell clung to him like a second skin, and he covered his nose with his hand. Something had clearly died in here. Every step raised a small cloud of dust as he walked down the hallway. He came upon the basement door. It was left open. He shone a torchlight, and it showed steps going down to an earthen floor. If he was running from the police, he wouldn't hide in a basement. Not here, anyway. Still, he went gingerly down the creaking steps, shining the beam around. Moist stone walls greeted his eyes, and the stench here was stronger, like an animal had died here recently.

Fighting the wave of smell, he waded into the darkness. Old shovels and spades were lined in one corner. A couple of broken

295

wardrobes stood next to them. He saw boot prints on the ground, but they could easily belong to the uniforms. He knelt on the ground and looked at the prints closely.

There was more than one type. The size looked the same, but Roy had learnt enough of boot print forensics to know someone else had been here, and recently.

The basement was devoid of life, and he moved the old crap around, and scared a couple of big rats that scurried away. He didn't find a trap door. He hammered his fist against the stone walls, but there was no hollow sound.

He came out of the basement. The upstairs was literally falling to pieces. The floor had caved in, forming large holes. In the middle of what had once been the main bedroom, the boards were rotten, due to rainwater coming in through the broken window. Part of it had crashed down to the floor below. There was no point in going in, even a couple of steps made the remaining floor tilt dangerously downward.

He heard the cooing of pigeons, and the sound of flapping wings upstairs. He went up the stairs, patches of open sky became visible, where the roof had disintegrated, leaving forlorn pieces of slanting timber standing like holes in a denture.

There was no way Damien would hide here, but there was a chance he had been in the basement.

Roy went down and found Jonty standing in the lobby. Roy took him down to the basement and showed him the boot prints.

"They're both fresh, but the larger boot is fresher," Roy said. He had already snapped photos on his phone.

Jonty took a close look. "Aye, those belong to Darryl, the lad who just came out. He's got big feet."

"I wonder if we can get a match with the others and the ones in the second crime scene. They found boot prints near the canal," Roy said. "He might've been here, but he fled before we arrived. Restrict this area for now."

They went outside. It was getting dark. A group of uniforms had gathered in the middle of the yard. The barns were empty apart from old junk.

"You think he's around here?" Jonty asked, scratching his head. "There's no sign of his car."

"Any other farms around here?" Roy asked.

"None that show on the map. But there could be older ones that were built without any planning approval. Always a chance."

"Well, he can't be far, if this is where this track ends. The car's not here, which means he's driven through the fields. He must know this area."

Jonty nodded. "We start searching again at first light."

Roy walked to the edge of the yard, and stood next to a barn, looking out over the hills. Damien could be out there, anywhere. They had their work cut out, trying to find him.

His phone rang, and he answered. "DCI Roy."

It was Rizwan, and he sounded excited. "I've got some news, guv."

CHAPTER 54

DC Walmsley," Oliver said, showing the clearly-worried woman his warrant card. Rizwan did the same. They were inside a shabby, two-storey building that housed a tanning studio, and had a beauty or massage parlour alongside it. New paint and some plastic flowers did nothing to liven up the interior. A few orange-skinned blondies smiled from the posters on the wall, their pearly white teeth at stark contrast to the ripe tans on their bodies.

"What do you want?" The young woman asked. She was dressed in a black uniform, similar to those worn by shop assistants in a chemist. Her anxiety-ridden eyes flicked from Oliver to Rizwan.

In response, Oliver took out his phone, opened up the photo of the deceased woman, and placed it on the desk. The screen showed a close up of her face.

"This woman died last night, not far from here, by the canalside. Do you know her?"

The woman stopped breathing as she stared at the screen. Her neck muscles contracted, and she staggered backwards. She sat down on the chair, and stared ahead at no one, like Ollie and Riz weren't present.

"You know her, don't you?" Ollie asked, glancing quickly at Riz. He had to repeat his question before the woman slowly lifted her shocked eyes to him.

"Yes. Yes, I do," she whispered. "Her name's Charly. She comes to work here, like."

"What's her full name? Was she here last night?"

Riz touched Oliver on the sleeve, getting him to pipe down. Riz lowered his voice. "You alright, love?"

The woman sniffed; her eyes focused on her lap. Riz said, "You got anyone else here now?"

She shook her head. "What's your name?"

"Danielle?"

"Okay, Danielle. We just want some information about Charly, and then you can go home, alright?"

Danielle looked up at them, her eyes red rimmed. She nodded in silence. Oliver repeated his question.

"No, she weren't here last night. Her name's Charly Butler. She lives in Attercliffe."

"Do you know her well?"

"Kind of. She came here now and then, like. I talked to her a few times."

"Who's the boss here?"

Danielle looked even more scared. "Don't worry," Oliver said soothingly. "Nowt's gonna happen to you. This is just routine enquiries."

"Debbie runs the place, but she's not always here. I see her most days, though. Not heard from her in the last couple of days."

"Debbie McPherson?"

Danielle's Botox-smooth forehead creased. "Yeah. How do you know her name, like?"

"She's the manager at Cliffe Massage Parlour, isn't she?"

"Yes, how did you…" Danielle's words died as her face contracted with sudden panic. "What's going on?"

"Don't worry. It's best if you go home and stay there. This place will be shut now, and anyone who turns up will be sent home. Do you have Charly's address, or phone details?"

Danielle wiped her eyes and reached for a diary under the desk. Rizwan looked inside the cramped office, which had a door to one side.

"Can we have a look through there?"

"Yes. It leads on to the room with the three tanning beds, and there's another two rooms for the massage parlour."

"Mind if we take a look?"

Danielle rose from her chair and opened the door for them. The tanning beds were standard affairs – beds that irradiated skin and did to skin what smoking did for lungs – caused cancer. The men went into the massage parlour, and Oliver whistled after he entered. Each parlour was a nicely decorated bedroom with gilded red cushions, and velvety drapes on the walls and windows. Then again, they hadn't expected anything else. Oliver looked at Danielle, whose cheeks were rapidly turning the same shade as the cushions.

"Nice place, this. Are the beds only for massage, or other treatments?"

Danielle looked to the floor and shrugged. "I'll be outside."

"Wait a minute," Rizwan stopped her as she tried to leave. "Are there any other rooms?"

Danielle shook her head. "No. But feel free to have a look around."

The establishment only occupied the ground floor. The two DCs didn't find anything after a thorough look around. A rear door led to a small garden, with a two-metre-high brick fence.

They thanked Danielle on the way out and drove to the address she'd given them. An elderly woman opened the door. They introduced themselves, and from the look on her face, Oliver knew she was expecting bad news. When she saw the photo, the woman broke down. Her name was Liz, and she was Charly's mother.

Charly had a three-year-old daughter, who was at the nursery. Oliver and Rizwan gave Liz some time to recover.

"I was on my way to get the little one from her nursery." She held her head and succumbed to a fresh bout of tears.

"I know this is hard for you," Oliver said, "But did Charly seem troubled, or upset recently? Or did she say anything?"

Liz thought for a while. Then she frowned. "No, there wasn't. I mean, she was busy with her work, day, and night. She worked in the supermarket, at the tills, you know. And at night, she did that tanning salon job."

Riz asked, "How often did she do that?"

Liz shrugged. "Life's not easy, you know. My pension is almost non-existent. We got a little one to look after, and this house to pay for. Charly was a proud girl – she didn't want to go on the dole." Liz's eyes reddened, and she wept again. Riz came forward and crouched in front of her, then touched her shoulders.

"We'll send someone to come and stay with you for a couple of days. She will be a family liaison officer. If you give me your number, I will text you her details."

Liz nodded and wiped her eyes. "I can't believe this is happening. But I was always worried about her. This place is not good. People get mugged at night, like. We want to move out." She shook her head. "That's why Charly was working so hard. Now she's gone."

Oliver said, "We will find who did this. We promise you." He looked at Riz, who agreed. "We will need you to come and identify her. Is that okay?"

Liz looked down at her hands and nodded. Oliver asked, "Can we please have a look at her room? We need to take samples of her clothes, if you don't mind."

Once they had finished their duties, they went outside and called Roy as they walked to the car.

"Excellent work," Roy said, and Oliver beamed with pride even though his boss couldn't see it. "If I had my way I'd put Attercliffe under curfew," Roy muttered darkly. "Just in case he goes back there tonight. We need to shut down all the brothels in the city, and I mean all of them. I'm calling Nugent now, to mobilise more uniform teams. Scour the area and scare them if necessary."

"On it, boss," Oliver said.

CHAPTER 55

Roy was exhausted, and starving, by the time he got back home. Anna opened the door before he could turn the key in the lock.

"Long day?" She raised her eyebrows.

"You could say that. How are you?" Roy trudged into the living room and collapsed on the sofa. He took the radio off his belt, and put it on the table, then stretched his legs out.

"Had a good day. Pearl stayed for dinner. We had pizza. Got some leftover if you want some."

"That would be good," Roy smiled. "I'll get changed." He took his tired body upstairs, and in the shower. When he came back down, his wonderful daughter had put beer in a glass, and set out a plate with salad, and a few slices of pizza.

Roy pointed at the food. "Alright, this is lovely. What do you want?"

Anna was watching TV, and she opened her mouth in mock horror. "As if. Thanks, Dad. See what I get for being nice?"

Roy took a deep pull from the beer. Anna had used one of his

IPA cans from the fridge. Just the drink he needed.

"Okay, sorry. Thanks, darling."

"You're welcome." Anna went back to the TV while Roy ate. Presently, she spoke again, turning the volume down. "I met someone today. A schoolteacher. Well, we met before, but today we went for lunch. Her name's Lydia Moran. She teaches at a school in Totley. She lives there too."

Roy listened attentively; his sixth sense suddenly alert. "Oh, really? What sort of a teacher?"

"She teaches history in the upper sixth. I've looked her up already, don't worry. She does work at the school. Her name's on the website."

Roy relaxed a little. "How old is she?"

Anna shrugged. "Older than you, I think. Fifties, maybe. She looks like a teacher."

"Hmm. You know what we discussed about strangers."

They were both quiet for a while, events of the recent past casting long shadows in their minds. Both of them were lucky to be alive.

"I know," Anna said quietly. "But this lady's harmless. She's small, and wears glasses."

"Just be careful. You know you can't take anyone at face value, especially if you know nothing about them. I'll look her up myself."

Anna frowned. "Yeah, but don't contact her or anything. That would be like, super-embarrassing."

"Don't worry, I won't."

*****

While the whole of Sheffield slept, one soul remained awake,

304

pacing the streets. He had gone through three of the massage parlours and found all of them shut. As he walked past them, a police car went by slowly, clearly patrolling the streets. The man walked with his head high, keeping his spine straight. Cops were looking for someone shady, and he always kept himself well-dressed. That helped. Looking respectable was one of the reasons people trusted him, and he liked that.

Once the police car had driven past, and turned the corner, he slunk into a dark alley, and leaned against the wall. He let go of the long breath he was holding. Tonight, for some reason, Attercliffe was deserted, and so was Burngreave. All the massage parlours were shut. He guessed the reason of course – they had found Charly's body. When he thought of her, his mind filled with remorse. He always felt sad after the act. It was the planning stage that invigorated him. He loved the thrill of the chase, identifying the women, plying them with some cash, earning their trust.

Of course, Tracey had been different. She was special. She understood the game better than anyone else. She wanted to expose Kevin and what he was doing, bring him down. She told him what Luke had planned, and it would've worked to perfection… But the stakes were too high. He couldn't allow that to happen. When Tracey confided in him, whispered those words of passion in the middle of the night, she didn't know that she'd been marked already. That excited him even now, despite the regret. He hid himself from her, like he did from everyone else. Tracey stayed with him at his house, shared the same bed. But she didn't know the real him.

Luke had big plans, but he was an idiot in the end. Did he really think using Tracey to bring Kevin down would work? He had done Kevin a favour, but of course, Kevin would now moan after his arrest. These closed brothels meant his business was suffering.

The man's thirst was not satiated. Blood begets blood. Tracey,

Charly… And he had his sights set on another. A woman called Heather. He had slept with her three times now. He thought she knew Debbie, he had seen them engrossed in a chat, more than once. He had done the usual thing with Heather, bought her some nice gifts, jewellery, and now she liked him. heather was worth the money, but she was also scarred. She used heroin, and she was a single mother.

All of a sudden, from nowhere, the vision blinded him. He was a little boy, standing over his mother's dead body. Her face was bloated and blue, tongue protruding. Vomit, blood, and spittle encrusted the corners of her lips. The tourniquet gripped her left elbow, and the needle lay on the bed. He was starving, hungry, cold. His mother's money went on feeding her addiction. He felt sick, but also fascinated. He had never seen a dead body before. He pushed her once.

"Mummy?" There was no response. He reached out and picked up the needle and syringe. He stared at in in awe.

Now, headlights swept past him, dispelling his vision. He blinked, coming back to reality. He was shivering and breaking out in a sweat. He took a deep breath, trying to control the fervour again building into a fever pitch. He needed to see Heather. Needed to touch her. Needed to cut her skin where the needle would make marks… And let her bleed out slowly.

But first, he had to make sure he was safe. He walked down the alley, patting the knives in his pocket.

CHAPTER 56

Roy heard the beeping but dismissed it as a dream. He couldn't be bothered. But the beeping was persistent, and it grew louder. He shook his head, trying to fling the sound away, and turned around in bed. The beeping was now a loud buzz, and it came from under his pillow. His eyes flew open. He was awake instantly, his hand diving under the pillow to retrieve his work phone. He rubbed his eyes and peered at the number. It was blocked.

"DCI Roy. Who's this?"

A low, raspy voice gasped. It was a woman. "Inspector Roy, help me."

Roy was immediately alert, sitting up in bed. He flicked on the table lamp, then screwed his eyes shut at the glare.

"Identify yourself. Who are you?"

"Deb… Debbie"

"Debbie McPherson?"

"Yes. Please come to my house. I'm being held—"

The voice was cut-off, replaced by the sounds of a struggle.

Then another man's voice came down the line.

"Inspector Roy. My name is Damien Russell."

"What do you want?" Roy stood, and pulled on his jeans, holding the phone on the crook of his shoulder, against his ears.

"We have a lot to talk about. I suggest you come alone to Debbie's house. If you alert others, or try anything else, I promise you, I will cut Debbie into ribbons."

"Damien, is this worth it? Hand yourself over, and we can—"

"Shut up," Damien shouted. "I'm not interested in what you have to say. You listen to me, now. Got it?"

"Okay, just stay calm. I'm coming over. Give me the address."

"Come alone, Inspector. Unless you want another dead body on your hands."

The line went dead. "Hello? Hello?"

Roy hung up and got dressed quickly. He took his radio and torchlight; he'd left the extendable baton at work. He went around the house making sure all the windows, and doors were locked. He wrote a note for Anna to tell her to stay at home til he got back, and if he didn't, then to ring Sarah. He slipped the note under her door. He stood outside for a while, watching. Dore Village was shrouded in nocturnal silence, the occasional streetlights casting penumbras of yellow light. No one stirred, save a cat that slunk under a car. Roy watched for a while, making sure this wasn't a trap to make him leave the house on a wild goose chase. He had recognised Debbie's voice, and he knew she was in trouble. She must have gone back to the house for some reason. Maybe to do with the kids. Damien had taken his chance. Still, the memories of what happened to Anna was fresh in her mind. He hesitated for a fraction, then sent Sarah a text. He told her what happened, and to keep an eye on Anna. Sarah would be asleep now, in any case.

Then he got in the car, and pulled out a dog eared *A to Z*. His car's sat nav was beyond repair. Under the car light, he plotted his route to Hillsborough, where Debbie lived. He knew these roads now; it wouldn't take him long to reach there. It was three in the morning. He stifled a yawn and started driving.

Debbie's house was on the outskirts of Hillsborough. It was on a hill, and the road was uneven, and littered with potholes. Roy muttered curses as his old car shuddered and banged as the front bumper hit a cavity on the roadside. He was close now, so he parked the car, and set off on foot. The houses here were detached, with some terraces, and they looked out into open fields. Roy slowed as he came up to number 55. No lights were visible inside.

Roy went around the back of the street, to see the rear of the property. It was a stark, black shape against the night sky. The houses on either side were also detached and looked deserted. The rear fence was of crumbling brick, and when Roy stood on his tiptoes, he could see an overgrown garden. His eyes had grown used to the dark. He couldn't see a dog, but that didn't mean there wasn't one around.

He grabbed the top of the brick fence, and heaved himself up, then swung his leg over. He waited for a while, but no barks sounded. He dropped himself on the other side, dropping on weeds and bushes that he prayed didn't contain animal waste. He cracked his ankles when he fell, and grunted in pain as he rolled over. He stayed in a crouch and watched the dark edifice in front of him. A wind whispered across the garden, filtering through the weeds.

Roy looked around him and found the fallen branch of a tree. He snapped off the twigs, and then held it in his right fist. It was light enough to carry around. He crept up to the rear door. He depressed the handle, and found it locked. He let go and went down the stairs. There was a left side passage, and he went along, looking all around him. He passed under a window and stopped. He could prise the pane open from its frame by reaching up. The frame was of old wood, set in stone, strong enough to take his weight. He shoved the branch into his back belt line, feeling a little stupid. The damn thing hurt his back. But he wanted to keep it with him.

He pulled himself up, and through the open window. He dropped into a bathroom. The tiles were slippery, and when he looked up, he saw the drip from the ceiling. He heard another sound, like the shuffling of feet outside the door. He froze and crouched. Slowly, he prised the branch loose from his belt. He didn't hear any more sounds. If there was anyone outside the door, he would have to take his chance.

He pulled the door handle, and it opened with a creak. A dark corridor met his eyes. He didn't open the door fully and watched for a while. Further away, he heard the shuffling sound again, now above his head. Then he heard a dull thud, and a muffled cry.

CHAPTER 57

Roy opened the door fully and crouched into the corridor. There was no light, but he could sense this space was empty. To his right, the hallways stretched into what could be a kitchen. The door was open, and through it, he could see a large window that looked out into darkness, and the garden. He turned left and the hallways widened into a lobby area. There was a bug front door ahead of him. Two more doors opened up on either side, and both were shut. A staircase went up to his left. He heard the thud again, and this time a human voice. It was a sharp cry, but it was stifled quickly.

Silent as a ghost, Roy went up the stairs. The landing on the first floor was wide, with rooms on either side. The sounds had come from his right. He crept up to a closed door and put his ear against it. The smell of dust and mildew was heavy in the air, as if the place hadn't been ventilated for a long time.

Roy wondered if Debbie lived here or had been brought here. He stiffened as he heard the voices again, too soft to hear the words. It came from inside the room. He turned the handle, and it opened with a loud creak.

"Come inside, Inspector," a male voice said. Roy opened the

door and stood on the doorstep. He could see a large bay window, and a shape standing in front of it. It was a man, and he held another person in a chair in front of him. Roy stepped inside the room. The windows were open, and a breeze filtered inside. His eyes were used to the darkness, and he could see a woman's shape on the chair. Her hands were tied to the arms of the chair, and so were her ankles.

She moaned once, and the sound was soft. She had a gag around her mouth, and the man had a hand over her face. Her head was held tight against his abdomen. In his other hand, he held something against the woman's throat. Roy could discern the woman's shape and features in the dimness – it was Debbie.

"Be careful," the man warned. Roy now recognised his voice. It was the man who spoke on the phone. Damien Russell.

"I've got a knife to her neck. Don't try anything foolish. Stop where you are. Drop that branch from your hand."

Roy put the timber down to the floor and raised both hands. He spoke calmly. "Damien. Let Debbie go. This isn't doing you any favours."

In response, Damien's hands moved, and the gag came off Debbie's mouth. She gasped and heaved, then her body jerked forward. Damien pulled on her hair, making her scream. He dragged her head back and kept the knife on her neck.

"Tell him, Debbie," Damien said. "Tell him everything."

Debbie coughed, and then spluttered. She heaved on to the floor, trailing mucus, and saliva. Roy tensed himself, as Damien was distracted momentarily. He could make a move now, catapult himself in Damien's direction… But he was too late. Damien seemed to sense what he was up to. He jerked straight, pulling again on poor Debbie's hair, who howled in pain.

Damien snarled and clenched his teeth as he spoke into Debbie's ears. "Tell him! Now!"

"What… What…?"

"About me and Kevin. And Luke. Tracey. All of it. Tell him what Kevin was up to."

Debbie gasped, her breath short. She was struggling to speak. Roy fought the urge to rush forward and tackle Damien head on. Debbie was in the way, but Damien could easily slit her throat. Did he really have time to wait?

Roy said, "Let her go, Damien. You can—"

"Shut up!" Damien shouted. He raised the knife and pointed it at Roy. "This is all your fault. Your bloody investigation. I did nothing wrong. Do you understand?"

Roy had inched forward, and Damien appeared to not have noticed. Roy was glad that Damien's attention was now focused on him.

"You shouldn't have run. If you spoke to us, we could've resolved all of this easily. But, like a coward, you tried to escape."

Damien appeared to swell with rage. He shouted like a crazed animal and stabbed the knife in Roy's direction.

"I'm not a coward!"

Excellent, Roy thought to himself. He stepped closer, focusing on Damien. "Yes, you are. You killed those two innocent women. And Gemma Jackson, from six years ago. Admit it, Damien. A man who does that is a coward."

Damien went to speak, and Roy was now close enough to leap, and grab the knife arm. But a blur of movement took them all by surprise. Debbie's spine snapped straight, and the chair lifted vertically. Debbie's head smashed into Damien's chin, and she thrust her legs backward, propelling Damien towards the open window.

Damien struggled, but Debbie had the element of surprise in her favour. Roy seized the moment. He practically flew through the air, locked in on the knife arm. He hit Damien's upper body, and his fist closed on the wrist bearing the knife. In the process, he lurched Damien back further. Both of them crashed into the open window, smashing the glass pane into smithereens. Debbie had already fallen off the chair, and she lay on the floor.

Roy's head smashed into Damien's jaw, and the man fell back further. His legs hit the wall, and his body lost balance, then he topped backwards through the window opening. He screamed, and Roy's arm shot out, grabbing his shirt. The cloth tore, and buttons ripped off. Roy tried desperately to hold on, but Damien fell through the gap, and tumbled down into the night air.

CHAPTER 58

The eerie blue glow from several police and ambulance cars lit up the night. Debbie was sat at the rear of an ambulance, a blanket around her shoulders. Roy handed her a cup of tea. She accepted it with thanks. The EMT carried on dealing with the small lacerations Debbie had suffered while Damien had overpowered her.

Roy went back down, and watched as the gurney of the second ambulance lifted a prone Damien into the back of the vehicle. Damien had his eyes shut, and his neck was placed in a soft cuff to immobilise it. There was a bandage around his head.

"Can I speak to him?" Roy asked one of the blue coated EMT's.

The man shook his head. "He's in a bad way. He literally fell on his head. He's got severe head trauma, and they're waiting for him. He needs an urgent scan, and if there's a blood clot in the brain, it needs surgery."

The gurney was loaded, and the ambulance took off, blue lights flashing. Roy went back to the remaining ambulance. The EMT had finished tending to Debbie. The female EMT turned to Roy.

"You've got some cuts and bruises. Sit down, please."

Roy shook his head. "Nothing I can't handle. I need a moment with Debbie, if you don't mind."

The EMT left, and Roy shut the door. Debbie sipped her tea, and shivered once, under the blanket. She spoke, her eyes on the ambulance floor.

"Kevin had set up a trafficking business. He was delivered women by Eastern European human traffickers. He used them in his brothels. Tracey found out from Damien and got angry. She confronted Kevin and threatened to expose him."

"And that's why Damien killed Tracey," Roy said. "What about Charly?"

Debbie shook her head. "He was always the weird type. Very quiet. Shifty. No one liked him, and he creeped out all the girls. He did get fixated on some of them. Poor Charly."

"Did Charly have any troubles with Kevin?"

"No. Not as far as I know, anyway. I did see Damien around Charly a lot. She told me he went to her house once. Followed her around."

Roy gathered his thoughts together, which was hard with his splitting headache. "Bianca Wilkins, the girl who died six years ago. Was Damien involved with her?"

"He was always around the massage parlours that Kevin and Karen owned, if you know what I mean. Yes, Damien knew Bianca. He slept with her a couple of times. I saw him coming out of her room in the parlour." Debbie lifted her eyes to Roy's. "You think Damien…"

"Yes. The MO is the same. The person who killed Tracey and Charly, also killed Bianca."

Debbie shut her eyes, and shivered again, and this time it didn't stop. Roy squeezed her shoulder.

"You're going to be alright, Debbie. Don't worry."

Keeping her head down Debbie nodded, then sniffed loudly. Roy handed her a tissue.

"I wish I'd been more open from the beginning. But I was scared. Kevin's a dangerous man. Their gang has a wide reach. I chatted to Luke about it. I knew him. He wasn't as bad as Damien and Kevin."

"When did you speak to Luke?"

"Last night, after I got out. He told me Damien was gone, and to stay at home. He said it wasn't safe in Ashstead anymore. That's what I did. But when Damien appeared, I…"

"He broke into your house?"

"Yes. I was asleep." Debbie lapsed into silence.

"Don't worry about Kevin anymore. Luke's going to be charged with possession. Damien will be lucky to come out of this alive. Kevin will go back to Spain for a while, I think."

"I hope so. I'm not working for them again. But I'm still scared."

"I'm going to put you in a different safe house, and then apply to the Protected Persons Service. Don't worry."

The ambulance door opened, and Sarah appeared. Her cheeks and lips were pinched tight with anxiety, her hair in a ponytail. She looked at Roy and relaxed a little.

"Are you two okay?"

"Fine," Roy said. "Let's talk outside."

He said goodbye to Debbie, who was going to spend the night at the hospital. Outside, Sarah's eyes searched his face, and then swept up and down his body.

"I came when I got the message. A team of uniforms is outside your house, so don't worry about Anna."

Roy rubbed his aching forehead and sighed. "Thank you. Who's with Matt?"

"I called John. He came around. It's not for long, so that's alright."

Roy nodded. They leaned against the stone fence on the roadside, and he told Sarah what happened.

"So, where was Damien hiding out in the fields?"

"We don't know. He clearly dumped the car somewhere, and we couldn't find it. It was getting dark, and searching wasn't easy. He managed to get back here, and attack Debbie."

"At least he won't be attacking anyone else."

Roy was silent for a while, his mind flickering around. Then he realised he was too tired to think. He needed some rest. Sarah gripped his forearm, sensing his mood.

"You should go home. Let's get back to it tomorrow."

CHAPTER 59

Roy was at his desk, sipping from a scalding mug of tea. Anna had made him coffee in the morning, so he had switched to tea for now. Coffee again at midday. Anna had clamped down on his three cups of coffee before midday, and to be honest, he felt calmer without it. His phone buzzed once, which meant a text had arrived. Probably Anna, he thoughts, letting him know she was going into town, and the library for a few hours. When he saw the message, his spine stiffened.

Does your daughter know about Robin? Wouldn't it be nice if they met? Or maybe not...

Roy ground his teeth together. He shoved the phone back, trying to get his mind back to work. It didn't happen. He got up and went outside. Times like these, he craved a cigarette, a habit he had kicked decades ago. He called Anna, who thankfully answered.

"Hi, Dad. I'm on the bus."

"Okay. Are you going to the library?"

"And some shopping. I'm out of shampoo."

"Okay. Let me know when you're done, and I can pick you up."

"Okay, bye!"

He wanted to tell her to be careful, but she hung up before that. He needed to hear her voice just to reassure himself. He took a couple of seconds to calm down, then went back in.

Riz and Ollie were at their desks. They looked up as Roy sat down and focused on the paperwork on his desk. Ollie looked up and snapped his fingers.

"Got it, guv."

Roy was looking at the medical report on Damien's condition. He raised a hand, and Oliver handed it to him. Roy placed it next to the report, which he continued to scan.

"Intracerebral haemorrhage causing midline shift along the central brain matter," Roy read aloud, and shook his head. "I'm no doctor, but that sounds bad to me."

"Internal bleeding pushed his brain to one side?" Rizwan ventured.

"Something like that. The report says chances of a recovery are slim. Surgery is not possible without making it worse." Roy stopped reading and raised his head.

"He's toast, basically. Perhaps a fitting end to his life."

"Aye," Oliver agreed. "Oh, I got something back from Dr Patel. Damien's DNA was found under Tracey's fingernails. Still waiting for Charly's sample to get a match."

"Good. Did we get any more CCTV evidence for Damien and Charly?"

Oliver pointed to Rizwan, who was already clicking on his laptop. He turned the machine to make it easier for Roy to see. The CCTV footage was outside Sunrise Massage Parlour. A man and woman were walking down the path in front of the parlour. They stopped and talked for a while. The woman raised a hand and walked away. The man stood there, watching, then walked off. Rizwan zoomed into the man's face. It was Damien.

"This was four days ago. The researchers analysed this late last night. Damien knew Charly."

"Still no sign of the murder weapon?"

"Nope. Do you still want the drain searched for Tracey's phone?"

Roy inclined his head. "It would be good – for the CPS. We can show Tracey's contact with Damien." Roy tapped his lower lip. "Go back to the night when Charly was murdered. Show me the CCTV of Damien walking with her."

Riz did as told. Oliver walked around his table, joining them. They leaned over Riz's laptop. The black-and-white image showed a man and woman walked down the road, and then going down towards the canal. Roy leaned closer.

"What's the time stamp? My eyes aren't what they used to be."

Riz peered at the screen. "Ten minutes past seven."

"Keep it there." Roy pulled out his phone and called Dr Patel. She answered on the fifth ring.

"DCI Roy? To what do I owe this pleasure?"

"A conundrum, if you will. The time of death of Charly Butler was between half-eleven and midnight, you said. Can you be more precise now?"

In the ensuing silence, he heard the sound of fingers clicking on a keyboard. "As it happens, I can," Dr Patel said. "The window comes to between midnight and 1 am. We can err closer to 1 am, rather than midnight."

"And we're sure about this?"

"The software takes into account moisture, temperature,

victim's body size and shape, sex, and about another ten factors. I won't bore you with the details. But it's correct 99.9% of the time. Are you worried about the CPS making a fuss? I don't think they will."

"Thanks, doc. Please let us know if there's a DNA match."

Roy hung up and swung round to face the two DCs, who were staring at him with interest. Roy pointed at the screen.

"So, Damien and Charly walk down the canal steps at 7 pm, but she dies after midnight. What were they doing down there for more than five hours?"

Oliver made an 'O' shape with his mouth. "That's a really, really, long shag. I mean, a marathon. A shagathon, to be fair."

Roy tutted, disgusted. "Shagathon? These are new lows, even from you, Oliver."

Riz gave his partner a withering look. "No signs of sexual activity, you idiot. Didn't you read the post-mortem report?"

Oliver opened his mouth and pointed inside the cavity. Then he grinned. Riz rolled his eyes, and Roy clutched his forehead.

"Good job the ladies aren't here," Riz muttered.

"Why not?" A female voice said. Melanie appeared and shrugged off her coat. "What are you lads up to?"

"These two can't take a joke," Oliver complained, then looked sulky.

"And you can't tell one to save your life," Riz said.

Roy raised a hand, shushing them both. "It's about the time of death of our latest victim. The killer and her headed down to the canal at 7 pm, but death occurred between midnight and 1 am."

Melanie frowned. "Does he come back up from the canal? What about her?"

Riz answered. "No, neither of them show up again. And the canalside is a CCTV dark spot."

"Maybe they walked up and down for a while. He didn't kill her til much later. Took his time, the bastard."

"Hmm," Roy said, and looked down at his feet. Shapes were flitting through his mind, some clear, others obscure. He dearly wanted to question Damien, but he knew he would never get the chance. The man was in a coma and would eventually die.

He looked at the two DCs. "And there's no CCTV of Damien and Tracey?"

Oliver said, "Nope. The street in front of Cliffe Massage Parlour doesn't have CCTV."

"Having second thoughts about our man?" Melanie asked.

Roy sat down at his table and steepled fingers in front of his face. "Bring up the video of the man following Bianca Wilkins, the cold case," he asked Oliver.

They went to his desk and watched the footage, as well as the close up of the man who went down the steps a minute later Bianca. It looked like Damien, there was no doubt. But he wore glasses, and the hoodie remained on his head.

"On the bus that he stepped off," Riz said, "he kept the glasses and hoodie on, because he knew he could be identified. Nothing on his hands or visible skin that's identifiable."

Roy said, "Damien knew Bianca as well. Debbie saw them together. All of it makes sense. He had the opportunity, and the means, definitely. As for motive, god knows what went on in his sick mind."

Melanie said, "He's our man, guv. I think you're overthinking this."

Roy looked to the ceiling and rubbed his forehead. "Yes, I'm sure you're right." He glanced around him. "Where's Sarah?"

Melanie grinned. "Didn't she tell you? She's got the day off. She's going to see Sheffield United play Liverpool today."

"Oh yes, game on today," Oliver said. "We're gonna smash them scousers."

Roy shrugged. "Oh, good. She didn't mention it last night."

CHAPTER 60

S arah was putting sandwiches into the box for later. Matt ran into the kitchen, wearing his Liverpool jersey.

"When's Dad coming?"

"He'll be here soon."

John had been waiting at home when Sarah got back last night. Matt had been in bed, fast asleep. She couldn't fault John. He had been good as gold, to be honest. He had left promptly after she came back and assured her she could call him anytime she needed.

She checked her watch. It was almost midday. John should be here soon. They would stop by a pizza place for lunch, a place that Matt liked. Matt in fact, had been so excited for today he had barely slept last night. After lunch they had time to tour the Sheffield United Museum. As Sheffield had been promoted to the Premier League this season, there was also a concert at the stadium, before the match started.

Sarah had to admit even she was looking forward to the events. She couldn't remember the last time she'd been to big match like this one. It wasn't every day that Liverpool came to play in

Sheffield. There would be busloads of Liverpool fans travelling to the city. Sarah's police mind wondered about the security. Many years ago, she used to be a uniformed constable. She had worked in crowd control after a match. If fights broke out between fans, it was never nice. But luckily, those days were mostly gone. She didn't expect anything bad to happen today.

Her mind turned to work. She had told Roy about today, she had decided after talking to Matt last night, and there was no time. When she met Roy after Damien's capture, she'd simply forgotten. She decided to call Roy now, while she had some time.

"DCI Roy."

"Hi guv, it's me. Sorry I forgot to tell you that I took the day off. It's the football match—"

Roy interrupted her. "I've heard from the others already. Have a good time. To be honest, I'm well jell. That means 'well jealous' in Essex, by the way."

Sarah grinned, and she could hear the mirth in Roy's voice. "You can come with Matt and me next time." The words had slipped out before she could stop them.

"I'll hold you to that." Roy went quiet, and so did Sarah. Then she changed the topic quickly, to avoid that awkward pause.

"Did you run through things with Mark?" Mark Spencer was their CPS legal advisor, the man who looked at their case and told them if it could be successful in the Criminal Prosecution Service courts.

"Will do that later today. First though, we need to bring Kevin back in. After Luke's arrest, we have grounds. We can't pin the drugs stash on Kevin, there's no evidence. But we can grill him on the human trafficking ring. Alleged, of course."

"It's not going to stick, is it? Look on the bright side. At least we got Damien. The streets are safer. We can tell the families, and they can get some closure."

"Yes." Roy paused, and his tone became hesitant. "Needed to ask you something else, actually. Did you get any feedback on that weirdo behind your house?"

Sarah's eyebrows lowered. "No. Has something happened?"

"I got another text. This one mentioned Anna. Specifically, it asked if I wanted Anna to meet my brother. And then called me a liar and a cheat."

Sarah touched her forehead and sat down on the sofa. She could see Matt outside, kicking a ball in the garden.

"They're not giving up, are they?"

"No. Even worse, this person knows Anna lives with me. I'm actually thinking of sending her back to London."

Roy continued. "Anyway, don't worry. Go and have a good time. It's a big day for Matt, right?"

"Yes, Rohan," she said softly. "See you soon, okay?"

"Bye."

Sarah hung up, then tapped the phone against her hand, thinking. She wondered who this person following Rohan could be. One of Stephen Burns's friends, without a doubt. Some freak intent on torturing Rohan. He was crazy enough to come up to her house. She stood and her eyes scanned the back fence. She walked out into the garden to take a look. It was all clear. She'd almost forgotten about that incident; it seemed a while ago.

CHAPTER 61

Anna put her bags down and scanned the library. She didn't see Lydia, but then the teacher often came later, and sat near the front, close to the counter. Anna went downstairs, where there was a small café on the ground floor. She had seen Lydia here in the past, but there was no sign of her. She saw a man staring at her as she approached the café counter. There was a queue for coffee, but the man was standing to one side, leaning against a pillar.

He was an Asian man, light brown skin, short black hair, clean-shaven. He wore blue jeans and a brown t-shirt, with trainers on his feet. There was something about the man that she found unsettling. First, the familiarity, like she'd seen him somewhere before. Secondly, the interest with which he stared at her. Anna was growing up; she was used to men staring at her. She also knew when not to encourage them.

Roy had taught her to discreetly observe and note particulars. Hence, Anna looked for any tattoos, or piercings. She noted some tattooed blue letters sticking out of the left forearm sleeve. She tried not to catch his eye when she looked at him, but she was acutely aware of his inspection. Eventually, she ignored him, and focused on getting her coffee. She felt a movement behind her, and shifted in case someone was trying to move past her.

It was Lydia, in fact. She beamed at Anna. "Hey, how are you today?"

"Fine, how are you?" Anna was pleased to see Lydia. She had worked hard on her latest essay, and she wanted Lydia to have a look at it. Lydia joined her for a coffee.

"Just got here," Lydia said. "Bus was late." She looked good in her blue dress, Anna thought. Her hair was done nicely. She wondered if Lydia was going somewhere from here. She looked like she was dressed for a job interview.

"You look lovely," Anna said.

"Oh thanks," Lydia flicked something off her sleeve. "Yes, had an appointment with the hairdresser yesterday. Do you like it?"

"It's really nice. Suits you well." Anna moved forward with the queue and turned to look for the man. He was gone. She looked around but didn't see him. She got her coffee and waited for Lydia to get hers. As they walked upstairs, she was still thinking about the man. Finally, a button clicked in her mind, and she suddenly knew why that man was familiar.

Yesterday, when she was having lunch with Lydia, she had seen the man across the road. He was sitting inside a café but was watching them. He looked away when their eyes met, but she remembered him. Anna thought hard. Was it the same guy, or was she imagining it? It was hard to be sure, but it bothered her. With a jolt of fear, she recalled her recent ordeal. Where she almost died. She shook her head, as if that would dispel the dark memories.

"Are you alright?" Lydia asked.

They were standing at the gates of the library, about to go in. Anna hadn't realised she had stopped.

"Oh sorry. Yes, I'm fine. Shall we go in?" She forced a smile on her face.

"You looked like you were miles away," Lydia said. She had a concerned look on her face. "Everything okay at home?"

Anna blinked. "Yes, it is. Why do you ask?"

"No reason. Sorry, I didn't mean to intrude."

"No, it's okay. I just saw this man yesterday when we were out at lunch. I'm sure I saw him again, downstairs."

Lydia's eyes narrowed. "Really? What does he look like?"

Anna described him. Lydia thought, then pressed her lips together. "No, can't say I noticed. He was downstairs just now?"

"Yes. I saw him staring at me, then he disappeared. I have to be…" Anna's words dried-up. She didn't know how much she could tell Lydia. Her instinct told her she could trust Lydia, but she wasn't one-hundred-percent sure. Lydia must've seen the conflict on her face. She pulled Anna to a quiet corner.

"You can talk to me. I won't tell anyone."

Anna hesitated, then decided she could do with Lydia's help. She could be an extra pair of eyes to watch out for this man. She told Lydia what happened to her last month. Just the basics, without going into details. Lydia listened, her eyes wide, then her hand went to her mouth. She touched Anna's hand.

"That's unbelievable. Gosh, I'm so glad you're okay."

"My dad saved me. Yes, it was really bad."

Lydia's expression turned blank on the mention of her father. Anna could see that she was curious, and perhaps it wouldn't harm to tell her more, but for now, she refrained. Her dad had told her not to talk about this stuff to anyone, and she had already broken that rule. But what harm could Lydia do? She was an older woman, and a teacher. Anna sighed, and stood, indicating the conversation was over. They walked back into the library.

"I'm here," Lydia pointed to a desk near the gates. "I'll see you later? Maybe we can go for lunch again?"

Anna nodded. "Sure, why not? Make the most of this weather."

Time passed by quickly as Anna got busy with her work. She wanted to show Lydia the essay, but she had some maths to get done first. After an hour and a half, she took a loo break. The toilets in the library were across the big lobby on the same first floor. The lobby was deserted as she crossed it. She halted when a man appeared from behind one of the pillars. Her eyes widened with fear when she realised it was the same man who was watching her that morning. He saw the panic on her face and raised both hands. He stood still, not advancing.

"I'm not going to hurt you. I just want to talk."

Anna's fists were clenched as she took a step back. "Who are you? There are people here, I can shout."

"I know, and that should tell you I'm not here to make trouble. I'm a well-wisher. I just need to tell you something about the woman you're chatting to."

Anna frowned. "What?"

The man said, "Is her name Lydia?"

A tingle of curiosity sparked in Anna's mind. "How did you know that?"

"I know her from many years ago. She was younger then. She's the ex-girlfriend of my father. Well, kind-of-father. He's a very dangerous man. She was close to him. You need to watch out for her. She's not who you think she is. She follows you around in her car. I saw her yesterday, doing just that."

The man had lowered his voice, but his words still hit home.

331

Anna thought for a few seconds. She didn't trust this stranger, but why would he be saying stuff like this? And what if it was true?

"What's your name?"

"Jayden Budden. I know your father. Is he Rohan Roy, the Detective Chief Inspector?"

Fear whiplashed against Anna's spine, and her head jerked straight. She stepped further back. "How did you know that?"

Jayden had a pleading look in his face. "I'm sorry, I didn't mean to scare you. Look, I'm a witness at a crime scene, and he interviewed me. I saw you yesterday with Lydia, then I saw you get into a car with Rohan Roy. I guessed he was your dad, or maybe your uncle or some other relative."

Anna's mind had gone supersonic, thoughts flashing past at jet-speed. *Who was this weird guy? What did he really want?* But he had given his name and had explained how he knew her dad.

"Why are you following me around?"

Jayden shook his head vigorously. "Not you. I have no interest in you. I was following Lydia. I saw you two purely by chance. If she's around, then I'm worried that my stepfather might also be around. Like I said, he's dangerous. You must not be near him."

His face changed suddenly, like he was drowning. His expression became a rictus of fear, and he stopped speaking. Colour left his face, and he shivered as if in a cold, dreary wind.

Anna tried to decipher the sudden change in the man and couldn't. But she could tell he wasn't acting. This was really weird.

"What's your father's name?"

"Jerry Budden. I ran away from him. Look it's a long story." The man ran a hand across his face. He tottered to a sofa nearby and sat down heavily. A couple of people walked past them, chatting. Anna got closer to the man but didn't sit down.

"What did your dad do?" she whispered.

Jayden slowly moved the hands covering his face. He looked up at Anna. He seemed calmer.

"I don't remember much. He's not my real dad. He stole... Look, I can't talk right now. Just be very, very careful of Lydia. Jerry might be around. You must tell your father who she is, okay? He might know, actually. There might be records." Jayden became downcast.

"Records of what?" Anna frowned. "Of what your father did?"

Jayden raised his head, and their eyes locked. "Yes."

"And what did he do?" Anna asked.

The terror returned to Jayden's eyes and seemed to convulse his entire body. Then he stood and walked away. He looked back one last time.

"Stay away from her. Tell your dad."

Then Jayden ran to the doors and disappeared down the stairs. "Wait," Anna shouted, and ran after him. But she didn't catch him. He had run through the double door of the lobby downstairs, and when she came out on the sunlit street, she couldn't see him anymore.

*****

Roy was in his office when the knock came. A uniformed constable poked his head in.

"Young girl at the desk, guv. Says she's your daughter, Anna. She looks worried."

Roy didn't waste any time. He barged past the constable and ran down the corridor. Anna stood when she saw him coming through the double doors. One look at her face confirmed his

333

worst fears, but he was relieved she was unhurt.

"What happened?" he asked.

"I met a man called Jayden Budden. He was in the library, but I saw him yesterday outside a café as well. Think he was watching me. He said he knows you. He told me Lydia was dangerous as she's the ex-girlfriend of his dad."

They had sat down, and Roy was confused and alarmed at the same time. "Jayden Budden?"

"Yes, that's what he said his name was. Do you know him? He said he was a witness at a crime scene."

Roy's mind was running loops at a nuclear rate. He felt dizzy, and closed his eyes, trying to concentrate.

"Okay. Slow down. Tell me word for word exactly what he said. Actually, start with what he looked like, and what he was wearing."

Anna told him and Roy listened attentively. "Jerry Budden," Roy uttered the words slowly, but they meant nothing to him. "And Jayden said he was a dangerous man. That you were unsafe if he was around. You, specifically?"

"Yes. He made that very clear."

"What did you do after that?"

"I was worried. I went back into the library, got my stuff, then got a taxi down here. I tried to call you, but you didn't answer."

"Yes, I was a in a meeting, sorry. You did the right thing. Come with me."

As they walked in through the double doors of the station, Roy tried Sarah's phone, but she didn't answer. Riz and Ollie were standing and chatting in low voices, and Melanie was at her desk. The men were surprised when Roy walked in with Anna. Mel didn't notice at first, she was engrossed in a document. Roy stopped in front of her table, and she looked up. Her eyebrows hiked north when she saw Anna.

"Can I have a word please? In my office." Roy tilted his head towards the closed door of his tiny space.

"Sure."

Roy got the attention of the two DCs. "Can you two please find me anything on a man called Jerry Budden. IC1 male, in his fifties or sixties. Scour HOLMES, all police databases in UK and Interpol. Anyone asks, given them my name as permission. Got it?"

Oliver sat down promptly and grabbed his laptop. Rizwan did the same. Roy followed the two ladies into his office and shut the door. He told Melanie what happened with Anna and Jayden.

"This is the same bloke you met at the crime scene? He's clear, isn't he? He didn't show up on any searches, and his alibi holds up."

"Yes. But this might not be related to our case. Or it might be. I just don't know. I need to get hold of him and have a chat. I need to ask you a favour." With his last words, Roy sat back in his chair, and felt uncomfortable.

Melanie glanced at Anna, who was looking nervous, hands twisting on her lap as she listened to the adults. Melanie dragged her focus back to Roy.

"She'll be safe here," Mel said. "Don't worry, I won't let her out of my sight."

"Thank you," Roy said, relieved. He knew Mel would help, but he still felt bad dragging his personal life into work. From Mel's face, he could tell she knew that.

"Don't worry, guv." She grinned. Then she turned to Anna. "Why don't you stay here and read a book or something? We can go to the canteen later, if you want."

Anna nodded. Roy left them to it and went to his desk. He pulled up the file on Jayden and scanned through it. No, he hadn't missed anything. He jotted down the home and work address. With any luck, Jayden would be at work now, at a garage in central Sheffield.

"Nowt on him, boss," Oliver said. "I checked HOLMES and all the PCN databases in UK."

"Interpol don't have any files on him, or on Jerry Budden," Riz confirmed. "To be honest, I can't find any record of a Jerry Budden. Nil on council tax lists anywhere in the country, or electoral rolls. Nothing in the home office, either. Have you got the name right?"

"Positive," Roy frowned, stroking his cheek. Something wasn't right here, and it was bothering the hell out of him.

"OK, we need to bring Jayden in, but I want to speak to him outside first. He's going to get a lawyer this time. I'll be back soon."

"Do you want us to come with you?"

Roy shrugged into his jacket, and checked his radio was charged. "I've got to do this on my own," he said, and left.

CHAPTER 62

He's not my real dad…

I ran away… He's dangerous…

Tell your dad, he might know…

Anna had told Roy verbatim what Jayden said, and the words reverberated, crashed against the confines of Roy's skull like surf pounding against rocks. He barely saw the traffic as he drove. His knuckles were white on the steering wheel, and a bead of sweat trickled down the side of his face.

What on earth was Jayden talking about? Anna said his fear was genuine. When he talked about his dad, Jerry Budden, he was scared. Roy sped through traffic, his eyes a blur, his mind straying.

Instinct told him Jayden was harmless. True, he had nothing to base that on. Jayden might not have a police record, or home office and foreign office warnings against him, but that didn't make him safe.

And yet, he had come of his own volition and told Anna to stay away from Lydia. Jayden could be a total nutter who was having psychotic delusions. Such things happened, and Roy had dealt with people who acted strangely, and the family had to call the police. Could Jayden have a mental health issue? Possible, but again… That old sixth sense of Roy's was ringing an alarm bell.

Jayden didn't seem like a paranoid schizophrenic. Not impossible, but from what he had seen, unlikely. Roy was in the one-way-system in the city centre, and he had to race through, jumping a couple of red lights, and getting flashed by the camera.

Finally, he screeched to a stop outside a street with a row of shops, residential flats, and a car garage. A couple of mechanics in the forecourt looked up. Roy showed them his warrant card.

"Is Jayden Budden here?"

One of the men was short, squat, and had an accent that Roy couldn't quite place, then realised it was Geordie. He wiped his hands in a dirty rag, then flung it over his shoulder.

"What's this about? He done summat?"

"I can't discuss that now. Do you know where he is?"

"He's not been to work for two days. Gilly, you heard from him?" The squat man asked his younger colleague. Gilly shrugged and said no.

"This is important," Roy said. He didn't want to overdo it, after all, he was here on a personal matter. "I need to speak to him ASAP."

"I told yer. He's not been around for two days. Not like him, though. He's normally here every day, first thing. I let him come over to mine and pick up keys and he opens up."

"You're the owner?"

"Yes. Grant's my name. Grant Bovril."

"Ok, Grant. How long have you known Jayden for?"

"Five years or so. Dependable lad. Does his work and goes home. Met him a few times at the pub an' all. Haven't we, Gilly lad?"

"Yes," Gilly said. "Jay's alright. Never been in trouble with the cops though. What's this about, like?"

"He's not in any trouble. He's a witness at a crime scene, and I need to ask him some more questions, that's all. Do you know if he's moved recently?"

"No, lived here for a while. Near Park Hill, last I knew. He's been there for ages.

That was the address that Roy had. He thanked the men and gave them his card. He jumped back in his car and drove off. The drive to Park Hill, a low-income suburb not far from Attercliffe and the city centre, didn't take long. Roy parked outside the brown brick terraced house that bore the number 34. It was one of those long, wide terraces that were turned into multiple flats many years ago. Jayden's address said Flat 3, and Roy pressed the buzzer, and waited. After three attempts, nothing happened. The place had six flats, and he pressed all of them till an irate voice answered. The man piped down once he heard it was the police. After a wait, a middle aged man opened the door. He wore a white tee shirt and jeans, and scratched his belly, looking at Roy anxiously.

"Owt's the matter?"

"Not much," Roy said, entering the musty smelling, tiny hallway. It was divided up into three doors that led into the various flats. His feet creaked on the floorboards, covered by a threadbare, brown carpet.

"Do you know the man who lives in Flat 3, Jayden Budden?"

The man screwed up his face, then shook his head. "Can't say I do. Why, what's he done, like?"

"Nothing."

The man showed Roy the way to Flat 3 on the first floor. He knocked on the door but didn't get an answer. He checked the doorframe and lock. They would give way. He hammered on the door and called Jayden's name. There was no response.

Roy went back down and made sure the door stayed open. Flat 3 was on the left, and the only windows would be to the rear. He couldn't find a way into the garden. There was no other option.

He went back upstairs, and hammered on the door again, with the same response. Then he lifted his foot and gave it a good kick. He had to repeat the kick twice, then slam his left shoulder into the door before the lock splintered, and the door swung open.

A narrow hallway led to a TV and dining room. Beyond that, there was a kitchen with windows facing the garden. There was a bedroom to his left, that also had a window that opened to the rear. The bed was slept in. The room was a mess, with clothes on the floor, and a pizza box under the bed. There was a TV at the foot of the bed. The desk near the window had a laptop, monitor and printer. Roy kicked away a few beer cans and got to the desk. He put his gloves on. The laptop was password protected but turned on.

He turned to the bed and flung off the sheets and pillows. Apart from a stained mattress cover, there was nothing on the bed. He did a quick search of the wardrobe, which had clothes stashed in it randomly. The window was shut, and the room smelled. He went out and searched the rest of the flat. There was another pizza box in the fridge, and a carton of milk, with some more beer cans.

Jayden was still living here. But where had he gone?

CHAPTER 63

Totley High School was in a nice part of Sheffield, next to a golf course. Lessons were being held, and all was quiet as Roy parked his car and strode down the main entrance. At the reception, he showed his warrant card and said he wanted to speak to the principal urgently.

A tall man in a blue suit appeared shortly. He wore glasses, and his left eye had a squint. He examined Roy's warrant card with interest.

"I'm David Burton," the principal said, shaking Roy's hand. "What's this about?"

"Do you have a teacher here called Lydia Moran?"

Mr Burton frowned. "As a matter of fact, I think we do. She teachers history and some classes in English as well, to the upper sixth form. May I enquire why?"

"This might be better in your office?" Roy spread his hands and raised his eyebrows.

"Of course. Sorry. Please come with me."

Mr Burton's office was on the ground floor. He shut the door behind him, and Roy sat down.

"What's going on, Inspector?" Mr Burton's lazy left eye remained fixed, but the other scanned Roy's face.

"It's come to our knowledge that Miss Moran's ex-partner is a danger to children and teenagers." Roy thought for a few seconds, but he'd already made his mind up to come clean.

"My daughter is sixteen and met Miss Moran at the central library. Miss Moran tried her best to befriend my daughter, even offering her help with her essays, and invited her to her house. Bear in mind my daughter goes to school in London and is here for the holidays. Miss Moran doesn't know her."

"Sorry, I'm confused. What does this have to do with Miss Moran's ex-partner?"

"A man then approached my daughter. He's the stepson of a man called Jerry Budden, Miss Moran's ex, or possibly current, partner. This man fled his former home, to get away from Jerry Budden. It is possible they had an abusive relationship. We are treating this as a serious matter. This young man has warned my daughter not to socialise with Miss Moran, in case she is still close to Jerry Budden. I thought you should know that."

There was silence for a few minutes as Mr Burton stared at Roy.

Roy said, "The Safeguarding Team of South Yorkshire Police will be involved. They will want to speak to Miss Moran."

Mr Burton sat back in his chair. Roy said, "I suggest you let me speak to Miss Moran immediately."

"Yes, I think so," Mr Burton nodded. He picked up the phone and rang his secretary. He put the phone down and waited.

"Just checking which class she's teaching now."

Roy nodded. He felt an itching on his skin, and a tremor. He didn't know why, but he was restless, and had to stop himself from standing and pacing the room. The phone rang, and Mr

Burton snatched it up.

"Yes. Yes. Okay, send her in. No, no need to tell her why. Just say it's important."

Another wait. Roy felt a bead of sweat course down the back of his neck. His feet tapped in silence, and he clenched and unclenched his fists. The door opened, and he turned. The secretary stepped in, and behind her, a prim and proper, thin woman of average height appeared. She wore glasses, and a pale pink dress that came down to her ankles. She looked worried, and her brown eyes moved from Mr Burton to Roy.

"Please sit down, Miss Moran," the principal said. The secretary closed the door and left.

They waited till the teacher sat down, a few paces to the right of Roy.

"This is Detective Chief Inspector Rohan Roy. He is here on a pressing matter." Mr Burton folded his hands over the table. He got straight to the point, which Roy liked.

"Are you familiar with Inspector Roy's daughter?"

The woman sat so rigidly that Roy wondered if she was having a stroke, or a seizure. Her face was ramrod straight. Not a muscle on her face moved. Her hands were still, shoulders straight.

"Miss Moran?"

Still, Lydia didn't budge. She seemed frozen into place; her feet nailed to the carpet.

"Miss Moran?"

Her lips parted, and she swallowed, once. "Yes, sorry. Yes, I heard. Who are you talking about?"

"My daughter, Anna," Roy said, not mincing his words. He didn't care if Mr Burton was offended, but he addressed the teacher directly. "You met her at the library. Are you Jerry Budden's girlfriend?"

Slowly, as if it caused her great pain to move her head, Lydia turned. She looked at Roy, her eyes dim behind the glasses.

"No," she said. "I'm not."

"But you used to be? You're his ex-girlfriend?"

"I'm sorry, Inspector. You have me mistaken for someone else." She averted her face, looking ahead, at no one in particular.

"But you did meet Anna, and invite her to your house?" Roy persisted. "You offered to help with her homework?"

Lydia made an odd movement of her neck, a partly inclined nod, a sign of affirmation, without actually looking at Roy.

"I met a girl called Anna Roy in the library, yes."

"Why did you invite her to your house? I understand that you two had lunch yesterday as well."

"We were just having a conversation about homework, that's all."

Lydia was bothering Roy. She was more evasive than a politician on TV, but it was more than that. She was actually scared of looking at him.

"Inspector Roy," Mr Burton called out. "If you wish to question Miss Moran further, I'm sure she won't object. However," he now addressed Lydia. "Until this matter is concluded, I would like you to take a sabbatical please, Miss Moran."

Lydia sat stock still for a few seconds, then nodded curtly.

CHAPTER 64

Roy was back at the nick, doing a deep dive into Lydia Moran. Her records showed she had lived all over Yorkshire. Leeds and Sheffield had been her main homes, where she had worked as a teacher in the schools there. First in primary, then in secondary, education.

She had lived in Chapeltown in Leeds, and also in Headingley. Over the last eight months, she had lived just outside Totley, not far from the school where she worked now.

Anna was still in his office, engrossed in her laptop. In a way, it was reassuring that she was close by but on the other hand he knew having a teenager at his workplace was not exactly good parenting. He needed to drop her back home, but he first needed to make sure he knew everything there was to know about Jayden and Lydia.

It still struck him as odd that Lydia, a grown woman, had tried to strike up a friendship with Anna. Initially, he had thought Anna had started chatting to Lydia, like she often did. But no... It had been Lydia. She took Anna out to lunch and paid for it. She offered to help Anna with her homework. Invited Anna to her house.

And this strange man called Jerry Budden who he couldn't find any sign of.

Roy got up and went to his office. He opened the door and walked in. Anna was sitting on the desk chair and had her feet up on another. She took her headphone off when she saw him. Roy sat down, facing her.

"This man, Jayden. Can you tell me again what he said, and this time, go right back to when you saw him outside the library, and he approached you."

Anna did so, haltingly. Roy stopped her eventually. "Tell me the part about what his father did again? And he said this Jerry Budden wasn't his real father?"

"He said Jerry wasn't his real father two or three times. He seemed sure about that. As for what he did… He said the man was dangerous, and…" Anna frowned, her words dying out.

"And what?"

Anna's head straightened, and a new light filled her large, beautiful eyes. "He said his father stole. That's it. He said *he stole, but I can't talk about this now.* And he got really scared then."

"Stole? Stole what?"

Anna shrugged. "I don't know."

Roy lowered his head, thinking hard. If Jerry Budden was a robber, why would Anna specifically be at risk? Or maybe Jerry used to be armed and dangerous, hence Jayden was scared.

But Jerry wasn't his real father, and he ran away from home… Roy shook his head, trying his best to piece it all together.

He needed to speak to Jayden again. He had asked a squad car to be patrol outside his house, and the garage. Jayden would surface at one of them eventually. And he had also asked Traffic to track Lydia's car, to monitor her movements.

346

If Jerry Budden had been a violent criminal, then why wasn't there a record of him? Unless… Criminals could change names, and identities. Roy stood; his mind fired up with a new possibility.

"When can I go home?" Anna complained. "This place is uncomfortable."

"But it's safe. Stay here for now. Jayden is still out there, and so is his father, for all we know."

"Did you speak to Lydia?"

"Yes, I went to the school. She knows you but denies all knowledge of a Jerry Budden."

Roy went outside and busied himself on the computers. He couldn't find any data on a name change to Jerry Budden, at least not anyone on the police databases. Another dead end. He tapped a pen on the desktop as he stared at the blinking cursor of the search box. Perhaps this was just a coincidence. Or Jayden could be a mental health patient in the grips of a psychosis.

His phone beeped, and he picked it up. "DCI Roy."

"Sergeant Bloomsdale from Traffic, guv. You told us to alert you if a Vauxhall Astra EP59TWR was leaving Sheffield."

That was the reg number of Lydia's car. Roy sat up straighter immediately. "Yes."

"The vehicle is on the M62 heading towards Manchester. Single female driver it seems, from CCTV. Do you want us to track?"

"Yes, definitely, and I'm coming up."

He ran up the stairs to Traffic Control. The huge room was full of officers leaning over computers, and watching the large bank of CCTV screens that occupied an entire wall. A low hubbub of voices mingled with the clicks and whirr of invisible machines. The lights were dim here, so the screens could be visualised well.

Roy went up to Sergeant Bloomsdale, one of the duty officers, who was sat in front of the screen wall.

"Ey up, guv," the younger man said, when he saw Roy. "Hold on, here she is. Drove fast, she did. Almost entering Manchester now."

Roy pulled up a chair and focused on the screen. It showed Lydia's car entering Manchester's city centre and heading for Manchester Victoria train station.

But instead of going into the station, the car drove past it, and then took a turn to the left.

"Bloody hell," Bloomsdale. "What's she going there for?" He turned to look at Roy, whose face was ashen as he stared at the screen. A bugle of panic was unfurling against his ear drums, getting louder till it drowned out any other sound. His heart almost stopped beating, and his chest contracted like an iron grip was crushing it.

Lydia's car was entering His Majesty's Prison Manchester, formerly known as Strangeways. It was one of the UK's seven high security men's prisons.

It was also where Steven Burns, the notorious child killer, and his brother's abductor, was jailed for life.

CHAPTER 65

G uv, you okay?" Sergeant Bloomsdale asked. Roy heard the words, but the sounds were like a whitewash in his ears, like the noise of a steady drizzle. He didn't register anything. His gaze was hooked on the screen, on Lydia's car as she drove inside the prison compound and followed directions to the visitor's car park.

"Guv?"

Roy startled, then stared at Bloomsdale for a few seconds like he'd just seen him. "Yes, sorry. Thanks for doing this. Give me a minute."

He ignored the funny look in Bloomsdale's eyes and pulled out his phone. He thumbed through to Dr Parson's number. Once he was outside, he called the psychiatrist. Luckily, the forensic psychiatrist answered.

"Dr Parsons? DCI Roy speaking. I need you to check something. Can you please see if a woman called Lydia Moran is on the visitors list today for Steven Burns or Keith Burgess?"

"Any reason?" The psychiatrist was his usual calm and unruffled state.

"This woman is trying to get close to my daughter, Anna. She keeps meeting her in the library."

"I see," Dr Parsons voice was more alert now. He knew about the terrifying ordeal Roy and Anna had been through. "Let me check and then get back to you. Shan't be long."

Roy paced the corridor as he waited, his mind slinging around like it was in a pin ball machine. He answered on the first ring.

"Rohan," Dr Parsons voice sounded more urgent this time. "You were right. Lydia Moran is a visitor of Burns, and she's waiting now to see him.

"Can we stop them?"

"On what grounds? I can order it, and so can you, but Burns can file a complaint, as you know. So can Lydia."

Roy clutched the phone so hard it creaked, and his teeth ground together. "Grounds? How about that... Lydia was trying to do god-knows-what to Anna? And that she's probably taking orders from Burns? I'd say those are bloody good grounds."

"I can try, but you know how it is. Prisoners have rights."

"Stuff their rights!" Roy shouted, not caring who heard, and ignoring the few heads on the corridor that snapped in his direction. "I'll tell the prison director myself."

"So will I, if that helps," Dr Parsons said. "We need to investigate this."

"Thanks," Roy said, sighing in relief. He hung up and went back to Bloomsdale. "Can you get on that car again, and keep an eye on it?"

"Sure, guv. It's still there," he pointed to the screen. "I'll alert you when it moves."

"If I don't answer, please tell the MIT." Roy led the Major Investigations Team, and he knew any messages would end up with Ollie, Riz, Mel or Sarah.

He thanked Bloomsdale and ran down the stairs. All of sudden, the missing pieces of the jigsaw were joining up, and the emerging picture was ghastly.

It was Lydia who was sending him the messages about Robin. It was she who had observed him at Sarah's house, playing football with Matt. The neighbour had described a slim young lad – a woman in fact, dressed in a hoodie and glasses. Lydia was taking instructions from Steven… That was horrifying, but…

Roy stopped dead in his tracks. He was going down the staircase, and his hands became limp on the railing. His knees buckled, and he had to sit down on the stair. His eyes blurred as the realisation finally dawned.

Jayden Budden… Or Jayden Burns?

Jayden had run away from his stepfather, a dangerous man. Lydia's ex-partner, Jerry. Was it a fake name? Did Steven just use that name so Jayden would never find out?

Which meant Jayden could very well be… *Robin.*

His long lost brother, Robin.

Roy's face became hot as his chest tightened. He couldn't breathe. Then, like a drowning man who just got pulled out of water, he sucked in a deep, long breath.

Could it be? Could Jayden really be Robin?

He stood, and took slow, unsteady steps down to the second floor. His mind was like a wind chime in a storm. The cacophony of noises were making it impossible to think straight. He sank down to his feet again, sitting on a step. He needed Sarah now. She could see through this mist, offer him advice. He pulled out his phone and called her. She didn't answer. He left a message asking her to call him back.

He didn't know where Jayden was. But at least he could get hold of Lydia. Roy got up and strode into the office. His phone beeped, and it was from Bloomsdale.

"DCI Roy."

"The driver just left Manchester Prison, guv. Heading back this way, down the M62. I'll keep you posted."

That was quick, Roy thought. Maybe Dr Parsons had got through to the prison director, as he was onsite. Lydia's visit to see Burns had been cancelled.

"Thanks, David," Roy said, using the sergeant's first name. "Can you please send me a live link, and I can track her myself."

"Sure, guv."

A live link meant he could follow Lydia and face her again. He couldn't wait.

CHAPTER 66

Roy stormed down the corridor, eager to pick up his coat and leave. He had his phone in his hand, and on the screen, he could see the small red dot that was Lydia's car moving on the map. He knew exactly where she was on the M62, and also the exit where he could hide to catch up with her. There was only one problem. Lydia might not know that she was being traced, but she did know Roy's car.

Riz and Ollie were not at their desks. As Roy walked past Nugent's office, engrossed in the phone screen, he didn't see the Super step out of his office. He did smell the unmistakable stench of nicotine that wafted down the corridor. He ignored it, but the man's gruff voice made him stop.

"Rohan."

He shoved the phone in his pocket and turned. Nugent came forward, a rare, but tight smile on his face. It seemed like he was forcing his lips to stretch.

"I hear congratulations are in order. You did well to catch Damien Russell. He was a key man for Kevin Rawlinson's crime empire, it seems. Lots of CCTV evidence of him hobnobbing with the senior figures of the Loxley Boys Gang, not to mention the Liverpool-based organised crime networks."

"Yes. Thanks. Look, you caught me at a bad time. I need to deal with a motorist incident."

Nugent's tight smile faded as he registered Roy's expression. "Anything important?"

"Yes, but nothing I can't handle. I'll report to you soon, Sir."

Roy rushed off, aware of Nugent's eyes boring into his back.

There was a general air of relaxation in the office. News of Damien's demise had spread, and the department as a whole felt a sense of achievement. The mean streets of east Sheffield were safe, for a while at least. Riz and Ollie were not at their desks. Roy saw Melanie, just the person he wanted. She was at her desk and didn't look up until he got closer.

"I need to go and see Lydia, the woman who was after Anna," Roy told Melanie in a low voice. "Where are the lads?"

"In the canteen, they just went to get some coffees."

"Thanks, I'll catch up with them. Can you please look after Anna till I get back?"

"No problem, guv."

Roy left the office and went to the canteen. It was almost empty, and he saw the two DCs chatting on a table by the window.

"Ey up, guv, all okay?" Ollie asked.

"Kind of. Look, I need your help with something."

Five minutes later, Roy was driving out in Ollie's brand-new Audi A5. He had to admit it was a pleasure to floor the gas and feel the powerful sixteen-valve engine surge the car forward. He had connected his phone to the car via Bluetooth, and he could see the red dot pulsating on the dashboard screen. He didn't have sirens, but for the first time in ages, he was driving a car capable of speed. He streaked towards the motorway, breaking every traffic rule in the book, while playing it as safe as he could.

His eyes kept darting at the red dot. On the M62, he pushed the needle to over 120 MPH, and felt the car respond as he overtook every other vehicle. He was getting closer. Then he realised Lydia had taken an exit, and he slowed down. He followed her into the Derbyshire Peaks, and he was forced to check his speed as the road became one lane.

Then he frowned. The red dot on his screen had stopped moving. A turning on his left appeared as the red dot got within touching distance. The exit led into a country lane with verdant, rolling hills in both directions. Clouds ringed the horizon where the blue hills smudged the skyline. Roy wasn't looking at the scenery. His eyes stayed on the screen.

Lydia's car had stopped. An anxiety started gnawing in his mind. He drove on, and the red dot remained still. Then he saw the car, a grey Vauxhall Astra parked on the grass verge next to a farm gate. Roy pulled over and jumped out.

The car was empty. The driver's door was locked. He tried the boot, and that opened. There was nothing in it. He slammed it shut, rage and frustration unfurling inside, spreading like a geyser about to burst. He jumped over the gate and landed on the other side. He ran around, then realised it was pointless.

Lydia was gone. He clenched his fists and roared at the sky. His rage echoed around the hills, but no one heard him.

****

Lydia Moran glanced at the driver. "Thanks for picking me up."

Kevin Rawlinson nodded. "No problem." He picked up speed down the dirt track, taking several turns, going deeper into the countryside. They stopped outside a stone house, at the end of a long track enclosed by fields.

Kevin looked at Lydia in a reassuring manner. That was difficult given Kevin's nightclub bouncer features, but somehow, he managed it. "Let's go inside. Don't worry, it's safe."

Lydia adjusted the strap of her handbag and followed. The went inside, and Kevin led them into the kitchen. He made two cups of tea and handed one to her. They sat down, facing each other.

"So," Kevin said. "It seems we have a common enemy. That big moron, Inspector Roy."

"Yes, we do. How did you know he was after me?"

Kevin smiled. "We have informers everywhere. We're keeping Roy under watch. One of my men tipped us he was going to your school. We followed him. Another little birdie told us he went to see you."

Lydia nodded in silence. Kevin's scarred face twisted into a snarl; the effect was like watching a jackal baring its teeth.

"Roy killed one of my best men. Damien was a good player. I need that Roy to be gone. Dead, preferably. But killed in a way that doesn't get back to me."

Lydia was shocked, and it showed on her face. Kevin smiled. "Don't worry. You won't have to do anything. All I want you to do is tell me what you know. I'll handle the rest. I'll teach Roy a lesson he won't forget."

Lydia swallowed and felt a fear spark in her chest. "Look, I hate him too, for what he did to my partner. But I don't want any violence."

Kevin raised a meaty hand. "Like I said, don't worry. I'll deal with him. The less you know, the better it is, actually. But give me the dirt on Roy. Why is he after you so badly?"

Lydia took a sip of her tea. Then she told Kevin, who listened with rapt attention. When she finished, a slow smile spread across Kevin's lips.

"Now then," he mused. "It's time we taught Inspector Roy a lesson he won't forget."

CHAPTER 67

S arah walked past Matt into the garden, warning him not to work up a sweat. She checked the back and side fences. It was a nice morning, sunlight filtering in through the leaves, blue sky overhead. She found nothing of concern.

The doorbell went as she walked into the kitchen. She opened the door to find John waiting with a bouquet of flowers and a package.

"For you," he said, handing the flowers to Sarah.

"No, thank you," Sarah said. She felt a little uncomfortable, and John seemed to read her mind.

"Sorry. I hope you don't mind. I thought the flowers would look nice in the house."

"It's fine. Come on in. We're ready. Matt," she called out. "John, I mean your dad, is here." She looked at her watch as John walked into the kitchen and said hello to Matt. They still had a half-hour before they had to set off.

"Would you like a cup of tea?" she asked John.

"Yes, please." He gave Matt the package, which looked like it was from a sports shop. "Got you some football boots. You said you needed new ones. Size seven, right?"

"Oh yeah," Matt said, his face glowing. "Thanks… Dad." He seemed shy again. John grinned, and they sat down next to each other as Matt opened his gift. Sarah watched them, happy.

Matt tried his shoes on. "They're perfect." He smiled at John. "Shall we play in the garden? I want to try these out now!"

"You start, and I'll join you," John said. Matt rushed out and John stood. He accepted the cup of tea from Sarah with thanks.

"What happened last night?" John asked.

"Just work stuff," Sarah shrugged. "My boss needed some help."

"Oh right." John didn't push it, and Sarah was grateful. "Hope you got some sleep after. You look alright," he smiled.

"Oh thanks," Sarah said. She'd dressed sensibly, in a long sleeved vest and slacks. Her hair was up in a ponytail and make up was minimal. She had Matt with her, and she also didn't want John to get the wrong impression.

"One of the builders at work lives in Attercliffe," John said, sipping his tea. "He said a lot of the streets were shut down, and police were everywhere. He said a body was found by the canal. Is that true?"

Sarah considered her response. Police had done a door-to-door, so it was normal that word would spread.

"Yes, it is."

John tried to look relaxed, but Sarah could tell he was interested. He wasn't stupid, he could put two-and-two together.

"And what happened last night…?" He raised his eyebrows.

Sarah sighed. Well, everyone would know soon. "We caught the man responsible for the murders. But please keep that to yourself."

"Of course. My lips are sealed." He shook his head and looked sad. "The world is so crazy sometimes."

"That it is."

"Well, at least you got him." John was standing near the concertina doors that led into the patio and garden. Matt was playing with the football.

John said, "I know you can't tell me anything, and I'm not trying to prod. But who was the victim?"

Again, Sarah thought, *this will all be out soon in the local papers*. "A sex worker."

John shook his head. "A prostitute? That's bad. They shouldn't exist. We as a society, need to ban prostitution." He looked at Sarah, his face suddenly animated. "These poor souls need to be liberated."

It was a strange comment to make, Sarah thought. She didn't quite understand the context, either.

"What do you mean?"

"Well, drug-taking, prostitution, all of these should be abolished. We need to stop it from happening."

"Not that easy. Class A drugs are illegal, but there's a big market for them. Criminals always find a way. It's our job to stop them."

Matt had come in, and he pulled at John's shirt. "Come on."

"It's almost time to go," Sarah said. "Stop playing now."

"Drugs are ravaging our society," John said. "These sex workers who died, drugs destroyed their lives as well. They would've died from their addiction, if it hadn't been the man who..." his words died out as he caught the look on Sarah's face.

Sarah was suddenly alert, her senses on fire. A strange feeling was fanning in her chest. She narrowed her eyes at John.

"You said *these sex workers*? How did you know there was more than one?"

John's face was rigid, and she noticed his hands were fists, knuckles white. "Oh," he tried to act casual. "The builder guy told me."

"He wouldn't have known," Sarah whispered. "And how did you know they were drug addicts?"

"Lucky guess," John said. His body was taut now, a gleam in his eyes she hadn't seen before. A vein throbbed in his forehead. He seemed like a different man all of a sudden. Like a wolf on the prowl.

Sarah's hands and feet were turning ice cold. A cold slab of fear was solidifying in her chest, making it impossible to breathe. Her mind grappled with impossible thoughts.

The murders started after John arrived in Sheffield. Six years ago, when Bianca Wilkins died and Gemma Jackson disappeared, John left Sheffield for Dubai.

It couldn't be… Could it?

Her eyes fell on Matt, standing next to John. John's did as well.

"Matt. Come here," Sarah said, trying to keep the tremor out of her voice.

John stopped Matt with a hand on his chest. "No," he said slowly. "He's fine here."

"Mummy?" Matt said, looking confused.

Sarah extended a hand towards her son. "Come here." She looked at John, her eyes now wide, fear bulging in her throat like a bomb about to explode.

John grabbed a kitchen knife that was on the counter before she could move. He clutched Matt's throat and placed the knife against it. Matt screamed in fright.

"No!" Sarah shouted.

John stepped back, dragging Matt towards the door. "Mummy!" Matt screamed and fought, but John was stronger.

"Let him go, please. I beg you, John. He's your son!" Sarah cried out and followed them. Her mind was searching for options and coming up with a blank. Her phone was somewhere in the kitchen. She didn't have her radio, or her mace spray and baton. It was all at work.

"You want to see him alive?" John said, his voice eerily calm, his eyes dead cold, flat. He held the knife closer to Matt as the boy screamed again.

"Don't hurt him. Please," Sarah fell to her knees. "Please don't." Tears bloomed in her eyes and rolled down her cheeks.

John held the knife and fiddled in his pocket with the other hand. He came up with car keys. He pressed it, twice.

"My car's right outside. It's a black Audi A5, the one you're looking for. But I painted it white and changed the number plates." John smiled. He looked like a shark about to bite off a swimmer's leg.

"Damien was a good fall guy. That idiot helped me more than he knows." His teeth bared. "Get in the car, in the back seat. I will sit in the front with Matt. Do you want to see your son alive?"

"Yes. Yes, please don't hurt him."

"Then do as I say. The car's open now. Get in the back, and I'll come right behind you."

Sarah cast a look at Matt, who was terrified, and crying. "Okay," she whispered. "I'm going."

THE END

Want to know what happens next?

Carry on reading in Book 4 – *Hold Your Breath*.

More books by ML Rose

<u>The Rohan Roy Series, in order (Free in Kindle Unlimited)</u>

My Brother's Keeper

Suffer The Torment

Don't Look Back

Hold Your Breath

<u>The Arla Baker Series, in order (read for FREE in Kindle Unlimited)</u>

The Lost Sister   https://geni.us/HFGU8

The Keeper of Secrets   https://geni.us/qXbvZ7

The Forgotten Mother   https://geni.us/cAeO

The Nail Collector   https://geni.us/g6XA

The Last Girl   https://geni.us/thelastgirl

Her Silent Obsession   https://geni.us/silentobs

The Forsaken Son   https://geni.us/forsakenson

The Vanishing Child   https://geni.us/vanishingchild

The Dead Voices   https://geni.us/deadvoices

To Die For   https://geni.us/todiefor

Last To Know   https://geni.us/lasttoknow

On My Skin   https://geni.us/onmyskin

AUTHOR'S NOTE

If you read this far, I'm hoping you enjoyed this book. Would you please mind leaving a review? It takes two minutes of your time, but less than one reader in one hundred leaves a review. Will you be that person?

Thank you very much

ML Rose.

Please get in touch, I love to hear from my readers!

Email - mlroseauthor@gmail.com

Facebook - https://www.facebook.com/arlabake

Printed in Great Britain
by Amazon

33234199R00209